"CASPAR IS GOING TO BE OVERSEER."

The Bondmaster announced to his black housekeeper. "This offspring of ours has persuaded me he can do it."

"Yo' does go'n make a slave de overseer!" Ella gasped in disbelief. "He go'n run de plantation? An' de niggers?

"Yes," Carlton beamed at Caspar. "And you can have the overseer's cabin, but you shall pay for it. With whelps, Caspar, whelps!"

"May I choose my own wenches?"

"No!" Carlton snorted. "You are half Batutsi and half white, boy. I have to cross you with a wench who'll produce quality."

"Da'," Carlton's little white daughter Laura rounded the corner of the balcony. She wore a hibiscus flower in her blonde hair and pouted prettily. "Can I be a wench?"

"What?" Carlton shouted, astonished. "You're going to be a young lady. Only slaves are wenches!"

"Does a young lady have black bucks to mount she like a wench, Da'?"

"A lady has slaves. You want to be a lady and have slaves, don't you, Laura?"

"Is yo' ah does want fuh meh slave, Caspar, when ah does be a lady." Laura looked up into Caspar's eyes and smiled.

"That's enough!" Carlton snapped. "Take the child to her room."

As she turned to leave, Laura glanced back and smiled at Caspar again. 'I *will* be a wench,' she vowed to herself. 'Even though everyone will think I am a lady . . .'

Books by Richard Tresillian

Blood of the Bondmaster
The Bondmaster

Published by
WARNER BOOKS

Blood of the Bondmaster

by

Richard Tresillian

WARNER BOOKS

A Warner Communications Company

WARNER BOOKS EDITION

ISBN 0-446-82385-6

Warner Books, Inc., 75 Rockefeller Plaza, New York, N.Y. 10019

 A Warner Communications Company

Printed in the United States of America

Not associated with Warner Press, Inc. of Anderson, Indiana

First Printing: November, 1977

10 9 8 7 6 5 4 3 2 1

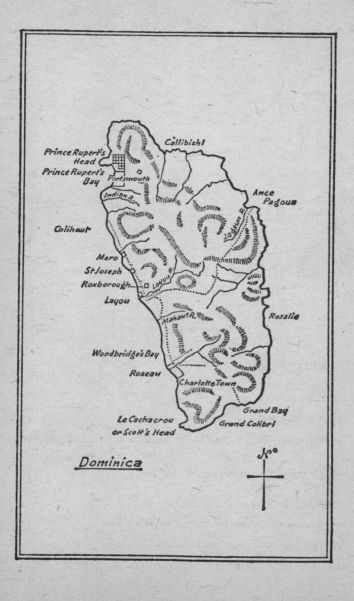

Dominica

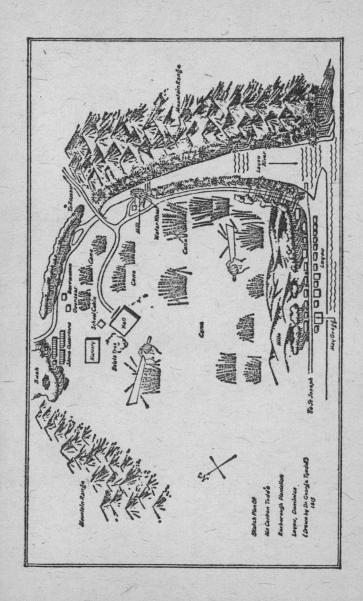

Sketch Plan Of
Mr Canton Todd's
Roxborough Plantation
Layou, Dominica
(Drawn by Dr George Tyndall)
1813

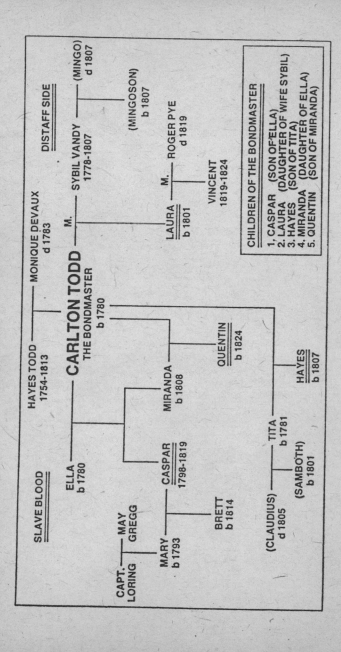

Table of Contents

"Roxborough Estate in the Layou Valley was the most productive of Dominica's sugar plantations until it declined at the end of the eighteenth century when the Todd family started the first slave warren in the British West Indian Islands.

"The Bondmaster, Mr. Carlton Todd, is reputed to have made a considerable fortune by his selective breeding of enslaved Africans for sale to the plantation owners of neighboring islands.

"A Roxborough slave became renowned throughout the West Indies as the elite of that subjugated race, and it is said that many of today's native citizens of prominence have descended from the line begun by the Bondmaster of Roxborough."

From: *A History of the British West Indian Islands* by Sir Verne W. Bissett, Bart. Published by Shankland & Box, London & Cambridge, 1913.

BOOK ONE

Caspar

1813

Chapter 1

CASPAR STROLLED ACROSS THE FRESHLY SCRUBBED boards of the deck to the ship's rail. He could feel the sun creeping under his high collar and scorching the back of his neck. He gripped the rail firmly with both hands, squinting at the sea as the ship glided through the water.

The ship was peaceful now. The squealing of pigs, the quacking of ducks, and the screaming of fowls which accompanied the ship's departure from Bristol six weeks previously had ceased. Only one pig remained; the rest, together with the ducks and the fowls, had been consumed by the passengers during the voyage. The sea, too, was a contrast to the vast ocean they had recently crossed.

Caspar clenched the rail and smiled, recalling the intolerable noise, the cracking of the bulkheads, the sawing of ropes, the screeching of the tiller, the trampling of the sailors, and the clattering of crockery as the sea had battered the vessel, everything above the deck and below deck all in motion at once. Now there was such tranquillity that Caspar knew he was nearly home.

Slowly, he raised his head to face the sun streaming over the densely wooded mountaintops of the island. The coast, as he scanned it for familiar marks, looked as inhospitable as any foreign shore. Yet the very intensity of that tropical jungle assured Caspar that he was home. Its overpowering verdure was brighter than he could recall after six years of the rolling, civilized countryside of England.

The *Sir Godfrey Webster* tacked to port, away from the island, throwing the sun behind him. Looking ahead, Caspar saw how one particular mountain range, as though bolder than its fellows, protruded farther out to sea than the rest. It was an awesome range with a waterfall scouring down the side of it. Caspar knew that waterfall; it was on the plantation boundary.

"So this is your tropical paradise?"

Startled, Caspar looked up quickly at the man who was placing his arm around his neck.

"I'm sorry, Doctor." Caspar drew himself up to his full height. "I didn't hear you." He wriggled his shoulders uncomfortably.

"Nor should I expect you to," said the doctor, keeping his arm draped around Caspar. "This island of yours is an awe-inspiring sight. All mountains, trees and . . ." He paused as the vessel began to tack again, revealing the Layou basin. "And such vast rivers!"

"Look, Doctor, look!" Caspar pointed with excitement into the depths of the valley. "Up there on the hill, sir. That's Roxborough Hall."

Doctor Tyndall followed the youth's outstretched finger with his eyes. "Yes, I see it," he said, when he caught sight of a roof and a house of sorts nestling on a ridge of flat land at the crown of a small hill. The house seemed in danger of being engulfed by the sugarcanes and the towering coconut trees which surrounded it.

Doctor Tyndall sighed and cast his glance down from the hills. He took in the majestic sweep of the river where it emerged from the jungle and spread into the sea. To the right of the river, there was a cluster of dilapidated cabins and stone warehouses.

"That's Layou!" Caspar was unable to conceal his excitement at being so close to home.

The doctor grinned at the youth, aware of the might of the sun scorching them both. "How now, Caspar, you cannot wait to cut a few steps in that townlet and display your English finery?"

Caspar grinned with pride. He had dressed that morning in his very best clothes. The silver buckles on his shoes glittered, his white stockings were spotless and the wine color of his breeches and jacket accentuated the gold and silver of his brocade waistcoat. He had a new yellow stock at his throat.

"In this heat I'll warrant your English trappings won't see much wear, Caspar."

"We does dress properly in Dominica, Doctor, even if we are miles from England."

"We does?"

"We do."

George Tyndall smiled, linking his arm through Caspar's and strolling with him across the deck to the other side of the ship. From there, they were able to see the buildings of the village and the people shuffling down to the jetty. The ship was lining up for her approach through the sandbars which encircled the basin.

His interest in Caspar helped George ignore his own confused emotions. When he beheld the vast jungle and mountains looming over the tiny vessel and realized that this was to be his new home, George had been stricken with doubt about his acceptance of this strange assignment. However, Caspar's excitement and the easy intimacy between them helped to drive those doubts to the back of his mind.

George kept his arm linked in Caspar's as the lad pointed out various buildings. "Caspar should find no difficulty in adjusting to life on this West Indian plantation," he thought as the boy chatted. "It is going to be easy for him. He'll have the same success with his charming personality that he had in the drawing rooms of London's nobility."

Reluctantly, George drew his arm away from Caspar's and sighed privately to himself. The voyage was coming to an end, but he had hopes that the attachment which had grown between himself and Caspar would not be shattered now that the youth was returning to his own world. George would always recall the weeks of the voyage with pleasure. He had helped Caspar with his questions, enjoyed games of chess with him, and they had read poetry together.

He glanced again at Caspar, now waving at the ill-clad scamps on the shore. George marveled at the youth's astonishing beauty. It was a masculine beauty, of that there was no doubt; Caspar had his father's determined features. What made him so appealing to George was his soft, tawny complexion which, in the morning sunlight, seemed to be glowing like gold beneath the black silk locks of his hair. George raised his hand to touch the boy, sliding his fingers under Caspar's collar and curling his hand around his neck, clasping him affectionately.

He was rewarded by the youth's turning to face him, his yellow eyes gazing frankly into his.

"Are you not pleased we have reached the end of the voyage, Doctor?"

"Yes." George sighed again, withdrawing his hand.

"There is much I can show you in Dominica, Doctor," Caspar said with a smile. "When we are ashore and settled in at Roxborough Hall."

"Well, Doctor, this is the hellhole you've signed up for! What do you think now, eh?"

George spun around in surprise at the sound of his new employer's voice. He bowed his head respectfully. "Good morning, Mister Todd," he murmured. "It seems a most pleasant spot."

"Aye, you'll find that for sure." The Bondmaster's eyes, yellow like his son's, studied him deeply. "It will be a new experience for you, Doctor. You'll see things here they never taught you in medical school."

"I expect that."

"Oh, yes, I'm sure you do. As long as you can heal the cut of a whip so it leaves no weal, slice a cord so neither dam nor whelp bleed to death, and lustrate the pox from a prime rutting nigger, you'll make out, Doctor Tyndall."

"Yes, sir!" George was disgusted with himself. He had vowed to stand up boldly to Carlton Todd, who called himself the Bondmaster of Roxborough. He wanted him to know that he did not own George Tyndall, even if he did have a herd of the best slaves in the Caribbean. He scowled.

"Doctor, you can lead a good life here. Work well with me, and I'll reward you well, make no mistake

21

about that. The life is hard, and lonely sometimes. I remember. No shortage of wenches, though."

The Bondmaster gazed toward the town as the ship prepared to drop anchor in the center of the river. "There are no other white men at Roxborough, Doctor, so the pickings are yours."

"You've been away a long time, Mister Todd. Don't you consider things may have changed?"

"Changed? At Roxborough? My father was there. He's only been dead these three months, may he rest in peace. My father built Roxborough, Doctor; the hall, the plantation. See this town of whores and blacks here." Carlton waved in the direction of Layou. "Every one of them owes their existence to Roxborough. Changed? No, Doctor. This part of Dominica will never change, so long as there is a Bondmaster."

Caspar moved to the prow of the ship, away from his father and the doctor. He tried to pick out faces he recognized in the crowd on the shore, but none of them seemed familiar. He had been ten years old when his father took him to England six years before. He looked eagerly at the boys at the river bank to see if any of them came from the plantation. All were strangers to him. Five naked boys who had been standing on the end of the jetty plunged into the river to swim over to the ship. Caspar leaned over the rail and hailed them.

"I say, you there! Who are you?"

The boys shouted at him in a language both foreign and familiar. Caspar frowned.

"You've forgotten that slave patois, boy?" Carlton laughed when he observed Caspar's confusion. "Quite a little English gentleman we've brought back, eh, Doctor?"

"I was wondering how he'll settle down after the life in England."

"He'll adapt," said Carlton. "So will I, so will you. There's so much work to be done here." Carlton's bright eyes gleamed. "There is a fortune to be made, Doctor, and that is where you will be involved. Everyone wants slaves in these parts, Doctor, and at Roxborough we breed slaves. With your help, I'll be able to breed the strongest, healthiest slaves ever created to cut cane."

"What about those blacks there?" George indicated the boys in the river treading water and shouting at Caspar. "Are not they slaves, too?"

Carlton regarded them contemptuously. "Damned free niggers! My da' always used to curse this town of Layou here. Of course, we make good currency selling our Roxborough rum in the casinos, but Da' said it was dangerous to have a settlement of free blacks on the plantation boundary."

George was puzzled. "How is it they are free? I thought all blacks were slaves."

Carlton planted his legs wide apart and surveyed the river bank defiantly. "They are free because some soft-hearted English puppy released their sires years ago. The English did not take kindly to plantation life, Doctor. They did not know how to handle slaves!

"My da' came from the cotton fields of Alabama, and mama was a French lady from New Orleans. My people knew about niggers." Carlton spat in the river, a glob of phlegm smacking into the face of one of the boys.

"The English who settled here around the time when America went independent scattered when the French invaded. Those English mice armed their

23

slaves and freed them before scuttling back to England. They were more scared of Dominica than they were of the French!" Carlton grinned.

"Not my father! He was a match for any man. Hayes Todd lived through all the invasions, *buying* slaves instead of freeing them. He bought land, too, when he could. He started Roxborough, and I'm going to make it great, Doctor.

"You see the house up there. That's where I was born. That is my home, and that is where I am going to live now. That is where I want to die."

It was the first time George had heard Carlton so eloquent. In London, George had met the Bondmaster occasionally at Almack's, the Assembly Rooms in St. James's presided over by a cabal of ladies whose morals were often no better than those of *demi-reps* but whose birth placed them in a leading position as the dictators of polite society. It was at Almack's that Carlton had broached the idea to George about coming to Dominica.

George had been as much impressed by Carlton's self-assurance as by his rugged good looks and obvious wealth. It seemed that Carlton attracted attention wherever he went, always attended by the charming Caspar. George was captivated. He was twenty-four, nine years younger than the Bondmaster. Recently qualified as a doctor, he accepted Carlton's proposition immediately.

"We have traditions here, Doctor. There are not many whites on the island. We have to set an example. Blacks are incapable of thinking for themselves, and without a white master they are lost. A free slave is worthless. Look at that!"

Carlton pointed as Caspar tossed coins to the boys swimming around the anchor chain. The boys were laughing as the coins fell and they leaped to catch them.

"See how they frolic like monkeys? Not a thought in their heads."

"Surely, that's because they are boys," observed George, "not because they are blacks."

"Aye," said Carlton with a wry grin. "I knew you'd be one for your theories. Caspar!" he shouted. "Stop playing with those dam' monkeys and order a boat to take us ashore!" He returned his attention to the doctor. "The one thing you need right now, Doctor, is a glass of Roxborough rum to welcome you. The place for that is May Gregg's tavern."

Caspar strolled down the deck as Carlton spoke.

"See how he walks," laughed Carlton. "Quite the English gentleman!"

"You must be proud of your son."

Carlton frowned. "Son, Doctor? That is talk for England. We are in Dominica now. Here Caspar is not my son. He is my slave. I am no longer his father but his Bondmaster. I own him, mind and body, Doctor. My father owned his grandmother, and I shall own his sons and his daughters."

Chapter 2

THE BONDMASTER JUMPED ONTO THE JETTY, clearing a path with his stick through the mass of naked blacks who surged around them. George felt an arm clasp his waist as he stumbled behind him. It was Caspar, holding him securely and shouting at the rabble.

"Make way dere, yo' black rascals! Move out de road. Don't yo' see is de Bon'massa done return?"

Caspar deftly hooked his foot behind the Negro nearest to them and gave the man a hearty shove in his chest. The Negro toppled backwards off the jetty into the river. Caspar repeated the action while Carlton scythed at the mob with his stick. A gap cleared around them and they moved forward onto the shore.

"That's a dam' warm reception, Doctor!" Carlton was laughing.

Appalled, George studied the black faces of the creatures jabbering around him. He was stunned by the contrast between the near-naked Negroes and Caspar in his silk breeches and brocade waistcoat, the Bondmaster in his elegant London clothes and he himself in trousers and fashionable coat. He moved forward gingerly.

The Bondmaster's cane cracked down on the outstretched palms, and Carlton roared with delight. The Negroes shuffled back reluctantly.

"Is dis de way yo' does welcome de Bon'massa?"

Caspar glared at the crowd, waving his hand to brush the blacks away. He began a harangue in a language which seemed like a kind of French to George.

"Hear how the boy's found his tongue, Doctor!" cried Carlton. "Six years in the drawing rooms of London society with Lady Mountjoy and Madam de Lieven, no less, and within ten minutes of being back with his people, the boy is jabbering at them in his own language as though he had never been away. Mark my words, Doctor, slave blood is bound to show itself!"

Some of the negroes slunk away and crouched down on their haunches in the shade of the warehouse, while others lolloped along the road through the town. George glanced around him beyond the circle of woolly heads. The trail to his right disappeared into the jungle alongside the river bank. A stone warehouse stood opposite the jetty, its walls partially obscured by tropical foliage. George pulled a handkerchief from his sleeve and dabbed at the perspiration streaming down his face.

"Aye, the heat will get you," said Carlton, wiping his own brow with the back of his sleeve. "No sense in staying here when we can wait for the horses in the comfort of May Gregg's. Boy!" Carlton addressed Caspar. "Run fast now to the house and have them send the wagon for the baggage and two horses for me and the Doctor."

27

Caspar stared at his father with an expression of disbelief. He had no intention of doing any such thing. That was the job of niggers.

He watched his father and the doctor stride along the path into town. He was aware of the boys gathering around him, putting out their hands to finger the hem of his coat. He turned toward them. "Where is de boy dat will run to de *cou*?"

"Fuh a quartah, massa?" The answer came quickly from a boy dripping water down his naked body as he emerged from the river.

"A quarter, is it?" Caspar grinned at the boy's eagerness. The lad was about his own height. "What's your name, boy?"

"Ah does be Samboth, sah."

"You know me, Sam?"

"Don't know yo' by name, but yo' does be from de *cou*. Ah done see yo' when yo' done come here from de big house wid de rum wagon."

"Fine." Caspar smiled. He remembered the days when he had accompanied Kingston, the bookkeeper, on his rounds delivering casks of Roxborough rum to the town casinos. "Come, Sam." Caspar led the youth away from the idlers squatting on the bank.

"You look a lively lad. I'll give you a quarter and more, if you help me properly. Run fast to the house. You know Ella?"

"Miss Ella? At de *cou*? Of co's."

"Right, well, tell Ella that her Bondmaster has returned. And her son Caspar. Tell her Caspar says to send the wagon and also three horses. Don't forget three horses, now. Then run back here, Sam."

The boy repeated his instructions. Caspar grinned and cuffed the boy's ear playfully. "Yo' catch on quick, *garçon*. How come yo' does be free?"

28

"Born free!" Samboth sprinted down the trail with a shout.

Caspar turned his attention to the *Sir Godfrey Webster* lying in the river mouth. His father, he mused, must have forgotten in his pleasure at being home that someone had to arrange for their baggage to be brought ashore. He scratched his head in bewilderment. What did his father mean by telling him, Caspar, to run up to the house for the horses? "Maybe he was showing off in front of the doctor and the town Negroes," he thought, dismissing the matter from his mind and walking back onto the jetty.

He climbed down into the ship's skiff, manned by two English sailors. "Right," he ordered, "you can row me back to the ship now."

"Aye aye, Cap'n," leered one of them.

"Aye aye," laughed the other, hitting the water with his oar and splashing a shower of spray over Caspar. "Beggin' yer pard'n, sar!" he sniggered, propelling the skiff out into the river.

Carlton Todd was enjoying his homecoming. Steering the English doctor down the street, he felt a surge of nostalgia flow through him. The town was exactly as he remembered it, although the faces were difficult to recall. Heads popped up at open windows, and doors swung open as eyes peered at him and the doctor. Old men, squatting in the shade of the wattle cabins, watched them in blank amazement. Women cooking over wood fires in the clearings by their *ajoupas* dropped ladles and bobbed quick curtsies.

George was intrigued to see white people as well as blacks at the doors and windows of the taverns.

29

Many of the whites were dressed in rags and, with their swarthy countenances, were almost indistinguishable from the blacks. Others were better dressed and raised their hands in cautious salutes which Carlton acknowledged with a wave of his cane. Cries greeted him from all sides. "The Bondmaster's back! Hello, Massa Carlton! Mas Carlton, yo' done come home?"

"Merchants, smugglers, deserted seamen, ruined overseers, French picklocks, what you will," answered Carlton when George queried the presence of white men in the town. "Don't be fooled by their ragged appearance, Doctor," he added. "Layou is a prosperous town. Thirty casinos and taverns here, and every one of them full when we ship sugar."

George observed that some houses were constructed solidly out of stone, while others were assembled with wood from old barrels, chests, and boxes. A few houses sported galleries from which their occupants looked down on the street. On one there were five white women who leaned over the railing to touch the two men as they passed.

"At last, at last!" cried one. "Real English gentlemen! English Rose is the girl to ask for, sirs."

"Angelique! Angelique!" called another. "Ze Fwench gairl fair ze jentlemens! *Demandez Angelique!*"

"They are a new attraction!" chortled Carlton. "Looks like you won't find it so lonely at Roxborough after all, Doctor, if you fancy a white doxy. Come."

They were standing outside a stone building with doors open onto the street. Although the sun was blazing down on the outside, the interior of the building was dark. George could see nothing, but allowed himself to be led down two steps into the building which, Carlton told him as he gripped his arm, was May Gregg's casino.

"What! What!" A shriek greeted them as they stood at the foot of the steps trying to adjust to the gloom of the interior. George stood nervously behind Carlton and peered at the far corner, which seemed to be the source of the noise.

"Lor' 'ave mercy!" The shriek gave way to a cackle of laughter.

"Come," said Carlton, "she's here." He plunged into the gloom, leaving George to follow. He felt his way cautiously past tables and stools. Shafts of light seeping through cracks in a closed jalousie outlined the obstacles.

"Lor' 'ave mercy!" cackled the large woman jammed into a rocking chair in the corner. "Me own Carlton is 'ere! And ain't 'e as 'andsome a man as ever 'e was!"

The woman shook her enormous bottom and prized herself from the rocking chair, which clattered to the floor as she stood up. She wrapped her arms around Carlton, enveloping him completely. Her shrieks and cackles smothered Carlton's protests.

"Doctor! She has me choking to death in her bosom!"

"Wooh! Lor', Carlton, ain't never been a man to complain of that before!" May Gregg released Carlton and flopped back into her chair. "Wooh! I'm all a-quiver. Can't believe it, just can't." She began to fan herself.

In the dark, George could not see whether the monstrous woman was white or black. "Why is there no light in here?" he asked Carlton. "Fresh air is what the lady needs."

31

"Hah! You hear that, May? This young sprat I have with me says that fresh air is what you need."

"Fresh 'air! Lor', Carlton, you'll be the death of your old May. A fresh man, maybe, but fresh air ain't goin' to tickle me doodah! Wooh!" She erupted with raucous laughter, subsiding only when she realized that Carlton was still standing in front of her. "Lor', whatever 'appened to you, Carlton? Sit down, for lor' sake, and 'ave a jar."

"It's so dark in here, I can hardly see to make myself comfortable, May."

"That never troubled you before, Carlton! I'm so 'appy to see you back, and no mistake. Open the back shutter if you like. It so early yet, ain't none of us awake."

As light streamed into the cellar, George looked about him in horror. Three men lay asleep on the floor close to his feet, while in a far corner what seemed to be a white man and a Negress were entangled in each other's arms. Tables were upturned, stools and chairs lying upside-down, barrels on their sides, and broken glass and wine bottles strewed the floor.

Glancing behind the bar, George caught sight of something lurking waist-high from the floor. He stepped back in alarm as the shadow became a shape which moved over toward him. When it reached the light from the open shutter, George saw the shape was that of a small but fully grown Negro perfectly proportioned in every way but less than four feet in height. The creature was dressed in a blood-stained shirt and pantaloons. He carried a tray with a pewter jug containing water, a decanter of rum, and three goblets. He set the tray down on an upturned barrel in front of May Gregg.

"Come, Doctor, meet May Gregg, the keeper of the most famous casino in the Caribbees."

George stepped forward and proffered his hand, which May Gregg, whom he now determined was white, squeezed quickly without apparent interest.

She seized the goblet Carlton filled for her and gulped at it. "Ah!" she belched happily. "Now I does be getting me wind."

Carlton poured rum in another goblet, passed it to George, and began drinking his own with obvious pleasure. "That's the rum I've been missing all these years, May, though methinks you water it considerably. Try the grog, Doctor."

George placed the goblet on the table untouched and knelt down to inspect the three men on the floor. Two of the men groaned as he prodded them. The third did not move. George felt for the man's pulse.

"This man is dead!"

"Oh, lor'! We don't need no doctor to tell us that."

George was pale. "He's been dead for hours. What about the authorities? What will you do?"

It was May Gregg's turn to look surprised. "I'll do what I always do with dead men, 'eave 'is body out the back window into the sea. 'E's a sailor, ain't 'e? I always buries sailors at sea."

"Drink your rum, Doctor," ordered Carlton, winking. "May Gregg looks after her business, and you look after yours."

"I would remind you, Mister Todd, that it is the health of people that is my business."

"Sit down, man, sit down!" Carlton glowered.

George hesitated, then slowly crouched onto a small stool.

"Your business in Dominica, my fine young physician, is to keep your mouth shut and to help me breed prime healthy slaves. That's what I brought you to Dominica for, Doctor George Tyndall, and I'll be obliged, sir, if you would remember it!" Carlton's eyes narrowed as he watched the sulky expression on the young doctor's face.

"Should you have other thoughts, Doctor, *Sir Godfrey Webster* is bound for Antigua with the tide and you are welcome to return on board. I trust, of course," added Carlton with a leer, "that your dear mother will be able to cover the cost of releasing you from your obligation."

"My mother? What has she got to do with it?"

"Very little, dear Doctor, if you conduct yourself according to our agreement. If you don't, though, someone has to pay to release you from your bond. Who else other than your doting mother in England?"

George was stunned. "I thought you were a gentleman!"

"Why, so I am. In England. And you are a doctor. And May Gregg here is a whore. Now drink your grog and remember that we are no longer taking tea with society ladies at Almack's. Niggers and whores are your companions here, Doctor, not lords and ladies."

Chapter 3

THE CASINO FILLED QUICKLY. CASPAR STOOD AT the entrance and peered over the heads of the seamen packed inside. He glanced at the white faces of the customers as he tried to find his father. He moved forward through the entrance, but Samboth put his hand on his arm to restrain him.

"Yo' does not be permit in dere, Mas Capar. Yo' does be dress like a white man, but dat place does be fuh de *bekés* only."

Caspar appraised Samboth. He supposed Ella had given him the old breeches which he now wore. "Listen, boy. I've just come from England. I can go where I want."

"Dat not be de way here, Mas Caspar. Yo' step in dere an' Ma Gregg gon' send she bucks an' she dogs behind yo' so quick yo'll climb de nearest coconut tree to save yuh balls being bit off!"

"Is that so, Sam?" Caspar raised his eyebrow elegantly in the manner of a Regency dandy. "Boy, in England I had noble ladies kissing my very hands. I escorted ladies of the finest character to balls and to the theater. No one can keep me out of a waterfront brothel in my own country."

"Oy, oy, Caspar! Yo' does think yo' does be white? Yo' does be a Roxbruh slave, nigger!"

"Stop that nonsense, boy." Caspar cleared his throat. "I'm going in."

Samboth shrugged his shoulders and squatted down on the flagstone outside the casino. "Don't know about yuh English ladies, Mas Caspar. We niggers don't git no privilege in dere. Ah does wait fuh yo' here, Mas Caspar. Yo' gon' leave dere in one big hurry. Fuh sure!"

Straightening the yellow stock at his neck, Caspar stepped inside. A group of sailors from the ship who were drinking at a side table murmured as he passed them. He squared his shoulders defiantly and excused himself around a cluster of Frenchies standing in the center of the casino. A black face blocked his path.

"What yo' does be doing here, nigger?"

Caspar gulped in surprise. "Who do you think you are talking to, boy?"

The crush of drinkers pressing around him prevented Caspar from pushing past the Negro. "Where is the Bondmaster of Roxborough?" he demanded quickly as the fellow bore down on him.

"Yo' does be one fancy nigger boy!" The Negro's face split into a menacing grin.

"The Bondmaster!" repeated Caspar, standing his ground.

The Negro paused, peering at Caspar and noting his splendid attire. "He does be in de corner wid May Gregg."

Caspar tried to squeeze around the Negro, but the brute stopped him. "Wait, boy. Help me wid dis business."

"What?"

36

"Jus' take de legs." The Negro indicated the man stretched out on the stone floor in front of Caspar. "May Gregg done say to move he out de way. I can't ax dem buckras to help, an' only me an' de pygmy Bambute here dis early."

Caspar swallowed the scolding he wanted to utter at the slave's impertinence and bent down to grab the man's legs. The body was heavy. He helped the slave lug it out of the window near where the Bondmaster was sitting.

"Ho, my boy!" Carlton reached out and grabbed Caspar's wrist.

"May! I want you to see the colt I took to England. Come, Caspar! Stand there. Ain't he an English gentleman?"

"Lor', Carlton! You can really pick a fine nigger. Why, that buck even 'as your eyes!"

"My get, May. His dam is my old bed wench, Ella."

May Gregg cackled with laughter. She addressed George, who was staring morosely into his goblet. "You 'aven't made the acquaintance of Ella, Doctor? She's the Black Queen of Roxborough, and no doubt! None of the slaves at Roxborough dare to disobey 'er. You'll see.

"You call yourself a doctor, but there is no physic invented to match Ella's potions and powers. That's what kept the 'erd of slaves in check while their Bondmaster was in England."

May Gregg turned back to Carlton. "So, Ella is this buck's mother? And you are the father!" She nodded her head, setting the flesh quivering under her chin. " 'Ow did you 'andle 'im in England? I 'ear tell that a slave is a freeman once 'e sets foot there."

"May, in England, Caspar was my son. But now

at home, he is a Roxborough slave again."

Caspar regarded his father with disdain. "The horses are here, *sir*!"

"Hold your tongue, boy, when I'm speaking."

"Yes, *sir*!" Caspar grinned impudently, unperturbed by Carlton's tone.

"If 'e is a slave, would you sell 'im?"

"May, you have me there. I plan to breed a score of light-skinned whelps from him first."

George reached between May and Carlton for the rum decanter, which he drained into his goblet. He added water and poured the draught quickly down his throat.

"It's a pleasure to see that you are taking our medicine, Doctor!"

"I can't understand it," muttered George. "Caspar is your son, right? In England you took him everywhere, gave him an education and experiences only the most noble of English lads are privileged to enjoy.

"He speaks English and French with fluency, is tolerable at mathematics, and can discourse with wit and intelligence. He is sixteen and could have a glorious future. Yet you talk as though he is some kind of breeding stallion. You do not even speak of him as though he is a human being."

"Well, he ain't human, Doctor, is he? His mother is a nigger, so he is only half human."

May Gregg, jammed into her chair, rocked backward and forward, shaking with wheezy laughter. She came to rest, struggled to control her gasps, and concentrated her tiny red-rimmed eyes on Caspar. He stood uneasily under her gaze.

"I 'eard the doctor say that you are a stallion, boy!"

"Dam' right, May. The buck is hung like a jackass swinging two coconuts."

"Wooh!" May accelerated the rocking chair.

"You want to see, May? Come, boy. Shuck off your trogs."

"Here?"

It was George who spoke in astonishment. "You want him to take off his breeches in here?"

"What better place than a whorehouse, Doctor? It is more private than a vendue, anyhow. At slave auctions, scores of strangers finger the wenches and handle the bucks. Caspar knows what's wanted, don't you, boy?"

"Yes, *sir*."

George was amazed that Caspar showed no surprise at his father's strange command. The youth was loosening the ties of his silk breeches without a murmur of protest. There was a look of boredom on his face.

"He does it all the time, Doctor," explained Carlton to silence the doctor's protests. "Any man who owns a slave is proud to show off the nigger."

"Wooh, Carlton! They are not like you and yours, not now," interrupted May, rocking her chair to a halt as she watched Caspar undress. "Slaves are 'ard to buy since you left 'ere, Carlton. Not many 'as niggers fit to show off."

Caspar peeled down his breeches and let them hang over his stockings.

"Drawers!"

Caspar hesitated before obeying his father's command and slipping down the undergarment.

May Gregg was unable to contain herself. "Oh, lor', Carlton! The boy's a colossus!" She jammed her chubby hand between her thighs.

"Quick, quick," she wheezed. "Cover that black broadsword before my girls see it. They'll never want a white dirk again."

"For heaven's sake, get dressed, Caspar!" cried George in embarrassment.

Carlton smiled wryly. "Doctor, I'll make a slave-master out of you yet." He faced Caspar. "Everything ready to go up to the Hall?"

Caspar nodded, stooping to pull up his breeches. "The wagon has taken the belongings up to the house already."

Carlton turned his back on Caspar brusquely. The doctor was right; Caspar did possess wit and intelligence. If he were pure white, he would be a worthy heir for the Bondmaster. But he was half-black and a slave.

Caspar swaggered out through the crowded bar. Samboth sat on the roadside while a groom in tattered clothes held the reins of three horses.

"Ah don't know how yo' ain't booted out de place on yuh backside!" Samboth laughed with relief when he saw Caspar.

"May Gregg won't throw me out of her casino, Sam. Not now she has seen me stripped. I think she wants to buy me, just like a slave!"

"Yo' done strip off fuh she? Ain't no one ever done inspect me. Ah don't have no massa."

"You don't like to be a free nigger?" Caspar was surprised at Samboth's despondent tone.

"Mas Caspar, even though ah does be free, is yo' dat does be de nigger wid de silk britches."

"Whose your mam?" Caspar straightened his coat as he stood in the sunlight, conscious of the people staring at him from the galleries overlooking the street.

"Ah does not know. Ah ain't got no home, nor mam. Ah does think ah gon' get myself thieved by a nigger-stealer. He can sell me in Trinidad as a slave wid my brand of ownership on my shoulder. Like yo' an' all dem Roxbruh niggers."

"Don't say dat, *garçon!*" hissed Caspar in patois. "Look out! The Bondmaster is coming. I'm going!"

"Ah'm comin' wid yo'!"

"Boy, you're too fresh! Stay away, do you hear? You'll make Mas Carlton vexed."

"Ah gon' ax he take me to de *cou* wid yo'-all."

"No!" exclaimed Caspar, turning on the boy as he grasped his sleeve.

"You can come with me if you want, but don't address the Bondmaster!" He jerked his arm free from Samboth's grip. Carlton and George stood blinking in the sunlight.

"Damme, Doctor! I had quite forgotten it was day." Carlton shielded his eyes with his hands. He squinted at the horses. "Caspar, are those my Roxborough horses? There's three of them. I asked for two."

"Yes, sir," Caspar answered with a smile. "The third one is for me."

"For you, dammit!" Carlton brought his stick down with a smack across Caspar's rump. "What do you mean by that, boy?"

Caspar gaped at Carlton. Samboth dodged to the other side of the road, where he watched nervously.

"I don't mean anything!" Caspar rubbed his bottom ruefully.

"I did not say you could ride back with us, did I, boy?"

"No." Caspar lowered his eyes to the ground.

41

"Exactly! Caspar, we are not in England any more. You have to accustom yourself to the ways of plantation life again. At Roxborough, you do nothing without obtaining my authority first, you hear?"

Caspar raised his head wanting to speak. He glanced at the people watching from the galleries and felt a flush of embarrassment creeping into his cheeks. He nodded silently.

"Fine! I want to see no more of this independence you seem to have brought back with you from England." Carlton studied the horses. "These are mangy beasts, Doctor. That nigger isn't much better. What's your name, boy?"

The youth holding the horses gawked at Carlton.

"Tell de Bon'massa yuh name, boy!" Caspar encouraged in patois. "Hold yuh head up high when yo' does speak."

"Ah does be Caliste, Mas Carlton, sah," stammered the slave.

Carlton shook his head sadly. "I feel my slaves have been neglected, Doctor. There has been no training and no discipline while I have been away." He took the reins from the groom's hand and mounted the horse easily, steadying the animal while George mounted his.

"I want a Roxborough buck to be bright and pleasing to the eye. The groom here is a disgrace."

"Caspar's bright enough," challenged George, "but you beat him for it."

"Don't misunderstand me, Doctor." Carlton dug his heels into the horse; the two riders moved off together. "I do appreciate Caspar's finer qualities. However, the boy seems to regard himself as an equal. He must learn and learn quickly to accept his position now we are back at Roxborough."

42

Caspar gazed after the two men trotting down the street, followed by Caliste running behind them. He stroked his cheek, smirking to himself.

"It seems my Bondmaster wants to use me as his whipping boy, now we are home," he thought. "We shall soon see who is the Bondmaster and who is the bondsman!" He chuckled aloud, taking the reins of his horse which Samboth handed to him.

"Sam, you've seen how the Bondmaster gets on. You still want to come to Roxborough?"

"Yassa!"

"If I am to be a slave again, Sam, I think I shall favor myself with a slave of my own."

Caspar jumped on the horse and held out his hand to help Samboth climb up behind him.

Chapter 4

ELLA SURVEYED THE KITCHEN SERENELY. EVERY-
thing was under control. Pip was decanting the rum
which old Massa Hayes had put to mature in a
cask the day Mas Carlton had left. From the aroma
and Pip's ecstatic expression, she knew it was all
right. Cleo, the wench who helped with the cooking,
was stirring a large pot on the grate.

At the long wooden table in the center of the
stone kitchen, a girl sat chopping chives. She worked
quietly, aware that Ella was watching her, excited
that the Bondmaster was coming home. Even Sophy,
whose usual job was helping Tita to look after the
children, was involved in the preparations and energetically polished a silver tureen.

A young boy with a stack of woodchips in his
hands burst through the back door. He tipped them
into a basket by the brick oven. He stood back.

"What next?"

"Boy, put some of dat wood on de fire." Cleo indicated the embers under the grate of the oven. "Not
so yo'r out it, Dontfraid."

Ella paused thoughtfully at the end of the wooden

44

table. She was trying to think what she had forgotten. She patted her hair to stir her thoughts.

"Oh, mah gawd! Look at me! Ah done prepare everything fuh Mas Carlton, but ah done fuhgit to prepare meself!"

"Don't matter, Miss Ella. Ain't nothing de Bon'-massa gon' say but he pleased he back home." Pip put the rum cask down on the floor and held up the decanter. "Dis rum hab de color of ol' gold."

He walked to the door and held the decanter to the sun. "See how it does be clear an' golden. It does be a shame dat Massa Hayes does be dead so he can't taste none."

"Yo' done taste he share!" Ella bustled over to him. "Yo' see dem comin'?" She peered over Pip's shoulder down the hill path.

"Ain't no cause to worry, Miss Ella. Ah done send boys down to Layou. When Mas Carlton does start he way up de hill, dey does run an' tell me."

"Mas Carlton sure gon' be pleased wid you', Pip." Ella put her hand on Pip's arm affectionately. Sophy was quick to observe the gesture as she polished the tureen.

"An' wid yo', Miss Ella." Pip winked.

"Ah does be pleased when dat Massa here!" Ella announced to the kitchen slaves. "De plantation ain't right widout a white man in de place." Ella squeezed Pip's arm and sighed with pleasure.

"Ah been waiting fuh dis day. Mas Carlton was be so sorrowful when he done go. He done hab plenty hate to lose out he heart!"

"Ah does rem'ber. Ah was be a house slave when he done leave. After he wife done die."

Ella looked at Pip sharply. "Ah does be talkin' too much. Let me go 'n prepare meself. Ah does hab a gown ah ain't wear since de day he done go away."

"Yo' think yo' still can wear dat thing?"

"Oh mah gawd, boy, ah so fat?"

"Go, Miss Ella! Ah does call yo' if he does come."

When Ella had bustled down the passageway to her quarters, Pip placed the decanter in the center of the table. "Dat does be de Bon'massa's special rum," he began. "Ain't nonè of yo' was be house slaves when de Bon'massa done go away.

"Ah does rem'ber dat day Mas Carlton done sail away. Ol' Mas Hayes done come down de kitchen heself. 'Boy,' he done tell me, 'yo' go down de still house an' ax Kingston fuh one puncheon of rum. Not nigger rum, but de best rum de does be. Yo' keep dat rum here fuh de day when de Bon'-massa does return,' he done tell me."

"What fuh de Bon'massa done leave Roxbruh?" Dontfraid was sitting on a bench, his elbows resting on the table as he listened to Pip in awe.

Cleo slapped his ears suddenly. "Boy, yuh tongue does be too big in yuh mouth fuh yuh size!" She drew back her hand to strike the boy a second time.

"He don't know, Cleo," said Pip. "Dat's a'right. De Bon'massa sail 'way when he wife, Mistress Sybil, done die."

"Ah does know dat," said Dontfraid, rubbing his ears to stop the pain. "Ah done hear dat in de quarters."

"Boy, what's yuh age?" asked Sophy haughtily.

"How ah does know? Maybe ah hab ten years?"

"Ah gon' ax de Bon'massa give yo' ten lashes," Sophy retorted. "Yo' don't hear Miss Ella say yo' must sweep de back yard? Stop yuh noise an' go about yuh tax, nuh!"

"Yo' don't know de Bon'massa no more dan me."

Dontfraid stood up. "Is yo' dat does be a quarters wench 'til Tita done carry yo' come help she wid de childrens."

"Hush yuh tongue, boy, an' get out de kitchen!" Cleo brought her ladle down sharply across his bottom.

Dontfraid scampered out, setting the chickens squawking away in fright.

Sophy stood up. "Ah finish down in dis kitchin. Ah gon' help Tita." Sophy headed for the front step.

"Let me tell yo'," Pip cautioned. "When de Bon'massa does be here, ain't no slave has de right to use de front step."

"Yo' think ah does be scared of dat white man! Ah does use de front step 'til de Bon'massa heself does tell me no!"

Sophy flounced out while Cleo clucked in disapproval.

"Unless Mas Carlton done change he ways, she in fuh one clash wid he." Pip nodded knowingly. He picked up the decanter and carried it to the back steps.

Roxborough Hall was not one of the Caribbean's great houses. Carlton's father, Hayes Todd, had constructed the house along the lines of plantation homes in Alabama when he had arrived in the island nearly forty years before. His plan to extend the house if he grew prosperous was abandoned when his wife died. The old house, which the slaves called the *cou*, served him for the rest of his life.

The kitchen, pantry, store, and quarters for the house slaves were solidly constructed from stone dragged up the hill from the river bed. The upper part of the building was wooden, painstakingly created under the supervision of a carpenter who, even in those days, had cost a hundred pounds.

The carpenter had built a magnificent gallery around the four sides of the house with elaborate carving to give it an air of distinction. The gallery afforded a view over the plantation down to the mouth of the Layou River. At the back of the house there were wooden steps for the slaves to use. The steps at the front were constructed of stone and led straight up from the front drive to the gallery and drawing room. The dining room, located at the back of the house, adjoined the drawing room with another door opening onto the back gallery.

When old Hayes Todd built the house, he had planned that the two bedrooms at the front, each with its own dressing room, should be for himself and his wife, Monique. The upper part of the house also had two guestrooms with access from the back gallery. One of these was now used by Carlton's two children, Laura and Hayes, and by Tita, their nanny.

"Yo' done tell Sophy dat she must use de back stairs now Mas Carlton does be comin'?" Tita's eyes flashed angrily as she stormed into the dining room to berate Pip.

Pip placed the decanter carefully on the oak dresser and turned to face Tita. "Ah does be de one dat say so."

"Who yo' think yo' does be in dis house? Not yo' dat does be Pipiritte, de kitchen boy? Maybe Ella does try to work she powers fuh yo', but yo' ain't de one to tell Sophy nothing about no front step." Tita paused for breath.

"Sophy does be nurse fuh young massa Hayes, dat's what. She ain't no kind of kitchen nigger like yo' an' Cleo an' Dontfraid. Don't yo' fuhgit dat!

48

Sophy gon' use what steps she does fancy to use, jus' like me!"

"So yo' does say, Tita."

"Ah does be Mistress Tita to yo' boy. If yo' please!"

"An' ah does be Mister Pip!"

"Mister Pip! Hah! Ah does be pleased when Mas Carlton does be here. All yuh freshness gon' stop, den. Ah gon' ax he send yo' back to de fields to cut cane."

"Ah ain't never been no field hand!" Pip spun around to face Tita. He saw she was dressed in clothes which had belonged to Carlton's dead wife. Her straight black hair was glistening, and she had powder on her face to lighten her complexion. There was rouge on her cheeks.

"Ah does be a house slave, Tita. Jus' like yo'." Pip spoke slowly. "Ah don't pretend ah does be white!"

Tita's light brown complexion darkened at Pip's words. She advanced toward him, flexing her fingers.

"How yo' does speak like dat? Ah does be de one dat suckle de Bon'massa's children! Ah does be de one dat does live in he wife chamber jus' like a buckra. Is yo' dat does be de kitchen nigger!"

"So yo' does say, Tita."

Pip stepped aside as Tita leaped toward him. She stumbled and clutched at the dresser to keep herself from falling. Pip caught her by her wrists. He held her firmly, his dark eyes level with hers.

"Let go of me!" she screamed. "Yo' bozal!" She spat at him. "Ah does know how yo' does molest Ella. She does be Mas Carlton bed wench. Mas Carlton gon' lash yo' when ah does tell he."

49

Astounded, Pip released Tita's wrists. Quickly, she seized the slender neck of the decanter and thrust it at him.

"Dat's de Massa's special rum!" Pip cried in horror. "Don't spill dat!"

"Ah gon' cut yo'l" Tita shrieked, lunging at Pip's face. He ducked, knocking the decanter out of Tita's grasp with his shoulder. It smashed on the floor, spilling its precious contents.

"Boy!" The voice cut angrily through the room. A white man with golden hair, wearing a brown coat and gray trousers, stood at the front door, a cane raised in his hand.

"De Bon'massa!" hissed Tita. She fell forward in a curtsey.

"What in hell's name is going on here?" Carlton strode across the room, ignoring the wench grasping his ankles. He glared at the black youth cowering in the corner.

"De kitchen boy, Massa Carlton, sah! He done break de decanter of old rum ah was be saving fuh yo,' sah. He was strikin' me blows wid it sah. Yo' done save me, sah!" Tita clasped Carlton below his knee.

Carlton shook his leg free vigorously. "Stand up!" There was something familiar about the long black hair and near-white features of the wench. She was a pure Fulani, he remembered. She was plumper and had aged. "You're Tita, ain't you?"

"Yas, mah massa," Tita purred triumphantly.

"What's this row about?"

Tita took her time to rise from the ground, touching up her hair and smoothing down her dress. She looked at Pip with scorn. "He does be de kitchen boy, Mas Carlton. He does be too fresh. Ah warn he a'ready. Ah done tell de boy ah does be a re-speck'ble nanny fuh yuh children an' he not sup-posed molest me. Dat nigger won't listen, sah. He done pick up yuh decanter wid de rum an' he done give me blows, sah. He does hit me so hard, it done break, sah." Tita buried her head in her hands, sobbing loudly.

"Is that true, boy? demanded Carlton as George walked over to Tita to comfort her.

"No, sah, massa sah."

"Ooooh! Hear how he lies, sah!" screamed Tita.

Carlton's cane crashed down across Pip's cheek. The slave raised his hands to protect himself. "Don't beat me, sah. She dat done do it, sah."

"Don't beat you, boy! You tell me, heh?" Carl-ton's composure snapped at the slave's whining. He sliced the cane across the boy's right cheek, sneering at Pip's cry of pain. His teeth clenched in rage, he beat the boy's head and shoulders with short, sharp thrusts.

"Carlton!"

The voice in its familiarity made him stop. He turned. The black woman standing at the door was holding out her arms. Her smile was warm and confident as she gazed at him with affection. Carl-ton stood without moving, remembering. Ella swept across the room, her long dress trailing in the rum and broken glass on the floor. She clasped him around his shoulders and hugged him to her, pressing her lips against his neck.

He tensed, ready to push her off.

"Oh, Carlton! I am so pleased you have come home at last. We need you so much." Her shoulders shook as she began to weep.

51

The cane clattered to the floor. Carlton seized the wench around the waist. "Ella!" he whispered into her ear. "Ella, my own Ella!"

Chapter 5

CARLTON RELEASED ELLA AND APPRAISED HER. Amazingly, she was still for him the tall, long-limbed wench he had loved so passionately as a boy. His absence in England seemed to have made no difference to his desire for her.

Ella was Carlton's age. She was royal Batutsi. Her proud, sensitive features reflected the high intelligence for which her tribe was renowned.

"Carlton," she murmured, her eyes bright with pleasure, one hand clasped in his. "The children."

He looked toward the doorway of the bedroom which used to be his wife's. A girl stood watching him, a faint frown on her brow. Her blond hair was long, brushed back from her parchment-white face.

She had, Carlton observed quickly, her mother's blue eyes and English features. It was like seeing a pale ghost of his dead wife. Carlton hesitated, letting Ella's hand fall.

The girl's frown cleared immediately. She took a step toward him. "Faddah?"

"Laura!" Carlton relaxed, extending his arms for his daughter to run to him.

She walked over slowly, standing in front of him so his hands fell on her shoulders.

"You've grown into a big girl, Laura."

"Of co'se. Ah does have twelve years of age, Faddah."

It was Carlton's turn to frown. "Child!" He shook her shoulder. "Is that the way you speak?"

"Ah does call yo' faddah de way Tita done tell me," Laura pouted.

Carlton glanced at Ella.

"She has no tutor, Carlton," Ella explained. "Tita is her nanny. I cannot interfere."

"Ah done teach she about yo', Mas Carlton," said Tita defensively. "She does be a good child."

"I'm sure," said Carlton. "But she speaks like a slave, Tita. You could not correct her?"

"Me, Mas Carlton? She don't git dat slave talk from me."

"What a beautiful daughter you have, Mister Todd!" George thrust himself into the dining room and beckoned Laura to him.

"Come, child." He crouched down to bring his face level with hers.

"To think such a pearl should be found in the midst of this nigrescence."

"Doctor Tyndall and I will soon have you speaking English properly, Laura."

Carlton caught sight of a boy peering out from the bedroom.

"Hayes!"

Carlton knelt down and beckoned the boy to come to him. There was no mistaking his son. Laura led him over, and Carlton embraced them both.

"Now, Doctor, you see my family."

"Two handsome children!" George contemplated

54

the boy. He was struck by the similarity of Hayes to Caspar. They had both inherited Carlton's eyes, although Hayes was lighter-skinned than Caspar. Hayes, however, was darker in complexion than his sister Laura, who had the pale cheeks of a traditional English maiden.

Tita hustled the children out of the gallery while Carlton and George sat themselves at the dining table. Pip, his face blotched by the blows from Carlton's cane, assisted Ella in serving dinner. Both men ate vigorously after weeks on ship's fare. It was sunset before they were finished.

"Come, Doctor!" said Carlton rising from his seat. "In the old days with my father, I used to sit on the gallery and watch the day end. 'Creolizing' we called it."

He led the way onto the back gallery with its view of the sun setting out at sea. Here were two wooden chairs with long arms and a hole cut in each arm in which to rest one's drinking glass.

"Pull your chair up to the rail, Doctor. Like this," Carlton sat down. "You can put up your feet on the railing so, and relax in perfect contentment, a glass by your side.

"That's creolizing."

"Admirable!" George leaned back with his feet up on the railing, marveling at the speed with which the sun was disappearing on the distant horizon. "One could become quite possessed by the beauty of this place."

"A rum will give you even greater appreciation, Doctor." Carlton clapped his hands for Pip.

"Boy, you say you have some old rum put aside for my homecoming? Let's have a screw."

The slave nodded and darted down the stairs.

George waited until the Negro had passed out of earshot. "Your maid, Tita," he said. "She claimed that young fellow there gave her blows with the decanter. I examined her when she was crying. There was no sign of blows at all. Strange, don't you think?"

"I suspected as much. Handling slaves is a curious business, Doctor. This boy, Pip. He was about fifteen when I left. We called him Pipiritte then, because he was so small.

"A cut from my cane this afternoon helped to remind the rascal who is the master now that I am back."

"You are not concerned that the woman was lying?"

"Niggers always lie, Doctor. If it's not a lie to save themselves, it's a lie to please you. Never trust a Negro, Doctor. The day you forget that might be the last day you live."

"You make plantation life sound quite perilous!"

"It is, it is. I have three hundred slaves here. Only you and I and my two children are white. What is to stop those slaves rising up and murdering us all?"

George frowned. "Good treatment? Make them feel they are better off cared for as Roxborough slaves than as runaways in the hills."

Carlton snorted. "Good treatment! That's a theory for you! It's fear, Doctor. Ella was able to run the place when I was in England because of fear, not good treatment. She is a slave, but the others move in terror of her."

"Why? She seems a most attractive and personable woman to me."

"You are looking at her as a human being, Doctor. Negroes are not humans! She is a devil in a wench's form, that Ella." Carlton lowered his voice to a whisper and leaned over to George.

"She is what the slaves call an obeah woman. She can work spells on their behalf, and put curses on them, too. That's how she controls them."

George was skeptical. "And you? How do you exert control?"

"Not through obeah, Doctor! A slavemaster has to be unexpected, cleverer than the wiliest Negro. Never let a nigger know what you are going to do next, and you will always have his respect."

George contemplated the changing colors of the sky. He was puzzled by the gloom which descended on the house with the fading of the sun. As the sky blackened, an atmosphere of foreboding hung over the house. He shivered in the breeze which swept up suddenly from the sea.

George was relieved when he saw Caspar coming up the back stairs holding a lantern. The youth was followed by Ella, who carried a tray containing a decanter of rum and glasses.

Caspar bade them good evening and quietly moved around the gallery and inside the house, lighting lanterns and candles. While the brightness relieved the gloom of the house, George was aware that the light only heightened the utter blackness of the night outside.

He could not dispel the feeling that there was something ominous in the influences hanging over Roxborough.

Ella was hospitality itself. It was hard for George to regard her as a slave when she graciously served him a glass of the special rum, smiling with pleasure like any society hostess.

Carlton sighed. "I was thinking." His voice trailed

57

away as though he, too, felt ghosts in the sudden dusk.

"Those days are done!" Ella's voice was emphatic. "This is a new life now, Carlton. You can begin again!"

"Aye, old Hayes is dead, and the slaves are breeding like rabbits, I hope." He chuckled, sipping the rum. "That's good grog. Tita did right to preserve it."

"Tita, Carlton? Pip saved that rum for you since the day you left. Tita is a foolish wench, Carlton." Ella paused.

"She may be giving your children her bad ways."

"Really?" Carlton seemed unconcerned. "What wenches have you got for me and the doctor tonight, eh?"

A flicker of disappointment crossed Ella's eyes.

George pulled his feet off the balcony rail and sat up abruptly. "Wench, Todd? What do you mean?"

"It is the custom at Roxborough, Doctor, for a guest to be given a bed wench for the night. Don't worry! Ella is well versed in a white man's tastes.

"The wench is carefully bathed and perfumed before being admitted to one's chamber. When you have finished with her, she will return to her quarters."

"I really don't think it would be proper," George stammered.

"Proper! Dammit, it's practical, not proper.

"I give you the use of one of my females for the night and in return I might get a light-skinned whelp out of the wench. I'm sure you could do with a young virgin after those weeks at sea!"

George gulped at his rum. Caspar had returned

and was standing beside him, while Ella waited in front of Carlton. George glanced at Caspar.

"Please do not concern yourself with me, Todd. The greatest pleasure for me after that voyage will be to sleep in a comfortable bed on dry land."

"Nonsense, Doctor! Ella, you have some wenches?"

"Yes, Mas Carlton."

Her icy tone was wasted on Carlton. "Go for them, Ella. Three or four will do. We'll make our selection." He turned his attention to Caspar.

"What ho, young fellow! Are you pleased to be home, boy?"

"Yes, sir."

"Why did you not serve us at dinner, boy?"

"I was supervising the unloading of the wagon," Caspar answered casually. "Your trunks are in old Massa Hayes's chambers, and I have put the doctor's belongings in your old room."

"Have you, dammit! And what about you, Caspar? Where are you to be quartered?"

"I shall sleep downstairs in the kitchen."

"Hah!" smiled Carlton. "You have remembered your place, boy."

"It will serve for tonight."

George was pleased that Caspar refused to be intimidated by Carlton. There was an engaging quality about the boy which was absent in his father, and it had nothing to do with the boy's youth. George wondered whether Carlton knew how fortunate he was in having a son like Caspar.

Ella returned, ushering three girls onto the gallery. They were each dressed in loose white shifts and were as black as midnight with hair gathered in tight braids across their scalps. George regarded their

59

full lips and squashed noses in horror. They lined up nervously in front of Carlton.

"Hah! Doctor, what a splendid collection of Africa's nubility. You want them to strip so you can finger them first? Choose the wench that takes your fancy!" He saw George shrink back in his seat.

"Don't worry about taking mine, dear fellow. It's your choice first, anything will do for me. It ain't no difference which one drains my water tonight!"

"You are very kind," muttered George, repelled by the sight. "I am not accustomed to such traditions. In Nottinghamshire, it is rather a different kind of life."

Carlton chuckled. "What is it? You don't like black loins? There's nothing your Nottinghamshire virgins have to match the sweetness of a black wench, I can tell you!" He smacked his lips.

"It does me good to see these three and to know that every one of them is mine to do what I want with. Come, man, take this one!"

George protested, glancing at Caspar for assistance. The youth looked amused. George coughed to cover his embarrassment.

"Put her in the doctor's room, Ella," ordered Carlton. "You, boy," he said to Caspar. "Come here!" Caspar moved awkwardly, holding his hands over his breeches.

"Hah!" said Carlton, brushing aside the boy's hands and grasping him suddenly.

"You see that prick, Doctor! It's as stiff as the barrel of a gun. You shall have one of these wenches tonight, Caspar. Fire your shots good, boy!"

Caspar brushed his father's hand away abruptly and stepped back. "Don't touch me like that, sir!"

"What!" Carlton angrily dashed his glass to the floor. "How dare you tell me what to do!" He rose from his chair and looked around him for his stick.

Caspar grinned. "If you hold me that way, sir, I'll break before I get to the wench!"

Chapter 6

GEORGE STAGGERED TO HIS BEDROOM, CLOSING the door rapidly. A lamp flickered a dim glow around the chamber with its large four-poster bed in the center. George stepped toward the bed with a sigh of relief. He stopped suddenly, aware of another presence in the room.

He pulled aside the curtain and peered into the shadows of the bed. In the middle of the mattress, a scowl of reluctance on her face, was a naked wench.

George felt a gush of nausea surging through him. His stomach tightened, his knees buckled, and he pitched forward over the bed. A stream of vomit erupted from his mouth, splattering the girl's ebony skin with yellow and red lumps.

The girl watched him in terror as he spewed over her, only twisting away when he quietened and lay inert across the bed. The door creaked open.

"What's wrong, girl?" Caspar slipped into the room.

The girl clutched at the bed curtain. "Don't beat me, sah! Ah done do nothin', sah."

Caspar nodded his head. "Go to the quarters, wench. Say nothing about this."

"Yassa!" The girl darted out onto the balcony.

Caspar bolted the door behind her and turned back to the bed. He smiled knowingly at the sight of the doctor sprawled across the counterpane. Taking a towel from the washstand, he dampened it and carefully wiped away the gobs of vomit from the doctor's face.

"The rum is too strong for you, Doctor," he murmured tenderly.

When he saw that the doctor did not stir, Caspar lifted him up and placed him properly on the bed with his head resting on the pillows. Slowly he unstrapped the doctor's boots, gently easing them off his feet. He untied the stock at his throat, removed his jacket and pulled off his trousers.

Caspar stood back to contemplate the white man. After six weeks of the doctor's company on board the *Sir Godfrey Webster*, Caspar believed he knew him as well as the doctor knew himself. He understood the doctor's feelings.

"How you will fare here, I do not know!" Caspar shook his head as he gazed at the man. "You look too soft for plantation life, Mas Carlton ain't going to understand why you don't mount his wenches!" Caspar touched George's shoulder. "I do, Doctor."

He withdrew his hand slowly, turned down the lantern, and crept out of the room.

Ella was waiting for him.

"The doctor is all right," he told her stiffly.

"Huh! Don't know how dat *beké* gon' be we doctor! Is me dat does know de remedy fuh all de sickness we does have here."

"Of course, Ella." Caspar embraced his mother

63

warmly. "Mas Carlton has learned a lot in England. So have I. The doctor is here as part of Mas Carlton's program to improve the Roxborough stock. The doctor won't be able to do very much without your help, Ella. Do you think you could care for three hundred slaves alone?"

"An' what ah done do fuh de past six years?"

"I know, Ella. Things will be changing now." Caspar accompanied his mother to the kitchen. He glanced around. "Mas Carlton did say I could have one of them wenches tonight, Ella."

"Shush, Caspar. Yo' don't want no *beké* discard. Dere does be wenches ah does be saving fuh yo' when yo' does be ready."

"I'm ready now, Ella!"

Impatiently, he paced the stone floor of the kitchen. He picked up a chicken leg from the dish on the table, gnawed at it briefly, then flung it to the floor. He licked his fingers, then straightened his stock at his neck and spun around, aware of Ella watching him.

"How do I look, Ella? This is the way I dress in England when Mas Carlton and I visit the gentry."

"Yo' look like a young English, Caspar."

"I think perhaps I will go and visit the gentry down at May Gregg's tavern, Ella. There is no one here to see how I am looking."

"No, Caspar! Yo' does be here, now. Yo' don't know when Mas Carlton gon' call yo'."

"There is Pip who can attend him. I'm home now, Ella. I'm not going to be running every time Mas Carlton whistles, just like his pet dog. I had enough of that in England. There are plenty of slaves here to do the Bondmaster's bidding."

Ella stared in disbelief. "Hush, Caspar! Yo' must

64

banish those thoughts from yuh head. Yo' is de Bon'massa's, Caspar, jus' like we. Yo' does be bound to obey he."

Caspar nodded politely. He knew Ella would not understand She had been reared in slavery and had never seen another life the way he had, "Yes, Ella," he smiled to reassure her. "You are right, of course."

He sat on the end of the table and appraised her affectionately She was a fine woman with her straight back, rounded bottom, full breasts, and her proud royal Batutsi face.

"It ain't funny!" retorted Ella when she saw the smirk on his face.

"I'm smiling at you, not at what you say, Ella."

"How so?"

"Because you are a woman to smile at, Ella."

Ella arched her eyebrow, sensing Caspar's mood. "Yo' done grow in sweet talk as well as body, Caspar."

"Yes." His voice was heavy.

"Ah s'pose we both does be disappointed tonight." Ella wanted to show she understood his feelings. He was swinging his legs over the table edge. She put her hand on his thigh.

"Don't be vex'. Caspar. Yo' see how Carlton done want some quarters wench fuh he first night at home? Dat gon' make Tita please to see he don't want me."

"Tita! Why do you fret about Tita?"

"She has she ways, Caspar."

"Mas Carlton knows all about Tita. He bought her for Mistress Sybil and kept her after she died to look after the children. Now he is back, he is going to educate Hayes and Laura himself."

Ella snorted. "Well, have a care wid Tita, ah does tell yo'."

"Yes, Ella, I understand." Caspar put his hands on Ella's shoulders as she stood in front of him, her eyes level with his. Her fingers idly traced a pattern on his silk-covered thigh.

"Ella," he breathed slowly, frowning. "Don't do that!"

Ella paused, peering knowingly into her son's yellow eyes. Her fingers crept up his thigh and her lips brushed his soft cheek.

Caspar tightened his grip on her shoulders, pulling her toward him. His lips met hers.

"Yo' does be a'right, Caspar?"

Caspar looked up sharply. Samboth stood at the side of the table, a puzzled expression on his face.

"How did you get here?" Caspar demanded.

"Through de door, of co'se."

Caspar glanced around the silent kitchen. Ella had gone. His body throbbed as he lay on the kitchen table.

"Ah done think yo' done pass out wid de rum, Caspar," Samboth said, jumping up to sit on the edge of the table beside him. "Yo' sure done look strange stretched out on top de table wid yuh britches down."

Caspar rolled over to inspect himself. His silks were creased, his brocade waistcoat was stained, and his breeches were sticky. He sniffed.

"So much for the English troggery, boy." He tugged off his stock and threw it on the floor.

Samboth dived off the table and retrieved it. "Don't throw yuh things, Caspar."

"I'm not throwing!"

"Where do I sleep, Caspar?"

"Huh?" Caspar slid off the table and frowned at his own appearance. "I am dam' tired myself," he muttered. "House slaves sleep down here. Come, boy."

Caspar led Samboth along the passageway from the kitchen. The pantry and store were locked. The room next to them was Ella's. He tapped on the door and called his mother by name. There was no answer.

He shrugged his shoulders at Samboth and tried the door opposite. It swung open. Samboth held up the lantern. There was one bed in the room.

Samboth shut the door and placed the lantern on the floor. Caspar peeled off his coat and waistcoat and threw them with a laugh into the corner. His stockings came next, rolled off his feet with a sigh of pleasure. Soon he was standing naked beside the bed.

"Now yo' does be dress like any other nigger," said Samboth.

"Huh?" Caspar was too tired to joke. "Blow out the lamp, boy." He threw himself down on the bed, waiting for Samboth to lie beside him.

Ella was happy. Tonight there were two buckras in the house and her own son. There were many things which Roxborough needed to return the plantation to its former days. Carlton would have to be ruthless with the slaves. The doctor was not a slavemaster, but at least he was white and the slaves would respect him for that.

She listened to the night sounds. Frogs were chirping in the valley. There was the sawing of branches as they waved in the breeze, and the caw of the crackcracks and crickets. Ella tilted her ear to the night to listen for noises from the slave quarters. All was silent.

Word that the Bondmaster had returned to the plantation had been passed from slave to slave. An atmosphere of tension was spreading among the slaves. The security of having no white man to beat them was vanishing. Ella gloated.

She absorbed the atmosphere of the night, drawing strength from its black depths. After an hour, she rose out of her chair and padded in her bare feet, her long dress trailing across the floorboards of the gallery, to the door of Carlton's room. She pressed her ear against it and listened.

When she could distinguish Carlton's regular snores from the noises in the bush surrounding the house, she unlatched the door and stepped swiftly into the room.

Carlton lay on his back, snoring gently. Ella glided over to his bed. How easy it would be, she realized, for a slave to enter his room and kill him. She bit her lip with concern. The *nègres marrons* were in the hills. Those groups of runaway slaves had attacked plantations before.

Ella slithered out of her dress and lay down beside him.

"You bitch!" Carlton's hands reached for her throat. "You thought I did not know you were here!"

Ella beat at his back with her fists.

He fell on her, gnawing at her breasts and pinioning her body to the mattress with his long legs.

Chapter 7

THE INSECTS IN THE FOREST AROUND THE HOUSE shrieked their morning chorus. Deep in bed, Carlton woke gradually to the sound. He considered it, and the irregular slap of the light rain on the shingles of the roof. He was happy to be home.

In England, Carlton had pursued ideas and studies which would be beneficial to him in running Roxborough. This was in contrast to the absentee planters, merchants, colonial agents, and factors who lived in England and constituted what was referred to by Parliament as the "West India Interest." Because of the great wealth of this West India Interest clique, its influence was considerable. Planters and merchants not only purchased immense property in Britain, they also rivaled the English aristocracy in splendid, ostentatious living.

Carlton had resisted the temptation to follow their example, using his time to improve himself. He knew from experience how the same absentee owners were being exploited by the attorneys who ran their estates on their behalf. Carlton was determined to prevent this happening at Roxborough, so when the news of his father's death reached him, he had hastened to return. Now he was anxious to put his learning into practice.

He rolled over in his bed to face Ella. She had kept the plantation and the slaves together, and now there was so much work to do. Discipline had to be enforced immediately. In spite of his quick temper, Carlton did not enjoy the whippings, imprisonments, or dismemberments which other planters considered necessary to maintain docility among slaves. For Carlton, slaves were property to be bought and sold. Inflicting injury as a punishment served to lower a slave's value.

Carlton was impatient for the dawn. He swung his legs out of the bed and stood up. Miraculously, his head was free of the after effects of the night before. He threw open the shutter and peered out. The range of hills which faced the house presented an impenetrable darkness, but over the sea there were signs that the sky was changing from black to dark blue.

"God damn me!" he said, addressing Ella. "It's almost dawn. Why ain't someone fired the morning shot to wake the slaves? On the east coast, they'll be up and in the fields already, I'll be bound."

"Mas Hayes stopped de gun." said Ella getting out of bed. She fumbled to strike a spark to set a candle flickering. "He done say he not trusting any nigger wid a gun."

"Right." Carlton smiled. "Da' did right."

"Down in de quarters," said Ella, holding up the candle, "one of de Wagenie fishermen does blow a conch shell to wake de slaves. We does hear de sound, too."

"Well, he had better change his timepiece," said

Carlton, surveying the sky again. "It will be daylight in less than an hour."

"Ah does go to de kitchen, Carlton. "Yo' does want a dish of coffee?"

"Roxborough coffee?"

"Yes, we does grow coffee still—enough for de house an' de slaves."

"That's too good for the slaves, Ella! Do you know what people pay for coffee in England? I'm going to appreciate Roxborough produce now I've seen what it costs overseas. The whites born here do not know their good fortune! Look at it, sugar, coffee fruits fish, meats!"

Ella slipped out of the room as Carlton surveyed the chamber The old mahogany furniture was in exactly the same place it was in when his father was alive. He imagined his father would burst through the door and demand to know what he was doing in his bedroom.

Carlton opened the wardrobe. Caspar had hung his clothes there. "Well," he thought glumly. "I won't have much occasion to wear those English fashions again." He picked out breeches, a pair of boots made in Jermyn Street, and a linen shirt. He divested himself of the clothes he had slept in, urinated in the utensil at the side of the bed, splashed his face with water from the basin on the washstand, pulled a comb through his fair hair, and slipped into his clothes. As he finished, he heard the low moan of the conch shell being blown in the slave quarters.

He stomped across the hallway and flung open the door to George's bedroom. "What, Doctor, not out of bed yet?" Striding into the room, Carlton pushed open the shutters. It was still gloomy. Carlton saw only one shape in the bed and he prodded it sharply. "What, Doctor, no wench?"

"Hah . . ." groaned the shape.

"Time to rise, Doctor. Work begins today."

"My head."

"You'll learn to drink your rum like a man, Doctor. Where's the wench?" He sniffed. "This room smells worse than a Cheapside brothel. You burst her?"

"No, no! I puked. The rum." George groaned again.

"Hum!" Carlton was puzzled. "Well, you'll see all the wenches today. Whichever one you want, just ask me, Doctor." He went out onto the gallery and leaned over the rail trying to discern movement in the gloom of the estate lands. In the old days, the slaves would be filing past the house to work in the cane fields. Now, although cane was still grown, sugar was no longer the mainstay of the estate.

Carlton assumed the slaves had other tasks instead. But what? The thought stunned him. What do you do with three hundred slaves if you don't grow sugar? Carlton shook his head.

"Ella!"

His shout cut across the whistling and warbles of the brightening dawn. The clear air carried his call right down the hillside to the slave quarters. The old slaves coughing and scratching themselves outside their *ajoupas* heard the shout. The gardeners preparing to go into the provision grounds in the heights paused at the sound. The youths who were small when Carlton left cocked their heads at the voice.

No one remarked about what they had heard, but it dawned on every one of them that the *cou* had become alive again. The threat of the Bondmaster and his hot-blooded whims had returned to terrify them. Like Ella's jumbies.

The presence of the Bondmaster worried Ketto. "Who is dis Bon'massa we does have, Mas Kingston?"

The youth waited while Kingston clasped his hands around the calabash dish. He raised it to his lips to sip at the contents.

"De coffee does be good, boy," said Kingston, staring straight ahead of him. "De Bon'massa, boy? Yo' ax ol' Kingston, who don't have no sight, who de Bon'massa does be?"

"De quarters folk does say, Mas Kingston," persisted Ketto, "dat yo' does know de Bon'massa best after de house slaves."

"Dat quarters *bagasse!*" Kingston spat in disgust. "Dey be right, though. Ah does know Mas Carlton better dan any of dem."

"Tell me, please, Mas Kingston." Ketto gazed at the old man. He used to be the bookkeeper for the mill before he went blind. Now he waited out his days as custodian of the works. Although he could no longer see, there was nothing that happened at the mill he did not know about. Ketto had become his eyes.

"De Bon'massa, Ketto, docs be de owner of dis plantation an' of every living creature on it, includin' yo' an' ol' blind me.' He spoke with a tremor in his voice. "Master Carlton Todd does be de best white man yo' ever done see. Ah'm proud to be he bondsman, boy."

"Yo' proud to be de slave of a white man?" Ketto was shocked.

"Of dis white man. Ah does be born in Jamaica.

73

Ah was be a Kingston slave. It does be old Massa Hayes who done buy me. When he done see ah can read and write he done put me in charge de rum. But it does be Massa Carlton who done see me worth. Ah was de one dat show he how to keep he registers All de slave registers dey does have at de big house does be de work of me an' mah Mas Carlton!" Kingston smacked his lips together proudly.

"How do yo' mean, de work? De Bon'massa does work?"

"Sure, boy. He ain't no attorney who does be afraid to dirty he britches Mas Carlton does be born here like yo' an' most de slaves dem. He more a slave dan we cuz he must to think as well as to work. He does lead de work heself. He got dese slaves here to work an' to believe in de righteousness of being a Roxbruh nigger. Ah proud to have dat man as mah Bon'massa. yas sah!"

Kingston's enthusiasm was unexpected. Ketto thought the crusty old Negro would seize on the return of his white owner to berate the people who lived in the *cou*, as he usually did. He had a very low opinion of the residents of the house, whether white or slave.

Kingston held out the calabash for Ketto. The youth removed it from his grasp and drank the remainder of the coffee in it.

"Yo' does be a good boy, Ketto. Ah done pick yo' out de paddock meself. Ah done check yuh ped'gree in de register when mah eyes near fail. Ah done know yuh sire an' yuh dam, so ah does know yo' be from good stock." Kingston scratched his head.

"Jus' like de Bon'massa. He mam was be a fine

French lady an' ol' Massa Hayes was be from England, though he done come here from Alabama.

"White does need good ped'gree like we blacks, yo' hear, Ketto. Dat woman Mas Carlton done marry, ah don't know about she ped'gree at all. She done be bad stock, though. She go wid dat nigger Mingo who Mas Carlton done buy from she father. Laura an' Hayes be she children so we does know only half deir ped'gree."

Ketto murmured to let the old man know he understood. He loved to listen to Kingston talk. When the other boys were rushing down to the river to bathe or hunt with their slingshots, Ketto preferred to stay at Kingston's side, keeping the old man's chair in the shade and encouraging him to tell about the past.

"De half we does know, Ketto," continued Kingston slowly, "dat does be de best. We does know Mas Carlton. He does be strict, but he does be human, an' he does know we niggers does be human, too, even though we black. Mas Carlton does know we have feelings an' failures jus' like he.

"It was be Mas Carlton dat does give every wench who make a child a bolt of material fuh a dress, on top she yearly allocation. De other plantation owners don't care about childrens, cuz it does mean de wench stay out de fields. But Mas Carlton does be pleased when yo' does tell he yo' does be full here!" Kingston patted his swollen belly and laughed.

"He does put de bucks to de wenches. He say to a young colt dat he must lay wid dat wench an' get he a whelp. Now, aint dat fine?"

"Ah think ah does be pleased he done come back, Mas Kingston!"

Kingston chuckled. "What's yuh age, boy?"

"Don't know widout yo' check it in de register."

"Come here, boy!" Ketto stood beside the old man. "Yo' here? Give me yuh hand. Right," he said, taking the boy's arm and pulling him closer. He reached from his chair to pass his hand up the boy's arm to his chest, then over his shoulder, up the back of his neck and through the tight wool of his hair. His hand settled on Ketto's head as he tried to judge the boy's height. Kingston let go his hand and sat back.

"Wait, boy." Kingston stretched out again and touched the boy's bare stomach. He rubbed his veined hand over the boy's pants and squeezed. "Yuh balls still small, boy. Mas Carlton gon' tell yo' wait 'til next year come. Den he gon' give yo' one filly fuh yuhself alone."

Ketto felt the blood surging through his limbs after the old man had held him. Next year seemed a long time to wait. "Ah gon' get mah own wench widout waiting fuh he," Ketto pouted.

Kingston turned in his chair to face the boy. "Ketto!" The old man's voice was stern. "Mas Carlton is de will at Roxbruh. Don't touch not one of de fillies in dis plantation widout he say. Is yuh grain he gon' cut if yo' do!"

"Hah! Don't fret yuhself, Mas Kingston. How he ever gon' know?"

"Ketto, please. Yo' does be a good boy. Yo' got a chance to be better dan de field hands. Ah'm goin' to recommend yo' to de Bon'massa fuh de book work. Ah gon' ax he learn yo' to read an' write so yo' can be a boss nigger like me. Never fuhgit dat de Bon'massa does know everything yo' ever do.

Now he does be back at Roxbruh, dem foolish niggers gon' see how quick things does change. Yas, sah!"

Kingston slumped back in his chair, gripping the arms firmly.

Later that same morning, the clatter of horses' hooves on the overgrown cobbles of the mill yard slowly penetrated Kingston's tired brain.

"Mas Kingston, Mas Kingston!" Ketto's voice hissed in his ear, his hand shaking his shoulder. "Dey does be here!"

"Who? Who, boy?" Kingston sat up in alarm.

"De buckras, dem!"

"Where dey be?" Kingston tried to rise from his seat.

"Dey does be at de grinding house, by de water wheel."

"He bring he daughter?"

"No. Dere does be two white men and dey have one high-colored boy wid dem dat dress in clothes de color of de sunlight."

"De boy have bright eyes?"

"Ah don't see de color but dey kind of seein'. Not dark like we Negroes."

"Dat's he whelp fuh Ella."

"Mas Carlton have yellow hair, Mas Kingston?"

"De same!" Kingston tried to rise again. "Come, boy, we gon' tell he how d'yo' do."

Carlton rounded the corner of the still as Kingston rose to his feet. The morning had been a disturbing one for Carlton. Instead of the well-run plantation he had left, Carlton was aware of fields and animals not cared for, fences not repaired, and the sugar cane having been abandoned. The plantation was dead.

77

Even the mill was deserted except for this old man.

"Kingston!" Carlton bounded down from his horse as he recognized him. "Kingston!" he said, clapping the slave on his shoulders. "Well, with you here, Kingston, Roxborough will survive!"

"Mas Carlton," sniffed Kingston. "Oh massa, ah hear yo', massa, though ah don't see yo'. Mah eyes done go tired wid all de figurin' and dey done fail me. May ah touch yo', massa?"

"Yes." Embarrassed, Carlton stood while the old man's fingers touched his chest and traced up to his neck and shoulders.

"Ah does know yo' now. An' ah hear yo' speak." He stepped back, Ketto holding him by his elbow. "Is de mill a'right, Mas Carlton? We done grind no cane fuh years. Only dis boy, Ketto here, does keep de place in order. Near finish de stock of rum, too, Mas Carlton."

Carlton nodded his head sadly at the neglect.

"Kingston, I want to thank you. Without you, there would be very little to come home to." He turned to mount his horse again.

"Ah done keep a register, too, Mas Carlton. Since ah blind ah done keep everything in mah head. Dis boy does help me rem'ber."

"Amazing," said George, touched by the genuine bond of feeling between the old man and Carlton.

"He is amazing, Doctor," Carlton climbed onto his horse. "Boy, what's yuh name?"

"Ketto, Mas Carlton, sah."

"Aye, that's the way to answer, boy. Caspar, mark that buck's name. Kingston, I'll be sending for you and the boy soon. We are going to need your help to grade all this stock we have here and to get Roxborough on its feet again."

"Ah, yas, sah! Yas, sah!" Kingston sank back in his chair, a smile on his face. He squeezed Ketto's arm at the sound of the men galloping off. "Yas sah, yas sah!'

Chapter 8

"DOCTOR," CARLTON TURNED TO GEORGE AS they rode out of the mill compound, "you see the state of this trail? I used to have road gangs to look after the estate trails. Caspar, we must set up the slaves in gangs."

"I agree. The slaves will be pleased to have something to do."

"I don't care about that, boy!" Carlton snorted. "We have to revive Roxborough, Caspar, not please the niggers."

"Why didn't you have a white overseer?" asked George. "Isn't that what most plantations do?"

"Doctor, most plantations have absentee owners, men who do not even know their estates. They put in hirelings to beat the hides off their niggers, ruin the soil with their thoughtless planting, and raid the treasury with their professional guile." Carlton urged his horse forward.

"It's only worthless whites who are available for hire to run a plantation, Doctor. Anyone with talent and ambition will try to steal all you've got, while those without ambition are not worth employing."

They reached a branch in the trail. The road to the right led into a grove of tall bamboos and wild plantation trees. "That's the trail to Roseau, the capital," explained Caspar.

"I doubt you'll get there by road, Doctor," chipped in Carlton. "It's a day's ride through bush and precipice. I used to drive slaves on that trail before, but no one looks after the road since the French left." Carlton beckoned George to follow him. "I want you to see the paddock, Doctor. With Kingston still alive, and the records my da' was keeping for me, I'll be able to grade all the stock. Your job will be to keep the whelps healthy, so we don't lose any."

The paddock was an acre of land fenced with bamboo poles with bougainvillea and flamboyant trees overhanging it. To George, it seemed that the children running in the compound were like cattle in a pen. It was an amazing sight. Even Carlton reined in his horse and contemplated the scene in silence.

There were children of all ages, shapes, sizes, and shades. All, including the oldest, were naked. They were running, jumping, romping, tussling, walking, or squatting by the fence. The noise of their shouts and laughter was deafening.

George looked at Carlton for an explanation.

"Here it is, Doctor. A living fortune!"

"Englishmen keep their fortune in the bank, Doctor," muttered Caspar with a grin. "This is the Bondmaster's savings account."

"All those niggerlings!' George shook his head in astonishment.

"A hundred whelps at one hundred English pounds a head, that's over ten thousand pounds romping right there!" Carlton beamed proudly at Caspar. "I'll wager there are threescore that are ripe for the auction block!

"Damme, Caspar!" he added. "There's so much to be done! We've got to grade the stock for market, get the gangs working again, start planting cane to make rum once more, get breeding underway. I don't know how we are going to do it."

"Well, you have me to help."

"Thanks, boy, but I need you in the house."

"What do you mean?" said Caspar in surprise. "I'm going to be more use to you in the fields than in the house."

Carlton ignored his impertinence. "What, Caspar? You want to be a field slave? You hear that, Doctor? Every nigger aspires to be a house slave, but this cocky fellow here wants to go to the fields!" Carlton spurred his horse forward, but Caspar rode up beside him.

"Perhaps not in the fields, itself," he persisted, "but certainly in the plantation."

Carlton snorted in disgust. "After six years in England, you're the best body servant a man ever had, Caspar. I'd be out of my head to put you in the fields."

"With respect, sir," answered Caspar, refusing to fall silent, "any likely lad can be trained as a body servant or house slave. I would think that on the plantation, you need someone of my talents who can carry out your commands as you want."

"That's enough of that!" Carlton waved his whip at Caspar.

Two boys ran to open the gate for them to enter the paddock. Scores of children clustered around the horses. George leaned over to pat some heads, but Carlton raised his riding whip to flick them away.

George dismounted from his horse. The children surrounded him immediately, laughing as they tried to touch him, tugging at his coat, and grasping for his hands. He chuckled with them, looking up at the Bondmaster still on his horse. "I've never seen such happy children," he grinned. "They are wonderful!"

There was a whoosh of air and a sudden crack above his head. The children were stunned into silence. George's hat jumped into the air, pitched forward, and tumbled to the ground.

"Happy children!" bellowed Carlton, his hand raised as the long thong of his whip curled back to him. He flicked his wrist again, lower this time, sending the whip snapping over the heads of the youngsters.

"These are slave brats, Doctor, not children. They are all descended from African animals, Doctor. From black beasts who roam the jungles of Africa standing on their hind legs, hunting, killing, and eating each other. These niggerlings can grow into high-quality slaves and bring profit to Roxborough. But if you believe they are children, Doctor, you'll be doomed."

Carlton wound up the whip, nodding his head proudly to Caspar. "I still got my aim, boy."

He dismounted and pushed his way through the children into the nursery building. Inside, babies were sleeping on a blanket spread out on the floor. Girls crouched in corners holding other babies and playing with toddlers.

"Those outside," asked George as he tried to take in the whole scene, "where do they sleep?"

"In here, of course." Carlton pointed to a pile of rags in the corner. "They have plenty of things to cover them with. And the floor is wood, not mud," he said, tapping the boards with his foot. "Maybe there are too many here, though, Doctor, I'll grant you. But that's our business, what?"

Carlton led George through the nursery and outside again where he indicated the kitchen area. Two women were peeling ground provisions, helped by some of the girls, while a group of boys cleaned a huge pile of fish.

"We used to have a hospital, as well, Doctor, but it's part of the nursery now. We'll organize a work gang so you can build your own hospital quarters. Don't tolerate sick slaves, though. If a slave is not prime and healthy, we don't want him here."

George was shocked. "What do you do with him?"

"Do?" Carlton sounded puzzled at the question. "Beat him until he gets better, of course!"

George looked aghast.

"Doctor!" Carlton gripped George by the elbow when he realized that the doctor took him seriously.

"I'm pleased that you are here. A man can get lonely on a plantation. Oh, there's plenty of wenches, but sometimes I yearn for someone to talk to. A white face across the table instead of grinning black ones," He chuckled.

"Often I do not mean all I say, Doctor. I am so used to dealing with slaves. I might forget that you are an English gentleman and start to talk to you as though you are a field nigger!"

George was touched by the Bondmaster's confession. "I think I understand." He smiled professionally. "Why don't you define my duties? Is this nursery to be under my charge?"

"Why, yes."

"Good. And what do you want from the nursery?"

"That's easy, healthy niggers."

"You shall have them, Mister Todd. But I am not a schoolteacher."

"They don't want education!" Carlton was bemused.

"No, I understand that. Yet they might want distraction."

Carlton frowned, considering the doctor's words. "I'll have them working. That will be the distraction they need, and it will be training for them."

"When we grew sugar, Doctor," Caspar explained, "we broke in our whelps in small gangs."

George sighed inwardly as he turned away from Caspar's eager eyes. "And with the breeding, Todd? What am I supposed to do for you there?"

"Inspect, Doctor," said Carlton. "See that every one of my breeders is free from pox. I want my whelps to be clean."

George swallowed quickly. "You do not want me to take part in the breeding program myself, I trust?"

Carlton guffawed. "Last night too much for you? No, Doctor, that's up to you. I'll sire the light-skin whelps, if necessary."

"Please don't misunderstand me, Todd. I am sure your gesture was the height of hospitality for a planter. I am just not accustomed to planter traditions." He smiled bashfully, encouraged by the sympathetic grin quivering on Caspar's lips.

"You will be, Doctor. When the sun seeps some sex into those limbs of yours, and you see our wenches creaming their loins for you."

George coughed. "I will need staff with all these

niggerlings to tend." He gestured helplessly at the children swarming around them as they spoke.

"Staff? Slaves, if you please, Doctor, don't call them staff, that's for humans. You have the old mares here who nurse the whelps. We use breeders as wet nurses for the newborn ones. We take the get from the dam as soon as possible after it's born. It would die otherwise."

"Why?"

"Because the dam cannot suckle her whelp if she has to work. Anyway, I believe it is better if the dams do not get attached to their offspring."

"May I chose my own staff?" said George, ignoring Carlton's theories.

"You may chose your slaves, Doctor, and punish them if need be."

George inspected the nursery and paddock. He was appalled by the primitive conditions the youngsters were living in. There was not a bed in the place. Water was carried up from the river. The bush beyond the fence was their toilet. Only a few had clothes. As he glanced around, it began to rain. The children scampered toward the nursery, diving under the building for shelter.

The Bondmaster was at the end of the veranda talking to Caspar. George saw Caspar pointing to a group of boys sheltering under a large scarlet-flowered flamboyant tree. The boys seemed older than the other children in the paddock, perhaps about Caspar's age. There were a dozen of them, mostly pure Negro with their dark faces, flat noses, and black woolly hair. They were watching the Bondmaster silently.

86

Caspar clapped his hands and beckoned the boys to come to the veranda. A few ran over immediately while the others hesitated at the rain and then, as Caspar called them again, darted out of their shelter. It was one of these who caught George's attention.

The boy was lighter-skinned than the others and had fine features. George walked along the veranda to take a closer look. The boy stood on the outside of the circle of youths gathered around the Bondmaster. His hair was unlike the thick black wire of African Negroes and appeared to be much softer. The youth's ears were small, and his nose was slender and pointed His lips were thinner, too. The boy saw George studying him and smiled brightly.

George grinned in response and was amazed to see the boy point at him and then back at himself, nodding his head up and down vigorously. The boy repeated the gesture, pointing at George and then tapping his own chest. George was not sure what the youth meant, but Caspar, who had seen the pantomime, sidled up to George. "He thinks you're looking for slaves," explained Caspar. "He wants you to buy him."

George was puzzled. "You mean he wants to be sold?"

"Of course. They all want to be sold, that's what Mas Carlton is telling them about."

"You are prime niggers now," Carlton was saying. "Soon you will go out from Roxborough to work on plantations. Those of you who work well will be given your own wenches. Some of you might become house slaves and wear fine trogs like Caspar here."

"Why does he tell them that?" asked George.

"To prepare them for the vendues," said Caspar. "If a slave doesn't want to be sold, he won't fetch a good price. When he is happy about it, he looks fit and healthy, and he does what he is told. He's easier to sell for a high price then."

"You know plenty about it," commented George.

"Aye. I know as much as Mas Carlton, Doctor. Remember, I'm supposed to be a slave, too." He laughed.

"What will happen to that boy if he's sold?" George pointed to the youth who had attracted him.

Caspar shrugged. "He'll be sold in a coffle. He'll cut cane for four years, then he'll die."

"Die!" George was shocked. "How? Disease?"

"No," Caspar replied with a chuckle, "old age. A nigger cannot take more than four or five years in the cane fields. That's why there's such a demand for slaves. If they lived longer, planters would not need so many."

"Won't they get a wench, like the Bondmaster says?"

"Wench?" Casper snorted with delight. "Never! The nearest they'll get will be the tail end of each other! Plantations ain't like this one, Doctor. Their wenches are for work, not breeding. The owners don't want to bother with whelps when it's cane to cut or coffee to harvest."

George stared over the heads of the Negroes to the youth at the back. The boy's face was bright and hopeful, and he smiled at George, his eyes pleading.

"Todd!" George stepped down from the veranda and walked over to the youth. He grasped his wrist.

Carlton peered through the rain at the circle of slaves.

"I want this one, Todd." George held up the youth's hand. "I want him."

Chapter 9

CASPAR GALLOPED UP TO THE HOUSE AND DIS-
mounted quickly He threw the reins of his horse to
Dontfraic and strolled into the kitchen.

"What's happening Ella?' He smacked his mother
playfully on her bottom. "What's the Bondmaster
doing this morning?' His voice contained a note
of sarcasm which made Ella wince.

"He does be upstairs studying he ledgers," she
said, sighing.

"That's all he has been doing since we returned!
I don't see the reason for it. I have ridden around
every acre of the plantation, and I've got the slaves
on their feet and working again. We've cutlassed
trails and a gang has begun to build a dispensary for
the Doctor' Caspar raised his eyes at the ceiling
and shook his fist.

"Don't do dat, boy'" scolded Ella. "Mas Carlton
does be figuring He bound to hab he book work
after all de time he done spend in England."

"I know that Ella." Caspar picked up a pancake
and stuffed it in his mouth He poured coffee from
the pot on the stove into a dish, blowing on it to cool
it down. "I'm just tired of waiting for him to put

me in charge. I can't do anything without his authority!"

Ella considered Caspar. His features were contorted with exasperation. "Pip," she said with sudden determination. "Yo' hab dat sangaree mix' up?"

The tall Negro flashed her a broad smile. He took down a pitcher from the shelf high above his head and sniffed at the contents. He inhaled deeply. "It does be mix' fine," he beamed.

"Two goblets." Ella held out her hand for the goblets and the pitcher. "Caspar," she said, "take dis sangaree up to Mas Carlton."

"Oh, Ella," said Caspar with a cluck of annoyance, "I'm not a house slave. Pip or Dontfraid can do that. Leave me alone."

"No, Caspar. No house slave can speak fuh yo'. Go 'n' drink sangaree wid Mas Carlton. He does hab need of yo'."

Caspar raised his head from the coffee dish and regarded Ella with curiosity. "Ella, you does be an old obeah woman, in truth," he grinned. "Give me the pitcher. I'll go and *yassa* Mas Carlton and see what he does for me."

Carlton was rubbing his hands through his hair, shaking his head from side to side before he saw Caspar standing beside him with the tray. "Boy!" he said. "You know me too dam' well." He snatched a goblet, speaking while Caspar filled it from the pitcher. "Caspar, tell me what to do!"

"What about?" Caspar placed the tray down on the saman table between the two chairs on the front balcony.

"Sit down, Caspar!" Carlton paused, glancing at the tray. "Have a drink. I see you brought two goblets."

"I thought the Doctor might be here."

"Caspar, don't bother to fool me. You know the Doctor is in the nursery. Now what do you want?"

Caspar poured himself a drink and sipped at it thoughtfully. He looked up at Carlton, who was waiting for him to speak "I have been inspecting the plantation myself" he began.

"Yes, yes boy. What do you think?"

"We have enough acres of cane to supply ourselves with sugar and make rum for trading. We have able-bodied Negroes to do the work. We have provision gardens which can be enlarged to supply all our slaves with food. We have three slave drivers and could train more. We need five gangs to maintain the estate. If you give me the authority to organize the plantation work I'll see that it's done." Caspar sat back in his chair, waiting for Carlton's reaction.

"Aye, you have told me that already, Caspar. It won't do. You are too young, and I want you here to serve me."

"I was not too young to accompany you through England for six years. I am a man now, sir." Surprised by Carlton's silence at his assertion, Caspar continued quickly. "I can easily find you a good body servant."

"Body servant! You make me sound like a spinster." Carlton sipped his drink, eyeing Caspar. "Perhaps I do not need a personal slave after all, Caspar. It is the household that concerns me. That's what the training you had in England has fitted you for. How do you think I can organize it without your help?"

"But the plantation! The slaves! They are far more important." Caspar's eyes blazed. "I know the niggers. I can do it!"

92

Ella strained her ears to hear Carlton's reply from her hiding place under the gallery floor. She heard the pitcher tinkling against the goblets and heard Carlton stand up and walk across the gallery. The suspense of not knowing what was being decided proved too much for Ella. She sidled around to the back of the house and climbed the stairs onto the gallery.

"Ella!" Carlton was smiling. "At last I think I have it worked out. Tell me, this Cleo wench in the kitchen, why is she the cook and not you?"

"When I was tending old Massa Hayes, we needed a cook."

"I prefer your cooking, Ella. That way, I know the food is safe!" Carlton winked at Caspar. It was not unknown for a planter to be poisoned by his slaves.

"Do we sell her?" queried Caspar.

"Yes!"

Caspar dipped the quill in the inkpot on the table beside him and wrote the cook's name in the ledger Carlton had given him.

"Sell!" Ella was disturbed. "But Carlton, now you are back, I need more wenches in the kitchen, not less."

"I'm sure you do, I quite understand, my dear." Carlton smiled to placate her. "You shall have a new girl from the paddock. Not one, but three. You can train three at a time until we sell them, and then you train another three."

Ella pondered the situation. "What about Pip?" she asked. "He is plenty useful in the house, Carlton."

"Pip should stay," interrupted Caspar. "He can always train new houseboys."

"Agreed! No objection at all. You see, Ella, this

93

offspring of ours, he is going to be the overseer. He has persuaded me he can do it."

"Yo' does make Caspar de overseer!" Ella gaped in disbelief. This was more than she had ever hoped for. "He gon' run de plantation? An' de niggers? He does say who gets punished?"

"Sure, Ella, all that. Don't you think it is a good idea? Of course, I don't know why I should even ask you." Carlton gripped his goblet with annoyance.

"Now what about the wench I see that Tita has with her, caring for Laura and Hayes? She could be sold, too. We'll get a good price for a nursemaid."

"Are you gon' sell Tita?"

"No, Ella. I know you don't like the wench, but Laura and Hayes adore her." Carlton poured himself another sangaree.

"Huh! If only old Hayes could see me now!" he grunted. "His son and heir discussing the future of Roxborough over drinks with the family slaves!" He raised his goblet to the sky, gurgling happily.

"Don't worry, Da'. Times change!"

"Why doesn't de Doctor live in de old school cabin?" said Ella. "If he is to tutor Laura and Hayes, he does not have to live in de house."

"Oh, my Ella! Why have I grappled with these plans alone when I could have discussed all the problems with you?" Carlton slapped the arm of the chair enthusiastically.

"You and Caspar really are part of me, part of Roxborough. I must accept that!" He studied the sangaree. "As you suggest, the Doctor will have the old cabin."

"What about me?" Caspar was emboldened by the sangaree and Carlton's good humor. "May I have the overseer's cabin overlooking the quarters?"

94

"My dear boy," beamed Carlton, "I have said that you are the overseer, therefore you shall have the overseer's cabin." He frowned suddenly. "Stand up!"

Caspar leaped to his feet.

"Yes, boy, you say you are a man. Well, you can have that cabin, but you shall pay for it."

"How?"

"Whelps, Caspar, whelps! We have to build our future."

"May I chose my own wenches?"

"No!" Carlton snorted. "You are half Batutsi and half white, boy. I have to cross you with a wench who'll produce quality."

"Da'?" Laura ambled around the corner of the balcony. She wore a hibiscus flower behind her ear and pouted prettily as she approached Carlton.

"Yes, dear?" Carlton was surprised by his daughter's presence.

"Da', can I be a wench?"

"What!"

Laura blinked at Carlton's shout. She put her hand to her mouth nervously and repeated her request. "Ah does want be a wench, Da'."

"Hush, child," said Ella, sweeping down and snatching Laura's hand from her mouth. "She does not know what she is saying, Carlton."

"Ah does know what ah does say!" Laura tugged her hand away from Ella. "Ah does want be a wench like de wenches dem. Ah want mah bolt of cloth when ah does hab a whelp."

"Come, Laura, let's go 'n' look for Hayes." Ella tried to steer the child back to her room.

"Wait!" Carlton frowned. "What did you say,

Laura? You want a bolt of cloth? What for? For dresses?"

"Yas!" Laura stamped her foot.

"You shall have it, Laura."

Laura regarded her father doubtfully.

"Yes, child, you shall have it. You want to learn how to be a young lady? That's better than a wench, you know. Only slaves are wenches."

"Does a young lady have black bucks to mount she like a wench, Da'?"

"God damn me!" shouted Carlton. "What has got into the child?"

"A lady has slaves," said Caspar softly, taking Laura's hand. "A wench is a slave. You want to be a lady and have your own slaves, don't you, Laura?"

"Is yo' ah does want fuh mah slave, Caspar, when ah does be a lady." Laura looked up at Caspar's eyes and smiled at him.

"That's enough!" Carlton snapped. "Take the child to her room."

Laura squeezed Caspar's hand and turned to go without waiting for Ella. She glanced back and smiled at Caspar again.

"I *will* be a wench," she vowed to herself. "Even though everyone will think I am a lady!"

Chapter 10

KETTO LED KINGSTON BY HIS HAND. HE LOOKED at him proudly. He had combed the old man's patchy gray hair and wiped his face. He had found the yellow shirt Kingston used to wear on Sundays when he could see and made him put it on. With his heavy register tucked under his arm, and his unseeing head held straight up, Kingston looked impressive.

"What, boy? Kingston gon' up de *cou*, den?" Prudence greeted them as she came up from the slave quarters and they met at the junction of the trails. "Mornin', Mas Kingston."

"Who dat?"

"Prudence, Mas Kingston. Yo' does rem'ber Prudence? Ah does be in de field gang wid Dukey dem."

Kingston sucked his lips. "Prudence! How de day?"

"Day fine, Mas Kingston. What fuh yo' does go to de *cou*, Mas Kingston?" Prudence wanted the news to carry to the girls who labored with her in Dukey's field gang.

"Plantation business, Prudence," Ketto answered

proudly for Kingston. "De Bon'massa done summon we."

"Oy! oy! oy!" Prudence wagged her head. "Mas Kingston, if it does be a vendue dey does be fixin', rem'ber Prudence does be a fine house slave, yassa! Yo' can't see me, Mas Kingston, though ah does be right pretty. Here!" She snatched Kingston's hand from Ketto and rubbed it over her breasts. The old man chuckled.

"Feel me! Ah does be prime!" She cackled with laughter, then left them to waddle on her way up to the field.

It took them an hour to reach the big house. Kingston walked uncertainly even though Ketto was guiding him and the trail had been cleaned and the bush at the side trimmed back. Ketto stood at the edge of the yard regarding the big house with awe.

"What de matter wid dat ol' slave?" A girl shouted at Ketto from the balcony. Ketto swallowed nervously.

"Who dat speakin', Ketto?" Kingston grasped the boy's shoulder for an answer.

"Ah don't know she," Ketto hissed. "She de color of de fresh milk de cattle nigger does send yo'."

"Why don't yo' answer me, boy!" The girl's voice shrilled out across the yard. She walked to the top of the steps and gazed across the yard at Ketto. "Answer quick, now. What yo' does be doing here at de house?"

"Beg pard'n, Missy." It was Kingston who spoke, hugging Ketto close to him and raising his head in the direction of the girl's voice. "Mas Carlton done send fuh me. Ah does be Kingston!"

"Kingston? Dat don't mean nothin' to me. Mah

da' ain't here." Laura stepped back onto the gallery. "Yo', boy! What's yo' name?"

"Ketto, ma'am."

"Ketto," repeated Laura with a giggle. "Ketto!" She put her hand to her mouth as she sniggered again, darting around the corner of the balcony out of sight.

"Take me to de back door, Ketto. In de kitchin dey does know where de Bon'massa does be."

"Kingston! I'm glad you are here." Carlton arrived suddenly, followed by Caspar, who gave Ketto a friendly smile. "Let's go upstairs."

Carlton grasped the old slave by the elbow and helped Ketto guide him to the front steps and up to the balcony. He ushered Kingston into a chair, taking a seat next to him. Ketto stood uncertainly at Kingston's side while Carlton held out his hand for the book Kingston was carrying.

"Give he de register, Mas Kingston," Ketto whispered in the old man's ear.

"Thank you, boy. Take a look at this, Caspar." Carlton passed the register across. "Years ago, my mother started this book, entering the name of every slave born here or purchased for the estate. Kingston has kept up the ledger since then."

Caspar flicked through the pages of the book. Written beside each name were two other names. "Dey be de dam and de sire," Kingston explained. "Mas Carlton done ax fuh dat so he can check who sirin' buck whelps an' who sirin' fillies."

"Right. You, boy," Carlton addressed Ketto. "Take Kingston down to the kitchen. You'll get refreshment there. Then wait, boy. I want Kingston here when we have the roundup."

99

"Yo' go down de back steps, boy," said Caspar, pointing the way around the gallery.

Kingston shuffled off, led by Ketto, who gazed around him wide-eyed with wonder. Up there on the gallery, Ketto saw all the way down to the river mouth where ships were anchored in the basin. He was trying to describe what he saw to Kingston, which must have made him careless. He did not see Laura hurrying around the corner. She collided with him before he had a chance to move out of her way.

Ketto felt the blood rush to his face in embarrassment. "Ah does be sorry, mistress. Ah not see yo'."

"What yo' does be doing up here?" Laura studied the boy with interest. She saw he was about an inch taller than herself. He had a freshly scrubbed countenance and was dressed tidily in clean plantation breeches and smock. His dark face was smooth and handsome.

"We does be goin' to de kitch'n."

"Yo' must call me mistress, boy." Laura wagged her finger at him. "Ah have to slap yo' if yo' disrespeck me."

"Ah don't mean no disrespeck, mistress." Ketto answered carefully.

"Dat's better. What's yuh name again?"

"Ketto."

"Mistress, dam' yo'!" Laura slapped Ketto's cheek so quickly he never saw the blow coming. "Dere!" she said, curling her young lips in a smile of triumph. "Now yo' see ah does be de mistress!"

"Yas, mistress." Ketto rubbed his cheek in astonishment.

"Rem'ber, Ketto, yo' must do what ah say!" Laura gloated mischievously.

"Yas, mistress."

"Now take dat ol' nigger bugger off de gallery." Laura pushed past them and ran inside the house. They could hear her giggling.

"She done slap me, Mas Kingston." Ketto touched his cheek.

"Ah hear," Kingston sounded sad. "She does be like she mother. Stay away from she, Ketto."

The roundup took place later the same morning. All the slaves who could walk were herded up to the house by the drivers. Caspar galloped through the plantation chasing the malingerers. In the slave quarters, counted the old Negroes lying on the ground too feeble to move. When he was satisfied that every able-bodied slave was rounded up and packed into the yard, he shouted up to Carlton on the gallery that he could begin.

Carlton scanned the mass of black faces below him trying to pick out the best-looking youths. He wanted to see what stock he had so he could decide whom to sell, whom to work and whom to breed. He beckoned Caspar to join him in the gallery and leaned over the railing to address the herd.

"Slaves of Roxborough," he began, "you all know Kingston here." He indicated the corner by the kitchen where Kingston was standing with Ketto. Carlton held up the old ledger. "Kingston has kept this register with the name of every Roxborough slave in it since you were born. But Kingston is old now and cannot see. Therefore we must start a new register.

"Caspar, here, will keep the new register. Caspar is the plantation overseer. Even though he is young and does not have whelps yet, you are to obey him at all times, you understand? He speaks for me."

An ominous silence greeted his words. Carlton turned to Caspar. "Why don't they say something?"

Caspar gazed at the meek mass of niggers shuffling and fidgeting below the balcony. A sneer quivered on his lips until a thought streaked into his brain which made him regard the assembled slaves in a different light.

"If these wretches had a leader," he realized suddenly, "they could rise up and destroy me."

He licked his lips nervously and looked at the crowd with a new respect, trying to identify the faces he knew and wondering what they were thinking behind their passive eyes. Did they believe that he had sided with the Bondmaster?

"They don't understand you," he lied to Carlton.

Ella pushed forward, surveyed the swaying slaves, and launched into a tirade of abuse in patois. Hanging heads snapped up to stare at her with eyes which blazed with emotion as she spoke. Sullen bodies stiffened as she harangued every one of the slaves in the yard, calling many of them by name. Ella wove into her creole curses the words which conveyed the Bondmaster's message. She wanted the slaves to accept Caspar as the overseer and to acknowledge the power this gave him over them.

Carlton was surprised how the slaves were exulted by her invective. "Huzzah! Huzzah!" they shouted, leaping up and down and clasping their neighbors with excitement. A drum began to roll, and old women erupted into rapturous wails while men pranced ecstatically.

The fervor seized Carlton. He clapped his arm around Caspar's shoulders, laughing with pleasure.

"You see, son! We have the happiest slaves in the Caribbees. What a fine breed!"

Caspar was silent, concentrating on thoughts of his own. "Ella swayed these fools," he pondered. "She has delivered them to me. But what will happen if the day comes when someone sways them against me?" He glanced quickly at Carlton. The man was flushed with his false triumph, waving to his slaves as though he was their owner by acclamation.

"Does he know what he is? Does he know that he only exists because the slaves—and I!—tolerate him?" Caspar scowled.

From her vantage point, Laura watched the uproar, seeking boys who appealed to her. Her glance returned to Ketto. The youth had left the blind man and was standing at the corner of the house. The counting of slaves had begun, with each Negro stepping forward to be graded when Caspar called his name.

Laura leaned over the side of the balcony and hissed at Ketto. He raised his head. Laura beckoned him.

Ketto hesitated, glancing around. Laura called him again. He climbed the back stairs warily. Laura was waiting at the top.

"Yo' should come quicker dan dat. Don't yo' know yet, boy, dat ah does be yuh mistress?"

"Ah does be sorry, mistress."

"Dat's de answer. Come!" Laura tossed her head and strutted around the balcony to her room. Ketto followed and halted respectfully at her door.

"Come in," urged Laura. "Come!"

"Mistress, ah ain't never been in de buckra house!"

"Hello," said a friendly voice.

Ketto stared inside the room. A Negro boy about six years old was watching him intently. A white boy the same age, with black hair and bright eyes just like the Bondmaster, ran over and stared at him.

"Who dat?" the white boy demanded of Laura.

"He does be mah buck, Hayes."

"He yuh slave?" Hayes eyed Ketto suspiciously. "Yo' gon' beat he, Laura?"

"Hush!" snapped Laura. "Yo'll bring Nanny Tita here. Come in, Ketto."

Laura pulled Hayes to her. "Look, Hayes. Don't yo' think Ketto does be nice?"

"Mingoson does be more nice!" Hayes glanced at Ketto. "Mingoson does be mah nigger," he explained.

Laura released her brother. "Now, hush now. Don't tell Nanny Tita ah done bring mah buck here!" She turned to the Negro child. "Mingoson, take Hayes on de gallery an' show he de slaves in de yard. Mas Carlton does be counting every one of them."

Mingoson grabbed Hayes by his hand and ran out with him.

"Mistress," stammered Ketto, recalling Kingston's warning to stay away from the girl.

"Dat does be all yo' does say?"

"Ah does be scared, mistress. De Bon'massa gon' lash me if ah does be here in de house wid yo'."

"Why?" Laura cooed softly. "Yo' ain't gon' touch me, is yo'?"

"Oh, no, Miss Laura." Ketto backed up to the wall as Laura reached out and shut the door. She sat on the bed.

"Oh, no, Miss Laura."

"Ah done see mah daddy string up a boy like yo' and whip he under de flamboyant tree. De buck

104

hung upside down widout he clothes on. He peed heself," she smirked.

"Don't whip me, Miss Laura." Ketto wished he could run.

"If yo' do what ah does tell yo' ah ain't gon' whip yo', Ketto." Laura parted her lips and tried to smile.

"Ah does be pleased to do yuh bidding, Miss Laura," Ketto muttered anxiously.

"Dat's good. Where yo' does sleep, Ketto? Why ain't yo' in de paddock wid de other young bucks?"

"Mas Kingston done take me out de paddock. Ah does be he eyes, he say. Ah does live wid he out by de still."

"Take off yuh smock, boy!"

"Huh?"

"Come on, boy, yo' don't want me to ax my daddy to lash yo', do yo'?" Laura bounced impatiently on the bed.

"Ah does be a'right, Miss Laura." He sidled along the wall to the door.

"Yo' don't go nowhere unless ah does say," Laura snapped.

"Yas, Miss Laura." Ketto stopped, wondering what he should do next. He could feel a strange heat spreading through his body. The girl was watching him closely. He wiped away the sweat which began to form on his brow.

"Dere!" Laura sounded triumphant. "Yo' see yo' does be too hot. If yo' take off yuh smock yo' does be more comfortable. Take it off, now."

Ketto scratched his ear. "Yas, Miss Laura." He began to untie the smock.

"Oh, come here, Ketto. Yo' jus' be foolin'." Laura indicated where she wanted him to stand in front of her as she sat on the bed. She raised her hands and began to unfasten the garment. Ketto watched in amazement at her white fingers so close to his skin. She released the smock and pulled it from his shoulders. She sniffed.

"Yo' don't smell ranky." She put her hand to touch his chest. He flinched. "Stay still, boy. Yuh titties does be small, boy. Dey does be blue!"

"Ooh," moaned Ketto. "Yo' does be ticklin' me, Miss Laura."

Laura laughed, rubbing her fingers over his chest. "Ah'll make yo' laugh, Ketto. Ah'll tickle yo' until yo' does love me."

Ketto bent his body toward Laura and put up his hand to ward off her prying fingers. The door crashed open. Hayes and his playboy Mingoson barged into the room. Ketto leaped away from the bed and crouched by the doorway.

"What de arse yo' mean coming in here like dat?"

Hayes halted at Laura's voice, and Mingoson collided into him. They fell to the ground shrieking with laughter, rolling over and over on the floor.

While Laura berated them, Ketto slid out of the door and ran down the back steps, leaving his smock on Laura's bed.

Chapter 11

CARLTON STUCK OUT HIS LEGS AND CAUGHT HIS heels on the lower railing of the balcony. Stretching out, he sat back in his chair and linked his fingers behind his head with contentment. Since his return to the island, his face had become deeply tanned, his blond hair bleached by the sun. His sunburned cheeks were lean, his jaw firm, and his lips thin.

When he was angry, Carlton's countenance could be fierce; his lips curled over his white teeth in a snarl, and his bright eyes blazed with rage. Usually, however, his eyes twinkled with good humor. His features, although tough, showed warmth and understanding.

As he stretched out in the long chair, Carlton tensed his stomach muscles and then released them easily. He flexed his legs before expelling air from his hard body with a yawn. He sat up, brought his hands down from behind his head, and smiled at Caspar, who was sitting on the balcony with him.

It was late afternoon. Soon the night would be swarming over the hills to engulf them. Caspar was making his report on the day's tasks.

Carlton approved. "We'll soon have this plantation flourishing again," he said. "You are doing a good job, Caspar."

"The slaves like the work. They can see that if they grow more dasheen, sweet potatoes, and tanyas, they will have more to eat themselves."

"You believe that, Caspar? The niggers work because they don't like the sting of leather across their buttocks in the hot sun. Do those drivers thrash them regularly?"

"Yes. That's all they know."

"You should practice, Caspar. There is an art in lashing a slave. If you break the skin, you are lowering the bugger's price. Buyers don't like a slave with a set of flog marks on his backside. It says the nigger is troublesome. Dust them, boy, and hurt them, but don't cut."

Carlton scratched his chin. "You know, boy, slaves are the only animals that take so long to mature. It takes twelve years from the time a slave is born before you can work him properly. Cattle, horses, they've given years of service by the time they are twelve."

"Our young bucks are mature." Caspar chuckled. "They are mounting each other in the barracoon. It's their habit to *back-a-juice* whenever they get the chance.

Carlton thought for a few moments. "Ella has the fillies stabled in the quarters. We'll set those colts at them. How many bucks are in the barracoon?"

"Fifteen."

"You know their pedigrees?" Carlton picked his nose.

"They are all Roxborough-born. Some are born

of dandas, others are from mixed tribes, mostly Coromantins."

"Set them at the fillies tomorrow. I want those bucks to understand that they have to get me healthy gets. Quickly. When a filly is full, we'll put her colt with another filly. Those who aren't breeders we'll sell. We don't want any rump-rutters or prick-pullers in the herd."

Casper blushed. "Our bucks are hot, that's all. I feel that way sometimes myself."

Carlton laughed. "Ain't no nigger backside going to take you up it, boy!" He leaned over and slapped Caspar's thigh. "Control yourself, Caspar. I'll set you at something you can breed with soon."

Caspar bounded down the front steps while Carlton gazed after him with pride.

The boy had developed in the short time he had been back at Roxborough. His muscles rippled under the calico shirt he sported in place of his brocade finery, and his thighs bulged under his breeches. His amber skin had darkened to the deep tone of copper in the sun which beat down on the cane fields.

To contrast with Carlton's own slender nose, fine lips, and bright eyes, the boy had inherited Ella's proud physique. The foppishness Caspar had picked up in England had been rubbed off by dealing with the slaves. The boy looked good.

The crick and rasp of the night insects echoed in Caspar's ears as he made his way from the house. He strolled easily along the path in the dark, knowing every turn and tuft of the trail. He was barefoot and moved silently. He carried a cutlass in his hand and in his waistband was the emblem of his status on the plantation, the triple-thonged whip.

A peal of high-pitched laughter made him pause. He lifted his head, detecting the sound as coming from the doctor's cabin.

"Who's the Doctor got with him?" he wondered. The laughter subsided to soft giggles which intrigued Caspar even more. "Is it a wench?"

He slipped off the trail and snaked his way through the undergrowth to the back of the cabin where the doctor was quartered. The shutters were closed. Putting his ear to the side of the shack, Caspar heard the gentlemanly tones of the doctor but could not identify the other voice.

He was puzzled. He stealthily circled the cabin, looking for a crack through which he could peep. He bent down and cautiously put his eyes to a small gap between two boards in the side of the cabin. A candle placed on a shelf above the doctor's bed threw a vague glow over the two people lying on it.

Doctor Tyndall was naked, his arms encircled around a youth whose naked body was turned away from him. The youth was giggling. Caspar recognized him as Athol, the slave who worked in the nursery.

As Caspar watched, the doctor gripped Athol by his waist and pulled him backwards toward him. Caspar gulped with disgust when he saw the doctor grease the slave and ram himself between the boy's buttocks with a shout of pleasure.

Sickened, Caspar pulled away from the peephole. He stared in anger as the cabin wall began to shake. He could hear the doctor's deep-voiced grunts and the slave's ecstatic whimpering. He was confused. It seemed that the sight of the white man draining himself into the slave boy had snapped the bond which held Caspar's obedient mind in check.

110

"The Doctor seemed an upright man," he mused as he slowly dragged back to the trail. "Am I so dam' *zezay* I don't know what whites are like at all?" He cursed himself in patois.

"Why can't buckras stick to their own kind and leave their slaves alone!" Caspar slashed wildly at the undergrowth with his cutlass, his eyes flashing in the dark.

"It is not me who is going to die for them, not for treachery of a white man," he muttered to the night. "I'll serve my master because he sired me, but whites are not my people.

"My people are the slaves."

Caspar's cabin was located between the nursery and the barracoon. But he hurried past it and headed for the open door of the barracoon. Hannibal was startled by his approach.

"Good night, Mas Caspar!" he wheezed.

"De bucks all here?" demanded Caspar with a new spirit in his voice.

"Of co'se, sah! Ain't none of dem does leave here before daylight an' de conch sound. No, sah, dose boys too hot to let run wild!"

Caspar put his head around the door and peered into the old barn. Some of the boys were already curled together on mats on the hard mud floor. Others squatted in a circle exchanging banter. One youth sat in a corner by himself. Caspar counted the heads; there were fifteen. These were the colts Carlton had ordered to be locked up until he was ready to cross them with the fillies he had singled out. They worked in the fields guarded by drivers during the day and at night were shut in the barracoon.

The boys were pleased to see him. "Caspar!" one

shouted, jumping up and flinging his arm around his neck. "Come an' sit wid we."

"Get off, *makak!*" Angrily, Caspar brushed the boy aside with his free hand. "Yo' too dam' hot!"

"Ah ain't hot! Ah does be burning!" shrieked the boy, tumbling into the group squatting on to the floor. "Ah want to know what we done do dat yo' an' de Bon'massa jus' keeping us here at night!"

"Benn does be right," said another. "When yo' does be locked in de hot house, yo' know yo' done do something like thieve an' yo' sure gon' get yuh punishment. But ain't none of we do nothing."

"Not now!" said Benn. "But if ah in here much longer ah'm jus' gon' jump on Prudence when she come wid de tea in de mornin'!" Some of the boys clapped Benn on his back as they laughed in agreement.

"You must be patient, boys. It's you that the Bondmaster wants to breed from. Don't you know that already?"

"Yas, Caspar, we does know dat. We does need wenches fuh to breed, though." Benn led the snickers of the others, not noticing the shadow of annoyance which crossed Caspar's eyes.

"Benn, you be careful!" snapped Caspar.

"I know you and me were raised together. I know we played together and hunted *crapaud* in the woods together. Now things have changed. You see this whip I have in my belt. One day I might have to take this to you and lash you if the Bondmaster tells me to.

"The Bondmaster put you in this barracoon, and he put me in the overseer's cabin. Don't make a joke out of what he is planning for you, Benn."

112

"Caspar, yo' does be right." Benn placed his arm around Caspar's shoulder.

"Yo' know ah don't have disrespeck fuh yo' an' de Bon'massa."

Benn winked at the others. "We gon' stand by yo', Caspar, an' do what yo' an' de Bon'massa does tell we."

Caspar inclined his head in acknowledgment. He knew Benn's tongue from the days when the buck used to sweet-talk coconut cakes out of the old cook in the kitchen. Benn was his own age, lithe and full of tricks. Caspar needed Benn, plus a few others like him, to succeed in keeping all the slaves under control.

"I've got news for you, Benn. Tomorrow, you'll be getting your filly to ride."

"To-mor-oh!" Benn leaped into the air, clapping his hands over his head. "Yo'-all does hear *dat*?"

Even the youth sitting alone in the corner perked up his head as Benn cavorted about the barn, pulling the covers off the boys who were trying to sleep and shouting at them all. "To-mor-oh!"

"Who we does be getting?"

"Can we chose de filly we want?"

"Ah don't want no Congo!"

The cries of the boys deafened Caspar. "Hold it!" he shouted above the noise, ignoring their questions. "You'll see everything tomorrow."

The youth who had been sitting morosely in the corner touched Caspar on his shoulder as he was about to leave. "Mas Caspar!" he said quietly. François was Caspar's age, a pure black danda from Africa. "We does have to take de wenches Mas Carlton does give we?"

"Of course." Caspar turned to go.

"Ah does have a wench ah does crave, Mas Caspar. She named Claire's Joan. Ah does ax if de Bon'massa can give me she."

"Have you mounted her already?" Caspar demanded suspiciously.

"Oh, no, Mas Caspar. Mas Carlton does have she in de quarters fuh one of we. Ah jus' hope it does be me what gets she."

"François, I have to do what the Bondmaster tells me. You must do the same."

Caspar spun on his heels quickly, bade the guard Hannibal good night, and stepped into the bush to walk across to his own cabin.

Samboth was on the tiny veranda peering in the direction of the barracoon. He grinned with relief when Caspar emerged from the blackness. "Ah say de boys done get yo' wid all dat noise! Yo' does be a'right?" Samboth touched Caspar's arm when he stepped on the veranda.

Caspar wiped his hands on the boy's head. "Sure, sure. Are we sleeping together, or have you brought me a nice dish for my supper, Sam?"

"De dish." Samboth jerked his head toward the cabin. "Ah done tell she dat yo' done send fuh she. She slow to come first, but she only afraid de dark."

Caspar kicked open the door with his foot. In the center of the cabin there was a table with a lantern which threw its glow over the bed at the side of the room. A wench sat on the bed waiting for him.

She was black as charcoal, a halo of wiry black hair crowning her polished round face. She eyed Caspar boldly. With her shift stretched tight across her lithe body, she looked to Caspar as wild a nigger as ever came out of Africa.

Caspar walked over to the bed and stood above

her so that his crotch was level with her eyes. He could feel himself swelling. He ripped open his breeches.

"Who are you, wench?"

"Ah does be Claire's Joan."

The girl parted her lips and thrust her mouth forward into his crotch.

Chapter 12

LAURA LIVED IN A FANTASY WORLD. SHE KNEW it. She rarely left the big house. It was much more fun to watch the plantation from the security of the gallery. Nanny Tita was always there to protect her and fetch her everything she wanted. Almost everything.

Since her mother died and her father sailed away to England, Laura had been content in her make-believe world. But now she sensed stronger emotions stirring within her. She wanted things she could not yet name, and which Nanny Tita was unable to supply. When she viewed the plantation from the gallery, the cabins and cane fields now assumed an irresistible glamor.

"Out there in the sun are *slaves!*" Laura dreamed. "Caspar mounted on his horse galloping down to the river, and Ketto at the mill all alone."

Laura prepared herself for the outcry when she announced to Tita that she intended to walk out and explore the plantation.

"Yo' ain't never walked on de estate before, Miss Laura," Tita whined. "Yo' don't know de way."

"Ah does be goin'!" Laura snapped defiantly. She was bored with Tita's nagging.

"Very well, den," Tita capitulated. "But yo' sure must have Sophy wid yo'. Dis plantation full of bucks who gon' jump yo' as soon as see yo'.

"Yo' does have twelve years now an' de blood flowing," she added "No nigger buck gon' respeck yo', nohow."

"Ah tell yo' ah does be goin'!" Laura picked up the hem of her dress and stepped over her brother, who was playing on the floor with Mingoson. She threw open the door, walked onto the gallery, and hurried down the front steps, followed by Sophy.

Gaining the trail, Laura slowed down for Sophy, who sauntered a few paces behind, swinging her bottom as the slaves in the fields stopped work and raised their heads. The hiss of a whip made Laura pause.

Gazing across the fields, she observed a driver flicking his whip over the backs of the slaves who had stopped work. She watched with fascination. "Yohoo! Yohoo!" she called, waving to the slaves. They stood up, and the whip sliced down. Laura laughed.

"See what stupid nigger-buggers dey does be!"

"Dey does be afraid de lash," Sophy answered with the confidence of knowing that she would not be so stupid.

"Ah does want a lash, too."

Sophy stopped in surprise. "A lash, Miss Laura?"

"Mais oui! How it does be dat ah don't have a lash like de drivers an' Caspar an' mah da'?"

"Ah don't know, Miss Laura." Sophy was worried.

"Where dey does keep de lash-whips?"

Sophy glanced around nervously. She wondered

how Nanny Tita would handle this unexpected development. "Why, over dere, Miss Laura," she said, her eye falling on the stable. "Yo' does really have need of one, Miss Laura?"

Laura sucked on her lips in exasperation. "When ah does have mah whip, yo' be de first ah does lash, Sophy. Yo' don't know ah does be de mistress here? What fuh ah must tell yo' why ah does need a whip? Yo' gon' see when ah does git it!"

Laura hurried over to the stables, "Boy!" she addressed the startled youth who was feeding the horses. "Ah does want a whip!"

Caliste regarded Laura with bewilderment. Occasionally he had escorted Miss Laura and Miss Nanny Tita to the river for a picnic. He had never seen the young mistress in the stables alone before.

"Beg pard'n, Miss Laura?" he gaped.

"A whip, boy!"

Laura sighted what she was seeking hanging on a hook inside the stable. Hitching up her dress above her ankles, she ran into the stable and snatched the whip down from its hook. She tried it for weight. The handle was small, and the leather thongs on it were short. It suited her perfectly.

She aimed a blow at a post and discovered how she could make the leather ribbons curl around on contact with the target. Trying again, she practiced jerking the stock so that the lashes snapped against the post with a satisfying thwack.

"Ah does like dis!" she giggled at Sophy. "Come, let's make haste. Thanks, boy!" she crowed, flicking the thongs in his direction.

Caliste was standing by a horse which bucked away at the sting of the lash on its rump. It trampled on Caliste's bare foot, causing him to howl with pain as Laura hurried out.

"It does be far to de mill?" she asked Sophy when they came to the junction which led to the slave quarters.

"We must walk down to de river an' den go on de path to Layou, Miss Laura." Sophy expected Laura to turn back, but she seemed bent on a secret mission of her own and sped down the hill, clasping the hem of her dress in one hand so she could run faster, and holding the whip firmly in the other.

"Dis does be such fun, Sophy!" she cried, pausing to catch her breath when she reached the bottom of the trail at the river's edge.

"Yo' does be one old slowpoke. Ah does have a mind to give yo' a taste of dis lash!"

"Oh, no, Miss Laura, ah does be hurryin' like yo'. Yo' don't feel de heat, Miss Laura?" panted Sophy, twisting a plantain leaf from a tree and fanning herself with it.

"Yes," Laura answered without concern. "The path here does be cool, though. See, over dere! Ah does see de mill!"

She jumped with excitement.

Kingston was dozing in his usual seat outside the still house when girlish laughter disturbed him. He sat up, alarmed, gripping the arms of his chair and trying to distinguish the source of the sounds.

Laura burst through the undergrowth into the courtyard and, seeing the old man glaring out at her from his chair, erupted into laughter again.

"Oh, do come, Sophy. Look, it does be dat old nigger-bugger who done come to de house fuh de roundup." Laura skipped over to Kingston and used the whip handle to tap him on the knee.

"Ah does be Miss Laura," she said. "Yo' s'posed to stand up when ah does address yo'."

Kingston's heart sank at the sound of Laura's voice. He sensed a calamity. "Ma'am," he shuffled to his feet as he spoke, "ah does be an old blind man. Forgive me, ma'am. Widout mah eyes ah does not see yo' coming, ma'am."

"Huh!" said Laura, gazing around the still yard. "Yo' does live alone here? Ah don't see no one about de place."

"Dere does be anyone special yo' does be seeking, ma'am?" Kingston clutched his chair for support.

"No, no," answered Laura with a smirk. "Dere ain't no one does be here to show me de mill. Ah does crave to learn how de sugar does be make an' de rum an' so forth."

"Yo' does need de boilerman, ma'am. He does be in de quarters now, de other side of de path, ma'am."

"How yo' does live widout yuh eyes, old niggah?" Laura persisted, trying to stifle her giggle.

Kingston shifted awkwardly. Laura prodded his belly with the whip.

"Dere does be a boy dat does help me," he muttered.

"Where de boy?"

Kingston squirmed. He was reluctant to involve Ketto in whatever it was Miss Laura wanted. Before he could answer, two youths trotted into the compound. They stopped abruptly when they saw Laura.

The taller youth plucked at his short trousers, which were in danger of falling around his knees. He bowed his head.

120

"Good day, Miss Laura an' maid," he said with a grin. "How de day be, mistress?"

Laura glanced haughtily over the shoulder of the fawning slave and stared at his companion.

Ketto was perspiring. He had run down the hill with Benn. Like Benn, he was clothed in roughly cut osnaburg shorts secured around the waist with a piece of rope. His chest heaved as he tried to catch his breath. His face, Laura noticed with a giggle, showed lines of worry.

"Ah does be Benn," the older youth was saying, anxious to get Laura's attention. "Dis buck here does be Ketto."

"Dis ain't no social occasion, yo' dam' fraish slave! No one ax yo' yuh name," snapped Laura.

"Dese boys does be able to show yo' de mill, Miss Laura." Kingston was relieved.

"Yes," said Laura thoughtfully. "Ah s'pose dat does be a' right. Come wid me, Sophy. Dose two niggers can show us de place."

"Wid all pleasure, Miss Laura." Benn winked at Sophy, stepping aside for Laura and her maid to pass. "We does go 'round here where dere does be de water mill."

While Benn prattled, Laura scrutinized Ketto from under her sunbonnet. The youth glanced at her, but he made no attempt to speak.

Benn was enjoying himself as he described the workings of the mill. It had occurred to Benn that he might be able to lure Sophy away from her mistress. He would have to act quickly before he was missed from the field gang and someone was sent down to look for him. He scanned the bush adjoining the mill, wondering what pretext he could use for taking Sophy down to the river and leaving Miss Laura by herself.

"Boy!" called Laura. "Yo' does be walking too quickly. Ah does be tired."

"If yo' does be tired, missy, yo' maybe like to relax yuh feet in de coolin' house." Benn grinned eagerly. "Wid yuh permission, Miss Laura, ah does take Miss Sophy to de river an' collect a cup of cool spring water fuh yo'."

Laura's eyes gleamed. "Dat's a' right, Sophy, Yo' go wid de nigger. Ah does stay here wid dis one to protect me from de snakes an' lizards!" She giggled again, grabbing Ketto's hand as soon as Benn and Sophy had disappeared into the bush.

"Let's go in dis house, boy," she said, pulling Ketto inside the cooling room. She sat on the edge of a stone vat, keeping a firm grip on Ketto's hand.

"Why yo' done run from de *cou* de other day?" she demanded.

"Ah done hear de Bon'massa calling me, miss," answered Ketto miserably.

Laura pulled him closer to where she sat on the vat, her long dress rucked up to her knees. "De Bon'-massa ain't gon' call yo' today, Ketto."

Deliberately Laura placed her whip on the edge of the empty bath. She held the boy by both wrists. "Dere ain't nobody gon' call yo' now, Ketto!"

"No, miss." Keto felt his mouth drying and the skin tighten across his throat. His flesh tingled as Laura placed his hand onto her thigh. She stroked his arm.

"Yo' black niggers have a lovely skin," she purred. "It does shine. Yo' does be black all over, Ketto?"

"Ya-ya-yas, Miss Laura." Ketto felt his limbs

weakening. He lifted his hands from where Laura had placed them on her thighs.

"Ah don't believe yo'!"

"Ya-ya-yas, Miss Laura!" He clasped his hands in front of his pants so Laura would not see the reaction she was stirring in him.

"Take down yuh trousers!"

"Miss?" Ketto gawked at Laura in alarm.

"Ah does want to see if yo' does be black all over, boy."

"Ya-ya-yas, miss. Ketto was rooted to the spot, squeezing himself frantically, longing to bolt from the cooling room and find somewhere in the bush to hide.

"Take dem off, Ketto. Quick."

"Ah does not want to do dat, Miss Laura."

"Why not, boy? Come on, move yuh hands, an' ah'll do it."

"Oh, no, Miss Laura!" Ketto pleaded. "Oh, no!"

"Oh, yas!"

Laura tugged at his hands. Ketto knew it was wrong to resist. He let his hands drop to his side and stood motionless before Laura, conscious of his *tuli* pushing out his pants in front of him. Laura reached for her whip and smacked it on the edge of the bath.

"Now yo' know yo' must do what ah does tell yo', Ketto, not so?"

Ketto surrendered. "Yas, Miss Laura."

"Take down yuh trousers!" Laura snapped the whip against the stone bath again. Her mind was racing at the possibilities of what was coming.

The boy slowly untied the rope around his waist. His trousers slipped down his legs to the ground. He cupped his hands in front of his *tuli*.

123

"No!" Laura brushed at his hands with the thongs of the whip. "Let me see!" She held one hand away with the stock of the whip and kept the other back with her own hand. Ketto hung his head with misery.

"What a funny thing! It does be dancing!"

Laura prodded Ketto with the whip handle, letting its thongs caress his thigh. With her tongue clenched between her teeth, Laura withdrew the whip and made a playful thrash across the boy's bare buttocks.

Ketto sighed, unable to move.

"It does be dancing!" Laura shrieked playfully, pitching all her force behind the whip as she brought it slicing down on Ketto's genitals.

Ketto tried to protect himself.

"No, Miss Laura!" He rolled over the edge of the vat and doubled himself up on the stone floor inside.

Laura clambered after him, slashing frenziedly at his naked body with the tongue of the whip.

"Oh!" she crowed. "Oh! Yo' see ah does be de mistress!" Her white cheeks flushed pink with excitement, and her eyes were glazed as she fell on him.

"Let me be yuh wench, Ketto!"

Laura's cry of ecstasy switched to a shriek of fright as a black hand clamped onto her wrist. An arm wrapped around her waist and hauled her out of the bath.

Caspar held Laura firmly without hurting her. Her whip fell to the stone floor with a clatter. Carlton climbed into the vat and prodded Ketto with his boot.

"What the hell's going on here?" he shouted. He glanced at the naked buck and at the whip which had fallen from his daughter's hand.

"He done take off he trousers, Daddy," sobbed Laura. "Ah does be protecting mahself."

Saliva drained from Carlton's mouth. He jammed his foot in Ketto's groin, lifting him off the floor and letting him crash down onto the stone slabs. He drew back his boot and aimed another blow at the boy's head. His foot smashed into Ketto's cheek, shattering his jaw.

"Sah! Sah!" Kingston, shouting frantically, groped his way through the doorway and fell onto the vat. Hearing Ketto's shrieks, he threw himself on top of the boy. Carlton's foot drove home and caught Kingston in his thigh. He yelped with surprise.

"It does be she, Mas Carlton," Kingston gasped. "De missy tell he take down he trousers or she whip he. Ah does hear, but ah does not see, massa."

Laura twisted away from Caspar. "Dat does be a lie, yo' stupid nigger-bugger!" she screamed. "Yo' does lie cuz de boy be yuh bed wench."

Laura fell on Kingston and pummeled him with her fists. Carlton shook his head, surprised at his daughter's words.

Caspar pulled Laura away from Kingston and told the old man to get up. He examined Ketto. The boy's face was bleeding, and he was clutching his stomach, gasping with agony.

"He is hurt, Mas Carlton," Caspar said curtly, trying to control his own temper which threatened to pitch him at the Bondmaster's throat.

Carlton was clenching his fists, his mouth set in a vicious snarl. His eyes blazed with anger as he stared at Caspar. Caspar stared back defiantly, shielding Ketto with his own body. No one spoke.

Carlton turned away from the bath and swung

around to face his daughter. "What you doing here, Laura? Who told you those things?"

"Oh, Da'!" she wailed, her sobs turning to tears. She leaned toward her father. "Ah does be so scared, Da'." Laura entwined her arms around Carlton's waist and laid her head on his chest.

A slight movement through the open doorway distracted Carlton. He glanced up in time to see Sophy emerging from the bushes with a slave. The slave kissed her on the cheek and then disappeared back into the undergrowth. Sophy giggled and smoothed down her dress.

"Oh, Da', Da'!"

Carlton thrust Laura away from him, cursing bitterly. He was disgusted by this sudden insight into the character of the girl he had fathered.

Laura tripped, toppling into the bath beside the broken Ketto. She began to howl.

Chapter 13

THE MOURNFUL BELLOWING OF A CONCH SHELL echoed over the plantation. A chill of fear buffeted the older Roxborough slaves when they heard it.

"What's that?" George lifted his head in concern, pushing away the book in which he was writing. Athol, polishing a microscope, blanched. "What's the matter, Athol? What does that dreadful noise mean?"

"Oh, Doctor, ah does be scared when ah hear de conch blow in de day. Before, it done mean de Bon'massa gon' punish a slave."

George's brow puckered with amazement. "Carlton Todd? That's not his nature. He's told me himself a mild flogging is all he finds necessary to keep his slaves under control."

"Ah don't know, Mas Doctor, sah. De conch does be calling we to de *cou.*

"Oh, very well," said George. "It must be dinnertime anyway. Let's go and see what it's all about."

Slaves streamed up the trail to the house, jumping out of the way as the doctor hurried through them. He was followed by Athol carrying his bag.

"My God, what's happened!" George pushed

through the crowd clamoring around the body of Ketto which lay on the ground under the flamboyant tree. George knelt down beside the boy, appalled. "Clear away from here!" he pleaded as the slaves clustered around. "What happened to him?" he demanded again.

No one answered. "Athol, this boy is hurt badly. Who put him here?" George appealed to the expressionless faces hanging over him, dark eyes staring back at him as he searched them for an answer.

"De Bon'massa, sah!" It was Samboth who answered.

"Todd!" George exclaimed. "I don't believe it!"

There was a hurried consultation between Samboth and some of the older slaves while George examined Ketto. "Mas Carlton done tell Caspar leave de boy dere an' sound de conch to call de niggers," explained Samboth.

"Well, we are not leaving him here," said George. "You, Samboth, take his legs." He held Ketto firmly under his arms while Samboth caught up his legs and they struggled to carry him to the kitchen. Pip barred the entrance.

"Where yo' gon' wid dat nigger?" Pip asked Samboth indignantly.

"Get out of the way, boy!" George pushed past Pip with an unexpected display of authority. "Put him on the table."

"Oh, mah gawd!" uttered Ella, bustling into the kitchen from the store. "Who done lay out a nigger on mah table?"

"Keep quiet, if you please, Ella!" ordered George. "This boy is dreadfully hurt."

"Huh! Dat ain't no concern of mine. Mas Carlton

128

done lay de boy under de tree fuh de niggers to see. He ain't got no place here at all."

"Ella, he is hurt. I have to treat him!"

The unexpected anger which had replaced the doctor's normally mild demeanor halted Ella. It was her kitchen, but the doctor was a white man. She shrugged her shoulders and peered at what the doctor was doing. "Ain't nothing wrong wid he dat a cup of herb tea an' *crapaud* paste on he face won't cure," she announced sulkily. Samboth giggled.

Upstairs, Carlton was pacing the length of the drawing room. Laura was sobbing in her bedroom and Carlton could hear Tita trying to comfort her. Hayes and Mingoson were romping on the outside gallery while below he could hear the lowing of the slaves as they gathered in the yard. He reached one end of the room, spun around on the balls of his feet, and began another circuit. Carlton did not know what to do.

The balcony door opened and Caspar entered. "The Doctor has removed the boy. He has him in the kitchen." Caspar seemed pleased.

"Zounds!" Carlton stopped in his tracks. "What's the Doctor meddling in this affair for?"

"He said the boy is hurt," shrugged Caspar, walking to the dresser and pouring two glasses of punch, passing one to Carlton.

Carlton waved the glass away. "Of course he is hurt. He's lucky not to be dead! Get that Doctor up here at once." Carlton resumed his restless pacing over the floor, wishing that the morning's events had never happened.

The doctor entered by the dining room door and began to speak before Carlton realized he was in the room. "I'm here, Todd, but I am not staying.

The boy is hurt very badly; his jaw is broken and he may be ruptured, to say nothing of the lacerations about his body. I have to attend to him."

"Dam' the boy, Doctor. Why did you move him?"

Carlton's voice was high-pitched, but the worry of the situation had extinguished the flames of his anger.

"To treat him, of course, Todd. My job is the care and health of your slaves. Even if you only regard the boy from a commercial point of view, Todd, he needs treatment. If he dies or is permanently maimed, then his value to you is going to be nil."

"Yes, yes, Doctor." Carlton sank into a chair, accepting the glass Caspar offered him again.

"You must understand, Doctor, that sometimes it is necessary to sacrifice a slave as an example to others and to preserve the salutary effect of punishment."

"Punishment!" The doctor's face flushed with anger. "What kind of barbarian are you, Todd? The boy is wounded, and you talk of punishment."

"Of course he must be punished. He was naked in front of my daughter."

"Hah! And so are most of the blackies you keep here!"

"He removed his trousers in front of her," Carlton chanted wearily. "Isn't that enough?"

Caspar was unable to keep silent as the two men glared at each other. "Kingston says Laura forced him to do it," he told the doctor.

Carlton turned a baleful eye on Caspar. "Do you want me to believe a blind black nigger over the words of my own white daughter!"

"If it's the truth!"

Caspar drained his glass and walked past Carlton with a scowl. He stood on the balcony.

"I saw her lashing the boy myself," Carlton appealed to George. "She was defending herself against his advances. He must be beaten until he is insensible!"

"He is that already, Todd. He is in shock, but he says he was only doing what Miss Laura told him. He's very young, Todd."

"Young! You don't know Negroes like I do, Doctor. They start to rut from three years old. It's the heat, the smell, the animal in them." He gazed through the balcony door at Caspar, who turned his back on him.

"Have you ever gelded a colt, Doctor?" Carlton asked suddenly.

The blood drained from George's face as he gaped at Carlton in horror.

"Carlton!" Ella clattered into the room, breaking the silence. She had been listening outside the door. "Have yo' axed why Laura was be in de mill by sheself alone? Where was be she chaperone, Carlton?"

Carlton sighed. "In the bush rutting with one of the field hands."

"Well, den," Ella leered. "She does be de one to be punished. If she done stay wid Laura, dere would be no ruckus nohow."

Carlton nodded his head as he made up his mind. "Caspar!" He watched him turn slowly to face him. "The maid is to blame," he called. Caspar walked back into the room.

"I must punish someone as an example to the cattle out there, Caspar. If the slaves feel the Bond-

131

master is weakening, we will soon be at the mercy of their churlishness."

Caspar realized he was caught between the wisdom of his father's remarks and his own reluctance to be part of any slave punishment. "The slaves are frightened already," he snapped. "Listen to them wailing down there."

"Yes, yes. They remember what happened in my father's day. We should string up that wench from a branch of the flamboyant tree and lash her with the cat-o-nine-tails. A scouring has a powerful effect on wayward niggers."

"It also leaves a pattern of welts on the slave's skin!" Caspar said irritably.

"Doesn't that lower a slave's price, Caspar?" the doctor asked with assumed casualness.

"Of course, Doctor. And that maid is a trained child-minder. Her value should be considerable."

"That's enough!" Carlton rose from his chair and carried his glass to the dresser. He poured punch into it as he directed Caspar to tell the drivers to seize Sophy and shackle her to the trunk of the flamboyant tree.

· He waved everyone out of the room and returned to his chair to think.

"Boy!" Carlton leaned over the railing and called Dontfraid who was standing outside the kitchen door. "Tell Ella take de knife she does use for shaving pigs."

A murmur of concern rippled through the crowd. Each pair of eyes, wide with fear, watched as Mercury clamped shackles on Sophy's ankles and fastened her to the tree. Mercury and the other drivers stood back laughing when Sophy tried to lift her feet. She dragged the chains as far from the tree as the links allowed.

"What ah done do, massa? What yuh Sophy do?" She shrieked in terror as the Bondmaster walked down the steps.

The slaves quickly observed that the Bondmaster had his pistols stuck in his belt and carried his long whip slung casually under his arm.

Carlton ignored Sophy. He faced the slaves jostling uncomfortably around the tree. "You have all seen that the boy Ketto nearly died," shouted Carlton at black faces. "He insulted my daughter, Miss Laura. He has been punished.

"This slut here, she is Miss Laura's own slave. But she left Miss Laura alone with Ketto so she could rut with a bozal in the bush."

Carlton put his hand on the bodice of Sophy's dress. Two of the drivers gripped her shoulders to prevent her from falling as Carlton yanked at the fabric. The bodice ripped open.

Carlton pounded Sophy's breast. "This wench was dressed in buckra clothes. But she has her nigger ways. So now she is a nigger again. Because the Bondmaster says so!"

Carlton grabbed Sophy's dress angrily, pulling it off her so the wench stood naked, straining at the shackles at her feet. Tears streaked down the dust on her worried black face.

"Hold her head," Carlton ordered the two drivers. "Ella, give me the knife!"

Sophy screamed when Carlton held the knife in front of her eyes. The slaves gasped.

Carlton knew his slaves were cowards. He waved the knife in front of them, enjoying their fear. He noted Caspar's worried grimace, and was glad that

133

the doctor was out of the way in the kitchen bandaging Ketto.

"Niggers ain't no better than wild hogs," Carlton shouted. "This slave wench is a sow."

Sophy had beautiful hair, the envy of every wench on the plantation. She combed it religiously each day. She wore it in long whorls plaited in the style of her native Africa.

Carlton grabbed the braids which crowned her head. He raised the knife above her eyes. Sophy shook with terror, sweat trickling down her legs. Carlton slashed at her. He sliced off a handful of her plaits and threw them to the ground in disgust.

"Here, Ella!" he called, thrusting the knife at her. "You finish the job. Shave the pig until she is bald. All of her!"

Chapter 14

CASPAR HERDED THE FLOCK OF BUCKS FROM THE barracoon down to the slave quarters. Carlton rode in front at the head of the coffle which scuffed its way past the shacks and *ajoupas*. When they were in the center of the slave section, Caspar saw the Bondmaster raising his hand to bring the procession to a halt. Caspar reined in his horse and relaxed, his whip hanging loosely in his hand.

"Mally Ibo!" Carlton hailed the old seamstress, who shuffled out of her cabin at the approach of the coffle. A girl stood beside her, nervously twisting the folds of her shift in her hand.

"Is that the filly I gave you to keep for my bucks?" demanded Carlton. "Who is she?"

"She does be Tency, Mas Carlton." Mally Ibo hitched up her old bosom and sniffed. "She does be pining fuh a buck too bad, massa!"

"Ah does be de one fuh she!" Benn retorted from the coffle.

Carlton looked at the bucks and snorted. "You'll all get your fillies!"

Caspar handed Carlton a ledger which he opened

and searched for Tency's name and the name of the buck she was to be crossed with.

"Who is Homer?"

The slaves exchanged glances, shouting with derision as they pushed a tall youth to the front. "Dis be Homer," said Benn. "But he does be too *maco* fuh she. Ah does be de one fuh yo', Tency!"

"Are you Homer?"

The slave nodded.

"Right. This is your filly. I want you to mount her until you get me a whelp. If you mount another wench without me telling you, I'll have you gelded."

Homer was prancing eagerly, his mouth wide open in a foolish grin.

"Hear me well, boy!" Carlton cautioned.

"And you, Tency, this is your buck. Mally Ibo will be watching and if you permit any other buck to mount you, I'm going to lash the flesh off your bones and stake out your carcass for the jumbies. Understand?"

Tency kept her eyes on the ground.

"She gon' drain dat boy dry, massa!" cackled Mally Ibo. "If she don't get yo' no whelp, is dat lanky poltroon dat don't have de quem!"

Chattering with excitement, the bucks were herded on to the next shack. Caspar rode up to join Carlton when they halted.

"There's one of those wenches who is awful black," he commented. "Her name is Claire's Joan. Which colt have you chosen for her?" Caspar tried to make his query sound of no consequence.

"Claire's Joan?" Carlton pondered. "I know that one, she's a Congo. François is the one for her. He's a Congo, too. I'll get me a pure breed."

"François!" Caspar burst into laughter.

"What's funny in that?" Carlton shifted in his saddle to look at Caspar. "Are you questioning my judgment?"

"Oh, no, Mas Carlton. Perhaps you don't know François though. I pray you look at him first." Caspar's gesture encompassed the heads of the slaves grouped around them.

"Look for the ugliest, blackest bozal here and that will be François."

Carlton cast his eye over the blacks. In complexion each nigger was different, ranging from the yellow of the Ibos and the lighter-skinned Mohamedians through the browns of the Pawpaws and Coromantins to the blue-black of the darkest Negro.

There was only one with the ugly features characteristic of a Congo, more like a monkey than a man. He was stoutly built with a fine physique. Carlton grinned at Caspar. "That one?" he said indicating the boy he had picked out as François.

"That's him. Isn't he blacker than a vile thundercloud at night? I venture to suggest that Claire's Joan would be better served by someone fairer, sir, to lighten up her breed."

Carlton leaned over from his horse and clapped Caspar on his back. "Like you, I suppose!" he roared. "Boy, you have the wiles of your father and the guile of your mother. Thank God it's me you're dealing with. You'd swindle the governor out of his own mistress if you had a mind."

Chuckling proudly, Carlton scanned the names in his ledger. "Yes, you can have her. I want a whelp quickly, though, boy. I had sired two by the time I was your age."

"Or course!" Caspar glanced at the doleful François. "And what will you give the bozal colt, sir?"

137

"François? An Ibo breed, I suppose. I'm not fond of them. They're foul feeders and pusillanimous. But a half share of Congo blood might produce a whelp that's stout-hearted for the cane fields."

"Do you believe those bucks will mount only the wenches you've given them?" Caspar broke into the silence engulfing the two men as they rode back to the house later that afternoon.

Carlton looked quizzically at Caspar. "Do you think they will disobey me?"

"Yes."

"Hah, maybe so! Threats alone are not enough, boy." Carlton sighed.

"I suppose it is impossible to control them all the time. I want to produce perfect slaves, Caspar, that's why I've selected those prime niggers. But with niggers from Africa being impossible to buy these days, anything born in bondage is bound to sell for a high price."

"Why don't planters breed their own slaves?"

"Economics, Caspar. A planter has slaves to work his land, not drop whelps. It is cheaper for him to buy a seasoned slave twelve years old ready to be worked than spend twelve years rearing a nigger himself."

Caspar scratched his head. "If that is the case, how can we make it profitable for Roxborough?"

Carlton appreciated Caspar's interest. "It pays because we have slaves in abundance who are hardworking and docile. The market for sugar is falling, and expenses are rising. If we were still in sugar, we would be in the same hard-pressed state as the others."

They were approaching the stables. "When we got

wind of the ban on slave-trading, Caspar, we started breeding. We have fifteen years' start on the sugar and coffee planters. It's only now that they are thinking about slaves for the future. We can name our own price."

Carlton dismounted, leaving the groom to catch his horse and stable it. He strolled immediately over to the house without waiting for Caspar, who had to scamper to catch up with him.

"Our niggers lead a good life. We work them hard and feed them plenty, and we thrash them when they idle. They have no mind to resist. Caspar, you must tame any slave who looks like being a leader. He could stir up the others."

"How do you do that?"

"Get him on your side, boy. Give him a whip and make him a driver!"

Caspar scowled. "Is that what you did with me?"

Carlton paused at the foot of the front steps. It was almost night, heralded by the squawking and cracking of insects in the trees around the house. He looked into Caspar's intense face. "No. One day, Hayes will inherit Roxborough. *What* he inherits will depend on you." He clasped Caspar's arm.

"You are my link with the slaves, boy. When my da' was alive, I was his link. I lived with the niggers as though I was a slave myself. I don't do that now. How do I know what the slaves are planning, Caspar? That foolish boy, Ketto, was Kingston's eyes. I need you to be my eyes and ears, son."

Carlton snapped the feeling of intimacy he could feel rising between them by tapping Caspar sharply on his shoulder.

"By the way, boy, think you can handle that

Claire's Joan? She looks like a *leggo beast* to me!"

The Bondmaster's crude laughter echoed through the night as he bounded up the steps. Caspar gazed after him, sucking his lower lip pensively.

Chapter 15

CASPAR HAD NO ILLUSIONS ABOUT HIS VULNERability at Roxborough. The Bondmaster carried an armory of weapons when he toured the plantation, but Caspar's only defense against potential danger was his cutlass and his whip. And Samboth.

Like the Bondmaster, Caspar needed a link with the slaves himself. Samboth, because he was a free Negro and almost a stowaway on the plantation, was that link. The boy roamed at will. He went to Layou frequently and carried reports to Caspar on what was happening throughout the island.

It was through Samboth that Caspar learned that a band of *nègres marrons* were camped above the Layou Valley, very near the borders of Roxborough itself. The *nègres marrons*, or maroons as they were called by the English planters, were escaped slaves and deserters from the island's Black Regiment. An order had gone out from the island's governor for their extermination.

As well as Samboth's warnings, Caspar soon had other evidence of the maroon menace on the plantation boundary. He was riding in the hills one morning in December, when he met Homer, one of the breeding slaves, racing down the track in search of him.

Homer reported breathlessly that he had found a cow with two legs hacked off it and the liver cut out. The slave believed the cow had been attacked by a *soucouyant* who had drunk its blood. However, when Caspar inspected the carcass he found the slaughter more like the work of an inefficient maroon butcher than an obeah witch.

Riding to his cabin later that morning, Caspar was surprised to see a kittareen parked outside the stables. Since his return to Roxborough from England, the only visitors had been revenue officers with tax demands. The Bondmaster dealt with these by giving the revenue man a keg of rum and a wench for the night and sending him packing the next day.

The stable boy, Caliste, was in a state of excitement. "Dat big *beké* lady wid de casino!" the groom announced, prancing around as though he was a nervous horse himself. "She has a wench wid she de color of cream an' lips de red of hibiscus. She done 'queeze mah hand!"

Caspar thumped the twittery groom in his stomach and strode over to the house. He took the steps two at a time and strolled onto the gallery where Carlton was sitting with the two visitors.

"Hah, Caspar! See what a pleasure an ill-wind has brought us. A visit from our neighbors from Layou." Carlton gestured at the two women. "You've already met May Gregg." He chuckled while Caspar bowed. "This is her daughter, Mary!"

Mary did indeed have the red lips which had so flustered the groom. Caspar smiled as those lips parted slightly. Mary extended a begloved hand

142

which he seized and kissed eloquently. He raised his eyes and found Mary appraising him with rather too obvious relish.

"This is Caspar!" said May, wheezing. "I would never 'ave recognized the boy. 'E 'as grown since you returned from England." May waved at the vast expanse of her bosom with a carved sandalwood fan clutched in her left hand, a glass of punch in her right.

"Lor! I suppose 'e 'as grown in the other directions, too!" She chortled, squeezing her tiny eye shut and letting it pop open quickly in an exaggerated wink.

"I've heard so much about yew!" crooned Mary in the drawl of the island-born whites. "Yew do not have to tell me anything about him, Mister Todd."

"If you had seen him in his English troggery with silks and satins and hair combed like a gentleman, you would have fallen for him, without a doubt," laughed Carlton in good humor.

"But I already have," said Mary, fluttering her long eyelashes at Caspar.

"Well, yes." Carlton coughed. "Caspar, May Gregg and her daughter have come to me because they are worried about the maroons. You see," Carlton turned to Mary, with an avuncular smile, "although Caspar is a slave, he is one I can trust."

Caspar considered Mary Gregg. Her fair hair tumbled below her bonnet to caress the back of her neck. Her lips were round and sensuous. Sitting with her hands demurely clasped in her lap, she seemed as pretty as her mother was grotesque. Caspar put her age at twenty. Had he not been to England, her superior air would have deterred him. But the ladies of Almack's had given him confidence and a perception with white women. This one was a whore.

"These maroons," said May Gregg, obviously continuing a tirade she had begun before Caspar entered, " 'ave quite terrified the free Negroes. They are camping in the 'ills and thieving from the *polinks*."

Caspar nodded his head in agreement, informing Carlton about the cow he had found butchered that morning.

"Ah, so you see," said May, her fan wilting at the task of billowing air across her enormous body. "They are coming for you, too. We must do something about it! We need protection!"

"Hmmm!" Carlton rested his elbow on the arm of his chair and supported his forehead in the palm of his hand. "What about all those sailors you have visiting you, May? Surely they are protection enough. I do not believe that those maroons would ever invade Layou."

"They massacred all the white people at Rosalie." May shuddered.

"Yes, yes, May. But the planter there, a fellow called Botts, was perversive with his slaves. It does not surprise me that the maroons found sympathy for their cause and his slaves revolted." He coughed.

"We have no trouble at Roxborough. We make sure our bucks are kept busy mounting the fillies, what?" He chuckled, but May Gregg was not in the mood to joke.

"Your father would 'ave led all the white men and free colored from Layou and 'unted them maroons until 'e 'ad killed every one!" May declared with a sniff of reproach.

"Da' was always hot-headed." Carlton brushed

away the challenge. "Besides, he did not have the advantages I have. Caspar will soon know if an attack is planned on Layou or on the plantation. He and Ella have their ways of knowing what is going on, don't you, Caspar?"

"What?" Caspar had been imagining the contours under Mary Gregg's stays. "I think I know what the mood of the niggers here is," he extemporized. "I'll intensify efforts to guard against an unexpected attack."

Carlton regarded Caspar skeptically. He assumed he was speaking in that manner to impress the visitors.

"Well, you see, May!" he flashed the madame a spurious smile to reassure her. "There really is no need to worry. Our slaves are loyal here. The maroons would get short shrift from my niggers. Layou is safe."

"Hmm," said May, her cheeks wobbling as she shook her head at Carlton's remarks. His mention of his slaves had caught her interest. "Those slaves, 'ow many do you 'ave?"

"At least three hundred."

"But that down right wicked, Carlton Todd! You don't even 'ave sugar no more. What you 'ave so many niggers for?"

"To sell, of course."

"Sell? Let's get on with it, then. I could buy 'alf a dozen meself."

"So you shall, May, so you shall. I am planning a vendue."

"An auction!" May's huge body lurched forward with surprise. There had not been a slave auction in the island for years. "Where?"

"Here, May."

"Oh lor' an' glory be!" May's pudgy hand shook as she drained her glass of punch. "An auction at Roxborough! You'll have 'undreds of people. They'll come fingering and handling and buying, they'll be so much money, and so many men. Oh lor! Carlton Todd, I love you." She lunged out of the chair and smothered Carlton, gobbling at his face like a plump pink pig.

"Oh, Ma." Mary stood up. "Yew and Mister Todd have your business to discuss, I'm sure. While yew do that, this boy Caspar here can show me the plantation."

"Yes, yes," said May without thinking. "Go on with you. Now, Carlton, you must let me do the catering for all those planters. Captain Loring can bring in some extra whores from Antigua."

Carlton's eyes were following Mary as she glided along the gallery behind Caspar. It had been many months since he had enjoyed a white wench.

"Your daughter," he asked May, "does she, eh, work at the casino?"

May's tiny eyes glinted. "She does."

"I must pay her a visit one of these fine evenings, May."

"You'll be welcome, Carlton. A lusty English whore knows 'ow to make love, not like your Negro wenches. Fat black sows they are, the way they lay back, part their legs, and let you drain yourself into them without a modicum of pleasure."

Pausing at the top of the step, Mary raised her parasol. She inclined her elbow to Caspar. He offered her his arm as they descended the steps.

Ella, spying from the kitchen, beamed at the ex-

146

traordinary sight of whore and slave playing lady and gentleman.

"Caspar!" whispered Mary huskily. "Where can we go?"

"Go?"

"Yes, we do not have much time. Don't yew have a cabin? I really don't think I could lie down in the middle of one of those cane fields."

Caspar's loins responded to the clutch of her arm in his. "Mah cabin does be 'cross de paddock."

"Let we hurry," Mary replied in the slave vernacular.

From the stable, Caliste followed the pair with his eyes, shaking his head profoundly. Samboth, who was relaxing on Caspar's veranda, saw them coming toward the cabin. He dashed inside. Claire's Joan was sitting on the bed, plaiting her hair.

"Get out, wench!" he ordered her, pushing open the back door leading into the cane field beyond. "Yo' haul yuh arse out de place fuh a while."

Samboth hustled the wench through the door and closed it quickly. There was a rumpled blanket on the mattress which he straightened out; he lined up the only chair in the room alongside the table, hastily closed the two side shutters into the fields, and then shut the two which opened onto the gallery.

He stood at the door like a butler as Caspar and Mary stepped onto the gallery.

"Good mornin', Miss Mary, good mornin', Mas Caspar, sah," he bowed.

François, about to pass the cabin on his way to the fields, darted off the path to hide in the cane when he observed Caspar and the white woman on the gallery. He saw Caspar lead the woman inside

147

the cabin and close the door, leaving Samboth standing outside.

Hearing a noise in the cane, François shifted his position to see who was behind him. He saw Claire's Joan sitting on a stone, her hair dishevelled, her body shaking as she sobbed.

The inside of the cabin was shadowy with the sunlight seeping through cracks in the boards and under the doors. Mary cast a glance around the place. She sniffed.

"It smells niggery."

"Only we niggers dat does live here," answered Caspar, sitting on the chair and tugging off his boot.

"I don't mean yew. Yew ain't a nigger." Mary hastily unlaced her bonnet. "Yew are a mulatto. If yew were a nigger, I would not be here." Her hair tumbled freely over her shoulder as she shook her head.

"No? Why not?" Caspar pulled off his other boot and looked across at Mary, who was fiddling behind her back to unhook her bodice.

"I might get raped!"

Caspar threw himself across the room onto the bed beside her. He grabbed Mary by her shoulders and pulled her down on top of him. He fastened his lips on hers, forcing her teeth open as he rammed his tongue into her mouth.

"Lor!" she said, pulling away from him. "Let me get my dress off before yew does rip it."

Samboth jammed his ear against the door. The rhythm of their tiny shrieks and sighs built up to a cadence which set the floor boards of the cabin creaking. Samboth stroked himself frenziedly, panting with

148

relief when he ejaculated over the veranda floor and the silence in the cabin indicated that Caspar had finished. He got up from his cramped position and walked off the veranda to urinate.

Standing at the edge of the field, Samboth became aware that a patch of canes seemed to be quivering. Thinking it might be an *agouti* he crouched down and stealthily threaded his way through the canes toward the disturbance. He parted the cane in front of him and peered through.

Claire's Joan was lying on the ground. She had her legs locked around the waist of a buck whose black arse rose and fell as he plunged into her. Samboth sighed, manipulating himself to ejaculation again in time to the buck's thrusts. He edged slowly out of the cane field before he was seen.

"Caspar!" Samboth heard Mary when he returned to the veranda. "How am I going to see yew again? People will suspect if I come here. My mam won't allow yew in the casino."

"Dam' what people think!" said Caspar, clasping her hand.

"I must see yew again." Mary slipped her arms around Caspar's waist. "Yew are going to mean a lot to me, Caspar."

"And you to me, Mary."

Years later, when the illusions had fallen away and he recalled the first reckless encounter with Mary Gregg, Caspar realized that the events which were to shatter his relationship with his father and destroy the tenor of life at Roxborough began the instant he uttered those words.

Chapter 16

CASPAR WAS TROUBLED. EVEN AS HE BEGAN HIS patrol around the plantation that night, Mary Gregg intruded into his thoughts. During the day he had kept her at bay by concentrating on the estate tasks, brushing away the feel of her limbs which stirred such emotions within him. But now, as he ambled soundlessly down the trail to the slave quarters, Mary Gregg refused to be banished from his mind.

In the darkness of the *porrie* trees lining the path, Caspar saw Mary's white face lying on his pillow, her red lips agasp. He remembered her cries and sighs as she rose with him only to collapse as though he, Caspar, was drawing the very essence out of her soul, not just emptying his juice into her.

Caspar blundered off the trail into the slave compound. He pulled up abruptly and stared at the shacks in surprise. He shook his head vigorously as though to tumble Mary out of his brain. A prickle of fear assailed him when he realized that for minutes his reverie had rendered him utterly defenseless. In neglecting the basic precautions of keeping all his senses alert, he was exposed to whatever evil, Negro or obeah, lurked at night. He shuddered.

It had been the presence of the murderous gangs of maroons so near to Layou which had brought May Gregg and Mary to Roxborough. The danger was real.

Caspar stepped into the bush which surrounded the clearing by the riverbank where the slave huts were located. Merging into the darkness and moving stealthily, he edged past cabins already shuttered against the night. Outside other shacks, small groups of Negroes were huddled around the lights from the *flambeaux*. Some of them were silent, some were muttering to themselves, some recounting *tim-tims* and others, captivated by the sounds of their own voices, were relating in expanding detail the occurrences on the plantation during the day.

Listening from the shadows, Caspar was surprised how rapidly the news of the impending auction had spread among the slaves. It was only that morning that Carlton had revealed his plan to May Gregg, yet now the slaves were themselves considering the proposal in detail.

"Dis action sale ain't no big t'ing."

Caspar identified the strident tones of Benn which he heard as he eavesdropped outside the shack controlled by Matilda. Matilda was a washer. Benn had been assigned to her to sleep in her shanty with Lilly, his breeding wench.

"Dat be how de *bekés* does call a vendue," Benn asserted.

"How yo' does know dem things, Benn? Yo' always have some kind of ol' talk to fool we."

"Good for Matilda!" thought Caspar as he listened to the woman berating Benn.

"Ah does have mah friends who does tell me

things," bragged Benn. "We here don't know nothing about de life outside Roxbruh."

Caspar edged nearer, alarmed by Benn's remark.

"Ain't nothing to know!" retorted Matilda. "Ah done be born in Africa an' done come here in a ship wid a Captain wid' a red beard. Does be Mas Carlton heself done buy me off de deck of de ship. Ah have seen life a'ready, an' dere ain't nothing better dan here at Roxbruh."

"Yo' does only say dat cuz yo' does be dry up an' don't have no life left," cried Benn. "Not like me! Ah does be beginning mah life an' ah don't gon' stay here a slave fuh ever!"

"How can yo' say dat?" demanded Lilly. "Yo' don't know if yo' does be sell at de action sale."

"Action sale? Ah don't think me gon' wait fuh dat."

"Dat's stupid nigger talk, Benn. Ah does be vex."

"Dat a'right, Matilda. Yo'll see de day when we slaves gon' rise up an' throw off we chains. Yassa!"

"We ain't got no chains." Lilly pouted.

"We have! We not free!"

"Dat's yo'!" Matilda was angry. "Ah does have mah provision garden in de *polinks*, mah *ajoupa*, an' ah does have any buck ah can get. Ah does have new clothes two times a year from Mas Carlton heself an' salt fish an' flour."

Matilda's voice rose to a shout. "Mah children done grow up in de paddock. Dey gon' collect big money at de action sale. Dey gon' live on a buckra plantation where dey get de same good life like me. Dis slavery does be de best life dere is, boy! In Africa ah does be dead by now!"

"Yo' does be a foolish ol' nigger, Matilda. De *marrons*, dem don't talk dat way. Dey say we slaves must rise up an' chop de buckra an' take we freedom." Silence greeted Benn's remark.

"Aw, yo' does be *sot!* Yo'-all stupid! Ah'm gon'!"

"Benn!" Matilda tried to restrain him. "Where yo' does be gon'? Mas Carlton done say yo' ain't got to go 'n' mount no other wrench when yo' does be wid Lilly."

"Mas Carlton dis, dat, and toder! De day does come when is me dat does say what me gon' do, not Mas Carlton. Yo' ain't gon' stop me gon' where ah does want, Matilda."

"Benn!" It was Lilly's voice which shriekcd after him when he shook open the rickety door of the shack.

"Don't worry, Lilly," Caspar heard Benn say. "Ah does give it yo' good tonight. Why ah does need another wench when ah does have yo'?"

Caspar stepped back in the shadows, hidden by the cane grass growing around the house. There was enough moonlight seeping through the branches of the trees enclosing the compound for Caspar to follow Benn.

The slave skirted the circles of dim light from the *flambeaux*. When he reached the trail which led up to the house, he branched off down to the river.

Benn was taking no special care to move silently now he was out of the perimeter of the slave quarters, and this made it easy for Caspar to track him.

At the riverbank where the trail disappeared into the river and emerged on the other side as a bridle path, Benn halted. His whistle interrupted the twittering of the night creatures.

Caspar crept closer to see whom Benn was calling. He crouched at the base of a giant fern tree about five paces from Benn. He glimpsed Benn as a darker shape against the background of light from the young moon reflected in the gurgling river.

An answering croak came from the other bank. Caspar took it for the cry of a *crapaud* until he detected a difference in the note. Benn heard it. He moved closer to the river and waited. After a few minutes, Caspar saw two shapes emerge from the darkness of the water. He gripped his cutlass securely in his hand and edged forward.

It was difficult to see the two maroons. They were both naked with locks of unkempt hair caked with mud sticking out all over their heads. Caspar recalled the prints of jungle savages from Africa which he had seen in England. He sniffed. The maroon's odor was distinctive, a scent of decayed foliage and excrement. The two stood on either side of Benn, jabbering in a guttural creole.

"We done get de cow."

"Ah does know," Benn replied. "Caspar done find de carcass. Why yo' not take all of it? Caspar does know now, an' he sure to ax who done loose it fuh yo'."

"Dat's yuh concern!" The maroons edged closer to Benn. "Nigger! We does have a powerful need of currency."

"Currency?" Benn sounded puzzled. "We slaves here don't have no currency." He made a gesture of helplessness.

"De Bon'massa does hab! Not so?"

"Ah don't know how to get dat," Benn whined.

"Nigger! Yo' does want yuh freedom, *oui?* Yo' does want to join us in de hills fighting de buckras, dem?" One of the maroons prodded Benn in his waist.

Benn stumbled. "Yo' does know dat."

"Nigger. Yo' gon' run 'way wid we. Tumba does know about yo'. He done say he hab need fuh a nigger like yo'."

"Tumba!" Benn uttered the name of the maroons' leader in awe.

"Tumba say yo' to take de Bon'massa gold an' he gon' make yo' a chief beside he." The maroon pushed Benn toward his partner.

"An' if yo' don't get de gold," said the second maroon, pushing Benn back, "Tumba say he gon' cut out yuh liver an' drink yuh blood."

As quietly as they had arrived, the two merged back into the night. Benn stayed peering across the river for minutes before slowly retracing his steps up the bank and onto the trail. Caspar fingered the blade of his cutlass as Benn passed close to him.

"Should I chop him? Should I chop him?" The question flashed through Caspar's mind. "It's easy!" he decided, rising slowly behind Benn.

"No!" The voice shrieked at him. "Why kill a slave? That's the Bondmaster's affair!"

Caspar sank back on his haunches, letting the troubled Benn, unaware of his presence, blunder past him.

Carlton listened grimly to Caspar's report. He sat back in his chair, his arms folded across his chest, studying Caspar's face in the glow from the lantern.

"Why, Caspar, why?" he demanded. "Benn! He's Roxborough-born. He's got no cause to run away and become a maroon. Don't I treat him well, Caspar? He has a wench. He's never been strung up and flogged."

Something occurred to Carlton, making him pause,

contemplating Caspar standing in front of him.

"Does he hate me, Caspar? Does he want to kill me?"

"I didn't hear him talk about that."

"Huh. I can't understand it. Haven't I been good to the slaves?"

Caspar kept silent. What did being good to slaves mean? He knew Carlton's reluctance to punish a slave was due to his desire to preserve the slave's value, not out of a desire to be good to them.

"Benn is such a prime slave, Caspar. You are sure it was Benn?"

"Of course. I grew up with him. He is my friend."

Carlton frowned, then raised his head to stare at Caspar. Caspar gazed down at him without flinching, waiting for the Bondmaster to decide what to do.

"No." Carlton considered his overseer carefully. "You wouldn't lie."

It was Caspar's turn to frown.

"Right." Carlton stood up briskly. "Go and get him."

"Now?"

"But yes, Caspar, now. Rouse Mercury and any of the drivers you need to help you. Benn won't be expecting any retribution at this hour!" Carlton sneered.

"Won't you wait until he actually does something?" ventured Caspar.

"He has! Contact with the maroons is enough! You heard what May Gregg told us this morning. Do you think we are safe?" Carlton clenched the gallery rail nervously.

"I am going to root out any of the slaves who let the idea of running away enter their thick woolly skulls. The niggers need to realize that they must never defy the Bondmaster."

"What if the maroons decide to attack the plantation?"

"The rangers will defend us. A packet sailed to Roseau this afternoon with a message for Governor Anslie from me and the white citizens of Layou. We have requested protection. The rangers will soon flush out Tumba. Now you get your wits about you, Caspar, and flush out Benn."

Carlton gazed out across the yard in the direction of the slave quarters. "Bring him to me in the stable," he called as Caspar clattered down the steps.

It was an easy matter to round up Benn. He was already in Lilly's arms when Caspar and the drivers invaded Matilda's shack and dragged him off the floor. While Matilda and Lilly wailed, Caspar urged them to stay inside. They and the other slaves in the quarters needed no persuading. Those who had heard Benn's shrieks cowered behind the flimsy walls of their *ajoupas*, grateful that it was not they who had incurred the Bondmaster's displeasure.

Caspar prodded Benn into motion, trying to ignore the boy's protests.

"You'll find out!" gloated the driver, Asaph, when Benn pleaded to be told what he had done.

Benn's panic grew at the sight of the brightly lit house which dominated the plantation in the moonlight. People were rushing along the balcony, hanging lamps which threw their light down into the yard and across to the stable.

When he observed the stable door open and the lamps hung inside, Benn was certain he was to be flogged. He trembled, lurching forward as Asaph cracked his whip across his shoulders to make him

157

walk. As a child, Benn had seen slaves hanging by their ankles, twisting like dead pigs from the stable beam, as Constance, the blacksmith, flayed their bodies with the cat-o-nine-tails.

Benn shrank back in terror when a lamp carried by Caliste illuminated the enormous shape of Constance standing by the Bondmaster at the door of the stable. Asaph's whip lashed across his shoulders as he faltered.

Benn hurried through the door, his eyes cast down on the floor to avoid Constance's gaze. Asaph thumped his shoulders, and he fell at the blacksmith's feet. He curled himself up with his hands shielding his face. He waited.

Constance watched the Bondmaster intently. Constance was totally deaf and dumb, chosen by Carlton, because of his prodigious size and strength, as the plantation blacksmith. He performed his duties conscientiously, forging shoes for the plantation horses and for those of neighboring estates. His superior physique and his inability to hear the screams of his twisting victims made him a natural choice to administer floggings to disobedient slaves.

Constance viewed Benn, stretched out on the stable floor in front of him, with relief. Many months had passed since his skill with the whip had been needed. He felt neglected. But now he followed the Bondmaster's gestures with excitement, trying to understand what was required of him. Slowly, glancing from Benn to the Bondmaster's hands, he realized.

His broad mouth hung open with delight. He barked, and the unnatural sound filled Benn with horror. Benn peeped upward between his fingers, only to see Constance lumber off into the darkness.

"Turn him over!" Carlton stubbed his boot in Benn's side. Benn scrambled into a kneeling position and grasped Carlton's ankles.

"Get the wretch off me, Caspar!"

Caspar flicked his whip gently across Benn's wrists. "Let go, Benn."

Caspar was himself puzzled by what the Bondmaster intended to do. He swallowed nervously. A flogging at Constance's hands would be painful for the horniest field hand to bear. A youth of sixteen like Benn, with his soft skin and young muscles, could not be expected to survive.

"Caspar!" Carlton was looking at him reproachfully. "This is not a game. See!" Carlton snatched Caspar's whip and thrashed Benn across his cheek. Blood oozed out of the raw welt and trickled onto his boot.

"This is life or death. Our lives or our death, Caspar."

Caspar turned away. He did not want the Bondmaster to see him wince. He was disturbed. When he had been younger, Caspar had seen the Bondmaster in a quick rage, striking out at anyone in his sight. This was a new side of the man: an evil composure more terrifying than any wild outburst of temper.

"See, Caspar, now the nigger cringes! Well, my fine slave," Carlton's voice sounded strangely beguiling, "you don't want to tell the Bondmaster any lies, do you, Benn?"

"No, sah!" Benn sensed there was hope. He shifted so he could see the Bondmaster better, trying to gauge his mood.

"You don't want to waste our time when we should all be in our beds sleeping, do you, Benn?"

"No, sah!" Benn thought of Lilly lying on the floor of the *ajoupa*, waiting. He would ride her the whole night as soon as the Bondmaster released him, no matter how the lash stung him.

"Well, Benn, there is no one here apart from you and me and a handful of house niggers. There is no one here from the quarters, Benn, so you can tell me the truth."

"Sah?" Bewildered, Benn fingered the trickling blood on his cheek.

"The maroons, Benn! Who else in the quarters is in contact with them?"

Benn's eyes flickered with renewed confidence. His expression assumed a mask of hurt innocence. "Mas Carlton," he began.

The whip sliced into the other side of his face. "No lies, Benn!"

In spite of the stinging pain in his cheek, Benn was lulled by the sweetness of the Bondmaster's voice.

"No one, sah," he murmured.

Benn reasoned to himself that if he told the Bondmaster what he wanted to know, he would soon be back with Lilly in her shack. He would take her with him and run away to the heights at dawn. He would join Tumba; Mas Carlton would never find him.

"Ah does be de only one, sah. Dey done tell me not to tell none of de slaves dem, sah."

Carlton crouched in front of him. "Go on, Benn. What else did they tell you?"

"Nothing, sah." Benn waited for the next slash of the whip on his face. Nothing happened. He peeped up. The Bondmaster's eyes were staring into his.

160

"Did you plan to run away, Benn?"

The voice was so gentle and kind that Benn felt ashamed of what the maroons had asked him to do.

"Did you plan to steal gold from me, Benn, and join the maroons in the hills?"

Benn gasped, twisting his face away to avoid the Bondmaster's eyes. "No, sah! No!" he shrieked.

A shadow fell over him as he groveled in the damp straw of the mud floor. It was Constance. Benn peered through his fingers. He saw Carlton nod his head, and the huge slave slobbered as he bent down. He picked Benn up in his arms as though he was a child.

"Dey said dey would kill me, sah!" Benn screamed. "Dey said Tumba would eat mah liver, sah!"

Carlton nodded again, walking beside Constance, who was carrying Benn out of the stable. "Do you believe he is telling the truth, Caspar? Are there other bucks who are in contact with the maroons?"

Caspar shrugged his shoulders.

"I'm sure he'll tell us," sneered Carlton. "It grieves me to do this, I can assure you, Caspar. Benn would have fetched a high price at the auction, I declare!"

Constance stopped at the forge. The fire was raging in the brazier as Dontfraid pumped the bellows. The blacksmith's irons were hanging beside the anvil. Constance threw Benn onto the ground and looked obediently at his master.

"Asaph! Mercury! Spancel the buck's wrists behind his back."

"What are you going to do?" Caspar grabbed the Bondmaster's sleeve.

"Give our runaway shoes so he can run, Caspar."

161

"But that will kill him!"

"Do you think so? Constance has never lost a horse and he has shod plenty."

The two drivers held Benn by his shoulders. His arms were pinioned behind his back. Constance bent down and grabbed one of his legs, bending it backwards. Benn hopped on his other foot to keep himself from falling, twisting around and resting when Constance held his foot between his own legs. Asaph and Mercury gripped him firmly.

With a grunt of glee, Constance removed an iron from the fire with his tongs. It was a glowing horseshoe which he had beaten down to fit Benn's foot. He glanced at Carlton for approval.

"See, he has made it the right size! I could name my own price for this slave, Caspar. He is an artist!"

Benn tried to pull his leg away from Constance when he felt the heat.

"Help to hold him, Caspar, there's a good fellow. Yes, by the leg."

Carlton walked around to face Benn. The slave was staring wildly through the door of the forge and out into the darkness. Benn's hopes of returning to Lilly were fading.

"There's none of your maroon cronies to help you now, runaway!" sniggered Carlton. "You can clip-clop down to the quarters in the morning and show the slaves the fine shoes the Bondmaster has given you. You can tell the niggers I'll shoe any who want to run. Are there others, Benn? Are there?"

"No, sah!" Benn's answer changed to a screech as Constance scorched the iron shoe onto his foot. His body arched off the ground, then plummeted to the floor. He twisted, trying to throw off the hands which gripped him, pain searing through him as the horseshoe burned into the hard flesh.

Constance held Benn's ankle calmly, removing a nail from the cluster he held in his lips. He poked the nail through a hole in the metal rim of the shoe and hammered it swiftly into the charred skin of Benn's foot.

"Oh, dear," said Carlton as Benn's head slumped forward. "He has passed out."

Caspar released Benn's leg and fell back against the wall of the smithy. He stared at Carlton, his nostrils flaring. The stench of Benn's burned flesh made him heave.

"No, Caspar. It is not a nice sight. But what else to do? I'm sure there'll be no more talk of runaways! See the job is completed properly. I'm going to bed."

Constance had already caught up Benn's other foot and was fastening the shoe to it as Carlton left. The drivers released Benn's body, which flopped lifelessly to the ground. They looked at Caspar. Constance knelt down and studied his handiwork, honking with satisfaction.

"What do we do with him now, Mas Caspar?" asked Asaph, kicking Benn's inert body.

"Carry him outside!" Caspar spoke quietly. "It's too hot in here. Mercury, run for water." He watched Benn lying on the grass outside the forge. Ella was moving along the balcony, turning down the lamps. Constance and Dontfraid were dousing the fire.

It seemed only minutes ago that Benn had been a carefree youth, full of hope and energy. Now he lay broken on the grass as Caspar stood above him.

Mercury brought water which Caspar poured over

163

Benn's feet. The shoes hissed, steam foaming around his ankles.

"Go now!" Caspar told the drivers. "Take Constance with you. Dontfraid, you go, too."

"What about you, Mas Caspar?"

"Me? What about Benn?"

"Benn?" The question was wasted on Mercury. He had done what he had been told to do. "He ain't gon' run no more!"

"Go!" Caspar cried angrily. "Leave me alone!"

When the forge was closed and Dontfraid had removed the last lantern from its hook and wandered back to the house, Caspar knelt down beside Benn. The moon cast a pallid glow over the slave's body. Caspar trickled water from the pail onto Benn's forehead. It spread into his eyes, ran over his stubby nose, washed blood from his cheeks, and drained over his throat into the earth.

Benn groaned.

Caspar bent his head low over the slave, peering into his eyes, blowing gently onto his lips. Benn's eyelids flickered. Caspar grasped his hand.

"Benn!" he called softly. "Benn!"

Slowly, Benn's eyes opened. He focused on Caspar's face pressed close to his.

"I'm sorry, Benn!" Caspar breathed.

Benn parted his lips as though about to speak. Caspar shifted his cheek to place his ear close to the slave's mouth to listen. A low moan began from the depths of Benn's body, almost from the soles of his mutilated feet themselves. It rattled through his frame, increasing in volume until it erupted from his throat in a howl of suffering.

Caspar recoiled from the slave's body in horror.

Benn did not move. Caspar approached Benn again, his cutlass poised above his shoulder.

"Caspar!" Benn pleaded. "Save me!"

Caspar chopped down the freshly honed blade of his cutlass into the slave's neck.

Benn fell back with a yelp.

Cursing himself for what he was doing, Caspar hacked at Benn's neck until he severed it. He flicked the slave's head away crossly. It rolled over the grass and came to rest against Benn's iron-shod feet.

Chapter 17

CASPAR PIROUETTED AROUND THE KITCHEN. Ella clapped her hands with delight. In his long coat cut away in the front with its wasp waist and high collar, and with his tight trousers, Caspar looked every inch a free man of color.

"Oh, Caspar! Caspar!" cried Ella happily. "Yo' does resemble de Doctor de day he done set foot here."

"Am I not perfectly handsome, Ella? The English gentleman, wouldn't you say?" Caspar twirled elegantly in front of the kitchen table. "Or a young mulatto merchant with a fortune? At least a free man of property?"

"Yas, yas! If it does please yo', Caspar." Ella bustled around the kitchen hanging the lamps as night descended. "Why yo' does be dressed so, Caspar?"

"To please a lady, mam."

"A lady?" Ella hung the lamp she held in her hand and turned to look at Caspar. He stared back at her.

Ella noticed how Caspar's eyes had shed their look of youthful innocence. She saw a toughness in his

166

face which had developed since his return from England, a defiant cut to his jaw, and lines of determination etched in each cheek. He held his head proudly, like a white man.

"Who is dis lady?"

"Oh, no, mam! I am not going to tell you yet. Do you think she'll like me dressed like this?"

Suspicion grew in Ella's mind. She sat down. "Yo' going to May Gregg's, Caspar."

"What if I am?" Caspar glared at his mother in surprise.

"Caspar," sighed Ella, "sit down, boy. Here, on de bench beside me." Ella waited for him to join her, wondering how to explain herself without dampening the ambitions of her son.

"Mas Carlton does know yo' does be going to May Gregg's?"

"Of course not, Ella. He would tell me to drain myself in my bed wench and get him a whelp."

"He does be right, Caspar." Ella put her hand on Caspar's knee, trying to restrain him.

"How is he right, Ella? I fail to see why you support him. Do you want to produce whelps when the Bondmaster demands one?"

"Ah mean dat May Gregg's whores are not fuh yo', Caspar. Yo' have all de wenches yo' need here at Roxbruh."

"But no white ones, Ella."

"Oh!" Ella raised her hand to her mouth. She glanced around the empty kitchen in alarm. "What will become of yo', Caspar? If yo' molest jus' one of May Gregg's whores, yo' gon' get yuh throat cut before yo' does pull up yuh britches."

"Why should I, Ella? Whores are whores. I have

167

money to pay." He chuckled. "Though I doubt that will be necessary."

"Caspar!" Ella cut off his laugh. "De wenches by May Gregg may be whores, but dey does be white whores. Yo' does not be a white. Yo' does be a slave!"

"A'right, Ella. I hear you. Don't worry. What can happen to me?"

"Death, Caspar. De Bon'massa bound to kill a slave who does lie wid a white woman."

"That is old talk, Ella, and you know it." Caspar put his arm around his mother's shoulders. "Mas Carlton has been in England. He has seen how civilized people live. Why, even ladies of quality in London have their black paramours who were once slaves."

Ella pulled away from Caspar in disbelief.

"And tell me, Ella. The Bondmaster thinks it's right for a white man to mount a slave wench, so surely a slave buck can mount a white woman."

The blood drained from Ella's face. "Caspar, ah fear fuh yo'!" She wrung her hands nervously in her apron. "Yo' must understand de mind of a white man, Caspar. A white man don't want he slave to have what is he own."

"Even a whore, Ella?"

"Even a whore, Caspar. Wait!" She put her hand out to stop him as Caspar began to rise. "Dere does be another thing." She paused to see if he was listening.

"A whelp does take de life of he mother."

"How?" Caspar feigned interest.

"If de mam does be a slave, Caspar, den de whelp is a slave, too, even if de father is free. But if de mother is free, like May Gregg's whores, den de

168

whelp does be free, too, even when de father does be a slave like yo'."

In spite of Ella's protests, there was no way Caspar could consider not seeing Mary Gregg again. Making sure that Carlton was engaged in conversation on the gallery with the doctor and unlikely to seek him out, Caspar mounted his horse and made his way to Layou.

From his earlier visit to the casino the day he had arrived from England, Caspar felt he knew what to expect. As he entered the casino, he steeled himself in preparation for the sarcasm of the casino's clients of seamen and assorted whites. Caspar believed that after his previous acquaintance with May Gregg, she was unlikely to consider turning him away. He was mistaken.

"Boy!" May Gregg growled at him as soon as he pushed through the crush of drinkers and gamblers and presented himself to her. "You're a bold one and no mistake. What are you doing in 'ere? Where's your master?"

At the sound of May Gregg's loud voice, people turned their heads expectantly. Caspar felt their unfriendly gaze on the back of his neck as he stood before the enormous woman.

May pursed her lips. "This is my busy time, boy. Carlton Todd should know better than to send you to me at this hour." She peered at Caspar. He was quite presentable, but some of her customers were bound to know that he was really a slave from Roxborough. Anything could happen in her tavern. If her clients thought that slaves were sniffing around her whores, business would fail immediately.

169

"You best go in the back room, boy. I'll come to you in a while," she told him urgently.

Caspar nodded and pushed open the door that May Gregg indicated. His hope of seeing Mary in the casino had been foiled. At that hour of the evening, the tavern was packed, making it impossible to see from one side of the room to another. There were several white women in the place, laughing gaily or embracing the sailors with exaggerated delight. Somewhere in the middle of the crowd, he assumed, was Mary.

In the room to which he had been banished so hastily there were two chairs and a mattress. Caspar sat despondently on the edge of one of the chairs. He scowled. He realized now that he should not have come to this squalid hole. Seeing the atmosphere in which Mary worked was profoundly distressing.

He stood up and walked over to the closed shutters. It was painful to consider that Mary might be in the casino being mauled and fondled by ignorant white seamen while he, a real man who had proved he could pleasure her, was hidden in the casino back room because of her mother's embarrassment.

Caspar considered opening the window and jumping into the alley beside the casino. Samboth was in Layou waiting for him. He would show him a tavern where he could relax without being spurned because he was a slave. Ella was right, as usual. He resolved to return to his cabin, where Claire's Joan was lying in his bed waiting for him, and forget Mary Gregg.

As he raised his hand to release the bolt holding the shutter in its place, the door of the room opened.

Embarrassed, Caspar swung around ready to deliver his contrived message to May Gregg and then hurry back to Roxborough.

"Caspar!"

"Mary!" he replied, surprised.

"Sssh!" Mary cautioned, raising a finger to her lips as a warning. She carefully closed the door, turned the key in the lock, and glanced around the room. Only when she was satisfied that she could not be observed from the alley outside did she allow herself to be embraced by Caspar.

"My!" She pulled herself away from his lips and examined him. "Yew look so elegant. Far too fashionable for the Gregg family bawdy house!"

"Well, I didn't want to look like a slave," he retaliated bitterly. "But the first words your mam uttered when she saw me were to ask me about my master!"

"My mam only thinks of the money," Mary said with a laugh. "No matter if yew are a slave or a tar. It is the menfolk who come here. Many of them are planters. What would they say if they thought she was pandering to niggers?"

"Mary, I just had to see you. I haven't stopped thinking about you since that afternoon you came to my cabin." He stared wide-eyed at her. "To me you are even more beautiful than I remember."

"That's the candlelight and my working clothes." She sidled up to him, her hands snaking around his waist.

"Caspar, I wanted yew so much."

Caspar inclined his head forward, brushing her cheek with his black hair as he nibbled the lobe of her ear.

"Fie, Caspar! I have a gentleman out there will

come bursting through this door if I dally one moment longer."

Caspar felt his heart lurch. It was sickening to think that a man was waiting to make use of her body in the same way that he pumped himself into his bed wench.

"Mary, we must talk."

"Lor, Caspar. It's not talking we must do. Look at yew." She placed her hand on his burgeoning crotch and squeezed him. "I want yew, Cas, I do, I really do!"

"Tell your gentleman to go about his business!"

"I am his business, Cas." She kissed him quickly and caressed his face. "How I adore your sweet nose!"

"Is there nothing we can do?" He tried to draw her to the mattress, but she broke away from his grasp, her eyes bright and her chest heaving.

"Let me think. It is too dangerous to go to my lodgings, because the girls are there with their clients."

"Can you foist your fogey on another whore?" demanded Caspar. "I have a solution."

"I'll try."

"And your mam won't know?"

"May Gregg knows everything."

Caspar bit his lip as he thought quickly. "Give whatever excuse you can. You know my boy, Samboth."

"Samboth? Of course. I helped to raise him when his mother abandoned him in our kitchen."

"Samboth will wait outside. Go with him. Behind the houses, not down the main street. I have the key to the sugar warehouse by the jetty. I'll be inside."

"It's dangerous."

"So am I, Mary," warned Caspar as he clasped her to him and gnawed at her mouth in a frenzied kiss.

"Let me go now." She squeezed out of his grasp. "Mam will suspect. I nearly forgot, I'm supposed to ask yew what message yew have for Mam."

Caspar told her some details about the auction, all the while fondling her bottom with his long fingers.

They broke apart. Mary smoothed her hair, took a deep breath, unlocked the door, and walked out into the casino. Caspar, keeping his hat held in front of him, followed. He bowed to May Gregg and edged his way out through the crowd.

The warehouse was a low-roofed stone building with walls eighteen inches wide. Using it was Samboth's suggestion. Its double doors opened onto the riverbank by the jetty where idlers squatted observing the river traffic. However, there was a rear entrance to the warehouse which was shielded from public view by the lush vegetation which had grown up around the building.

Caspar and Samboth made a preliminary investigation of the warehouse. They greased the hinges of the back door so it would not squeak and attract the attention of anyone idling at the front of the building. They brought two blankets down from the house to serve as a covering on the mud floor. Because of its thick walls, it was unlikely that a passerby would see the candle glow or hear voices inside the warehouse. It was an ideal solution.

Caspar waited impatiently in the darkness of the interior. The back door was slightly ajar so that he could listen for Mary's arrival. Caspar had arranged for Samboth to guide her to the warehouse through the forest behind the town so that no one would observe her. He was helped in his plan that evening by heavy clouds which hung over the moon imposing the blackness of night on the town. It would be difficult, Caspar thought, for Samboth to find his way to the warehouse without a lantern. Certainly, no one would spy Mary walking with him.

At a rustle of the branches outside the warehouse Caspar reached for the knife at his belt. He poised behind the door, ready to strike. A hand softly tapped twice upon the door and then a voice called his name.

"At last, Mary!" he breathed, opening the door wide. "Keep watch, Sam," he whispered as the boy put Mary's hand into his. "Did anyone see you?"

"I haven't seen anyone myself," said Mary. "It's so dark along that trail we could have passed within inches of a revenue man and he would think it was the breeze."

Caspar closed the door noiselessly and put a light to the candle. The glow flickered around the empty warehouse and illuminated the corner he had furnished with blankets.

"We don't need that," said Mary, leaning over his shoulder and blowing out the flame. "I need yew."

Their embrace was an experience for Caspar. It added a dimension to rutting that he had not known existed. Mary teased his senses in a way no wench on the plantation had ever done. With her hands, her lips, her legs, she sought out every sensitive nerve in his body. He trembled with desire for her.

Caspar understood what he had been pining for

since that interlude in his cabin the day she had visited Roxborough.

Mary weakened as he gripped her with a passion she recognized as genuine. He took her with an unhurried, animal strength. Whether it was his generous size, the excitement of the secret encounter, or some other quality with which Mary had yet to come to terms, Caspar's lovemaking inspired her more than that of any white man she could recall.

Exhausted, they clasped each other, neither wanting the other's grip to loosen.

"Cas, I don't know what is happening to me." Mary's fingers strayed lovingly through his soft black hair as he lay beside her.

"Yew've showed me something I've only heard about. I think I am falling in love with yew."

"I know," he whispered. "That's how I feel, too."

Mary had no idea how much time had passed. Perhaps she had even fallen asleep in his strong arm, wrapped so securely around her. She jolted up suddenly.

"Cas, I must go."

"Stay."

"No, I must. I have a gentleman. He is waiting."

"Ah, yes," he sighed.

"Don't be vexed for that, Cas. He'll be gone tomorrow."

"You'll come here tomorrow?"

"Yes, if I can. But that's not what I meant. Yew must understand me, Cas. I know what yew are, and yew know what I am. Neither of us can change ourselves. That doesn't matter to us, does it?" She curled a lock of his hair around her finger.

"Even though yew were born a slave and half black, it will not stop me wanting yew. Yew must not be vexed because of what I am and what I am bound to do. It is what I was born to. Just like yew."

"Yes," he said softly, helping her to her feet. "What we can't change, we have to accept. Mas Carlton wants me to breed whelps to enrich the Roxborough coffers. You have to keep your mam's casino prosperous." They laughed ruefully, holding hands as they eased out of the door.

Samboth rose up at their feet. "I shall wait here tomorrow," Caspar said. "Sam will escort you to your *gentleman*."

"Would that he were yew, Cas."

While he closed up the warehouse and waited for Samboth to return, Caspar pondered the possible outcome of the relationship into which he had so willingly entered.

Were he in England still, he would be free to enjoy whatever emotional opportunities came his way. He had seen several white ladies of quality who had taken up with their darling blacks, as they called them. Indeed, he himself had enjoyed a similar but furtive arrangement on occasions.

But at Roxborough, as Ella always reminded him, he was a slave. If his relationship with Mary ever became known, it could kill the Bondmaster, nurtured as he was on the restricting notions of bygone traditions. It could kill Caspar, too.

It puzzled Caspar why, when he was himself the offspring of a white and a slave, he could not expect to achieve a similar liaison himself. A solution suddenly occurred to him.

"I should ask the Bondmaster to manumit me," he declared to himself. "If I was free," he thought, "instead of a slave, an *affaire de coeur* with Mary would be tolerated."

He scratched his head as he saw the obvious flaw to his scheme. Mary, too, would have to be freed.

While he loitered at the warehouse waiting for Samboth's return and brooding about Mary, Caspar was completely unaware of a similar drama which was being enacted in his own cabin.

Claire's Joan lay on his bed, not alone as she should have been, but with François at her side. They were both naked; François's drawers lay on the floor beside the bed. The cabin was in darkness as François reached for Joan.

"No, François, no more," she whispered.

"Please," she sighed in meek protest when François climbed onto her again. "Caspar does be coming jus' now."

She wriggled away from him reluctantly. "Yo' mus' go!"

"Ah does shit on de nigger's mother!" François growled. He lunged at Claire's Joan as she rolled away from him.

"No," said Joan firmly, jumping off the bed. "If he does come, yo' sure gon' get yuh head chopped jus' like Benn."

François made a sound of annoyance. "Dat Caspar done mess wid me in truth. He done tell de Bon'massa give yo' to he when Massa say yo' is fuh me. Caspar done say ah does be too black fuh yo'."

"Caspar does say we must have a light-skin whelp because light-skin niggers are more valuable."

"Dat's he talk."

"Ah must do what he does say."

"Ah does want yo' fuh mah wench, Joan." François clutched Joan's waist. He leaned forward and kissed her tenderly on her stomach. "Ah does need yo'."

Joan felt her flesh tingling. "François, yo' does make me scared. Caspar does be coming, ah does know it. Ah don't want yo' dead."

"A'right, ah does be going." He tugged on the pants Joan handed to him. "Yo' lek dat *beké* nigger, Joan?"

"No, man." Joan sucked in air in a cheep of protest. "He does be laying wid me to get a whelp, dat's all. Yo' got yuh breedin' filly, too!" she challenged. "If yuh wench does drop a whelp, Mas Carlton gon' give yo' a gold piece."

François put his arm around Joan and sought her mouth with his lips. She edged away from him toward the window.

"No, François!" she said, opening the shutter and peering out into the darkness of the cane field at the back of the cabin.

"Yo' does git me scare', François. Caspar does walk quiet like de devil in de night. Any time now he gon' come in an' meet yo' here."

"A'right, Joan, ah does be going." François hitched himself up to the transom. "Ah does be watching yo'. Ah gon' come when he does go out again!" François's words sounded like a threat as he disappeared into the night.

Joan hastily banged the shutter closed and walked over to the mattress. She sighed sadly before lying down and fingering herself to sleep.

Chapter 18

THE DAILY ROUTINE THAT THE BONDMASTER ES-
tablished on the plantation suited Caspar's affair
with Mary Gregg. Caspar was required to join the
Bondmaster on the gallery around five o'clock every
evening. The tasks for the day were completed by
that hour, and he made his report while taking a
glass of sangaree with Carlton. Together, they
watched the sun set across the sea to the west of
Layou at about six o'clock. Within minutes, darkness
fell on the plantation.

This was the time for Caspar to leave Carlton and
begin his patrol of the slave quarters to see that
nothing was amiss. When Carlton was abed, Caspar
dressed, took his horse from the stables, and galloped swiftly through the night to Layou. There, in
the warehouse, he waited for Mary.

Carlton was becoming accustomed to this torpid
routine. Occasionally, he did yearn for the excitement he had enjoyed in England, but plantation life
demanded that he forsake such existence for different pleasures. After Caspar had delivered his account of the day's work, Carlton was usually joined
by the doctor for a leisurely supper, glasses of rum,

and bouts of conversation. By eight o'clock, the lamps were turned down and Carlton was in bed.

However, Carlton had no inkling of Caspar's nocturnal jaunts to Layou. This troubled Caspar, as his capacity for deceit was small. Caspar felt that he was entitled to live his life as he wanted to, within the framework laid down by the Bondmaster. But he needed Mas Carlton's approval to ease his gnawing conscience.

Ella, who knew about Caspar's trips to Layou in the same way that she knew about everything which occurred on the plantation, counseled silence. She foresaw only calamity in Caspar's willful behavior.

One evening when Carlton seemed in a particularly good humor, Caspar broached the subject which was troubling him. The doctor had joined them early on the balcony, and Carlton had been reminiscing about the nights he had spent with the ladies of London society at Almack's Assembly Rooms.

"I don't really miss it," he assured the doctor. "It was pleasurable, to be sure, but to what end?"

"Ah," said George, sipping at his sangaree. "The end was the pleasure itself. Do you not yearn for the company of ladies instead of wenches?"

"Fah!" chortled Carlton. "I have my pick of the wenches here, and there is one snuggling up to me in my bed every night. Almack's never provided that!

"During the day, I am engrossed with plantation affairs; in the evening we have our banter. I am occupied, Doctor. Yet, should I be thirsty for the taste of white company, there is May Gregg not a mile away with her doxies."

"I miss London, Doctor." Caspar spoke up boldly.

"I miss the balls, the drives through the park, and most of all, I miss the attention of the ladies who saw me as a man able to do my wont, not a slave as I am here."

"Caspar! Such bitterness in your voice?" Carlton tugged at his ear in concern. "Do you not have more privileges than any other slave you have ever known? Why, it is you who are in charge of this plantation!"

"If I have privilege, Mas Carlton, what would be your views on my riding to Layou of an evening and tasting May Gregg's doxies, too?"

The doctor sucked in his breath in surprise. He glanced quickly at Carlton, searching for the narrowing of eyes under a heavy brow which usually forecast the Bondmaster's imminent rage. But Carlton's face was calm as he stroked his cheek pensively and considered Caspar.

"Ride to Layou of an evening, boy? Hmm! I doubt there is objection to that. In my father's day, of course, every slave needed a ticket to leave the plantation gates. But you are the overseer." He paused.

"What makes you speak of May Gregg's doxies, Caspar?"

"It was you who mentioned them."

"Aye, so I did. And I have right, too. Caspar, if it is white meat you crave, May Gregg's is not the place to seek it. That's for white men of my standing.

"White whores for Negroes are two for a bit in the rum shops by the riverbank. That's for free Negroes, of course," Carlton concluded, as though settling the matter.

Caspar scowled. He supposed he could not have hoped for more. "Mas Carlton, what would happen if I was taken up by a white lady who is not a nigger's harlot? In England, white ladies of quality desired me. Why not here also?"

"Caspar! England is so totally different you must banish such ideas from your head immediately. Oh, Doctor." Carlton turned toward George. "What complexities have I created here?

"If a white lady takes a fancy to Caspar, am I to remind him he is a slave who must keep his station and not offend public decency, or am I to lease him to that lady for our mutual profit?" Carlton's chuckle had an ironic ring.

George blushed. He looked at Caspar sitting opposite him, his firm thighs open and his crotch bulging provocatively. "It depends on the lady, I suppose," muttered George. "If she is unattached and amiable to an arrangement, it might be possible."

"You don't know our traditions, Doctor, so you speak that way. Before I went to England I would have strung up by his balls any slave who even thought of cavorting with a white lady."

Carlton glanced meaningfully at Caspar. "Let's have no more talk of this, Caspar. You have your duty to me, boy. Is your wench full yet?"

"It is possible."

"Good, the doctor will inspect her. If she is, you can have your choice of whatever you want, even a virgin whom I might be saving for myself. Is not that better than fantasies about nonexistent white ladies, Caspar?"

"Yes." Caspar drained his glass and stood up, bidding the two men a polite good night. He ran down the steps and out into the darkness.

"Doctor, don't reproach me," cautioned Carlton. "I well know how the boy feels. He has settled in admirably. But there are traditions he must learn to acknowledge and conform to.

"I think he understands me and we will hear no more of this nonsense about white women. Let's talk about the auction."

The day of the auction was a fine one. Carlton was up before daybreak, scanning the sky anxiously for signs of rain but, for once, the usually wet weather which gave the island its astonishing fertility was absent. It had taken five weeks to complete the preparations with round-the-clock activity.

Seamstresses had been working all day and at night by candlelight to produce special auction smocks which could be raised quickly so potential purchasers could inspect the slaves with ease. In the yard in front of the house, a gang of carpenters had constructed a vast stage on which the Negroes being offered for sale would parade.

Hogsheads of rum were brought up from the still, and Ella and Pip spent days training hand-picked bucks and wenches to serve drinks and food. Ella recruited girls to help in the barbecueing of a cow, roasting pigs, and boiling the goat water stew. Bush growing at the side of the trail leading to the house was cut down and was dispelled the gloomy aspect of the approach to the house revealing an impressive drive lined with royal palm trees.

Handbills advertising the sale had been circulated to every plantation on the island. Buyers began to arrive two days before and were lodged with great conviviality in Layou and the neighboring township of St. Joseph and the nearby villages of Mero and Barroui. Schooners were anchored in the Layou basin while more lay in the Mero anchorage.

As dawn broke and Carlton gazed, first at the ships anchored off the shore, and then around the neat layout of the plantation, he felt proud. Today Roxborough would become renowned throughout the West Indies for the superb quality of its slave stock. Today also he would add substantially to his fortune.

Surveying the yard where the auction was to take place, Carlton observed Caspar hurrying up the path. The boy was already dressed for the vendue. He wore a shirt, tight-fitting trousers and boots, English style, and carried his coat over his arm.

As though aware of Carlton's gaze, Caspar raised his head. "Good morning, sir!" he hailed Carlton. "A fine day for the fete!"

"Fete be damned!" Carlton bellowed, returning the boy's wave and sitting down for Caspar to join him for a dish of coffee. Carlton speculated idly on how much he would accept for Caspar, considering the expense he had lavished on training the buck. Carlton was acutely aware that he could not run the plantation without Caspar. His dependence on Caspar meant that he was obliged to tolerate in Caspar behavior which would be unacceptable from anyone else, whether slave or freeman.

"Coffee?" Caspar carried over the singing pot and placed it on the saman table between their chairs. He sat down immediately and crossed his legs, waiting impatiently for Carlton to pour out his own cup.

"There are so many strangers in Layou! There must be three buyers for every slave we have on sale. There will be hundreds of people here!" Caspar pounded his knee in excitement.

"If they have gold or currency, they are welcome.

184

Credit is a damned pesky mode of doing business, boy, and I expect some buyers will want a mortgage on the slaves, secured against this year's sugar crop. I'm telling Jonas Henderson that cash buys my slaves before credit."

Carlton sipped his coffee. "You were in Layou last night?"

"Oh, yes," Caspar spoke with confidence. "I strolled down to look at the prospective purchasers." He smiled at the Bondmaster while he poured his own coffee.

Carlton scowled. "Sometimes I wonder who is the master here, boy, you or me."

"I'm sorry, sir, I don't understand?" Caspar sat back contritely.

"You strolled down to Layou? Who said you could stroll down to Layou, boy?"

"Why, no one, sir. After our words a few weeks ago, I did not think it was a matter of such importance that I should disturb you about it."

"You are correct. I had forgotten." Carlton sighed. It was pointless remonstrating with Caspar. The buck always had an answer.

"I will be taking Laura to Trinidad after the auction, Caspar. I must put her in a school. She is growing wild here."

Caspar blew on his coffee to cool it down, listening eagerly as Carlton spoke.

"I'll spend a few weeks in Port of Spain," he continued. "After today's sale there will be no idle slaves on our hands. You'll have to take care of the plantation for me. The Doctor will be here as the white presence required by law. You have Ella's experience to rely on."

"I hope to acquit myself satisfactorily during your

absence." Caspar gripped his coffee cup to stop its chattering against the saucer. He was stunned. With the Bondmaster out of the island, he could ask Mary up to his cabin every night.

The sound of slaves singing as they trooped into the yard drifted up to the balcony. Carlton rose and looked down at them. He was amazed. Every slave, male or female, was attired in a loose smock. Each slave shone from the daybreak river bath and the scrubbing they had given each other. There was a festive air as Ella and her crew of kitchen girls dished out a calabash of coffee and johnny cakes to each one.

"Give a gill of rum to every one," Carlton ordered Caspar. "That will make them dance onto the dais."

The slaves were herded into the stockade which had been erected in the yard. Caspar went down to check the names on his list, sending back to their quarters those who had tried to stow away. Every slave, it seemed, wanted to be sold.

"That's good," Carlton assured Caspar. "It means they won't look morose and contrary. A cheerful nigger is bound to sell for a higher price than a surly one."

Buyers arrived at the house soon after breakfast. They came on horseback, by carriage, and on foot. They crowded around the stockade exclaiming in amazement at the quality of the slaves. Carlton, watching from the balcony, beamed with pleasure at their enthusiasm. He was disturbed by his son Hayes, who came running around the balcony chasing Mingoson.

Tita was following Hayes anxiously. "Ah does be

186

sorry, Mas Carlton. Dey does be too excited today wid de vendue."

"That's all right."

Carlton caught Mingoson as he tried to edge past him. He stood the boy on the floor and automatically ran his hands over his chest and shoulders and down his legs, appraising him as he did all the slaves.

"My goodness! What a sturdy little nigger your boy is growing into, Tita. He is really fancy. He's inherited your brown complexion, and see how fine his features are. Even his hair is soft. He'll be a superb specimen."

"What about me, Da'?" Hayes tugged at his father's hand, pushing Mingoson away.

"De massa does be inspecting me, boy. Hold yuh tongue!" Mingoson glared at Hayes.

"That's right," said Carlton. "You should wait, son. You are not a nigger, so I don't have to inspect you."

He patted his son's tight curls. "You don't have my hair, son, but your eyes are bright like mine. You look more like me than your dead mother. Thank God!"

"Yo' does see he does be a bonny young buck, Mas Carlton." Tita knelt down beside Hayes, cuddling him proudly.

"Aye. Where's Laura?"

"Laura, she does be a handful, Mas Carlton. Ah does try to keep meh eye on she, but she does slip away. Right now, ah declare she done escape me fuh sure!"

"Doctor," said Carlton to George as he came up the steps. "Send that boy of yours to find Laura. I'd like you to take her, and Hayes and Mingoson and their nanny, Tita, over to the paddock. I want you to keep them there today with the niggerlings."

"Of course, I'll be pleased to."

"Doctor," Carlton cautioned, "send any stranger who comes to the paddock to me immediately. Not one of those whelps in the nursery is for sale. That's Roxborough's future. We don't want them stolen, either." He turned to Tita.

"Tita, I'd like you to help the Doctor look after the whelps today. And you, young Master Hayes, must help the Doctor guard your inheritance." He patted the boy on his head again.

"Yes, Da!"

Hayes, chased by Mingoson, ran off after the doctor with shrieks of laughter. Tita glanced at Carlton with an odd smile of gratitude before she followed the children down the steps, humming to herself.

Chapter 19

A SLAVE AUCTION NEVER FAILED TO ATTRACT large numbers of potential purchasers as well as those who had no intention of buying but were itchy for the opportunity to examine Negroes. The inspection routine was an important part of the auction and Carlton had provided for it. He knew that no man would buy without examining the slaves first.

Each slave carried a placard hanging around his neck bearing a number. A catalogue handed to each potential purchaser as he arrived contained the name of every slave, together with age, tribe, work, and other information such as "virgin" or "childbearer" or "breeder." Prospective purchasers leaned over the rail of the corral, painstakingly marking in their catalogues. The slaves, inspired by the attention they were getting, paraded and pranced when the spectators shouted out their numbers.

Jonas Henderson, the white auctioneer Carlton had engaged for the day, was accompanied by two rough-mannered stewards armed with truncheons and whips. The stewards supervised the inspection routine which took place in a booth constructed at

189

the auctioneer's end of the stockade. The sides of the booth were covered with branches from coconut trees, enabling the inspection to be carried out in privacy.

A gentleman in the dark clothes of a cleric swaggered up to the auctioneer and demanded to be allowed to inspect the slaves marked on his catalogue. He had picked out four of them.

"You have chosen well, Reverend," commented the auctioneer dryly.

"Huh, Henderson! It is very kind of you to say so. I fear others may share my choice and force the price beyond the purse of a poor cleric."

Henderson smiled discreetly and passed on the Reverend's order to a steward.

Henderson was familiar with the Reverend Audain, the Anglican minister of Roseau. A singularly eloquent preacher in the pathetic style, Audain rarely failed to draw tears from his audience. His manners were fine and gentle and his appearance even venerable. He was known to be hospitable to the rich and gave alms to the poor. But Reverend Audain was frequently absent from his church due to his extra-pastoral activities of privateering and slave-smuggling.

The Reverend carried a pistol stuck jauntily in his belt. His schooner was anchored in the river.

"You are not on the Lord's business today, Reverend?" taunted Henderson, who was a Methodist.

"But, of course, dear fellow! A man must live to serve the Lord, and what better way for a man to live but with slaves to attend him?"

"And to sell at a substantial profit in Nevis, some say," rejoined Henderson.

"You have had an approach from Nevis?" Audain asked anxiously. "Oh, dear. It seems that the whole of the Caribbees wants the Lord's dusky creatures."

"Come, Reverend," the steward beckoned curtly. "I have your virgin for you."

Audain bowed his head to the auctioneer and followed the steward into the cubicle. A Negro girl of about fourteen years stood trembling in the corner. Her dark eyes were wide, and her confusion increased as she contemplated the white stranger facing her.

Audain looked at the steward. "You stay with us?" he queried.

"For your protection, Reverend."

"I hardly feel that this young chit is going to assault a man of the cloth," said Audain. "You have no such thoughts in your pretty woolly head, have you, girl? Of course not. You may leave us, my man."

"The Bondmaster's own orders, Reverend, are that I am to be present at the inspections. Lift your smock, wench! Make haste."

"Oh!" Audain looked at the steward with disdain. "You have no need to be so brutal with the child. Yes, my dear girl, raise your clothes, if you please."

A stool had been provided for purchasers and Audain lowered his portly frame onto it. His cheek twitched as the girl lifted her shift over her head and stood naked before him.

"Come, come," he said, flapping his hands. The steward prodded the girl in her backside with his truncheon.

"Yes, yes," said Audain, smacking his lips. "Fine

specimen, dark hue, supple torso." As he spoke, Audain rubbed his hands over the girl's body, lingering at her young breasts before bringing his hand down between her legs.

"Ever known a buck, child? Here?" His fingers slipped into her crotch. He panted. The girl, her eyes glazed, shook her head.

The Reverend repeated the process with the other young girls he had asked to see. After the fourth had been prodded back to the corral by the steward, Audain sat on the stool mopping his brow.

"That's all for you, Reverend," muttered the steward sarcastically. "There's others what be waiting for a fingering, too."

"Yes, yes," said Audain, rising and walking awkwardly out of the cubicle. "Well, well, what a splendid quartet!"

Carlton, attended by Caspar, strolled through the crowd. There were rough, red-necked overseers, pinched-faced attorneys, English fops, and French dandies clustering around the stockade rail and queuing to get into the inspection booth. Carlton accepted the words of praise for the quality of his stock with polite nods.

"It's their gold I want," he whispered to Caspar, "not their praise. See how some have come only to finger the wenches. If we had this auction in Roseau, the factor's yard would be jammed with parsimonious libertines jostling for a free feel of my wenches' thighs."

"I say, Mister Todd!"

Carlton checked his progress through the crowd as a tall middle-aged man stepped toward him. He had the face of a working planter, tanned and lined through spending his days in the open air.

The man extended his hand in greeting. "I'm Jabez Williams," he announced. "But recently arrived from Jamaica."

Carlton was impressed by the openness of the stranger's expression.

"We have plenty in common, Todd. I'm an American, like your father, I believe. I settled in Jamaica with the Loyalists."

Carlton welcomed the man cordially.

"Fine stock you have," Jabez replied. "Won't waste your time. This boy here, he's for sale?" Jabez indicated Caspar.

"What! You have perception, Williams! You obviously know the best. I am not selling out, Williams. This is my annual sale. Only those in the stockade are being auctioned today."

"I'll give you your price, Todd."

"No, sir!"

"Are you a poker player, Todd?"

"Not for stakes as high as Caspar."

"Very well, Todd. I see you are resolved," Williams replied briskly. "Now, tell me this. Do you have a young Negro, about thirteen or fourteen? He must be obliging, intelligent, and house-trained. I want to educate him, Todd. My cane fields are full of bozals. They work well, but I need new blood in the house. If I can't have your slave here, I'll buy something younger and mold my own."

"You have studied the catalogue?"

"I have indeed. A variety of women from virgins to viragos. Broad-shouldered colts, doubtless fine working beasts, and some whelps of honest potential. Nothing I fancy."

"Excuse me, sir," said Caspar, who was rather flattered by the American's attempt to purchase him.

"If you check the lot reserved for the scramble, you may see something."

"The scramble?" Jabez Williams stroked his long gray hair. "Is not that the reject lot?"

"Not really," said Carlton. "I have included the scramble more for the buyers than for my benefit. As you know, with seasoned slaves so hard to buy these days, I could sell each nigger individually without difficulty. But some purchasers like competing with each other as sport.

"I have put twelve niggers in the scramble lot. We will sell shares. Those who purchase a share can claim whom they want. One or two of those niggers, perhaps, have been a little troublesome, but otherwise they are fine stock. For instance, there's a nursemaid there called Sophy and a boy called Ketto."

"He's the one I am thinking of," said Caspar.

"Ketto?" Carlton was dubious.

"Yes."

"What makes you recommend him, Caspar, when your Bondmaster seems so doubtful?" Jabez looked at Caspar quizzically.

"He was seasoned by our old bookkeeper, who went blind. He had to be punished once, but he recovered and cared for the old man until he died quite recently."

"The slave has a strong pedigree," conceded Carlton.

"Hmm." Jabez stroked his chin. "With your permission, Todd, I would like to see him and then perhaps we can negotiate privately instead of me having to take part in your quaint scramble."

Caspar took leave of Mr. Williams and wandered through the crowd. He was looking for Mary. He had expected her to come early, for the night before they had made a plan to slip away from the auction yard and spend some hours in the comfort and privacy of his cabin.

Caspar worked his way through the cluster of people, looking in vain for Mary. As he approached the dais, where he hoped to get a better view, a red-bearded man emerged from the cubicle, walking bowlegged and grinning like a happy gnome.

"I was fingering this wench," he chuckled to his companions, "when she reaches down and starts to finger me!"

"Fancy!" said the lanky young man who was next in the queue, raising his hands in mock horror. "I can't wait to see my sample!"

He turned to his companion. "You do mean that I can buy absolutely any one of these gorgeous blackies and do anything I want with him?"

"That's what a slave is for, my lord," his escort insisted.

Caspar scowled as the young man minced into the booth. He was dressed in the fashion of a Regency beau, his head kept high with a starched stock under his chin. His companion, the attorney for an estate on the other side of Roseau, exchanged glances with Caspar, whom he mistook for a free mulatto.

"He has recently inherited a plantation." The attorney winked conspiratorially. "God preserve us!"

"Oooh, he's very big!" the young man exclaimed as the steward ushered François into the cubicle. "And isn't he black!"

"We don't 'ave no red, white, and blue ones, me lord," growled the steward gruffly.

The beau threw up his hands. "Oooh, what do I do now?" he squealed.

"Strip!"

"What?"

"Not you, me lord," said the steward. "The nigger."

"Ooh!" The young nobleman sank onto the stool, his eyes agog as François curled his lip at him and lifted his smock up to his shoulders.

"Move, boy." The steward prodded François with his truncheon to make him step toward the white man.

"Ooooh! What a black sausage he has there!" the beau said, his hands fluttering. "I never did!"

"Are you going to inspect 'im, me lord, or do you want me to send 'im back. This is Lot Fourteen what you asked for."

"I'll inspect him, of course. But what do I do?"

"You touch 'im, me lord, to see if 'is body is sound."

"Touch him?"

"Yes, me lord. 'E won't bite."

The nobleman slowly put out his finger and prodded François's stomach. When François did not stir, he touched him again, fascinated by the Negro's solid stomach muscles.

"You can pull back the prepuce, me lord, to see if 'e's a breeder." The steward sounded bored.

"I don't believe I'm going to breed, but he is rather gorgeous." The man gripped François's penis. "Oooh, what a monster." He began to jerk it backwards and forwards, sucking his lips between his teeth.

"You ain't supposed to 'andle the merchandise before you buy, me lord," said the steward, coughing to indicate that for a small consideration he would oblige by turning a blind eye. François was unable to stop his prick responding to the man's touch.

"Yes, yes!" The white man released François. "I'm all of a dither. Such muscles on the beast. Oh, look what I've done. He's got all excited."

"That shows 'e's a breeder, me lord." The steward sighed loudly.

"Do you speak ze English?" ventured the man.

"Yassa." François scowled. "Ah does be a breeder, sah. Ah does have two wenches wid deir bellies full fuh me."

"How disconcerting!" exclaimed the man. "You are rather brutish. Would you like to be my personal slave?"

"Yassa." François sneered.

"Oooh, how uncouth!"

" 'Ave you finished, me lord?" The steward indicated to François that he should pull down his smock.

"You can 'ave 'im to take 'ome tonight, me lord, if you bids more than those that want a strong nigger like that to cut cane for them."

When the auction began, the slaves needed no encouragement from the steward's truncheon to make them run up the steps to the dais. They each had a dream of being purchased by a wealthy white man who would take them off to lead a life of luxury as breeding niggers. They did not know that their fate lay in the cane fields of far-off plantations. There, the eccentricities of the Bondmaster and his breeding program would be replaced by the relentless cruelty of new owners bent on extracting value for the high price they had paid.

The English law which prohibited the slave trade doubled the price of slaves in the West Indies. The price of sugar remained static. Therefore, a planter had to get more work out of his slave to make his purchase worthwhile. If the planter could also get a whelp out of the slave, it was a bonus.

"This specialized breeding program of yours," the Reverend Audain commented to Carlton during a lull in the auction, "will eradicate the poor quality of Negroes in Dominica. Our consignments from Africa were very meager parcels, you know, Todd, the refuse of Barbados."

Audain plucked Carlton's sleeve enthusiastically. "Now that you have established this conservation of superior Negroes, you'll improve the whole race, dear fellow. It's an excellent idea! I am sure the good Lord would approve."

Carlton laughed, for he had heard of Audain's nefarious exploits. The rector broke off the conversation to bid for one of the virgins he had inspected. Carlton supposed that the rector would smuggle the wench to another island and sell her for double what he had paid.

"If her virginity does not prove too much for him," he thought to himself with a smile.

"Alas," Audain told Carlton. "I am competing with the richest planters in the region today. I cannot hope to secure more. I will come and visit you on another occasion, my friend, and we will discuss some business."

The Reverend took his slave wench by the arm, beckoned to three members of his crew who stood by, and pushed his way out of the crowd.

The bidding proceeded at a furious pace. Carlton mounted the steps to scan the crowd from the balcony. He picked out the main bidders. Two appeared to be overseas agents who were obviously buying for resale. There was a pair of Roseau factors snapping up the lower-priced lots, while a few gentlemen planters were competing with each other for the more specialized stock.

The prices were higher than Carlton had anticipated. Even the kitchen boy, Dontfraid, whose disposition was pleasant enough but whose efficiency as a house slave was minimal, went under the hammer for a hundred and twenty guineas.

As he surveyed the mass of people in the yard, Carlton caught sight of Caspar. He was standing at the edge of the crowd and appeared to be pleading with a woman who twirled a parasol above her head. Carlton could not see her face. She wore an exquisite dress of white lace and although all he could see was her back, Carlton sensed in the woman's bearing a voluptuousness which made his loins tingle.

He watched curiously as Caspar gestured emphatically to the lady.

The woman turned, acknowledging the smiles of the men at the edge of the crowd. Carlton chuckled to himself when he realized it was Mary Gregg who had caught his attention.

She was chatting to Caspar with an easy familiarity, laying her hand gently on his arm at times. It seemed to Carlton that Mary had a vivacity he could not recall from the time she had visited Roxborough with her mother. There was a ruddiness in her cheeks and a zest in her walk.

Idly, Carlton wondered who the man was who had inspired such a change in her. "I wouldn't mind a taste of that myself," he thought, stroking his crotch casually.

Caspar was leading Mary away from the crush of the men bidding for slaves.

"Where are we going, Cas?" Mary murmured. "I like it here!" She smiled at another gentleman who raised his hat to her as he walked past.

Caspar scowled. "I'm sure you do. See how many men you are attracting."

"But, of course, Caspar. Some are my customers. My ma would be vexed if I did not take advantage of my visit here. She only agreed to my coming because she knows it will be good for business."

"Take my arm, Mary. Let's stroll down by the river."

"No, Cas. You know I must not be seen with you for long. People may suspect."

"Hah! That's nonsense." Caspar smiled. "Who should be escorting you around the plantation but the overseer? There's nothing less suspicious than you and I being together."

"Well, we must not be seen to be *so* together, Cas. I will not take your arm!"

"Mary!" Caspar pleaded. "What is wrong with you today?"

"Quiet, Cas. You'll attract people's attention."

"Yes, I will!" Caspar raised his voice. "It is damned silly. You don't mind loving me in the depths of night when you cannot see me but here in bright daylight in my own home, you treat me as though I am untouchable."

Mary stared at Caspar, clutching his arm in panic. "Pray be quiet, Cas. You'll ruin us both. Don't you see?" She smiled brightly at a Roseau merchant who gave a slight bow in her direction.

"Damme! There's another one. Have you had them all, Mary?"

"Caspar!" she beseeched. "Why do you make yourself so unhappy? I am not asking you which of these wenches you have mounted to give your Bondmaster another whelp to sell. Let's have no more about it, now, Cas. I want to enjoy today."

"You will, Mary. You will, when you come to my cabin. As we planned last night."

"Yes, Cas. But not now. We cannot walk away from here together."

"When?"

"Later, about four. Before I go. Wait for me in your cabin. I will come."

"What am I to do until then?" he pouted.

"What I will do. Move around and meet people. Talk and be gay!"

"I know why you want to meet people!" Caspar scowled.

"Hush, Cas." She squeezed his wrist. "I am yours, you must believe that."

Caspar nodded his head forlornly as Mary swept away from him. He watched her join a group of planters arguing about whether the slave they had bought was a virgin or not. The red-bearded man Caspar had seen earlier leered at Mary, pushing forward his cheek for her to kiss. Caspar heard Mary's laughter and spun around on his heels in disgust.

Every time he glanced at Mary during that long afternoon, she was laughing and joking with different groups of men. It was as though she were deliberately tantalizing him. Although Caspar had little time to consider her behavior, as the auction and the serving of dinner to the purchasers kept him occupied, jealousy nagged at him.

"Going well, boy, going well!" Carlton shouted

at him at some stage during the afternoon. Caspar nodded obediently, dodging around to the kitchen for a quick glass of punch. Although he thought the hour would never come, he suddenly realized that it was nearly four.

He glanced round the crowd from his position at the kitchen window, hoping to sight Mary's parasol. The last few lots before the scramble were being auctioned. Caspar knew that he must find Mary quickly. Soon the auction would be over and she might have to leave before she had a chance to go with him to his cabin.

"Have you seen Mary?" he demanded as Ella hurtled back into the kitchen from serving in the courtyard.

"Mary?" Ella plonked her tray down on the kitchen table. "Caspar, who is Mary?" She held him by his shoulders. "Do yo' know what yo' does be doing, Caspar?"

"Of course, Ella. Mary is the white lady in the lace dress. Have you see her?"

"Dere does be many people here, Caspar." Ella frowned. "Perhaps she done leave a'ready?"

"No! She cannot go yet!"

"Cannot?" Ella was taken aback by his tone of voice. "Caspar, I can't help you." She sounded sad.

He dashed out of the kitchen and ran into the middle of the throng. The scramble was about to begin, and everyone crowded around the stockade to watch as four portly merchants rushed inside to grab their choice of slaves from those who remained.

Caspar pushed his way to the front steps and climbed up for a better view. He scanned the top hats and bonnets, but nowhere could he see the pink parasol of Mary Gregg.

He was desolate.

"Where can she be?" he asked himself angrily. "Has she gone off with one of her customers? Is that the kind of thing she would do?"

He gazed at the crowd again. The red-bearded man was there, and the Roseau merchants, and the Colihaut planters. Everyone she had smiled at was engrossed in the excitement of the scramble.

The faint sound of Mary's carefree laughter which he knew so well from their moments together in the sugar warehouse made him relax. The laugh came from in the house itself. "The hussy!" he thought happily. "She is playing a trick on me and hiding somewhere."

He left the balcony and walked into the house. The drawing room and dining room were empty. He was puzzled. "She can hardly be in one of the bed-chambers," he thought, standing still and trying to hear her laughter again above the roars of the crowd as they cheered the merchants scampering after the frightened slaves in the stockade.

He heard the laugh again. It was smothered instantly.

A vein in Caspar's throat began to throb. He stared increduously at the Bondmaster's room. Mas Carlton, he suddenly realized, was not with the others in the courtyard below.

Choking with fury, Caspar charged the Bondmaster's door. He flung it open. Mary was on the bed, her lace dress drawn up to her hips, her legs locked around Carlton's waist as he plunged into her.

Carlton, his trousers bunched around his ankles, continued to jerk himself up and down on Mary. He glanced casually at Caspar.

"Get out, boy," he panted. "Can't you see I'm engaged!"

Caspar stared at Mary. Her eyes were open. She waved him away frantically, turning to kiss Carlton professionally as he rose to his climax.

A huge roar of delight went up from the crowd in the courtyard. Caspar lunged at the bed, landing on Carlton's back as the Bondmaster sank, spent, into Mary.

"Oh lor!" shrieked Mary as Caspar began to beat Carlton's shoulders. She struggled to get out of the way of the flailing arms and legs, throwing herself onto the floor and crawling out of the room.

The cheers from the throng downstairs drowned her shrieks. She looked back briefly at the two men rolling over the bed, shook down her dress, snatched up her parasol, and rushed out of the house and down the back steps.

Carlton, dazed by Caspar's weight on his back and bruised when Mary wriggled out from under him, pitched across the bed to escape the blows. He picked up the pillow and twisted around, beating it over Caspar's head. The pillow burst. Feathers fluttered round the room. Downstairs the shouts of the crowd continued.

Carlton was defenseless. His ankles were tied together in the tangle of his own trousers. He had been seized at the point of his lowest resistance. His only chance, if he could not shout some sense into Caspar, was to reach the pistol which was in the drawer beside the bed.

It was as though Caspar read his thoughts, for he pulled at Carlton by his shirt collar and flung him down in the center of the bed, far from the drawer. He jumped on his chest, breathing heavily.

"Why?" Caspar shrieked. "Why?"

Carlton choked, staring up at Caspar's wild eyes, aflame with fury.

"You're mad, boy! Get off me at once. Get off!"

Caspar responded to the Bondmaster's command by instinct. He eased the pressure he had been applying to Carlton's chest with his knees. It was enough. Carlton struck out with his fist, landing a blow squarely under Caspar's chin. The boy fell back, shaking his head to clear it.

In that fraction of a second, Carlton leaped across the bed and pulled open the drawer. If he could grab the pistol, he could hit Caspar over his head with the handle and shout out of the window for help.

Caspar was faced with the naked backside of his father as he fumbled to get his hands on his pistol. He stretched himself calmly over the full length of Carlton's body, pulled his hand out of the drawer, and slammed it shut.

He jerked Carlton back onto the bed, lifting him up by his shirt and holding him so close to his face that his nose almost touched Carlton's. Sweat from his face splashed onto Carlton's cheek.

"Why? Why?"

"Why, Caspar? It is I who should ask why. Stop this foolishness and let me go. You'll be flogged within an inch of your life for this!"

"It's you who should be flogged!" Caspar was almost weeping.

Sensing that Caspar was wavering, Carlton raised both fists simultaneously and jabbed them with all the force he could muster into Caspar's ribs. Caspar fell backward and Carlton dived again for the pistol, spinning his body off the bed and tumbling onto the floor. He crouched on the floor and tried to prise the drawer open.

Caspar drew his knife from his belt. "Don't touch that drawer, Mas Carlton!" he pleaded. "Please!"

Carlton threw up his arm to protect himself at the very same instant that Caspar moved forward to remove Carlton's hand from the drawer handle.

Caspar slipped, the knife clenched in his hand.

"Aye!" cried Carlton, clutching his arm.

Caspar looked in amazement at the blood trickling down Carlton's shirtsleeve.

Carlton sank to the floor, gazing up at Caspar as his son stepped carefully off the bed and lunged at him.

The crowd in the courtyard watching the scramble shrieked with delight as a slave slipped from the grasp of his clumsy pursuer.

Blood began to seep through the floorboards of Carlton's room into the kitchen below.

Chapter 20

"**E**LLA! ELLA! MAS CARLTON'S DEAD!" CASPAR burst into the crowded kitchen shouting wildly.

Ella raised her head from the table as a drop of blood spattered onto it from the ceiling above. She took in Caspar's glazed eyes and the blood on the front of his coat. She cursed. A hush fell on the kitchen.

Pip and the serving girls edged backward in alarm as Ella rose from the table. Her face set in determination, she caught hold of Caspar's arm. "Come," she said, jerking him along with her. "Yo' others, stay here!"

She asked no questions as she hustled up the back steps, Caspar chasing behind her. She marched across the drawing room floor and paused at the open door to Carlton's bedroom. Her eye fell on the knife lying in the pool of blood beside Carlton's inert body. She glanced questioningly back at Caspar before dropping on her knees beside Carlton.

His head was slumped forward over his chest, his shirt ripped open to his waist. His pants were bunched around his ankles, his once proud penis shriveled in between his pathetic thighs. The flow of blood from the cut on his arm had slowed.

Ella put her ear to his nose and then to his chest. She reached across his body and plucked the knife out of the blood on the floor. She handed it up to Caspar.

"He ain't dead!" she said grimly. "Yo' want to finish the job yo' began?"

Caspar stared at her in disbelief. He looked at the blood-smeared knife in his hands, then at Carlton's crumpled body. He shook his head.

Ella was kneeling beside Carlton, her face raised, waiting.

"Yo' can cut he throat across here," Ella murmured, tilting Carlton's head back and drawing her fingers across his neck. "Or yo' can stick de knife in here," she pointed at his chest, "or slice he here." She patted Carlton's hard stomach.

Caspar swallowed. "He's not dead?"

"No." Ella shrugged. "Yo' want me to kill he fuh yo'?"

Caspar backed away as though shocked by her suggestion. "He's not going to die, Ella?"

"Not unless yo' chop he properly."

"I don't want him to die, Ella!"

Ella stared skeptically at Caspar, frowning as he shrieked at her.

"Can you make him live? Bring him back to life, Ella! Please!"

She shrugged her shoulders again. "He done faint. He never could stand the sight of blood, especially he own."

Caspar knelt down beside her.

"Ah tell yo', boy. If yo' don't kill he now, Mas Carlton gon' cut yuh body into quarters an' throw yo' to de Ibos to eat."

Caspar looked puzzled. "I didn't mean to hurt him, Ella. He was trying to get his pistol to shoot me."

"Yo' are dead, boy, when Mas Carlton recovers." She stiffened. "Unless yo' join de maroons, dem in de hills."

"Make him live, Ella! I want him to live!"

"He does be yuh massa, Caspar. Yo' does be he slave. If he does be dead, yo' does be free to run away."

"Ella!" Caspar stood up abruptly. He wiped the knife on his kerchief and stuck it back under his belt. "He is my father, Ella!"

Ella nodded wisely. "Yes," she sighed. She slapped Carlton gently on his cheek. "Run to de paddock an' tell de Doctor come bandage de Bond-master."

Caspar bounded out of the room with a sense of relief. Ella looked into Carlton's weary face. Slowly she lowered her head to his thighs. She opened her mouth and slipped out her tongue to rasp against his lifeless penis. She closed her lips gently over it, sucking the soft flesh into her mouth.

Carlton stirred.

Ella withdrew and smiled at him, her mouth overflowing. Carlton pulled up her head and put his mouth to hers, forcing her sticky lips to open so he could drink the contents. He swallowed and sighed.

Ella laid her hand on his brow. "How yo' feel?"

"Dam' sore!" He raised his arm, regarding his bloodstained shirtsleeve with distaste. Ella helped him to stand, untangling his trousers from his feet.

"Yo' gon' to lie down on de bed?"

"Whatever for? Take trousers from the wardrobe for me. I must have fainted." He sat on the edge of the four-poster bed, gripping the corner post for support as Ella picked out trousers for him.

"Caspar done run fuh de Doctor." Ella spoke with caution, trying to measure his mood.

"He'll need a doctor when I'm finished with him! Ella, he attacked me. Caspar, of all people. Your son!" He glared at Ella for an explanation.

She passed him the trousers and spread her hands open in front of her to indicate her ignorance of Caspar's behavior.

"I was riding a filly when he burst in here and jumped on my back, Ella. Then he knifed me. He could have killed me!"

"No!"

"I tell you that's what happened, Ella!" He pulled the trousers over his feet and stood up to put them on. He buttoned up and sat down on the bed as Ella spoke.

"No, he could not kill yo', Carlton. He done have yo' at he mercy, Carlton, but he say yo' be he father and he would not kill yo'."

"Hah! He will wish he had killed me when I get my hands on him. I'll have Constance string him up and lash him till his hide is as full of holes as a whore's lace dress. Then I'll stretch him out in the sun and roast him. I'll cut off his grain and gouge out his eyes."

"Hush, Carlton!" Ella put her hand on his brow to calm him. "Who was de filly yo' done have here?"

"That whore for May Gregg!" snapped Carlton. "What's that got to do with it?"

"Mary?"

"Something like that." Carlton clenched his fist.

"She does be he wench, Carlton. Dat's de reason he done pull yo' off of she."

"His wench! I don't believe you!"

"Is true." Ella shrugged.

"Look, Ella." Carlton patted a spot on the bed for Ella to sit down beside him. "Caspar is a slave. He does not have wenches unless I assign them to him."

"Yo' don't know he have a white wench?" Ella challenged. "He does be in Layou wid she every night."

Carlton pursed his lips. "Perhaps he mentioned something about it. I don't recall. But it ain't right. And he knifed me, Ella. He has to be punished."

"Ah does not say no, Carlton." Ella rested her hand on his wrist. "He not mean to cut yo', Carlton. He done think yo' wanted to kill he."

"You weren't here, Ella. The boy was possessed. I'm not safe with him around."

"What yo' gon' do?"

Carlton fell silent, his wounded arm cradled on his lap.

The doctor bustled in, followed by Caspar carrying his bag. He lifted the arm, snorted with derision, and proceeded to clean it. Carlton kept his eyes on Caspar.

"I thought you were dying, Todd, the way Caspar told it. A slight cut, doesn't need more than a bandage. So you and your son were fighting over a wench, eh, Todd!"

George took advantage of the Bondmaster's temporary dependence on him to give him a piece of his mind.

"I'm surprised at you, Todd. You have the pick of every wench on the plantation, or so you tell me, and money enough to pay any whore, but you chose the one your son loves. The lad did right

211

to give you a thorough pasting!" He pulled the bandage tight.

"Now rest that arm, and no excitement, do you hear?"

Ella and Caspar stared open-mouthed at the doctor. They had never heard anyone address the Bondmaster that way. Caspar seized the initiative to break the silence when he saw Carlton considering the doctor's words.

"I am sorry, Mas Carlton, about the knife. I thought you wanted to kill me. I do love Mary Gregg, you see, and she says she loves me. But what can I do? Every buckra on the west coast seems to have laid with her. Even you!"

Caspar fell to the floor on his knees in front of Carlton. "Help me, father!" he pleaded, laying his head in Carlton's lap. "Help me!"

"Doctor, Ella, get out!" Carlton waved them away, speaking softly. "Out!"

"I'm going!" said George with disgust. "I've no wish to stay, but remember, Todd, absolutely no excitement."

Carlton nodded his head up and down without speaking. He ignored the pleading gleam in Ella's eye, waiting for her to close the door of the bedroom before he spoke. Grabbing Caspar by the tight curls at the back of his neck, he forced the boy's head up from his lap.

Carlton gazed down at his own bright eyes shining up at him from Caspar's youthful brown face. He hawked. The phlegm rose into his mouth and he rolled it around his tongue, spitting it out venomously onto Caspar's mouth. The gob trickled down Caspar's chin.

Caspar waited.

212

"What are you, Caspar?" Carlton jerked his head back to shake out an answer.

"Your son, sir."

"My slave, sir!" Carlton slapped Caspar's cheek with his good hand, knocking him backwards onto the floor. "Get up, boy! I'm going to help you to remember what you are.

"Go to the forge and tell Constance to light his fire."

It was agreed that the scramble put the seal of success on a magnificent day for all who attended the auction.

"It was enormous fun," said one planter enthusiastically to Caspar, whom he met running down the front steps. "Please convey my respects to the Bondmaster."

"With pleasure, sir," answered Caspar politely.

"Where is Todd?" demanded another planter.

"He is . . . eh . . . engaged at present," Caspar replied with a forced grin.

"Trust that Carlton Todd!" guffawed the planter. "The man has had so much money off me today, he is ashamed to show his face!"

Slowly the planters, merchants, traders, and slave speculators drifted away from the auction ring. Caspar found that he was trapped into representing the Bondmaster, apologizing for his absence, and bidding the visitors safe journey, as night began to fall. When he spied Samboth hanging around the stockade, he called him over and told him to instruct Constance to light the forge fire. Jonas Henderson, the auctioneer, was one of the last to take his leave.

"Here are the accounts, Caspar," the auctioneer

said with a patronizing leer. "Be sure to give them to the Bondmaster, there's a good boy. This coffer," he indicated the box being carried by the steward, "contains the proceeds."

Caspar accepted the coffer and the key, signed his name with a flourish in the auctioneer's book, and directed the steward to place the box in the drawing room. He invited Henderson onto the balcony to take punch with him and engaged him in polite conversation, chuckling with him over the events of the day. Henderson softened in his attitude toward Caspar, captivated by the youth's manners and charm.

"Goodbye, Caspar!" he said almost with regret when his carriage was ready for him to depart. He extended his hand. "I'm sorry Todd is indisposed. I would fain congratulate him on his stock. And on the conduct of his overseer!" He shook Caspar's hand firmly.

"Boy, you could almost be white!"

When Henderson had gone, Caspar stared out from the balcony. The fireflies danced like sparkling green gems against the impenetrable backcloth of the night.

He sipped at the glass of rum in his hand, relishing the numbness he felt creeping through him.

Samboth whistled to him from the courtyard. "Constance does say de fire does be ready."

Caspar waved the boy into silence. He heaved a sigh under the burden of his troubles before shuffling slowly to Carlton's door. He stopped in front of it and raised his eyes.

He remembered the sight of Carlton astride Mary when he had thrust open the door earlier that very afternoon. He swallowed resolutely now, squaring back his shoulders and pounding on the door with his fist.

"Mas Carlton!" he called boldly. "The fire is ready."

The door swung open and Carlton came out. He still wore his torn, bloodstained shirt. He glanced sleepily at Caspar, hitching up his belt in which he had placed two pistols. He straightened himself, then marched across the room to the dresser. He poured two glasses full of rum from the decanter, handing one to Caspar. He drained his own down his throat, eyeing Caspar while he did likewise.

"Jonas Henderson delivered the proceeds of the vendue." Caspar indicated the coffer in the center of the room. "The account book is in your bureau."

Carlton glared at Caspar, all interest in the auction drained from him. He beckoned Caspar with a baleful glance to follow him as he strode down the steps to the forge.

Carlton approached the forge briskly, Caspar only one step behind. Constance was standing at the door, his arms folded across his huge chest, sweat pouring down his gleaming body into the cloth he wore tied around his thick waist. His eyes flickered over his master and Caspar. He gazed around puzzled, searching for the slave he was expected to punish.

Carlton ushered Caspar into the forge. He waved his hand to indicate that Caspar should lie down in front of the fire. Caspar hesitated only long enough to remove his coat and fling it over the anvil. He lay on the ground with his face up, crossing his ankles. He clenched his teeth, determined not to flinch regardless of whatever cruelty Carlton inflicted.

215

Constance regarded the two with amazement.

Carlton knelt down beside Caspar, his injured arm dangling at his side. With one hand he tugged at the stock at Caspar's neck until it fell apart. He ripped open the silk shirt, exposing Caspar's chest and stomach. His hand wandered down to the boy's trousers which he fumbled to unfasten. He gripped Caspar's balls tightly in his fist, shaking them in a silent fury.

Caspar's penis danced at Carlton's touch.

Carlton released Caspar and looked up at Constance snuffling, like a black ox, at his shoulder. Carlton pointed to the branding irons hanging on the wall by the fire. Constance followed his gaze and smiled.

Constance took down the irons one by one, holding each one up for Carlton to indicate his choice. The iron with a small letter "R" for Roxborough received Carlton's nod of approval. Constance plunged it into the flames.

"What are you, Caspar?" demanded Carlton.

"Your son, Mas Carlton." Caspar spoke boldly.

"You are my slave, damn you. You are never going to forget that! Nor is anyone else," Carlton pronounced dourly. He held out his hand for the branding iron.

Constance wrapped a chamois leather around the handle and plucked the iron from the fire. The letter "R" glowed a fierce red in the shadows of the forge. His wide lips broke into a smile of bliss as he passed the handle to Carlton's outstretched hand.

Carlton gripped the iron firmly, his teeth bared. He passed the iron so close to Caspar's face that

Caspar was forced to close his eyes to avoid being blinded by the heat.

"Caspar, *what are you?*"

Caspar opened his eyes. He was mesmerized by the glowing branding iron as it waved in front of his face. He blinked, wondering what part of his body Carlton was going to plunge it on.

"Your son, Father!" he shrieked.

"Damn you, damn you, damn you!"

Carlton drew back his arm, poising the burning iron above Caspar's forehead. He was ready to ram it down and scar the Roxborough slave brand forever on Caspar's brow. Constance knelt down behind Caspar and gripped his head between his thighs so he could not move. Carlton plunged forward.

The brand hissed past Caspar's ear. With a sickening smell of scorched flesh, it sank into Constance's thigh.

The iron clattered to the ground as Carlton fell on top of his son. "Dammit, Caspar," he croaked. "I love you, my son. I love you!"

Caspar clasped his arms around his father, squeezing him, burying his head in the crook of his father's neck. His father's tears fell upon his shoulder.

At midnight that night, arm in arm, father and son paced ten steps from the corner of the house in the direction of the old *balata* tree. Carlton handed Caspar the shovel, and he dug a deep hole. Helped by Ella, Caspar dragged the coffer containing the auction money to the edge of the hole. He tipped it in.

"Gold, French coins, currency, sterling!" chanted Carlton gazing at the casket. He stroked his chin, uncomfortably aware of Ella and Caspar facing him. "I hope the niggers will be all right," he added lamely.

Caspar stepped forward silently. He raked the earth to fill the hole, burying the money and, with it, the memory of one hundred souls bartered that day by the Bondmaster.

Chapter 21

CARLTON JOGGED EASILY ON HIS HORSE ALONG the trail from the slave quarters. The morning had been spent with Caspar taking an inventory of the cabins and their inhabitants. He was pleased that as a result of the auction there were now fewer worthless slaves on the plantation to feed and house.

From traders attending the auction, Carlton had learned that he could get even better prices for his slaves if he shipped them to Trinidad and sold them there. Although a trading ban had been in force since 1807, Carlton was prepared to risk traveling to Trinidad with a personal retinue of hard-pricked niggers which he would sell on arrival. Carlton looked forward confidently to the future. He had drawn up an extensive program to ensure a supply of prime slaves for the next two decades. By allocating different bucks every three months to cover the fillies who were not full, Carlton hoped to have new litters from his various sets of breeders four times a year. It was a production cycle which could keep him supplied with a whelp a week.

With his markets guaranteed through trips to

neighboring islands, and occasional sales by private treaty, Carlton knew that he could make more out of selling his slaves than by working them on sugar.

He reined in the horse when he reached the paddock and waited for a boy to open the gate. He rode through the tumbling black infants with pride, jumping off his horse at the nursery. Stepping onto the veranda, he passed through to the doctor's new dispensary and sank gratefully into a chair.

"Damned hot this morning, Doctor," he gasped.

"I have some Madeira wine acquired from a schooner that was here a few weeks ago," said George, reclining at the end of his examination bench. "Athol, bring me the bottle and two glasses." He threw the slave his keys.

"How's that arm, Todd?"

"Capital." Carlton followed the slave with his eyes. He was an appealing Negro, well-behaved, polite. "You trust that nigger with your keys?"

"Of course. He's responded excellently under my guidance. I've managed to teach him to read as well."

"Really?" Carlton was interested.

"Yes, when I instruct Laura and Hayes, he sometimes attends the lessons. I hope you don't mind about that, Todd." George stuck out his jaw defiantly.

"Not at all. Does he behave himself?" Carlton picked his nose thoughtfully.

"Why, yes."

"My daughter is an attractive girl, you know, Doctor. Especially to hot-blooded young niggers."

"Athol would never do anything!" George was shocked. "In fact, Todd, if I may say so, it is your daughter Laura who exhibits an unequivocal interest in the opposite sex."

"Healthy attitude, Doctor, don't you think? Providing the opposite sex isn't black, of course."

Athol returned with the Madeira and placed the bottle on a table near Carlton. Carlton poured himself a measure while studying the slave. The boy was slender in contrast to the other Roxborough bucks with their broad shoulders and sinewy arms.

"Is he healthy?" Carlton gestured with his glass toward Athol.

"Of course, Todd."

"You examined him?"

George felt himself blushing. "Well, yes, of course. I've examined every one of your slaves, Todd. On your instructions," he added boldly to disguise the alarm he was feeling at Carlton's probing.

"Yes, I know, but have you given him any special examination? I mean, he looks sort of . . . well, wispy, if you see what I mean."

"I assure you he is quite healthy and strong, Todd."

George refused to be drawn, although he knew what Carlton was implying.

"Say something, boy, let's hear your voice."

Surprised, Athol glanced at George for guidance. It told Carlton what he wanted to know.

"Damme, boy! I am the one who is your Bondmaster, not this nigger physician here!" he shouted.

"I'm sorry, sir. What would you like me to say, sir?"

"Oh-ho, you speak English, do you?" Carlton smiled as he heard the bass of the boy's voice.

"Was it you who gave him the special raiment, Doctor? Shoes and stockings and so forth?"

"Why yes, Todd. I bought them for him myself. It is important to be properly dressed when dealing with the sick, even sick slaves, Todd. It reduces the chances of infection, of course. Bare feet are most unhealthy."

"You like the boy, don't you, Doctor?"

"Why, yes, of course I do. He is an excellent helper."

"Get out, boy!" While he waited for the slave to leave, Carlton sipped at his Madeira, regarding George over the top of his glass.

"Do you keep any poisons in your cupboards, Doctor?"

"Yes, there are some medicines here which are poisonous."

"That nigger has access to the keys of those cupboards?"

"Why, yes." George was offended by the question. "Athol is perfectly trustworthy!"

"Let me tell you, Doctor," retorted Carlton, stretching out his feet and adjusting his crotch. "Trustworthiness is a characteristic not to be found in the Negro race." He waved his glass in emphasis.

"By nature, a Negro is good-humored to the highest degree. His eyes will sparkle and his teeth will flash. He'll bid you a happy 'How d'ye, massa!' and go about his business. He cannot be silent, Doctor; he talks in spite of himself. For that reason, Doctor, he cannot keep a secret.

"There must be scores of slaves on this plantation who know of those poisonous mixtures in your cabinet there. They must know that your fancy nigger controls the keys.

"These are troubled times, Doctor. The maroon menace is abroad! Rumors of emancipation stalk the islands! Niggers are being goaded by the mistaken ideals of Parliament's abolitionists fed with lies by their God-snickering cohorts in the colonies." Carlton coughed, disturbed by his own words.

"Put trust in one Negro, Doctor, and you invite slaughter from all!"

Carlton raised his hand to still the doctor's protest. "I know you think I am exaggerating and that you feel you have established a special bond with your nurse-boy Athol. The bond is irrelevant.

"By their very nature, Doctor, Africans are not reliable. They come from jungle conditions where everything is accessible. They have no need to think or prepare for the future. They lack the logic of responsibility.

"There is no force exerted on them by nature to do something today so that they might benefit tomorrow. They have no instinct to plant, because in their jungles they find fruit and vegetables growing without any persuasion and care from man. They do not need to rear animals for meat—they can take a spear and go and hunt when they are hungry.

"They have no insight, Doctor, into preparation for the future." Carlton put his glass down emphatically on the doctor's workbench.

"Consequently Negroes are creatures of impulse. They have no restraints, like the white man, to be otherwise. Every passion acts upon them with a strange intensity unknown, even incomprehensible, to us, Doctor. Their anger is sudden and furious and even quite catastrophic. I've seen it, I know.

"Afterwards, they will cool off because they lack the sustained intention to be anything more than damned inconvenient. If you don't believe me, then look at their happiness, Doctor. Their mirth is clamorous and excessive, their curiosity audacious, and their love, Doctor, their love is the sheer demand of one ardent animal for another!"

Carlton picked up his glass and took a final sip of Madeira. He regarded George quizzically. "You appear flustered, Doctor. Doubtless you disagree with me. I would expect you to. You are a typical pure idealist with a few weeks in the tropics, sticking your gender into black torsos and not, I hope, retching too much at the stink!

"At the end of your contract, you will doubtless return to London and speak on public platforms about the evils of slavery and the wickedness of the Bondmaster of Roxborough, who sells Negroes by the score, wallops them when he is in a foul temper, and ravishes by right every virgin on the plantation."

"Sir, I assure you I am not of those views at all!" George found his voice at last.

"You are not, Doctor? Well, you should be. What happened to the ethical English gentleman I shared reels with at Almack's?"

"I like these blacks, sir. I think I understand them."

"Oh-ho!" sneered Carlton. "A nigger-lover, forsooth! You like their meek obedience and the chance to sodomize them. No, don't stammer a protest and challenge me to a duel. Tell me, do you like them as slaves?" Carlton wagged his finger in George's face.

"Do you agree slavery is the only form of existence for these creatures? Or do you share the views of those who want to free every nigger so he may grow into a black white man?"

"Todd, I must protest! Your view of my own association with your slaves is unacceptable. I ask you to withdraw it."

"Oh, yes, I was speaking metaphorically of course," Carlton answered coolly. "Now state your position, Doctor!" he demanded.

"The slaves I have met here, Todd, are treated in the manner in which they should be treated. I could not say that the Roxborough slaves would fare better if they were free men."

"You are convinced of that, Doctor?"

"Why, yes." George wondered what was coming next.

"Were I to be absent, Doctor, would you do everything to maintain my traditions and uphold my interests? You would not interfere with any punishment being meted out to recalcitrant slaves by my overseer? You would, in short, do nothing to change the running of Roxborough?"

"In your absence, sir, I would endeavor to act precisely as I know you would want me to," George affirmed, still baffled.

"Dammit, Doctor, you're not such a slouch as I thought!" Carlton rose from his seat.

"Splendid wine, Doctor. See you this evening." He paused. "By the way, I am taking Laura to Trinidad next week to put her in a school there. I want you to keep your eye on the plantation. I'll need a personal slave with me, of course. Caspar will be staying here as the overseer."

Carlton walked to the door of the nursery, carelessly brushing aside the children romping on the floor. "Methinks I will take that nigger of yours with me. Athol, is it? Yes. He's the one. Well, good day, Doctor."

George stared open-mouthed after Carlton as he walked along the veranda and mounted his horse.

"What does be de problem, Doc?"

Athol's words jerked George into action. He ran out of the door, along the veranda, down the steps and across the paddock, catching up with Carlton as he reached the gate.

"You really mean that, Todd?" panted George.

"Really mean what?" Carlton answered archly.

"Taking Athol to Trinidad with you?"

"Of course!"

"You won't sell him?" George wrung his hands anxiously. "He is learning so well. Who knows? One day he might become a doctor. He is bright enough for it. Think of it, Todd, a Roxborough slave becoming a doctor!"

Carlton blinked. "Huh?" He scratched his head. "Yes, that is a thought, and no mistake. The boy will be my personal slave for the trip, Doctor. You can have him back when I return. Send him to Caspar to organize trogs for him."

A tranquillity foreign to Roxborough descended on the plantation with the departure for Trinidad of the Bondmaster, Laura, and their retinue of eight slaves. Coming so soon after the slave population had been reduced by a hundred, the absence of Carlton and his tempestuous daughter emphasized the estate's comparative desertion.

The slaves reacted by performing their tasks lethargically. They accepted meekly the frequent lashings from their dedicated drivers. At night, they sat morosely outside their shacks staring into the darkness and thinking of those who had been sold.

The house, too, was in a state of quietude. With Laura out of the way, Tita was able to devote her time to the care of Hayes and Mingoson. The two children had been inseparable since birth, and Tita loved them as though both were her own. She delighted in walking them about the plantation telling Hayes that one day the estate would be his.

Ella knew of Tita's influence over the young Hayes and grieved about it. Her hope was that soon Carlton would send Hayes away, too, perhaps to a school in England.

George performed his role of token white man on the plantation with care. Every evening, he was joined on the balcony by Caspar and together they watched the sun set before Caspar made his rounds of the Negro cabins.

Caspar concentrated on providing sufficient supervision to remind the slaves that he was there so that the estate would keep functioning. He allotted the wielding of the whips to the head drivers, Mercury and Asaph. He now had time to resume his courtship of Mary Gregg.

Caspar's initial reaction after his inopportune discovery of Mary with his father was to finish with her. He had persisted in this view up to the time of Carlton's departure for Trinidad. But now, without his father's strict influence, Caspar found his limbs yearning for Mary again.

He decided to invite her to the plantation. His preparations began with the eviction of Claire's Joan from his cabin. To his relief, she was pregnant at last. It was not until the whelp was born as black as a Congo that Caspar realized that François, and not he, was the father. By then it did not matter.

With the wench out of the way, he decorated the cabin, hanging curtains on the windows, putting a cloth on the table, a counterpane on the bed, adding a couch removed from the *cou*, and laying a rug on the floorboards.

When his preparations were complete, he despatched Samboth to Layou with a note inviting Mary, accompanied by a chaperone, of course, to visit Roxborough to view some young female slaves she might be interested in purchasing. He worded the letter so that Mary could show it to her mother.

Samboth brought back the reply that Mary accepted the invitation and would call the following afternoon.

It was Caspar's plan that whoever accompanied Mary would be lured away on some pretext so he could make love to her in the cabin. He was sure Mary would agree. Caspar was amazed, therefore, when Mary arrived at the plantation with not one chaperone but two, together with a coachman and a little black girl as her attendant.

Caspar concealed his disappointment. He bowed as he held open the door for Mary to descend from her carriage. He invited her into the cabin.

"Are we not going up to the house, Caspar?" she asked, declining to alight. The two chaperones fluttered their fans and cooed at each other.

"I thought we might be able to have a private talk about our business here in my office," Caspar suggested, trying to get his intention through to Mary without her companions realizing.

"I'm sure yew did, Caspar." Mary spoke without humor. "I feel we would rather take tea at the house, if yew have no objections." She indicated her companions. "Rose and Angelique have been dying to see the famous Roxborough bucks. They were thrilled when my mother suggested they accompany me today."

"Very well," sighed Caspar. "I see." He swung up beside the driver. His only consolation, he reflected, was that Mary must have some plan of her own. He exchanged a rueful glance with Samboth, who ran behind the phaeton as it took off up the trail.

At the house, Caspar bided his time and played the part of the perfect host. He ushered the ladies up the grand steps, settled them in the drawing room, waited on them with tea, and joined them in polite conversation. All the time he was wondering how he was going to get Mary to bed.

"Shall we take a walk over to the nursery to see the whelps?" Caspar asked. "Rose and Angelique could stay here. I'll call Ella and Tita to keep them company."

"Oh, I'm sure they would love to come, too," said Mary brightly. "They are both interested in purchasing a little dolly like my own here." Mary indicated the girl who lay on the floor with her head resting on Mary's lap.

"She is such a pet, Caspar. Mas Carlton sent her to me as a present after the auction. Wasn't he kind?"

His brow darkening with frustration, Caspar forced himself through the performance of showing Mary and her pair of May Gregg's whores around the nursery. Every time he tried to get Mary alone, she summoned Rose or Angelique to her side. It was impossible when the doctor joined them, too.

"I have enjoyed this afternoon, Caspar. It was so kind of yew to ask me to visit," Mary said coyly when the tour of the nursery ended. "My girls have been thrilled."

"More than some!"

"What do yew mean, Caspar?" Mary fluttered her eyelashes.

"Nothing!" His eyes searched hers, trying to fathom the reason for her off-hand behavior.

Was he wrong to expect Mary to contrive a chance to be alone with him the moment she arrived? She appeared to be avoiding him deliberately.

The doctor walked with the party to the phaeton. He helped Rose and Angelique into their seats and stood talking. At the other side of the carriage Mary ushered in her slave girl. She accepted Caspar's hand as he helped her up, and he squeezed her fingers imploring her to stay.

The phaeton door closed. The doctor waved farewell. Mary leaned out of the open window. Her eyes blazed with anger.

"Caspar!" she hissed.

He turned his face to hers, his features contorted with disappointment at his foiled plans.

"You ogre!" she said, her voice quavering. "I'm pregnant!"

Mary fell back into the arms of her slave as the coachman whipped up the horses and the carriage drove off in a cloud of dust.

Chapter 22

CASPAR RUBBED HIS EYES TO CLEAR THE DUST from them as the phaeton disappeared down the drive to Layou. Mary's voice was still hissing in his ears.

"Ogre!" he thought with despair. "Is that what the sweet talk has come to?" He shrugged his shoulders, scuffing his feet in the dust. Suddenly, the horrific import of her accusation stunned him.

"My whelp!" he exclaimed aloud. "What will Mas Carlton say to that?" Caspar moistened his lips pensively, standing outside his cabin with one hand on his hip, the other cradling his chin.

Samboth, like a faithful puppy, sat on his haunches in the shadows from the tall cane grass, watching his master eagerly. Without glancing at the boy, Caspar swung around listlessly to enter his cabin.

"Hello, Caspar!" Ella's greeting surprised him when he pushed open the cabin door. She was sitting where he had hoped Mary would sit, on the couch. He blinked at her.

"What are you doing here?" he demanded sharply.

"Yo' done make dis ol'. cabin passing pretty," Ella murmured. She gazed around. "Now ah does be wondering why yo' done make yuh shanty so comfortable, Caspar?"

"What do you want here, Ella?"

Caspar shook his head, bewildered. Ella sat calmly, her hands clasped in her lap, watching him.

"You know!" Caspar threw himself down on the bed, uttering a low groan of despair as he rolled onto his back.

"No." Ella raised her eyebrow. "Ah don't know anything unless yo' tell me."

"About Mary?"

"De *beké* whore, Caspar?"

"Yes, Ella. The buckra's white wench forbidden to black boys like me." He sat up facing his mother.

"I thought she would come back to me, Ella! I never spurned her. I stopped seeing her after the auction because I wanted her to know that I had feelings, too, like a white person. I did not reject her. She used to say she loved me, that she needed me. What happened to her, Ella? I need her myself, now!"

"Yo' send fuh she to come here today? Yo' pretty up yuh cabin fuh she?"

Caspar nodded, collapsing back on the bed and burying his head in the pillow.

"Why she not stay wid yo', Caspar?"

"She is pregnant with my child!"

"How do yo' know dat?"

"She told me, Ella. She called me an ogre."

Ella snorted with scorn. "How do yo' know she does be pregnant fuh yo', Caspar? She does have different white men every night. Any buckra could be de father of she whelp." She paused. "Even Mas Carlton heself!"

"When the whelp is born black, you'll see. The whole island will know!" Caspar rolled on to his back angrily. "Mas Carlton is going to be so vexed after all I have done to him."

"Not Mas Carlton yo' have to concern yuhself wid, Caspar. Yo' does have he heart in yuh hand. Is May Gregg! She gon' ax Carlton fuh yuh hide, fuh sure! Yo' done wreck she business. No white buckra gon' pay fuh she whores when dey does know dat nigger slaves does rut wid dem, too!" Ella sighed.

"Carlton have to hang yo' fuh she, Caspar!"

Five weeks were to pass before the Bondmaster returned to Roxborough. They were the worst days Caspar had ever known. He trudged around the plantation in misery, barely able to concentrate on the tasks he was supposed to supervise. His nights were spent in torment, writhing in bed, gripped with melancholy. He was unable to sleep or to service the wenches Samboth brought over from the quarters.

Caspar did not want to be sacrificed at the behest of Mary Gregg. Neither did he want Mas Carlton to be placed in the position of having to decide on his death. To Caspar, there seemed to be no solution.

The Bondmaster's return precipitated another crisis before Caspar could acquaint him of Mary's condition.

Caspar was at the house when Carlton galloped into the yard unexpectedly. He jumped off his horse and strode up the steps with a swagger. He embraced

233

Ella fondly. He scooped Hayes off the floor and swung him around until the boy cried for him to stop. He greeted Caspar, clapping him on his shoulders with delight.

"Did you pass a profitable visit, sir?" Caspar was nervous.

"Boy, more than you know!" Carlton threw himself into a chair on the balcony as Caspar carried over a jug of sangaree.

George came rushing up the steps from his surgery in the paddock. He bounded onto the balcony.

"Doctor!" Carlton paused in his teasing of Hayes. "How nice to see you so agile. Won't you sit down and have a glass of sangaree with me? You must tell me all that occurred in my absence."

"Where's Athol?" George's chest heaved as he tried to catch his breath. "I see you came back alone. Is Athol coming with the baggage cart?"

"Sit down, Doctor. Have a drink with me. I take it nothing untoward happened while I was away? Did you find someone to help you in the dispensary? Some of my young niggers have good heads; I've always said so. I'm sure you found someone to help you, didn't you, Doctor?"

"Why should I?" George took a seat and accepted the glass which Caspar handed to him. "I've been waiting for Athol to come back. Where is he?"

Carlton laughed. "Athol? Well, Doctor, Athol is in Trinidad." He smiled wryly. "I came back without any slaves at all, actually. Damned inconvenient, I can tell you. I won't travel without a slave again, whatever price I am offered. You hear me, Caspar?"

Carlton sipped calmly at his sangaree while

234

George stared at him in disbelief. "You sold him? You sold him! You sold my Athol!"

Carlton grimaced at the doctor's raised voice. "Doctor, take heed of yourself. You are fortunate that my good humor makes me willing to ignore your presumption. Did I hear you refer to *your* Athol, Doctor?" Carlton turned to Caspar, his eyebrow raised.

"I was under the impression that every wretched creature on this plantation is mine, not so, Caspar?

"Not only are they mine, Doctor, but all the slaves, including Athol, are mine to do with exactly as I please." Carlton banged his glass down on the table to emphasize his words.

"Yes, I have indeed sold Athol. I might add, purely for your elucidation, for an astonishingly large sum of money! You trained him excellently, Doctor. Splendid! I shall assign two new bucks to you from today so you can instruct them in the same way."

George was silent, opening and closing his fists as he fought to keep his feelings under control.

"Caspar." Carlton turned away from the doctor. "In Trinidad, it is truly impossible to buy slaves! Plantations abound in the island, but there are no slaves to work the fields.

"It was impossible to ignore the demand, so I had to part with my entire retinue. Each slave sold for triple what he would fetch here. That buck Athol was outstanding. Imagine! Merchants mobbed me for the opportunity to purchase him. Every gentleman seems to want a fancy slave to keep around the house."

Carlton cocked his head in surprise as George stood up abruptly and stomped off the balcony.

"Now what is wrong with the good Doctor?"

Leaning over the balcony railing, Carlton followed the doctor with his eyes as he scuttled across the yard, darted into his cabin, and slammed the door shut behind him.

"Oh, dear," Carlton mocked. "The Doctor isn't feeling well."

When George did not come to the house for supper that evening, Carlton was not worried. Caspar left the table early with an excuse about having to check on the quarters. Carlton was content to spend the evening on the balcony playing with Hayes.

The voyage had been a success and provided a new outlet for his slaves. "I'm happy tonight, Ella," he mumbled as he staggered to his bedroom much later.

"Life is good. See, I have a son and heir in Hayes. Laura is in a school learning how to be a lady. In Caspar, I have a first-rate overseer who costs me nothing. I have a successful stud farm with niggers galore and gold sequestered for the future. And you." He kissed Ella's cheek.

"I'm going to secure the house, Carlton." Ella slipped easily from his grasp. She knew that tonight she must take advantage of his mood, for Caspar's sake.

Carlton stumbled about his bedroom, humming to himself and tugging off his clothes. It was good to be back at Roxborough, he mused, blowing out the lantern and plunging into bed. Ella slipped into the chamber, removed her robe, and lay down beside him. He groped for her in the dark.

Ella toyed meticulously with Carlton, coaxing and restraining before clawing his passion out of

236

him. He arched and bucked and finally subsided, his mastery spent.

"Caspar has a wench impregnated for he," Ella whispered casually.

"About time, too." Carlton yawned, exhausted.

"Not a Roxborough wench, Carlton."

"No." He showed no interest.

"It does be Mary Gregg."

Carlton hugged Ella closer to him. "I thought so." He yawned.

"Yo' does not be vexed?" Ella was surprised.

"I saw it coming. I hope he can get me some black whelps as well."

Carlton drifted asleep, a smile of contentment on his face.

A furious clattering of iron-clad wheels on the cobblestones of the cart track disturbed Carlton's reverie. He was sitting alone on the gallery blowing steam off his daybreak coffee. He peered over the balcony rail as a phaeton bounced up the trail to the house. The coffee scorched his mouth when he gulped at it in surprise.

"It does be May Gregg," said Ella, who had rushed up from the kitchen. "She does have she daughter with she. What yo' gon' do, Carlton?"

"Send the whores packing!"

He rose from his seat angrily but kept silent as Pip and Samboth ran to help May Gregg descend from the carriage. He narrowed his eyes as he watched.

May Gregg puffed her way up the front steps, stumbling each time she raised her fat legs. Mary held her arm and pulled while Ella helped by pushing from the back.

"Well," May belched with achievement when she reached the top, "I made it." She collapsed panting into the chair which Ella hastily held under her.

Carlton signaled to Pip to bring the decanter of rum. Mary, Carlton noticed, was dressed in white and wore a fixed expression as though trying to convey injured pride.

"I would 'ave come before but we 'ad customers," May blurted, struggling to get breath. "Wanted to see you immediately!" She moistened her lips with her fat pink tongue.

Pip brought in the rum decanter and placed it on the table. Carlton poured a half-gill measure and passed the glass across to May. He looked at Mary, but she shook her head firmly.

"I thought only your clients had the honor of seeing you so early in the morning, May."

"That won't get you far, Carlton Todd! Only the monstrous ruination which your nigger 'as perpetrated could get me out of bed at this hour. Not that I've been in it!" she snapped.

"No, I 'aven't slept a wink for nights, knowing as 'ow my darling daughter 'as been compromised."

"Oh, yes?" Carlton smirked. "Do tell me how she knows. I had no idea morality was one of Mary's virtues."

"She knows 'ow by 'er belly, Carlton Todd! Look at 'er! She's with child, Carlton. That's 'ow she's been compromised."

"You're not suggesting that I had anything to do with it, are you, May?" Carlton glared at May threateningly. "I'd be rather surprised if you could attribute that state of affairs to any one particular man."

"You'd be rather surprised, would you? Oh, yes,

you would!" May fanned herself aggressively, perspiration seeping through her dress under her arms.

"It's that fancy buck of yours 'oo is the one, Carlton Todd. Not one particular man, but a nigger! He raped my Mary!"

"Did he really?" Carlton put his glass down on the table. "Who was that nigger, Mary?"

"It was Caspar." Mary did her best to look tearful.

"What did Caspar actually do to you, Mary?" Carlton decided it was time to end the play-acting.

"He raped me, Mister Todd." Mary sniffed.

"Really! When exactly was that?"

"Every night for four months, Mister Todd."

"May Gregg!" Carlton tried to conceal his amusement. "We know each other too well to go through this drama. I suppose the next act is for Mary to break down in tears and then you demand that I string up Caspar by his balls. And, of course, you'll put in your claim for compensation." He leaned forward.

"Do without the histrionics, May. How much?"

May's chins trembled and her cheeks puffed up with outrage. She was about to answer when Pip slipped onto the balcony and passed a letter to Carlton.

"A boy done give it to me, sah. He say de Doctor done tell he carry it fuh yo', urgent."

"Doctor?" Carlton glanced at Ella standing behind Pip. She shook her head to indicate she knew nothing of the doctor or the contents of the note.

He tore open the letter, reading it quickly. His mouth tightened, and Ella noticed his cheek twitching as he read the letter through a second time. He

239

pulled his nose thoughtfully; then his expression changed, and he beamed at May Gregg.

"Oh yes, yes," he said. "Let's get this straight, shall we? Dear Mary here is going to give birth to a child, right? You claim the child is that of my overseer, Caspar, who, Mary claims, raped her repeatedly for four months."

"Yes," said Mary quickly.

"You've got to 'ang that nigger for sure, Carlton Todd. My name is ruined."

"I've got to do what I want to do, May, not what the madam of a wharfside bordello demands. Another rum, May?" Carlton poured a large measure into her glass.

"It happens that this letter here is from the Doctor. It seems the good physician has jumped his bond and left my employ and is even now on his way."

Carlton gazed out to sea where a schooner was maneuvering out of the Layou basin. "Yes, he says he is on that ship sailing for Trinidad. Well, that's too bad. But perhaps I could offer Mary a position."

Carlton turned in his chair. "How about it, Mary? Take some months off from your duties in the casino and watch over those whelps in the paddock instead. Have your child here. If it appears less than the purest white and has Caspar's features, you will renounce all claims to it." He eyed Mary before continuing.

"I will take the whelp and pay you one hundred pounds currency. However, should you birth a seaman's bastard, you can haul your pretty strumpet's arse out of Roxborough and back to your madam!"

"What about the business I will lose when she's

240

not at the casino looking after clients?" May said promptly. "Make it two hundred pounds, in gold."

May had never seen a sneer so mean as that which curled across Carlton's face. "Get out, May Gregg!" he snapped. "One more word from you, and you will lose your dam' casino so fast, you'll rue the day you ever thought of blackmailing Carlton Todd!"

From the veranda of the overseer's cabin, Caspar watched the phaeton clatter away from the house. His heart lurched at the sight of Mary sitting haughtily beside her mam. He stared after the carriage until it disappeared from sight. He scowled.

"Come on, Samboth!" he called to the youth by his side. "We'll patrol the hill boundary today. I want to see the provision gardens."

Samboth laughed. "Yo' ain't gon' see Mas Carlton?"

"No. He can send for me, but he'll have to wait till tonight. For five weeks I've been dreading this day. Now it's here, I don't care, Samboth. I just don't care."

Caspar maintained his arrogant attitude until the evening. He took his supper with Samboth in his cabin, then sat on his veranda gazing out at the slave quarters. All was quiet. Occasionally, he glanced up at the house.

He could see Carlton sitting alone on the veranda with a glass in his hand. He observed when Carlton got up, walked to the veranda, and stood staring into the night, as though looking for him. Eventually, Carlton gave up and left the balcony.

It was then, as Pip was dousing the lights of the house, that Caspar decided to stroll up to the *cou.*

241

He was satisfied now that whatever fate the Bondmaster had decided for him, he, Caspar, had shown by keeping the Bondmaster waiting that he had a will of his own, too.

He opened the door to Carlton's room without knocking. "Well," he demanded crossly, "am I to be hanged?"

Carlton was sitting up in his bed, a candle burning on the table beside him. In his hand, pointing at Caspar's heart, was a pistol.

"Hanged? Or shot like a manicou?"

"Close the door behind you, boy," Carlton said calmly. "And lock it, if you don't mind."

Caspar was puzzled. He had expected the Bondmaster to be in a rage. Fury would have made it easier for him to ignore his own sorrow. He wanted to shout and curse his father's old-fashioned attitude, condemn him for his hypocrisy in being part of the buckra system, and abuse and defy him. Caspar wanted to do everything possible to numb the pain of knowing that he had betrayed the Bondmaster's love for him.

"I'm sorry about the pistol, Caspar," declared Carlton, placing it back in the drawer. "I heard your footfall on the floor. These boards creak so much in this old house. Over the years, I've learned to relax lightly. Do step forward and sit down, Caspar. Here, on the bed beside me."

Caspar licked his lips nervously, his defiance drained by Carlton's friendliness. He stepped forward and sat on the bed, frowning.

"I believe I know how you feel, Caspar."

"How can you?" Caspar's voice was husky.

"Ella has told me. It's over. I bought off that pair of whorish fortune hunters. You are not to be hanged, shot, or castrated. If the child is yours, we have an additional whelp but, in law, as the mother is free, so is the offspring. Mary has renounced all claim, though, so the brat will be born in bondage." Carlton smiled.

"It should be the kind of bright-skinned nigger who'll fetch a high price in Trinidad when he's five. Bless my boots, I'll even make a profit!" He slapped Caspar on his thigh.

"Is that all I am to you? A begetter of whelps to sell for a profit?"

"Caspar, why do you have to torture yourself? You know full well what you are to me." Carlton reached up his hand and placed it on Caspar's shoulder.

Caspar sighed, perplexed.

"Come, Caspar," Carlton tugged at the boy's neck. "Lie with me tonight."

Caspar turned to face Carlton.

He saw the sun-beaten features and the smile of a man he adored. He felt tears of shame pricking at the corners of his eyes.

He bent his head to blow out the candle, then lay on the bed beside the Bondmaster. He reached across his father's chest and pulled him gently toward him, seeking forgiveness.

BOOK TWO

Laura's Love

1815-1819

Chapter 23

LAURA LEANED OVER THE EDGE OF THE BALCONY rail and gazed at the ships anchored in the harbor. She was excited. The wharf and roads were jammed with vessels of all kinds. She studied each one carefully, wondering which had her father on board.

A messenger had arrived at the Academy that morning as Laura and the five other girls who constituted the enrollment of Mr. & Mrs. Micot's Academy for Young Ladies, were sitting down to breakfast. The messenger had informed Mrs. Micot that Mr. Todd of Dominica was awaiting permission to land from Governor Sir Ralph Woodford. He would be calling on Mrs. Micot shortly.

It was two years since Laura had seen her father. She had spent that time in the care of the Micots, who had been entrusted to instruct her in elocution, writing, arithmetic, and geography, as well as music, drawing, and needlework. A few of the wealthier members of Port of Spain society sent their daughters to the Micot's Academy. Laura had enjoyed her stay, and she was saddened by the thought of leaving her companions.

"Come, come, Miss Laura, we must do our work

even if our daddy is coming to see us today!" Mrs. Micot bustled out onto the veranda clapping her hands.

"But Mistress Micot," said Laura, pouting. "What is the point if I am to leave the Academy today?"

"Leave!" Mrs. Micot threw up her hands. "You are not halfway through your education. Why do you talk of leaving?"

Laura thought to herself that the loss of fees was more in Mrs. Micot's mind than disappointment that Laura would not complete her curriculum.

"I can read and write, Mistress Micot, and curtsey, bob, and serve tea. I can speak English as befits a creole. I can sew and keep household accounts. I can even sing a fair ditty." Laura grinned.

"If I am not halfway through my education, Mistress Micot, it is a husband I need to complete it, not you and yours."

"Fie, Miss Laura! At such a tender age you talk of wanting a husband."

"What is tender about my age, Mistress Micot? I am all of fourteen years. Look at Cecilia Graham. Only last term she married an officer in the militia, and she was barely thirteen."

"That child was born in Trinidad, Miss Laura, and she was advanced for her age. Not like you when you came here! Such a stubborn and rude creature you were. You had no respect for anyone. Your father will be delighted when he sees what a gracious young lady his spoiled hoyden has become."

"Was I really so awful, Mistress Micot?" Laura smiled, fluttering her eyelashes demurely in the manner she had learned from the other girls.

"Yes, yes, Miss Laura. Come now, the King's Wharf is chockablock with ships today. You can not expect to make out your father in that melee. All those Spanish refugees from the war in Venezuela! Your father will have difficulty getting through the crush."

"You don't know my father," said Laura, following Mrs. Micot into the drawing room which served for their classes during the day. "He is a very determined person."

"Glad to hear it, Miss Laura. I'm sure he'll have respect for our customs. Life in Port of Spain is not like the heathen existence of the island plantations. Come now, girl, to your books!"

The sounds of the activity on the King's Wharf below the Micot School drifted through the windows into the classroom. Usually, Laura found the lessons interesting and was able to concentrate without being disturbed by the noise. This morning the creak of the boats at the wharf, the clatter of cargo being unloaded, the cries of the Chinese street vendors, and the clamor of refugees around the soup kitchens distracted her. She waited for her father with growing impatience.

It was not until the afternoon that a commotion on the stairs of the Academy heralded the arrival of Carlton Todd himself. The door to the classroom burst open. The girls hid behind their books in delight and began whispering. Mrs. Micot rose swiftly from her seat like a mother hen, advancing toward Carlton with clucks of annoyance. Laura, suddenly nervous, glanced shyly at her father.

"You did not tell us your daddy was so handsome!" shrilled one of the girls in Laura's ear. "I do declare he resembles a co-respondent!"

The girls giggled as Laura glided over to embrace her father.

"Laura, is this you?" Carlton held her happily in his arms. "I have been longing for this day, my daughter. Let me look at you." He held her hands as she stepped back from him.

"If this is what two years with Mistress Micot does for a girl, I would I had more daughters to entrust to her zeal and care. Your servant, ma'am."

He appraised Laura professionally, aware that his daughter had the attributes of a most eligible lady. Her young femininity was appealing, heightened by her blond tresses and her blossoming figure. Carlton was satisfied.

He had written recently to an acquaintance of his, the Earl of Philbert, inviting him to spend some weeks at Roxborough. Carlton's scheme was that the Earl should take Laura for his wife. Her beauty and manner now convinced him that such an arrangement was indeed a possibility. Laura was enchanting.

Laura was anxious to parade through the streets of Port of Spain at her father's side. Carlton had to explain that it would be several days before he completed his business in the port and secured a passage on a vessel to Dominica.

"I have been fortunate in finding accommodation with Mrs. Bruce at her hotel at the corner of Queen and Frederick streets," he told her. "With the refugees huddling in doorways at night for want of accommodation, I feared I might have to sleep aboard a vessel in the harbor."

"You have attendants with you?" Mrs. Micot sounded anxious.

"Why, yes."

Mrs. Micot indicated that Carlton should step out of earshot of her pupils. "I suppose you do not have among your entourage a buck of serious demeanor who could serve as a steward for this house? It is impossible to acquire slaves anywhere in Trinidad these days."

"You are asking the right person, Mistress Micot," Carlton avowed. "I sold my slaves the moment I set foot on the dock. The Roxborough breed is rather special, you know. The letter R branded on the shoulder of my Negroes has won a reputation." Carlton frowned briefly.

"But, ma'am, do you think a Roxborough slave would be the best servant in an establishment such as yours? Unless he is gelded, of course."

"Oh, *M'sieur* Todd, such talk in front of my young ladies! If ever you happen to have such a specimen, a slave of that ilk, please do remember us."

"If you care to order one, ma'am, you can let me know your preference, shade of color, age, and height. I will endeavor to oblige."

Port of Spain was renowned as the most cosmopolitan port in the world. Its varied Spanish, French, and English history had created a community in which all nationalities were to be found, especially at this time when the city was inundated with refugees from the Venezuelan mainland.

The Governor, Sir Ralph Woodford, was energetic in his campaign to make the town safe. Carlton noted the full casks of water placed outside each house as a precaution against fire. The mud streets of the town were covered with gravel and paving stones had been placed for pavements in the main

251

streets, all under the Governor's directions. At night, the wharf by Laura's school, as well as King's Street and Marine Square, were all lit by coconut oil lamps, an astonishing sight to Carlton, who beheld them for the first time in a public place.

Port of Spain's streets were thronged with people, not only refugees, but large numbers of free mulattoes attended by their own slaves. Chinese vendors appeared to be everywhere with their poles over their shoulders, a basket filled with fish on either side, and their pigtails hanging down behind them. *Marchands de pain doux* roamed the streets with their cakes and bonbons, which were eagerly bought by the office clerks.

Carlton wandered through the town fascinated by the activity. The Spanish and French women, with their gay costumes, foreign speech, and unusual vivacity, gave the town the appearance of a bustling fair. After two years confined to his Roxborough slave warren, Carlton was ready to indulge himself. He plunged with relish into a round of fornication and gambling.

One evening he was in a billiard saloon where thousands of dollars were changing hands as a result of the Trinidadians' excessive fondness for gambling. To Carlton, the billiards and *brelin* of the saloon were lacking excitement. He declared as much to an English army officer who stood beside him drinking at the bar.

"You should try one of the native bordellos if you want excitement," guffawed the soldier. "From the black of the devil to the sun-kissed white of a Mediterranean goddess, you can choose any wench you wish."

"I've had them all already!" Carlton quaffed his

measure of rum. "I have over fifty sable mistresses on my plantation and not one of the dingy belles here can equal them."

"Animals meet your fancy? They have horse-racing on the plains of Lapeyrouse this very afternoon."

"My interest in sport is in the male form. No fighters here? It's many years since I saw a real fight. To the death."

"Trinidadians are forever seeking to blow each other's brains out at the most trivial misunderstanding," retorted the soldier. "But dueling is illegal."

"What about nigger fighting?"

"Niggers are too valuable for that, sir."

"There are some Negroes that does fight," interrupted the barman, a mulatto. He regarded Carlton shrewdly.

"It does cost a contribution to attend, sir, there being a number of expenses to defray. A group of Trinidad gentlemen I does know have a fight in hand for this evening."

With the mulatto barman, an engaging rascal called Louis, as his guide, and Captain Grell of the Light Dragoons as his companion, Carlton was soon heading for a cane field on the outskirts of Port of Spain. As they drove in their carriage past the shanties at the edge of the town, Carlton was alarmed to see the outline in the dark of enormous birds perched on the branches of trees.

"They are vultures, we call them *corbeaux*," explained Louis. "They does devour to the very bone any refuse, animal, or dead slave they does come upon."

"The shooting of those damned birds is punishable by imprisonment," scoffed Captain Grell. "Saves the cost of scavengers, what!"

The fight was to take place in a clearing which had been cut in the sugar cane. It was a bright night, with a full moon and a sprinkling of stars in the clear tropical sky. A breeze wafted over the canes from the sea, ruffling the lights of the *flambeaux* held by slaves attending the spectators.

Groups of men emerged from the darkness as the preparations for the fight got underway. Carlton paid the burly Spaniard who was the organizer three dollars each for himself and his companions. It seemed an excessive amount, especially when he learned that there was to be only one bout.

"The Negroes, I cannot get them," whined the Spaniard. "They shoot them on the mainland, they whip them to death in the islands, and here in Trinidad they let them buy their freedom." He wrung his hands.

"What is there to do? There are no fighters any more!"

Carlton inspected the specimens to see whom he would back to be the winner. The Negro who was reputed to be the Port of Spain champion was the crowd's favorite. He was a muscular buck with broad shoulders, a thick trunk, and massive hands; his hair, though bushy and crimped, was not woolly but soft and silky. He was a Mandingo.

"Mandingos think themselves superior to other Africans." Carlton aired his knowledge to Captain Grell. "I find them prone to theft and disinclined to work."

Carlton was forced to agree with the Captain, however, that the Mandingo seemed likely to retain his status when he saw the challenger. The boy was a young colt, barely sixteen.

Carlton called for a slave to hold his *flambeau* closer to the boy's body so he could inspect him in the dark.

"What a superb specimen," gulped the captain, watching Carlton handle the boy's flesh. "Fine torso on him, what!"

"Exactly, Captain!" Carlton's eyes flashed. "He's a rare breed of nigger, pure Yoruba. See the bright intelligence in the eyes and face. See that potential strength in his physique. But the boy has no weight."

Carlton moaned, turning away. "He is too young to fight."

"You know a great deal about this?"

"Years ago, I used to fight niggers. I owned a Yoruba once, and I would be proud to own this one. I would feed him and train him. In no time at all, he would become the Champion of Dominica." Carlton cupped the Yoruba's balls in the palm of his hand, weighing them thoughtfully.

"I would breed from him, too. A pure Yoruba strain would enhance the meager Congo stock I've got."

The Yoruba regarded Carlton blankly. The other white men in the circle were praising the prowess of the Mandingo. Carlton alone recognized his qualities. There was a murmur of surprise among the group when Carlton agreed to back the Yoruba against the champion.

"I say, old fellow!" exclaimed Captain Grell as the Spaniard totted up the stakes. "You have wagered on this nigger more than five years' pay for a captain of the militia!"

"If he wins," said Carlton, elated by the challenge, "I want the nigger, too."

"You really believe he will win?"

"I like his pluck. See how he is prancing! He is eager to get at the Mandingo. He is not scared of him and seems to hate him, too. He is more confident now that I'm backing him." Carlton chuckled. "A Yoruba is bright. He'll give a damn good account of himself."

"He'll lose, of course," declared Louis.

"Maybe, maybe not. See his eyes. He doesn't want to die."

When he was satisfied that he could milk no more bets from the small crowd, the Spaniard ushered the planters, merchants, and assorted Europeans into a circle encompassing the two fighters. A small boy acted as the Yoruba's second while the Spaniard himself prepared the Mandingo. Carlton stood at the side of the Yoruba.

"The Mandingo will kill you!" he hissed into the Negro's ear. "Unless you kill him first."

"If ah does kill Don Juan's champion, Don Juan gon' shoot me, sah! Is dat he done buy me fuh. He does make back me purchase price from yuh stakes, sah. Ah don't have no chance now."

"Yes, boy! Bite off his ear, screw out his eyes, and crush his balls with your knee in his crotch. I guarantee you my protection if you kill the Mandingo!"

Carlton stood back as the small boy attending the Yoruba rubbed him quickly with snake grease. Don Juan sneered at the preparations. He let his kerchief flutter to the ground, pushing the Mandingo to the center of the ring to start the fight.

"*Al muerto!*" he shouted.

The Yoruba leaped out of his corner and dived at the champion. He knocked him off balance by his unexpected agility, sending him crashing to the ground. The group of men broke into a roar of approval.

"Good!" shouted Carlton. "The Mandingo is winded at the outset!"

The boy jumped on the champion's chest and pummeled him with his fists.

Carlton groaned. "He's fighting him like a child. Throttle the bastard, you black ape! Squeeze the bloody life out of his throat!"

As though ridiculing Carlton's advice to the Yoruba, the huge Mandingo rose off the ground and placed his hands around the Yoruba's waist. He lifted him up as though he was as light as a doll, with a hand under his buttocks and the other grasping his neck. The Yoruba struggled helplessly.

Holding the boy aloft, the Mandingo marched proudly in front of the circle of spectators. He paused when he was face to face with Carlton. A glimmer of contempt flickered in his eyes. He raised the Yoruba high above his head and hurled him down at Carlton's feet with a crash which made Carlton shudder. The Mandingo leered quickly at Carlton, then pointed his penis down at the Yoruba's face and urinated into his eyes with a flourish. As the spectators jeered, he stalked back into the center of the ring.

"The bounder!" yelled Captain Grell. "To your feet, man! Thrash the savage!"

"Up, *garçon!*" shrieked Louis. "Get up!"

Carlton knelt down and whispered into the Yoruba's ear.

The boy wiped his face and pulled himself into

a crouching position. The champion had his back to him as he flapped his arms and crowed with jubilation to his supporters. The boy jumped for his neck, clawing at his face. No one saw the sharp-edged stone which Carlton had slipped into the Yoruba's hand.

The stone tore into the Mandingo's eyes. He was knocked off balance and crashed to the ground. As he fell forward, the Yoruba clung to him desperately, grinding the stone into his eyes until they were a fleshy mass of blood and pulp.

The Mandingo reared up with a shout of anger, tossing the boy off his back. He lunged at him, trying to hold his head, but the urine and grease prevented him from getting a proper grip. The boy slipped away, and the crowd exploded with shouts of excitement.

Sensing his advantage, the Yoruba sashayed into the center of the ring. He goaded the champion with shrieks of abuse. Blindly, the Mandingo pounced, but the boy was too fast. He stepped to the side and stuck out his foot. The Mandingo toppled over, his head bashing against a stone.

"Wait, boy, wait!" yelled Carlton when the Yoruba began to close in. "He'll twist your leg off!"

Surprised at the advice, the Yoruba paused.

"Now!" Carlton screamed as the Mandingo began to rise off the ground. The boy saw the chance and kicked the champion's head as he raised it groggily. The Mandingo fell back in agony.

"Damn me! The boy will win!" bawled the captain.

"It's not certain, Captain. Now you'll see the Mandingo get really angry."

Carlton was right. In a fury, the Mandingo lifted

himself off the ground, smeared the blood from his eyes with the back of his hand, and lashed out. He outreached the Yoruba boy, who dodged around the ring for safety. The boy was tiring.

"The boy can't get near him," said the captain anxiously, grasping Carlton's arm.

"Good thing, too," said Carlton. "If he does, the Mandingo will crush him." Carlton was ready to concede defeat.

He shrugged his shoulders. "He was a spunky nigger."

A shout went up from the spectators as the Yoruba fell to the ground, apparently exhausted. Caught by surprise, the Mandingo tumbled over the boy's limp body. He reached quickly for the boy's leg. Picking it up in his hands, he began to bend the knee against the joint, almost tenderly. The crowd chanted, waiting expectantly for the sickening crack of bone.

"He'll tear him apart, piece by piece!" grumbled Carlton.

"Are you not going to do something about it?" The captain spluttered indignantly, drawing his pistol. "I will put a ball through the Mandingo's head and arrest the Spaniard for fighting without a license!"

"No, no, no!" said Carlton. "Leave the Yoruba to die proudly."

Neither Carlton nor any of the spectators realized what was really happening. The boy had faked his apparent exhaustion so he could get inside the barrage of the Mandingo's punches. With the champion trying to crack his knee, the boy slipped his hand quickly between the Mandingo's bare buttocks.

He jabbed a stone he was holding sharply into the champion's anus.

With a scream of pain, the Mandingo released the boy's knee.

Seizing his chance, the boy sprang at the Mandingo's chest. He slashed at his throat with his forearm, at the same instant jamming his groin mercilessly with his knee. The Mandingo went down on his back. The Yoruba waited for an agonizing second, then jumped, landing solidly with both feet on the Mandingo's neck. There was a crack. A sigh went up from the crowd as the Mandingo's head lolled to one side.

Realizing what he had done, the boy rushed to Carlton, throwing himself at his feet, clinging to his legs.

"Save me, sah! Save me!"

The captain pointed his pistol at the crowd, hoping to hold them at bay.

"There's no need for that!" growled one of the spectators. "It was a good fight. Here's your money!"

He thrust a purse at Carlton. Others followed suit, chattering with excitement.

Carlton grinned as he looked around the clearing in the light of the *flambeaux*. Don Juan had disappeared.

"Don't fret, boy!" he chuckled. "Don Juan's made good his escape. He's left you behind to pay his debt." He patted the boy's head.

"You're a Roxborough slave now!"

The Yoruba raised his head and glanced at the black shapes of the vultures crouching in the trees. He shuddered. The Mandingo's body lay stretched out, forgotten in the dust.

Carlton found, to his surprise, that he enjoyed his daughter's company. They spent afternoons together strolling through the streets of Port of Spain, visiting shops and buying cloth, jewelry, and souvenirs. They were accompanied by Bute, the Yoruba, who showed no after effects from his fight.

Carlton provided Bute with a blue jacket of permistone, a shirt of duck, osnaburg trousers, a hat, and a blanket. The boy followed Carlton and Laura at a respectful distance, waiting patiently outside the shops and houses they visited.

Laura declined to acknowledge the slave's presence. "We were taught at the Academy," she explained to Carlton one day when they took tea at Mrs. Bruce's, "that one should not be familiar with one's slaves.

"It is unfortunate, Mistress Micot told us, that standards in Trinidad have changed so much in recent years. Why, you will even hear of a master and his slave playing cards together!"

"Disgraceful," muttered Carlton, enjoying his daughter's small talk.

"Indeed it is. Mistress Micot told us that the manager of an estate here had to be upbraided by the Chief Justice himself for his familiarity with a Negro." She sipped daintily at her tea before continuing.

"It appears that a Negro was playing cards with his master when the Negro became incensed over his master's finesse at the game. The slave lifted the master off his feet, threw him to the ground three times in succession, and gave him a blow with his fist which made him spit blood for three whole days."

"Terrible, Laura. What did the Chief Justice do?"

"He sentenced the Negro to fifty lashes of the cat-o-nine-tails!" Laura laughed gaily. "Do we have a cat-of-nine-tails at Roxborough, Daddy?"

"Why, yes. I hope not to use it. Roxborough is a very orderly plantation now, Laura. The slaves are happier when it is so, and they breed quicker when they are content."

"What about the maroons, daddy?"

"They have been disbanded. Governor Anslie's measures broke them." Carlton smiled at his daughter.

"The plantation flourishes, Laura. We've had two good cane harvests, and the warehouses are packed with hogsheads of rum and sugar. The nursery is abrim with whelps, and the demand for slaves is greater than ever." He beamed with satisfaction.

"It seems I am returning to a perfect paradise, Daddy. But I shall miss my school friends here."

"School days are over now, Laura. It will soon be time to find a husband."

"That," said Laura, with a shy smile, "is in my thoughts, too."

Chapter 24

CARLTON HAD BEEN APPREHENSIVE WHEN HE sailed from Dominica to collect his daughter. He had feared he would meet an older version of the girl he had sent away. His pleasure at the apparent change in Laura increased when they returned to Roxborough and Laura immediately expressed an interest in the house, the plantation, and everything that was going on around her.

After supper on the first evening of Laura's return, she sat in the drawing room talking delightedly about being back.

"I missed home so much, Daddy," she concluded, astonishing Carlton, who was unaware that his daughter had any attachment for Roxborough. "Where am I to sleep?"

"What? Well, I had not considered that." Carlton stroked his chin.

"You didn't think to put me back in that gloomy room with Tita and Hayes surely, Daddy? I am old enough to have my own boudoir now!" She leaned forward in her seat.

"I have so many lovely things, I would not want Hayes to interfere with them, and then there are my studies. You must realize, Daddy, I am a young lady now."

"Yes, of course. I'll ask Ella."

"Why ask Ella, Daddy?"

"Well, she's the housekeeper."

"I know. But I am here now. I will be able to supervise such things. You don't have to depend on your slaves for personal matters any more. I am so looking forward to being able to help you.

"Besides," she added, to forestall Carlton's objections. "It will be good practice for when I am to be married."

"Do you mind if I have a drink, Laura?" Carlton asked tartly.

"Oh, Daddy, let me do that for you!" Laura laid her hand on Carlton's arm to restrain him, rising to carry the tray with decanter and a glass over to him.

He chuckled. "Mistress Micot made sure that I got my money's worth. If you go on like this, I may have to geld a nigger for her to show my gratitude!"

Carlton poured a measure of rum and sat back in his chair to contemplate his daughter.

"You want your own chamber? There should be no problem in that. You'll want a maid, too?" Laura smiled in agreement.

"I suppose you should have my old chamber. It used to be your grandmother's. There's a dressing room where your maid can sleep.

"You shall choose your maid from the nursery wenches tomorrow. You'll have to train her."

Laura leaned down and kissed Carlton on his forehead. "It is so nice to be back.

"Hmmm," grunted Carlton, pulling his nose and

wondering what changes Laura's return would bring to Roxborough.

He did not have to wait long to find out.

At breakfast the next morning, when he came in from his daybreak patrol of the plantation, Carlton was amazed to see the table set for four. Laura, in a pretty check dress she had bought in Trinidad and with her hair freshly brushed, smiled at him radiantly.

"Good morning, Laura," he said politely, clearing his throat. "I did not expect you to be up yet."

"We are having breakfast together."

"We? You and I? That's very nice. Who are the other two places for, Caspar and Ella?" Carlton snorted dryly, sitting down at his usual place at the head of the table and reaching for the coffee pot.

"You should wait until we are all seated, Daddy. Mistress Micot taught us to say grace before every meal."

"Grace?" Carlton put back the coffeepot as Hayes burst out of his bedroom followed by Mingoson.

"What are you doing out of your room so early, boy? How many times must I tell you not to disturb me before I've had my breakfast! Tita!" Carlton bellowed. "Get these boys out of here."

"Now, Daddy, that's not the way it should be done. Mistress Micot taught us that family life is very important. Hayes is nearly ten now. He is old enough to have breakfast with us." She beckoned Hayes.

"Come, Hayes, you shall sit here on your daddy's right. I shall sit at the end of the table. Mingoson, go around to the other side."

"What!" Carlton thumped his fist down on the table, making the cups and cutlery shiver.

"Why's that boy sitting down at my breakfast

table?" he roared, pointing an accusing finger at Mingoson.

"What's wrong in that, Daddy?" Laura fluttered her eyelashes innocently.

"Nothing wrong, dear Laura, but he is a slave, and I do not breakfast with slaves!"

Mingoson stared wide-eyed at the Bondmaster, his lip trembling as he shifted in his seat. Hayes began to whine.

Tita, who was watching from the bedroom door, spoke up before the Bondmaster put the blame on her.

"Miss Laura done say dat Mas Hayes is to sit at de table, Mas Carlton, sah. Mas Hayes done say he not sitting at de table unless Mingoson does be wid he."

Carlton sank his head in his hand. "Damme, Laura, what kind of nonsense is this?" He lifted up his head to stare at Tita, wagging his finger at her.

"That boy, Mingoson, is a slave whelp even if he is Hayes's playboy. He's not black like a bozal, I know, but he ain't white!'..

Mingoson started to cry. Hayes got up from his chair and ran around the table to put his arm around him. "Don't cry, Mingoson, yo' does be a'right dere."

"No, he ain't! Hayes, a slave does not sit down to eat with his master!"

Carlton turned to his daughter. "Do you remember, Laura, you said Mistress Micot warned you to avoid familiarity with slaves?"

"Yes, Daddy, but Mingoson has grown up with Hayes. He is his playboy."

"That is so. But Hayes is not a child now. He has got to grow up and you can help him. Teach him to speak like you instead of like a slave. Teach him how to behave himself." Carlton rapped the table.

"Hayes is my blood. One day he will be the Bondmaster of Roxborough. Mingoson will be his servant."

Hayes cocked his head on one side. "When I does be de Bondmaster, can I do what I like wid de slaves?"

"Of course."

Hayes hugged his playboy. "It does be a'right, Mingoson. Yo' go down to de kitchen an' eat wid Nanny Tita and Ella. When I does be de Bon'massa, ah gon' give yo' yuh freedom an' den yo' does eat up here wid me."

Bewildered, Carlton shook his head, reaching for the coffeepot with relief. He filled his cup while Laura ushered Mingoson and Tita out of the dining room.

"Laura, I see I have neglected Hayes for too long. Tita appears to have been working on the boy's mind. Of course, Mingoson being her whelp, she wants to see the brat get privilege. You must not encourage her."

When breakfast was finished, Laura accompanied her father to the nursery to select a wench as her maid.

Caspar was waiting for them at the entrance to the paddock. He bowed as Laura approached. "Good morning, Miss Laura. I'm pleased to see you back home."

Laura flashed him a dazzling smile. In Trinidad, she had thought often about Caspar. He was a

267

slave, but he was her half-brother. Suddenly, she felt nervous in his presence.

She glanced at his face anxiously, searching for some resemblance between them both. Caspar's sun-weathered skin was in contrast to her own white complexion. She expected that. But she had not anticipated the familiar yellow eyes shining out of his dark face. His stare was riveting. She gasped breathlessly at how handsome he was.

Abruptly, she turned her back on him so he would not see her blush.

"Daddy," she exclaimed to hide her confusion, "why did you buy that nigger in Trinidad when you have Caspar here? I declare he seems stronger than an ox!"

"Huh!" chuckled Carlton with pleasure. "He has a brain inside that body. Caspar is too valuable to lose in a fight, Laura. Roxborough revolves around him."

Laura strolled through the paddock as whelps clustered around her. Caspar snapped his whip to drive them away. He sorted out a dozen or so females and lined them up in the shade of a flamboyant tree for Laura's inspection.

Laura's eyes strayed beyond the frightened group of girls to a gang of naked boys gamboling in the grass. Caspar noticed her gaze and let his whip fly out. It cracked above the boys' heads and flicked one of them on his bottom.

"Move yourselves!" he yelled. "Come, Miss Laura, don't worry about the bucks. There's a fine selection of wenches for you here. You want them to strip down?"

"She's looking for a maid, Caspar, not a bed wench."

Caspar shrugged his shoulders.

"I don't think that's important, Caspar," soothed Laura. "I'll choose one, and if she's sickly I'll send her back."

She scanned the faces of the females lined up in front of her. A wench about thirteen years old with hair laid out in braids across her head attracted her. Her brown eyes danced with a knowing twinkle.

"Who are you, wench?" asked Laura.

"Ah does be Harodine, missy," the girl giggled.

"You'll do."

"Go to Ella at the *cou*, girl. Tell her that I sent you to be Miss Laura's maid. She will show you what to do," instructed Caspar.

Laura looked at her father quizzically. "Do you let Caspar give the orders, Daddy?"

"Of course, Laura. With a plantation like this, there has to be an effective chain of command. Caspar has responsibility, and he has to carry it out. The drivers come under him, and under them come the gang leaders.

He walked Laura toward the nursery building. "Come inside and see the whelps. I've raised over thirty new gets so far this year."

"What a strange thing!" Laura exclaimed pointing at one of the babies crawling over the floor of the nursery. "How did he get here? Isn't he white?" She lifted up the boy who had caught her attention and cradled him in her arms.

"You think so?" Carlton glanced at Caspar.

"That's my whelp, Miss Laura," Caspar said dryly. "His mother was white."

Laura studied the baby closely. Sure enough,

the child's hair was black and curly, and the boy did have the familiar yellow eyes.

"I wouldn't have known he had slave blood in him," she murmured.

"His name is Brett." Caspar waited nervously for Laura's reaction.

"I think he is gorgeous," Laura sighed. "Why do you keep him out here with the paddock whelps, Caspar? Shouldn't he be inside the house?"

Carlton answered brusquely before Caspar could reply. "Too many brats in the house!" He gestured to Caspar and Laura to follow him.

"We don't want him to get any silly ideas about his status. Do we, Caspar?"

With the help of her new maid, Laura transformed her gloomy bedroom into a glittering boudoir. Carpenters constructed new furniture, and she hung material from Trinidad to add color to the room. It was not only the old bedchamber which Laura transformed; she changed the entire house as well by introducing a note of domesticity which had been missing.

To Laura, it was important that she should have a home. In Trinidad when she visited the homes of school friends, she saw an atmosphere of security and love which she herself did not know. From the day her mother had died when she was six to the time she began at Mistress Micot's Academy, Laura's sole influence had been her embittered slave nanny, Tita.

The Academy had liberated Laura and with her days at Roxborough growing into weeks, Laura soon yearned for the stimulating companionship of her Trinidad friends. She sought a substitute in the companionship of the women in the house. She realized that Ella had a wealth of knowledge, especially about cooking, and was happy to spend hours with her in the kitchen. This charmed Ella, who had feared that Laura was trying to oust her in favor of Tita, her archrival.

Laura understood that her father was consumed by his passion to produce perfect slaves. She watched him from the gallery sometimes as he exercised Bute, the Yoruba he had brought from Trinidad. Carlton made the youth run around a course he marked out for him in the courtyard. He ordered Ella to massage the youth every day with a revolting mixture of snake's grease and lime juice. He supervised the boy's diet and measured his chest, his waist, and his thighs regularly to see if he was putting on more size.

Watching this daily performance from the gallery, Laura was determined to create a haven in the house where her father's love of niggers did not intrude. She desperately wanted her father to be like other planters or merchants, who came home in the evenings to relax with their families. What he did on the plantation or when he went to bed was not her concern, Laura reasoned, but she demanded the attention for herself and Hayes which she felt a father should give.

For his part, Carlton found himself absorbing Laura's changes without protest. He was lonely. To be able to relax in the evenings with his children was a pleasure. He no longer found it necessary to drink himself into a stupor before going to bed.

Hayes responded to this sudden surge of adult attention by listening to his father and sister with fascination. There was a world outside the confines

271

of the house that he did not know about. It sounded interesting.

It was when she lay in her bed at night that Laura, too, began to feel the searing thrusts of plantation loneliness. At the Academy she was constantly surrounded by friends. At Roxborough, there was only her maid to keep her company. At night, she sighed herself to sleep, wondering what was wrong.

Frequently she had dreams of Caspar striding through the plantation, or of Bute, the Yoruba fighter, lolloping naked around the yard doing his exercises. One night, as she lay in bed stifling in the heat, Laura found she could not sleep because of the image of Caspar's massive thighs which kept entering her mind. She opened her eyes to listen to the night. Her maid was stirring in the dressing room.

"Harodine!" she called softly.

"Yas, Miss Laura?"

"Do bring me some water from the cooler, please. I am so warm tonight."

The girl padded into Laura's room dressed in her night shift, her short hair plaited across her head. She had a sweet little face, rounded cheeks, and big brown eyes that seemed to be adoring Laura.

"Yo' want de lantern turn down, miss?"

"Yes, please, just a low glow. I feel restless tonight, Harodine. Sit on the bed and talk with me!"

"Yas, Miss Laura."

"Are there nights when you cannot sleep, Harodine? When your mind and body seem to be in a turmoil?" Laura patted her maid's hand.

"Some nights does be like dat, miss."

"What do you do, Harodine? When I was at the Academy in Trinidad I had a special girlfriend who would sleep with me. I would feel much better when she was in bed beside me."

"Is true, Miss Laura. When ah was be in de nursery we wenches does sleep together."

"You used to sleep with the other girls?"

"Of co'se, miss."

"How do you feel when you are sleeping in the dressing room there all by yourself?" Laura held her breath in suspense.

"A'right, miss."

"You don't feel lonely?" Laura fondled the girl's wrist. "If you do, wouldn't you like to lie here in this bed with me?"

"A'right, miss."

Laura shifted to the other side of the bed and patted the spot beside her. "Get in here, Harodine."

"A'right, miss."

"You did bathe this afternoon, Harodine?"

"Oh, yas, miss. Miss Ella done tell me to bathe every day."

"What else did she tell you?" Laura reached over and pulled the girl to her.

"She done tell me to do whatever yo' does ax me to do. An' also to smile even if I vex'."

"You're not vexed now are you, Harodine?"

"Oh, no, Miss Laura."

"Do it to me."

"What, miss?"

Laura took Harodine's hand and laid it on her breast. "Touch me here, Harodine!"

"A'right, miss."

Chapter 25

Rain splattered on the mud outside the kitchen door, forming pools of water under the back stairs. It bounced noisily off the pans placed outside for washing and swirled in torrents across the yard.

The sound of the rainfall reverberated through the house, engulfing the occupants with its deafening roar. The massive leaves of the wild plantain, the green ribbons of the cane stalks, and the fans of the young coconut trees dripped with rain. Ella stared gloomily out of the kitchen.

Pip was decanting rum in the storeroom. A girl peeled a mound of dasheen for the day's dinner. At the end of the long kitchen table Tita sat with Mingoson.

Ella turned to face Tita, nodding her head at the rain. "Dat rain bound to keep yo' down here fuh a while. Mingoson, take a knife and help de wench clean de dasheen and fig."

Tita put her hand on Mingoson's shoulder. "Stay dere, Mingoson! Yo' ain't no kitchen slave." Brushing at her long hair with a haughty wave, Tita scowled at Ella.

"Mas Carlton ain't never say dat Mingoson must

to clean de food. Is only de rain does keep we down here."

"Dat so?" said Ella, her mouth curling down in a sneer.

"He done say dat yuh precious Mingoson must to eat in de kitchin, though. Not wid Mas Hayes no more. If he does eat wid we niggers and not wid de buckras dem, is work he does work!"

Ella placed her hands firmly on the opposite end of the table and stared down its length at Tita. "Yo', too!"

Pip popped his head out of the storeroom to see what the commotion was about. He saw Tita rise from her chair like a squawking hen.

"Yo' only vex' wid Mingoson because Mas Carlton done put de whelp of yuh son Caspar in de paddock. Is dat where yo' does want Mingoson to go, nuh?"

"Ain't no neverminds, mam. Ah does do dat fuh Ella." Mingoson stood up. "Hayes does be out wid Mas Carlton. Dey don't want me wid dem."

"Sit down, boy!" commanded Tita crossly.

"Yo' see!" Ella scored a point. "Hear de boy! Mas Carlton done tell Mingoson he don't want he wid he. De boy right. Let he help here. Ain't nothing else fuh he to do in dis rain."

"Mas Carlton does be ridin' de estate wid he son to show he fuh de future." Tita was on the defensive. "Mas Hayes gon' tell Mingoson everything when he does come back!"

"Mingoson is a slave like we, Tita. Ain't no special privilege yo' does get because he does be playboy to Hayes," Ella continued.

"Ah don't see what use Hayes does have fuh a playboy an' a nanny no more!"

275

Tita advanced toward Ella indignantly. "What yo' does say, Ella! Yo' Batutsi *cochon!* Ah does be a Fulani, an' ah don't need no obeah to make me de one dat Mas Carlton does need!" she shrieked.

"Is yo', Ella, dat Mas Carlton don't have no use for! Is de *beké* whelp of yuh Caspar dat does be in de paddock. Mah whelp does be here in de Bon'massa's house!"

Tita crackled with abuse as the long-smoldering rivalry between herself and Ella flared up.

"Yo does think yo' does be bettah dan me! Yo' think because yo' does be a royal nigger wid a son by de Bon'massa yo' is de Black Queen.

"Not yo' alone does have de son. Yo' will see!"

Ella was puzzled by Tita's final remark, but she ignored it. "Yo' does be one stupid nigger, Tita. Ah does order yo' to get out mah kitchin."

"Oy, oy, oy! Yo' does be de Bon'massa!"

"Dis does be mah kitchin, Tita. If yo' not gon' let Mingoson do de work ah done ax he, yo' best move out mah way. Ah does have de dinner to think of." Ella moved toward the stove.

Tita blocked her path. "When mah Hayes does be de Bon'massa, Ella, yo' gon' to de cane fields!" She pierced the air with her finger in excitement.

"Yo' does be full of talk, Tita! Move out mah way!"

Ella snatched at Tita's arm, intending to guide her out of the kitchen. Tita reacted instantly, slashing her hand across Ella's cheek, cutting into the soft flesh with her long nails. Ella replied with a stunning blow to Tita's jaw with the side of her forearm. Tita stumbled backwards.

"Mam!" Mingoson leaped up in panic. He tugged at Tita's skirt as she regained her balance.

Tita turned on the boy and cuffed him viciously on his ear. "Yo' ain't de one to call me mam, boy!" she shrieked.

Wielding her fingers like claws, she lunged at Ella's eyes. Ella grabbed the coffeepot from the stove and pitched the steaming contents into Tita's face.

"Now yo' does be as black as me, Tita!" she screeched.

For seconds, the hot coffee blinded Tita. She staggered about the kitchen frantically dabbing her eyes with her hands.

Ella cackled with laughter. "Next time yo' does tell Ella about wha' gon' happen when Mas Hayes is de Bon'massa', rem'ber yo' does be in de fields yuhself one day! Yo' gon' be dere dead wid de worm nibblin' yuh flesh!"

Ella held Tita firmly by her shoulders and shoved her toward the kitchen door. "Now yo go'n' cool off in the rain!"

Tita stumbled on the step, lost balance, and fell headlong into a puddle in the mud under the back stair. Mingoson stood and watched her, turning away silently as Tita sobbed for help. The rain poured down, soaking them both.

Ella closed the kitchen door triumphantly. "De bitch! She bound to cause trouble. Miss Laura done done wid she, an' now Mas Carlton does be taking Hayes under he control. She does be finish here."

"Why she does be vex' wid yo'?" Pip poured a shot of rum into a glass and handed it to Ella. "Take dis fuh yuh feelin's."

Ella sniffed, accepting the rum and draining it quickly. "She does be a spoiled nigger! She don't

277

have no cause. She does be an evil influence on young Hayes. Ah done tell Mas Carlton fuh years Tita no good!" Ella looked around the kitchen defiantly.

"Lor', Pip." She remembered. "Miss Laura gon' want she sweetmeat an' sorrel dis morning." Ella hustled to prepare the tray. "Take dis fuh she, Pip, while ah does clean up dis mess."

In her boudoir at the front of the house, Laura lay on her bed, trying to read the small print of the novel she held in her hands, listening to the pounding of the rain on the roof. She found it hard to concentrate.

She climbed down from her bed and walked over to the window. The shutter was open. The roof of the gallery kept the rain from falling inside the boudoir. She leaned out. There were four women walking down the path toward the river, shrieking with laughter. She ignored them and scanned through the curtain of rain for some males.

As she watched, one darted across the yard in front of the house, the rain drenching his ebony body, his short trousers spattered with mud. His heels kicked splashes of rain onto his back. Laura followed the boy greedily with her eyes until he disappeared behind the stable. She sighed.

The sudden knocking on the door delighted her. She stepped swiftly across the room. It was Pip.

"Oh," Laura said with a leer. "Do come in."

"Miss Ella done send dis fuh yo'." Pearls of rain dappled Pip's bushy hair and streaked down his face. Laura eyed him eagerly as he placed the tray on her table.

He was dressed in breeches which fitted tightly

278

across his bottom. As he turned to go out, Laura's eyes fell on his bulging crotch. She felt a blush creeping up on her, sure he had seen her glance. Pip was in his twenties, a lithe and handsome boy with friendly eyes.

"A lot of rain today, Pip." Laura spoke quickly to stop him leaving the room. The red sash he wore around his waist accentuated the lean hardness of his body.

"Yas, Miss Laura. It does be de season."

"Oh, dear," she sighed. "The rain makes me feel so bored."

Pip wore his shirt open, exposing the masculine lines of his chest and the tiny curls of black hair around his nipples.

"What do you do when you are bored, Pip?" Laura's eyes strayed down his body.

"Ah does work, ma'am." Pip waited patiently by the door while his mistress sat on the edge of the bed. "Yo' does need anything, ma'am?"

Laura smiled wistfully at him. "Maybe, Pip, who knows?" She shrugged her shoulders, dismissing him. "Thank Ella for the sweetmeats."

When he closed the door, Laura flung herself across the bed, burying her face in her hands. "What can I do?" she thought. "Oh, what can I do?"

The rain finished as suddenly as it had begun. The sun seeped through the clouds and began to dry up the sodden plantation. Pools of water steamed in the yard as Laura stomped through the mud to the stables. She ignored the water which showered her from the leaves of the flamboyant

279

trees. She waited impatiently for Caliste to saddle her horse.

"Mas Caspar done ride out to de heights, Miss Laura."

Laura nodded and mounted her horse. She urged the animal to break into a trot, following the trail Caspar had taken. She felt free now that she was sprung from the confines of the rotting plantation house.

"Caspar," she thought, "is the only person of any intelligence in the whole of Roxborough, apart from Daddy. I cannot stay shut up in that house a moment longer!" She gritted her teeth with determination.

In front of her, guiding his horse carefully up a rough part of the trail where water was gushing down in a rivulet, was Caspar.

His shirt was soaked with perspiration and from the rain which splashed on him from the overhanging branches. His wet breeches were stuck to his thighs, his leather riding boots daubed with mud. He wore no hat, and his hair dripped with rain in the sunlight.

"Caspar!"

Caspar turned as Laura urged her horse up the trail toward him. He smiled. "She rides like Mas Carlton," he thought, noting her determined stance. She had secured her flowing hair under her bonnet and wore a cape over her dress.

"Is anything wrong?" He caught her horse's bridle in his hand when she rode up beside him.

"I'm damned sick of all this rain, that's what's wrong, Caspar! The house is so dull. Daddy is at his books, the slaves are preparing dinner, so what is there for me to do?"

"Needlework?" He grinned mischievously. "Read poetry? Engage in those ladylike pursuits you learned in Trinidad."

"Caspar, I could beat you!" She raised her whip with a chuckle of delight. "You see, you've cheered me up already. May I ride with you?"

"It is my pleasure." He dropped her bridle, spurring his horse out of the rivulet rushing around them.

"Where are you going?"

"There are some slaves clearing a new garden. Follow me with care, Laura. The rain has dislodged stones. Your horse may stumble."

Laura felt so good with the fresh air on her face. She wanted to speak, but Caspar's busy manner as he negotiated the trail deterred her. "Has he forgotten I am here?" she asked herself. She was piqued when he did not turn to see if she was still behind him. But suddenly he stopped.

He raised his finger to his lips, cautioning Laura with his eyes to stay silent. He grasped her bridle and urged the horses off the trail into the bush. Drops of rain flew about her, drenching Laura. She put her hand out to grip Caspar's, her eyes pleading to know what it was about. From his gentle smile she assumed they were in no danger.

She watched the trail patiently as he had indicated, almost unaware that her hand was still clasped in his.

After some minutes, a wiry Negro came trotting down the track, a log of wood balanced on his head. He was followed by another, also carrying wood. Laura counted ten slaves burdened with timber, scurrying and sliding in the mud. None

281

of them were roped or chained. The driver came last. His whip was furled under his arm, and he ran jauntily after his slaves. Caspar watched the procession without speaking.

"Why didn't you hail them?" Laura whispered after the driver had passed out of earshot.

"It wasn't necessary," he smiled. "You saw for yourself that they are working. I feared they may have been sheltering in the rain. Come." He released his hand from hers and led her horse out of their hiding place and back onto the trail. A clearing lay ahead of them.

"This is where we are laying out a new provision garden," he told her as he dismounted.

Laura gazed about her. Trees had been felled for a wide area in a spot where the land leveled out. Part of the garden was already cultivated. An *ajoupa* with thatched sides and a grass roof had been erected on the plot. Caspar walked over to it.

"What's in there?" Laura jumped off her horse and ran over to him. She held his arm as she peered through the doorway.

"Sometimes the slaves sleep here," explained Caspar, standing aside for Laura to walk in. "There's no one here now." He followed her. "Every one of them has gone down to the quarters." The door swung closed behind them.

Daylight filtered into the *ajoupa* through gaps in the *vetyver* thatching. There was a pleasant warmth inside after the splashing of the rain on them from the forest trees. The whistles and chattering of the birds seemed to emphasize their isolation.

"Oh!" said Laura, unlacing her bonnet and removing it, shaking out her hair over her shoulders. "This is pleasant."

"May I take your cape?" asked Caspar. "I can put it in the sun to dry."

Laura handed the cape and bonnet to him and sat down on a log which served as a stool. Caspar stepped outside, returning almost immediately, having shed his shirt, which he hung up to dry. The door closed behind him. He stood in front of Laura, his legs wide apart, wiping the back of his neck and face with a red bandana. Laura's eyes were level with his thighs.

She raised her head and gazed up at him. Caspar observed the fullness of her breasts under her tight-fitting bodice. Her pale throat was bare, her lips slightly open as she scrutinized him. She reached up and held his hand.

"Won't you sit here for a few minutes, Caspar?"

"That was my idea," he murmured. "I am watching you."

"And what do you see?" Laura tilted back her head as Caspar sat down on the ground beside her.

"I see a young woman," he said.

"A white woman, Caspar."

He frowned. "What do you see?" he demanded. "A black slave?"

"No." Laura reached out and ran her finger through the wet hairs on his chest. "I see a man. My half-brother. Do you mind me touching you?"

He gazed at her without speaking.

She circled her finger around his nipples with a sigh. His sudden laughter relieved the tension as she dived at him, running her hands playfully over his chest and under his arms. She tickled him. He fell backwards, wriggling to escape.

"I have you now, Caspar!"

"Stop!"

Laura was not to be deterred. She climbed on top of him, rubbing his naked chest, rolling on the ground with him as he tried to fend her off.

"You'll get your dress muddy," Caspar stuttered between giggles. He reached out to grab her.

"Laura!" he begged, grasping her firmly around her waist. "Laura!"

She stopped as he touched her. The hard hands which gripped her waist sent shivers through her body in spite of the warmth inside the shack. She was squatting on the ground face to face with him. She stared into his eyes in alarm. Her hands fell in front of her, resting on his arms.

She felt his fingers slowly released from her waist and his hands withdrawn from her body. The panic faded from her eyes, and she relaxed. She bent her head forward to rest on his naked shoulder.

Caspar's flesh tingled as Laura's lips brushed against the side of his neck. He winced. He grasped with his hands at the empty air behind her back, experiencing emotions soaring through him which he had not known since he had lain with Mary Gregg. He swallowed nervously.

"Laura!" he croaked, folding his arms loosely around her shoulders. "Are you sure?"

"I want you, Caspar. I'm not frightened now."

With a decisive tenderness, he drew her head away from his ear, placing his mouth over hers. She parted her lips in ecstasy, sucking on his tongue when it forced its way inside her. She clawed with her long nails into the hard muscles of his shoulder, clinging desperately to him.

284

"Caspar," she moaned as she lay with him on the mud floor of the shack and the rain began to fall again outside. "My brother!"

Chapter 26

LAURA GAZED AT THE MOON. IT HUNG ABOVE THE house like a pale sun, dominating a sky shattered with stars.

Laura was unable to sleep. It seemed that whenever she closed her eyes, the leonine features of Caspar floated into her mind. Her limbs ached from his presence in her body, her head reeled with the exhilaration she had discovered in his arms that morning.

She lowered her eyes, observing how the brightness of the moon illuminated the trail. The trail which led through the undergrowth to the overseer's cabin at the edge of the slaves' quarters. Laura smiled with determination.

Pausing only to wrap a cloak around her, she trod swiftly down the steps from the shuttered house. She moved soundlessly across the cobbles of the yard, gathering her nightdress above her ankles so it would not snag on the path. The formidable shadow of the house outlined against the moon glow was behind her. She reached the edge of the courtyard and plunged onto the trail to hasten as fast as she could to Caspar's cabin.

A hand seized her arms, clasping it firmly.

Laura gasped, clawing at the black hulk looming over her, blocking the path. "Who are you?" she demanded nervously. "Let me go."

"Maybe," said the voice. "After you tell me where you are running to at this hour."

"Caspar!" Laura cried with relief. "What are you doing here?" She fell forward as his arms encircled her tenderly.

"I was gazing at you, Laura."

They sank to the ground. Minutes, or was it hours, later, Laura stared up at the moon haloing Caspar's head. She put her trust in him, vowing to remain her brother's for always.

She nibbled the tiny lobe of his ear with pride.

Laura and Caspar recognized the need to be circumspect about their relationship as it developed during the blissful weeks which followed. They contrived to meet every day, whether it was in the forest when Caspar patrolled the plantation or in his cabin during the long afternoons after dinner when Carlton dozed on the veranda.

Laura tried to conceal her feelings toward Caspar when they were in the presence of others. However, it was impossible to hide from Carlton and Ella the changes which had come over her. Where before she was moody, she now sang brightly. Where she had been revolted by Carlton's obsession with fighting niggers, she now took an interest.

One morning, as she sat in her boudoir working on a sampler, a shout from below caused her to rush to the window. She had expected to see Caspar striding up the steps, but instead her gaze met the odd spectacle of Pip exercising the Yoruba. Pip had a long whip in his hand which he cracked down behind Bute's ankles to make the fighter run fast around the track marked out on the courtyard.

Laura watched in fascination, fearful lest Pip misjudge his distance and slice the whip into Bute's back. Pip was laughing.

Laura studied Bute's body as he trotted around the yard. He was much more of an animal than Caspar. His black torso was caked with dust and sweat, whereas Caspar's russet skin was always smooth and clean to her touch.

Bute's muscle-heavy limbs contrasted with Caspar's lean thighs, and his spreading nose and fat-lipped grin were a mockery beside Caspar's fine features. But, Laura noted idly, Bute surpassed Caspar in one respect. She was curious to know what difference that made to lovemaking.

She lifted her dress above her ankles and ran out of the boudoir, tripping carefully down the stone steps.

"Give me that!" she ordered Pip, holding her hand out for the whip.

Pip's laughter died. He handed the whip to Laura, frowning. "It does be a game we does be playin' to make Bute run more fast, Miss Laura."

"Fine, I like games," Laura smiled at Pip to reassure him. "Show me how to get the right swing so I don't belabor his back."

Pip stuck out his hand and moved his wrist up and down. "Yo' does flick de whip like dat."

Laura tried the same gesture but the long lash fell limply to the ground. "It doesn't crack," she moaned. "Stand behind me, Pip." She moved her body close in front of his.

"That's right," she said when he began to step back nervously. "Don't move. Now put your arm around me and hold my wrist and I'll hold the whip. Flick my hand the way I am to flick the wrist, so I will know."

With Pip close behind her, Laura did not know what was exciting her more. Was it the feel of Pip's taut body pressed against hers as he guided her whip-throwing, or the sight of Bute scampering clear in case she lashed him?

"Yo' does have it now, Miss Laura." Pip released her wrist and stood back rapidly, clasping the front of his breeches.

Laura tried again. The leather tongue of the whip uncoiled into the air and snapped over Bute's head. It cracked down, dusting Bute's ankles.

"You must run faster, boy!" Laura shouted, dancing with excitement.

Bute maintained his same pace. He had little experience of Miss Laura and was unable to judge her seriousness. He hoped that she was aware that the Bondmaster wanted him as a fighter and not as a whipping boy for his daughter. The whip cracked behind him again.

"Run, boy, run!"

Bute felt sweat trickling down his body. He wiped his brow with the back of his hand. The whip whistled over him, passing but a hair's breadth from his shoulders. He heaved.

"This is fun!"

Bute's black marble shoulder, rippling with muscles, was such a tempting target. Laura drew back her hand, aimed carefully, and brought down the whip with a snap.

"What a ripping circus! A fine black stallion

stepping high and the fairest ringmaster a chap ever did see."

A tall young man was standing at the corner of the house, removing his cape and shaking the rain from it. He pulled off his hat as Laura looked at him in astonishment. Bute, too, stopped running and regarded this white stranger with interest.

"Forgive me for arriving unannounced. I have no horse, so I walked up."

Laura recovered her poise, panting to regain her breath as well. She handed the whip to Pip and glanced around. There was no one else in sight. She scrutinized the stranger closely. He was fashionably dressed and had a pleasant face.

"You're wet!" she observed.

"Indeed I am. The rain caught me as I was walking from the ship." The man stopped shaking his cape and smiled at Laura.

"You must remove your clothes."

"What an appropriate suggestion." The man chuckled. "But I have no others here. They are still on the ship."

"You could borrow something of Daddy's."

Laura was sorry that her friends from Mrs. Micot's could not see this apparition. The man sported a black mustache with the ends waxed to points. His eyes, Laura saw as she moved towards him, were blue.

"It is not often we have strangers arriving without an escort or a messenger to bring news in advance. But you are nonetheless welcome for that."

"Enchanting," he said. "I had anticipated life would be different from England, but I must admit that I had not considered that I would be received with an entertainment of a tropical circus, instructed to remove my clothes, and then told I am welcome for being a stranger.

"I have come as the guest of the Bondmaster himself. Is that august gentleman at home?" The man looked up at the house.

"He is not," said Laura. "He is inspecting the slaves. I am his daughter. If you will tell me your business, perhaps I can be of assistance."

"Business?" The man offered Laura his arm as they strolled toward the steps. "My business is purely the pursuit of pleasure, or impurely, if you wish.

"I have not seen your father for some three years —since when he was cutting an impressive swathe through the London salons with his talk of life in the tropics. If you, my dear, are one of the rewards of such a life, he neglected to do you justice."

Laura laughed the way Mrs. Micot had taught her. "You flatter me, sir!" She walked with the stranger up the steps. At the top she paused, wondering if it was ladylike to tell a slave what to do in company.

"Pip," she called. "Come. See that Bute continues his training."

"Is he to be an athlete or a dray horse, your Bute?"

"Oh, he's not mine." Laura giggled. "He is Daddy's. He wants him to be a fighter. We were just playing a game when you arrived."

"Then I hope, ma'am, that you and I never have recourse to amuse ourselves by such frolics. I do not canter very well. The brute Bute, though, looks an exceptionally well-built black chappie." The man glanced at Bute now doing press-ups on the ground below the steps.

"Do you know anything about Negroes, sir?" Laura wanted to make the stranger feel welcome.

"Pip," she said as the slave appeared at her side when they entered the drawing room, "a pitcher of sangaree at once."

"I know they are black of visage and heart. Is there anything else to know?"

"Daddy can tell you that." Laura indicated a chair for the visitor. He remained standing, holding on to his cape and hat.

"How remiss of me," said Laura. "Harodine!" she called. The maid put her head around the boudoir door.

"Come quickly, girl, and take the gentleman's cape and hat. Give them to Ella and ask her to dry them at once, please."

The man handed his things to Harodine and waited for Laura to be seated before he took the chair opposite her. "It is a privilege to be entertained by one so solicitous as yourself."

"I love to hear you talk," Laura tittered politely. "You speak just like an English gentleman."

"I flatter myself in thinking I am. It appears your good father is not around to introduce us. I am the Earl of Philbert."

Chapter 27

THE EARL OF PHILBERT LIKED ROXBOROUGH. HE rose late every morning. If the weather was fine, he rode around the plantation with Caspar. If it was inclement, he, Laura, and Hayes passed the morning in the school cabin where Philbert good-humoredly endeavored to improve Hayes's English. After dinner with Carlton, Laura, and Hayes, the Earl liked to nod on the balcony in the dead of the afternoon. The evening was the time for the Earl to sit with Carlton on the gallery, attended by Pip with the rum decanter.

"It's such a pleasant life you have here, Carlton!" Philbert emulated his host by drawing his chair up to the railing of the gallery and elevating his feet into the air upon the highest rail.

"I cannot share your interest in slave blood, Carlton," he drawled. "Blackies make tolerable servants, but give me an English butler any day." Philbert twisted the end of his mustache.

Carlton chuckled. "Do you think an English butler would stay two days here? If he could endure the heat, he would remove himself to Roseau and open an emporium with slaves of his own. I tell you, Philbert, you cannot find better than a good slave, providing he is tractable and remembers his work. If he doesn't, then you beat him."

"Ho! Ho! A wife's not much different."

It was the first time during the three weeks that Philbert had been at Roxborough that the opportunity had arisen to discuss marriage. Carlton seized on it immediately.

"One would expect a good wife to bring more to the home than an uncultured and impoverished nigger."

"Indeed, indeed. But if such a wife were to upset her husband in some way, shouldn't she taste the force of his palm on her *derrière?*"

"Of course," said Carlton, smiling. "Are English ladies inclined to irritate their husbands, Philbert? A creole wife would never do such a thing."

"You seem to hint that a creole wife is to be recommended?" Philbert brought his legs down from the railing and shifted in his seat to look at his host before continuing.

"Were such a wife who has the fairness of an English damsel, the credentials of a dignified ancestry, and the support of an ample dowry to be found in these Caribbee islands, Carlton, it might be a proposition that even an English nobleman such as myself would entertain." Philbert twiddled his mustache pompously. "She must be chaste, of course."

"I believe such young ladies exist." Carlton leaned toward Philbert and poured another measure of rum into his glass.

"They are not in abundance, you understand. In fact, they are rather rare flowers. A gentleman, even a nobleman such as yourself, would be fortunate to be able to pluck such a rare bloom. One such as my daughter, Laura, for instance." Carlton sat back in his chair to judge the effect his words had on Philbert.

The Earl scarcely faltered as he raised his glass. He contemplated the amber liquid, bathed in flickering gold from the lantern swinging at the corner post of the veranda.

"That seems to be a proposition on which reasonable men such as ourselves could discourse." He gulped down the rum. "Damn it all, Carlton. I think it's a capital idea!"

"My dear Sister," wrote Philbert when he retired to his room later that evening, "I am to be married. At last! You may exclaim, but when you meet my bride, I know you will agree with me that the years of searching have been worth the while."

He paused as he scratched the words onto the page and looked around the cheerless guestroom for inspiration.

"My bride to be is Miss Laura Todd, a young lady of distinguished parentage and immense wealth. In addition to this latter and most important consideration, she is blond and attractive, if a little high-spirited.

"When I arrived here, she was whipping a blacka-moor as 'sport.' Fear not, dear sister, my choice is wise, for she is doing no more than following the traditions of this curious place."

Philbert stroked his mustache, wondering how much he could write without offending the sensibility of his sister in England.

"This is a slave plantation," he scrawled. "Some plantations raise sugar, others coffee, but Roxborough concentrates on the production of slaves. These slaves are not the oppressed creatures of whom you have heard from Mr. Wilberforce, but simple folk leading a carefree existence.

"They have no great matters to boast nor, considering their habits, is much required. They live in cabins made of mud and thatched with palm. For a bedstead they have a platform of boards, and the bed is a mat covered with a blanket.

"A small table, two or three low stools, an earthen jar for holding water, a few smaller ones, a pail, an iron pot, calabashes of different sizes serving very tolerably for plates, dishes and bowls, make up the rest of their furniture."

Again Philbert paused and his eyes wandered around the room. "So much for the slaves," he continued, "who are wonderfully cared for by mine host, the Bondmaster, Carlton Todd. His own house, where I am now writing this, has the massive furniture so esteemed by creoles.

"In this room there is an ancient family four-poster with heavy, handsomely turned pillars as well as a ponderous mahogany wardrobe. There are some costly Chippendale furniture, mirrors, and china which were sent out by the West Indiamen. There is a fine clock by Thwaites and Reed of Clerkenwell.

"We dine heartily each day and the mahogany table of the Bondmaster fairly groans with costly plate and native delicacies prepared by a sable *cuisinière*. Todd, my bride-to-be, and I are joined at table by Todd's son, a little tyrant by the name of Hayes who speaks the creole dialect with an accent indistinguishable from that of his slave companions.

"Indeed, everywhere one turns, there are slaves, and were it not for the breezes which blow in from the surrounding hills, their odor, which pervades the plantation, would be overpowering.

"Laura, my betrothed, I hasten to assure you, is not of this. A purer, prettier, and richer maiden would be hard to find. She has been schooled in Trinidad and hence has the manners and graces befitting a young lady. She is witty and intelligent, and I know you will adore her.

"Before agreeing to come out here, I commissioned an investigation of the finances of my host and I can assure you that once I am wed, there will be a veritable fortune at our disposal."

Philbert continued his letter with some instructions on family matters before concluding. "Tomorrow I am to be treated to a display of fisticuffs, Negro version. Todd has a young blackamoor whom he fancies as a fighter, and an exhibition has been arranged for me. I shall pretend to enjoy it, for the sake of my father-in-law and his fortune. As soon as I am married and have secured the treasury, dear sister, we shall sail for Bristol."

Laura raised her head from her sampler and listened carefully. There was a faint rap on the door. She leaped up from her chair and fairly flew across the floor. Surely it was Caspar? When she flung open the door, her smile vanished and she gasped in surprise. "Why, Father! I did not expect to see you."

"Apparently not, Laura. I am sorry to disturb you. I knocked softly in case you were already sleeping. May I come in?"

"Of course."

Laura stood aside while Carlton entered. She shut the door behind him, her brain racing. "Is anything wrong, Daddy?"

"No, my dear. Far from it." He bent down and picked up the sampler which had fallen to the floor. He glanced at it before handing it to her and sitting down in her chair. Laura, still mystified, stood by her bed.

"Laura, it's all arranged!"

"What is?"

"The Earl of Philbert has agreed to marry you."

Laura clasped the bedpost, blood draining from her cheek. She stared at her father.

"Come now, daughter. Your display of modesty is touching. A kiss of congratulation for the excellent terms I have arranged might be more appropriate, what?" He extended his arms toward her.

Laura shrank away. "Marry me?" she whispered.

"Why, of course, Laura. Devil of a job it was to get him to agree, too! I thought you'd be more grateful!" Carlton sank back in his chair eyeing Laura reproachfully.

"I don't want to marry him." Laura's voice was shaky but, having spoken, she found her confidence returning. She held the bedpost and drew herself up to her full height, raising her head.

"I don't want to marry the Earl of Philbert, Daddy!"

"Oh, I see!" Carlton snorted. "You want him to woo you, do you? You want to be a reluctant bride, blushing prettily as you walk up the aisle? I understand, Laura, but we have to be practical." Carlton leaned forward in his chair.

"It's cost a lot of money to bring the Earl here. He's a damn good catch. It means you'll be a Lady

298

and your son will be a Lord. Imagine, the grandson of Carlton Todd, an English Lord!" he chortled.

"We must snap him up, Laura, while he's warm! There's no time for your romantic tomfoolery. He'll propose tomorrow. You can swoon then if you will. Afterwards, it's a hasty wedding and off you go to his estates in England."

Laura was silent as Carlton finished speaking. Her thoughts were on Caspar and the tender way he clasped her as they embraced and the gentle words of endearment he breathed into her ear. He had never needed persuasion to love her.

"I am not marrying the Earl of Philbert, Daddy." Laura sat down defiantly on the edge of her bed. "You must believe me!"

"Now, now, now, daughter! You are distressed. I see I surprised you. It's my fault. I thought you were prepared for this news. Sleep on it, Laura. In the morning you will be begging me to expedite matters. Dream of a husband, Laura." Carlton rose from his chair, walking over to the bed to kiss Laura's cheek.

She moved out of his grasp. "No, Daddy! I know my own mind. I am not a slave wench you can mate with whomsoever you choose. The Earl will not be my husband. If he asks me, I shall refuse."

Carlton's hand twitched. He wanted to strike Laura across her face to stop this nonsense.

"You shall refuse, Laura? What right have you to refuse? You are my virgin daughter, Laura, not a slave wench. You are not being mated at my choice. I am doing my duty to you as your father in finding an acceptable suitor for your hand.

"You will oblige me by accepting the Earl with alacrity. I want to hear no more of your contrariness." Carlton shook his finger in Laura's face, then spun around on his heels.

"Did you say virgin daughter, Daddy?" Laura asked breathlessly.

Carlton stopped, snorting with annoyance. "I did. You are. The Earl, like all gentlemen, was emphatic about his prospective bride's chastity.

"Thank God, I was able to tell him truthfully that you are as chaste as the day you were born!" Carlton stepped out of the bedroom and slammed the door shut behind him.

Laura fell back on her bed with a groan, covering her eyes with her hand. "What a predicament!" she thought. "The Earl wants a virgin and he wants me. I am not a virgin and I don't want the Earl."

She rolled over on the bed, grappling with her thoughts. If she told her father she was not a virgin, he would want to know who had deflowered her. If she told him the truth, then Caspar would surely be put to death. She shuddered.

Laura could not bear the thought of anything happening to her Caspar. And she was certainly not going to be married to some white English ninny without an ounce of spunk in his pantaloons!

Laura spent a night of anguish, beating at her brains to find some way to resolve this terrible situation. She longed to rush through the plantation to Caspar's cabin and seek refuge in his arms. Mercifully, exhaustion overtook her as daybreak began to spread over the hills. She sank into sleep, awaking much later with a grim smile on her face as a solution slipped into her mind.

Ella was anointing Bute's body with snake oil when Philbert descended the front steps. Bute stood naked while she slapped on the grease and rubbed it into his skin. Carlton supervised the process carefully.

"Do the buttocks well, Ella," he urged. "There's flesh there that provides a hold. The oil will make him slippery and harden the skin."

Carlton raised his head when he heard Philbert's cough. The Earl was holding his hand to his nose.

"Don't mind the aroma, Philbert. That's the scent of money. This boy Bute is going to make me a fortune. See." Carlton touched the boy's arms. "Flex your muscles, boy."

Bute needed no encouragement. He assumed postures in rapid succession in the form of a native dance.

"I taught him those poses," boasted Carlton. "When I take him to Roseau, he will do that in the market square for everyone to see. Then I'll invite challengers. When I've finished training this nigger, there will not be a fighter in this island who can beat him!"

Laura, spying on the scene from the gallery, was intrigued. She knew Bute was being stabled in the barracoon away from the wenches. The Bondmaster claimed a wench would drain his fighting strength.

Her projected husband-to-be, noted Laura, was standing on the step with his handkerchief to his nose. He is doubtless a gentleman, she mused with a giggle, but could he compare with Bute inch for inch? Would such a man be able to quell the riotous passions which bedeviled her?

"Caspar!" yelled Carlton. "Where's your challenger?"

Caspar hurried from the side of the house where

he had been administering tips to Homer, the slave he had selected for the fight.

"He is ready. Are you?" he demanded mockingly.

"You will not see a fair exhibition, Philbert," said Carlton, sauntering toward the steps. "Bute here is my prize nigger. You can see he is in perfect condition. As soon as he has won some fights, I'm going to breed from him. He looks like a breeder, doesn't he?"

Philbert shrugged his shoulders.

"Caspar's picked out a field hand for this bout," continued Carlton, blind to Philbert's lack of enthusiasm. "You must not expect much style because his buck is untrained. It will doubtless be over very quickly.

"Just as well, perhaps," Carlton concluded, gazing at the clouds swirling over the mountains at the other side of the river.

"Rain is bound to fall this morning."

Caspar led Homer into the center of the yard which had been selected as the arena. The ground was muddy from the rains of the past few weeks, but it was firm enough for the fighters. Carlton conducted Bute to the center to stand by Homer.

From the gallery, Laura compared them. Homer was taller than Bute, and not so well-endowed. He was not so handsome, either, she decided. He was watching the Bondmaster nervously.

Tita glided onto the balcony beside Laura. She sucked air through her teeth, exclaiming, "Dat nigger don't have de spirit. See he eyes, dey scared de Bon'massa. De other be more proud."

"The other is well-built, isn't he?" Laura purred.

Tita gave Laura a knowing look. "He does have plenty, Miss Laura." She winked.

Laura blushed. She turned back to watch the fight with interest. Carlton and the Earl sat on chairs placed for them by Pip. The two combatants were circling each other cautiously. Caspar danced around with them. Laura smiled at him affectionately.

"Go on, Bute!" yelled Carlton. "Don't wait for him, attack!"

Bute lunged for Homer's chest, but Homer was ready for him and deflected the blow calmly. Bute lunged again, and again Homer was able to defend himself.

Homer was feeling less nervous now and, as he circled around with Bute, he closed the gap and slammed his fists into Bute's stomach. Unprepared for such an attack, Bute staggered back. Homer rushed with a right fist straight to his jaw, but Bute deflected it and brought his leg up to kick Homer in the crotch. Homer grabbed the foot quickly and twisted it, throwing Bute off balance.

Carlton and Philbert cheered. "I'm backing that field nigger," said Philbert. "Twenty guineas he'll win!"

"Agreed," snapped Carlton happily. "Where Caspar found the bugger, I don't know. He's got guile, but he cannot beat Bute."

Laura watched anxiously as the two slaves tumbled on top of each other. She grasped Tita. "Do you think Bute is hurt?"

"Hurt! Of co'se not, miss. Yo' like Bute?" Tita squeezed Laura's hand.

"He might be pleasing." Laura hardly dared to speak, she was so nervous about the plan she had in her mind.

"Some *beké* ladies does like niggers, Miss Laura." Tita crooned. "Dey does be de best dere does be."

"So I have heard, Tita." Laura could not stop her blushes. "I am to be married soon, Tita. I will never know."

"Oh, Miss Laura! It does be easy fuh yo'. If yo' does want . . .?" Tita glanced cautiously at her mistress, wondering if she had already gone too far.

"Whatever do you mean?" Laura clasped her bosom anxiously. Tita was playing into her hands.

"De boy Bute, Miss Laura. Ah can tell he come to yo' any time." She winked.

Laura's heart thumped, excited by the idea as much as by the way her plan was working. "Not here in the house?" she said aghast.

"In de school cabin. Tell me when yo' does want he dere an' Tita gon' arrange it fuh yo'."

Laura clutched Tita's hand at a cry of pain from one of the fighters. Homer broke away from Bute's hold and crouched low waiting for Bute to attack him. His face was streaming with sweat. Now his nervousness had vanished, and his eyes blazed with hatred.

A wave of cold air enveloped the fighters and, as Carlton and Philbert scurried for shelter under the gallery, the rain roared down.

"Keep on with the fight!" screamed Carlton above the noise of the rain pounding the house.

He need not have spoken. Caspar, as engrossed as the two fighters, was circling with them, his silk shirt already drenched, and his trousers sticking to his legs.

Water poured off the skins of the two as they clinched again. Homer slipped and dragged Bute down on top of him. They rolled over and over in the wet mud. The rain blinded them and made

304

their bodies so slippery they were unable to grip each other.

"Squeeze his bollocks," yelled Philbert, dancing with excitement under the gallery.

"He won't know what you mean," Carlton said with a chuckle.

Bute tried to get a firm footing, and was about to lift Homer off the ground, when he slipped and fell backwards with Homer on top of him. Homer pounded Bute's chest with his fist, mud splattering all around them.

Bute slithered out from under Homer, kicking him in the jaw with his knee. There was a crunch, Homer struck out blindly and grabbed Bute's prick. He pulled. Laura squealed.

"No, dammit!" cried Carlton. "Don't maim the boy! Stop the fight, Caspar!"

Caspar grinned and clapped Homer on his shoulder to make him stop. Homer looked backwards in surprise only to reel as Bute swiped at his jaw. He clutched Caspar for support, and the three of them toppled into the mud. Laura screamed louder.

Philbert crowed with laughter, smacking Carlton on the back. "What a damn good fight! You've not won, old chappie, and neither have I. Splendid sport!"

Carlton growled his disappointment. "Pah! Leave them to it. Let's go for a punch, and you can propose to my daughter."

Chapter 28

BUTE FOLLOWED TITA AS SHE HURRIED IN THE dark up the path to the house. She had summoned him from the barracoon as he was lying on his mat trying to sleep. He grabbed her by the elbow. "Who done send fuh me, wench?" he demanded.

"Shh!" Tita flicked her elbow away from his grip. "Don't touch me, nigger! Yo' does talk too much. De night has jumbies who does hear all yo' does say."

He stopped in the middle of the path. "Ah not coming wid yo' 'less yo' does say why."

"Yo' does be a *zayzay*, Bute!" hissed Tita crossly. "Is Miss Laura done send fuh yo'."

"Miss Laura!" Bute uttered the words in awe. "Miss Laura!"

He followed Tita without further protest. He had seen Miss Laura standing with Tita watching him that same morning from the balcony when he fought Homer. He thought of her all the time. Under his sleeping mat he had a plantain leaf sachet containing an amulet fashioned out of a lock of her hair and parings from her fingernails, which her maid Harodine had collected for him. He had worshiped

306

Miss Laura since the day he saw her with the Bondmaster in Trinidad.

"Is true?" he asked Tita, clutching at her elbow again.

"Boy! Yo' does make me vex'. Hush, now! Yo' don't want Caspar to discover yo' does be out de barracoon.

Tita hastened up the path, urging Bute to keep in the darkness of the trees so they would not be seen in the moonlight. She skirted around the paddock and along the side path to the school cabin. Outside the door she stopped.

"Yo' must go in dere an' wait," she whispered. "Don't show any light at all. Miss Laura does be in she boudoir. Ah gon' tell she yo' does be here."

"Tita, what she does want me fuh?" Bute felt a nervousness gripping his stomach. He could not believe this was really happening.

"Yo' great bozal!" Tita hissed. "Ah thought yo' niggers from Trinidad does be smart!"

Suddenly Tita was gone, swallowed up by the night. Bute peered around him, shuddered, and groped his way up the steps to open the door to the cabin. He slipped in, closing the door gently behind him. He paused, listening. His nose took in the aroma of dampness. He was alone in the cabin. He sank quietly to the floor to squat on his haunches while he waited.

Tita tapped on the balcony door of Laura's chamber. Harodine opened the door, and Tita slipped into the tiny dressing room. "She does be in dere?" Tita indicated Laura's boudoir with a nod of her head.

"Yes." Harodine sniffed suspiciously.

Tita opened the bedroom door and slithered into

307

the room. Laura was lying face down on the bed.

"Miss Laura," Tita said softly.

"Oh! I didn't hear you knock, Tita." Laura stood up, trying to control the trembling she felt in her legs.

"He does be dere, Miss Laura!"

"Did any one see you?"

"No one, ma'am. He does be axing about yo', Miss Laura. It does seem he have a strong desire fuh yo'." Tita cackled.

Laura froze, her lips stretched in a sneer of distaste. She tried to concentrate her mind on Caspar. Yet she knew she was intrigued by the forthcoming encounter with Bute. She prayed that everything would work out according to her plan.

"Where is he?" She felt her heart racing as she recalled Bute's naked body bespattered with mud and locked in a clinch with Homer that very morning.

"In de school cabin. Ah does take yo' dere. We go through de back door and down de front steps while de *zayzay* Earl an' de Bon'massa does be drinking deir rum."

"Oh, Tita," whimpered Laura as they hurried through the darkness across the yard to the cabin. "I don't know what to say to him."

"Don's say nothing," Tita counseled. "Jus' hold he."

Laura hesitated at the front of the cabin steps. She was a mass of nerves. Urged by Tita, she trod the steps in a daze, her hand trembling. She touched the door and it swung open.

"Who dat?" Bute's deep voice startled her. She wanted to run down the steps and into her Caspar's arms.

"Who dat?" the voice asked again, softer now. "Bute?"

"Yas, Miss Laura?" Bute stood up in the center of the room, his flesh tingling.

"I can't see you."

"Ah does be here, Miss Laura." Bute put out his arms to guide Laura. His hand connected with her shoulder. She fell forward as he gripped her with his strong arms.

Her cheek nestled in the crook of his neck. She sniffed the strong odor of his body, so different from the clean scent of Caspar. She pulled her face away in disgust.

Bute clutched her body, frightened by her closeness and yet unable to release her. Laura held her hands stiffly by her sides. Bute guided her hastily to the back room and pulled her down onto the bed with him.

Suddenly, as though wanting to be done with it quickly, Laura became the aggressor. She ran her hands rapidly down Bute's body and seized him with a gasp of amazement. She hitched up her dress and forced Bute's head down to her. She arched and strained as he caressed her. Pulling his head up, she locked her legs around his waist and urged him to enter her.

He began to take her with the long slow thrusts of a vicious animal, heedless of her cries.

Caspar halted when he heard the noise. Harodine had told him that Laura was waiting to see him in the school cabin. He was puzzled. He listened again. It was a female's cry. He sensed that it came from the cabin and moved swiftly over to it. He put his eye to the hole in the board at

309

the back. The cabin was swaying with the thrash and vigor of a couple rutting.

Caspar ran back across the yard and up the house steps. Carlton and the Earl were sipping sangaree on the gallery.

"Come quickly, sir." he panted. "Bring your pistol. There's a buck wenching in the school cabin."

"A buck wenching, Caspar. Isn't that all they ever do?" Carlton leaned back in his chair, about to put his feet up.

"In the school cabin? Surely you're not going to allow that." Caspar sounded shocked.

"You're right, dammit!" Carlton sat up. "These niggers are taking too much advantage these days. They feel that they own the whole dam' plantation and can mount their fillies where they please." He stood up, turning to the Earl.

"Coming for a bit of sport, Philbert?"

"Why, yes, what will you do?"

"Tie the pair of them together and whip them around the quarters, I shouldn't wonder."

Carlton took up his pistol from his bedroom. Caspar carried his cutlass and a short whip. He held a lantern with a low flame.

"We must hurry to catch them."

The trio set off down the steps, watched by Tita, who had been an unwitting participant to Laura's plan. She shrugged her shoulders as she stroked Hayes's hair.

"Where's Daddy going?" the boy whined. "Why he don't take me?"

"Yuh daddy gon' see a truth, Hayes." Tita cackled.

Through the trees, Tita saw when the lantern

310

Caspar carried stopped weaving in the dark. There was silence. Tita imagined that Carlton and the Earl would be listening with their ears tightly pressed to the side of the cabin. Carlton would be growing agitated as the sighs and grunts grew to a climax. Tita sighed, although she shed no tear for Laura's behavior.

"I wish I could witness the dam' thing in daylight," hissed Philbert. He stood beside Carlton just as Tita had imagined.

"There must be two jackasses in there judging by the noise they are making!" he sniggered. "I could never poke a blackamoor, Carlton, but I do declare the heat they are generating is stirring my own loins!"

Carlton snorted angrily. "Open the door, Caspar. Let's see who the black wretches are who want the comfort of a bed for their rutting."

He aimed his pistol into the air and fired. The crack roused the birds in the trees around the house, set dogs barking, and doors at the house banging. Carlton blinked. He had heard a voice he recognized before the cacophony of the disturbed night spilled around him.

Caspar yanked open the door and rushed into the cabin, his lantern held high and his cutlass ready to chop.

"Caspar?" Carlton called from the doorway. He was worried by the abrupt silence. "Who we caught?"

He groped his way through the cabin, followed by Philbert. "Who is it, eh?" He poked his head around the partition, jostling Caspar out of the way so that he could see for himself.

Laura lay on the plantain-leaf mattress, her eyes

311

closed, a tremor of a smile on her lips. Her white legs were stretched wide open. Bute, his eyes glazed with terror, lay at her side.

Carlton pitched forward and vomited over them.

The Earl of Philbert took in the scene, shaking his head sadly. "Oh, dear!" he said. "Such a waste."

Caspar scooped up Laura and carried her brusquely in his arms across the darkened yard to the house.

"He raped me, Caspar," scolded Laura. "You came too late!"

Ella was waiting for him at the front steps. Together they carried Laura up to her bedroom and laid her out on the bed. In her confused state, Laura barely knew what was happening. She smiled at Caspar and Ella. Harodine came rushing into the room.

"Stay out of this!" warned Caspar when he saw her. "Wait down in the kitchen." Harodine backed out of the room reluctantly.

Ella eyed Caspar with a frown. "Laura does be a'right, Caspar. Let she sleep."

"Stay with her, Ella. That's a strange kind of rape. Harodine said Laura sent for me. Harodine knows something about this."

"Caspar!" Ella's voice stopped him as he was about to leave the room.

"Yes?"

"Dat was be rape, Caspar!" She glared at him with such intensity he was forced to listen to her. "Fuh de Bon'massa, fuh Laura, fuh de sake of Roxbruh, dat was rape, Caspar."

Caspar's mouth tightened. He glanced at Laura, who was beginning to shiver with shock. He nodded his head slowly, wondering.

He ran out of the house and across the yard back to the cabin. "What are you doing here, Sam?" he demanded suspiciously.

"Mas Carlton done send me fuh de chains."

Caspar entered the cabin. Bute was cowering on the floor in the corner of the bedroom. He was whimpering. Carlton stood over him with his pistol at his head. Philbert was still shaking his head in amazement.

Bute opened his mouth to utter a plea to Caspar but was cut short as Carlton clouted him around his ear with the pistol. No one spoke. The lantern flickered, throwing grotesque shadows of the naked Bute on the walls of the cabin.

When Samboth brought the shackles, he helped Caspar to chain Bute by his ankles and wrists. Caspar's rage was building up within him as he listened to Bute's whimpering. He forced him to walk to the stone cell near the nursery. Several times Bute tried to protest his innocence, but each time either Carlton or Caspar silenced him with a blow.

Pip, who had hurried down from the house with a key, opened the heavy door to the small jail. It was many months since the cell had been opened. There were scurrying sounds as lizards and rats were disturbed. Bute was thrust into the black depths of the cell and the door slammed shut. He began to yell.

Carlton did not speak until he reached the house and had climbed the steps and sat down on the gallery. Caspar handed him the decanter of rum and a glass without a word. Carlton poured a half-gill and handed the decanter back to Caspar, who served himself with a similar measure. The two men stared at each other before gulping down the rum. Carlton tried to read the expression in Caspar's eyes. He sighed suddenly.

"Why, Caspar, why?"

Caspar scowled. He dared not let Carlton know that his anger was for different reasons from Carlton's. Jealousy gripped Caspar. He passed the decanter quickly to Philbert.

"Grisly business, what, Carlton!"

"The marriage is off?" Carlton stared out into the night as he spoke, his voice heavy with disappointment.

"I'm astonished that you ask, Carlton. No dowry of slave money could let a chap overlook that his bride was not a virgin!"

"It was rape, you know." Carlton's voice was insistent. He turned to Caspar. "That's what it was! Rape!"

"Yes, that's what Laura said." It was Caspar's turn to stare into the night.

"Rape or romancing, old chap, it makes no difference to me. Laura has been sullied. And by a blackamoor, too!" Philbert toyed with the end of his mustache. "What are you going to do with him, Carlton?"

Again, Carlton sighed, leaning forward to rest his head on his hand. "Rape is a capital offense. We have our own law here, Philbert. The Governor's law takes too much time, too much talk. Same thing in the end. Death. We'll deal with the nigger in the morning, first light."

Philbert excused himself, bade Carlton good night, and strode off to his room. Carlton sank back into his chair.

Caspar slipped away around the balcony to

Laura's room. Quietly, he opened the door to the dressing room just as Ella crept out of the bedroom. Laura raised her head when he walked in.

"Thank God you've come, Caspar!" Laura seemed to have recovered from the ordeal. She sat up in bed, her dress falling open to reveal the creamy whiteness of her bosom. She held out her hand for him.

Caspar ignored her. He leaned against the bedpost and eyed her with suspicion. "Why did you send Harodine to call me, Laura?" he demanded.

"Oh, Caspar," she chided with a sweet smile. "Not a word of concern for what happened to me? If you had not taken so long, Bute would never have got so far."

"No? What was he doing in the cabin, anyway?"

"Raping me."

"Dam' you, Laura!" Caspar slapped the bedpost with the palm of his hand. "You let that Trinidad nigger touch you, Laura. I'll kill him! I should kill you, too!"

Laura was shocked. "You are the one to blame, Caspar. You came too late."

"I came when Harodine said you were waiting."

"Don't you understand!" Laura sniffed. "I wanted Daddy to find me with Bute so he would see I'm not a virgin and wouldn't make me marry that odious Earl. Then I could stay here with you. How could I tell Daddy that you took my maidenhead, Caspar? I wanted him to think that Bute raped me," She sighed. "I didn't know you would take so long to rescue me!"

"You've broken Mas Carlton's heart, you know that?"

"Daddy? He doesn't care about me. He thinks

315

I'm one of his slaves. It is not my fault Bute actually did rape me, is it?" she snapped.

Caspar was silent.

"My God, Caspar!" Laura looked at him with disbelief. "What do you think I am, some kind of nigger's whore?"

He slapped the bedpost again. "I don't know what to think, Laura. I only remember those sighs I heard as I stood outside the cabin and the smile I saw on your face when Bute was mounting you."

"I smiled when I saw you, Caspar. If I resisted Bute, he would have killed me. He killed a champion Mandingo in Trinidad."

Caspar was silent again.

"If you loved me, you would be giving me your sympathy instead of quizzing me like this." Laura glared at him. "You think I'm a whore, don't you, Caspar?" Her eyes flashed angrily. "Well, you'll see! You'll see!"

Laura threw her pillow at his head as Caspar turned his back and walked sadly from the room.

Chapter 29

ELLA WAS ON THE GALLERY CONFERRING WITH Carlton. She spoke in a low voice, her lips close to his ear. He was slumped in his chair. There was a hush as they heard Caspar leave Laura's bedroom and tread across the creaking floorboards of the drawing room. Ella waited until Caspar passed through the dining room and down the back steps before she continued.

"Laura done say Bute done lure she to de cabin."

"I know, I know," Carlton replied listlessly. Like Caspar, he wondered if he could ever erase from his mind the smile of ecstasy he had seen on Laura's face.

"She's like her mother!" His voice croaked. "It was Caspar who showed me her mother being mounted by a slave. I thought I had purged that terrible night from my mind, Ella. Now it has happened again. With my own daughter!"

Carlton rested his face in the fold of Ella's dress as she stood beside his chair. She ran her long black fingers through his gray-gold locks.

"If only she could have waited until after Philbert had married her!" he grumbled.

Carlton spent the night on the gallery, racked with doubt. Ella tried to console him, carrying soursop tea for him to drink so he could sleep and calm his thoughts. But he stared sleeplessly at the night as it changed slowly from its evil darkness to the mysterious dark blue of the pre-dawn. The mountains which seemed to have entombed him in a cavern of perpetual blackness were haloed with light as dawn broke. Chattering birds took over the bush chorus, and the sounds of the crickets, crack-cracks, and *crapauds* faded away.

Carlton's face was haggard as he rose unsteadily to his feet. He clutched the balcony rail and peered out through the gray dawn at the plantation.

"Caspar," he called wearily. "Caspar!"

In the kitchen where he had spent the night dozing fitfully on a bench, Caspar heard the Bondmaster's call. He sipped at the dish of coffee Ella handed him, feeling the warm liquid put determination into his body. He ached after the restless night. Samboth was at his side.

"Mas Carlton does be callin' yo'."

"I hear, Sam. He'll be vexed if I don't come, won't he, boy?" Caspar continued to sip at his coffee. "What do you think he will do, Ella?"

"He done wid de brooding now, Caspar. He done make he decision. Ah gon' be sorry about Bute, though." Ella's eyes rolled upwards.

"What about Laura? Are you not sorry for her?" Caspar drained his coffee and put down the dish.

"Laura?" Ella shrugged her shoulders. "She done get what she ax fuh! She like she mam befoh she. De buckra women dey like de nigger prick too much."

"They like our bodies, Ella. Not our brains."

318

"Brains? Niggers ain't got brains, Caspar. Slaves like we have nothing in we heads, yo' does know dat!" Ella smiled grimly. "Take dis coffee up de stairs before Carlton does string yo' up wid Bute!"

Carlton glowered when Caspar handed him the dish. Not speaking, he sipped morosely at the coffee. He motioned to Caspar to pass the rum bottle, tipped most of its contents into the coffee dish, and sipped again. He felt himself coming to life. He stood up and stretched his arms wide above his head, shrugging off the misery of the night.

"I'm not interested in how it happened last night, Caspar. I know what Bute was doing. So do you. So does the Earl of Philbert, which is more important. I don't want to hear any of your arguments," Carlton said emphatically. "Bute is to be punished."

"Of course."

"You agree?" Carlton was surprised.

"Naturally. He is a slave. She is your daughter. There is no reason for mercy at all." Caspar's voice was hard, his mouth firm.

"He is such a princely nigger. It will hurt me." Carlton looked questioningly at Caspar, who was watching him sternly without speaking. Carlton sighed.

"Very well. Rouse the slaves. Assemble them in the paddock. See that Ella has every member of the household there, too. Including Laura and the Earl!"

While Caspar summoned the slaves, Carlton strolled down to the forge. He found Constance there and explained to him with gestures what he wanted the blacksmith to do. To emphasize

319

the urgency of his instructions, Carlton lashed the blacksmith across his massive shoulders with the lancewood switch he carried in his hand. Next, Carlton sent Samboth to tell the drivers to unlock the cell and bring Bute to the paddock.

The plantation was slow to stir. Carlton slashed angrily at the grass around his feet as he sat on the nursery step waiting for Laura and Philbert. Sleepy-eyed children regarded him with awe. As dawn seeped through the trees, the slaves shuffled up to the paddock fence and stood silently watching the Bondmaster. Fear hung in the air.

Suddenly there was a commotion. Asaph and Mercury pushed Bute through the gate, whipping him to make him move faster. The slaves wailed.

"Put him there!" Carlton stood up and indicated a spot in the center of the paddock. Asaph struck Bute in his back so he fell where the Bondmaster indicated.

"Cut four stakes," Carlton ordered crisply.

He gazed around the fence at the black faces staring at Bute. There was a livelier interest now that the slaves saw who was to be punished. Carlton sensed their approval that his wrath had fallen on an imported nigger and not on one of them. Some of the slaves were even grinning.

Bute was pleading with him, but he took no notice. He looked up to the house impatiently. Laura was late.

"Spread him out on the ground face down," he ordered. "Secure his legs wide apart, and tie each ankle to a stake. Stretch his arms out and fasten each wrist to a stake, too." Carlton indicated how he wanted Bute laid out before him. The crowd of slaves rumbled with speculation.

320

"Good morning, Philbert!" Carlton called cheerfully when the Earl stumbled over the grass toward him. He was huddled in a cloak to ward off the freshness of the early morning air.

Pip followed the Earl a few paces behind, escorting Ella. Tita, a grim smile on her face, hovered in the background, dragging a sleepy Hayes with her. Mingoson, Carlton noted, darted ahead to stare at Bute with curiosity. The boy knelt down and started to question Bute, ignoring Carlton's frown of annoyance.

"Where's Laura?" Carlton snapped.

"Upon my soul, Carlton. Her whereabouts is hardly my concern, is it? Damnably early hour, Carlton, to drag a man from his bed!" The Earl hugged his cloak closer around his body.

Carlton flicked the lancewood switch impatiently against his thighs. "Ella?"

"Caspar does be calling she."

"We'll wait for Laura. She must be here."

Mingoson was listening intently to Bute. He patted him gently on his shoulder and stood up. He looked at the Bondmaster and then at Tita, wondering what to do. Mingoson was frightened by what he had heard. Bute had told him that it was Tita herself who had brought him to Miss Laura.

Mingoson ran over to Hayes and whispered the news into his ear. Hayes regarded him stupidly.

"I does want to see the nigger punished, Mingoson. Hold your tongue, *garçon*."

Caspar trotted into the paddock, panting heavily.

"Where's Laura?" Carlton demanded angrily.

Caspar halted, his eyes blazing with hatred as he contemplated Bute. "She's gone!" He kicked Bute in his waist with rage and frustration.

"Gone?" Carlton clutched Caspar by his shoulder. "What do you mean?"

Caspar turned to Carlton with a sneer. "I mean your daughter has fled. I knocked on her door and called her. There was no answer. I thought she was sleeping soundly, so I roused the Earl and Hayes. There was still no answer when I went back to her room, so I took my cutlass and smashed down the door." He paused, kicking Bute again.

"Her bed was not even slept in. Her clothes are there, but she has gone. Her maid has disappeared, too."

"Impossible!" Carlton shouted. "I was on the gallery the whole night. I would have heard her."

"And I was in the kitchen!" retorted Caspar. "She did not take a horse; I checked the stable. She must have walked."

"Then she's not far. We'll get her, by God!" Carlton turned away crossly.

Caspar put his hand onto Carlton's arm. "Where you going?"

"To look for my daughter!"

"But the nigger. He is the cause of this."

"He ain't! He ain't!" Mingoson's shrill voice startled them. Tita slapped him quickly into silence.

The interruption served to trigger Carlton's wrath. He flayed at Mingoson with his switch, cutting the boy across his chest. He turned to the Earl, who was trying to hold himself straight but with his mind and eyes still hazy with sleep.

"This nigger here," Carlton said, stabbing his foot at Bute, "wronged both you and Laura." Carlton raised his voice so the young bucks gathered on the nursery veranda, and the slaves at the railings, could hear.

"He must be executed. I want all the whelps, bucks, fillies, and every accursed black nigger slave on this plantation to see what can happen to them. There just ain't no cause for a slave to lie with a white lady." He glared at Caspar.

"Ever!"

Carlton grabbed a whip from one of the drivers and tossed it at the Earl. "You have been shamed, Philbert. Take your revenge."

Philbert caught the whip in his hand, his eyes clearing. He shook the sleep from his head. The whip's thong was plaited cowskin; its effect would be devastating. He twirled his mustache with relish.

"Go on Philbert, go ahead. The nigger cannot run."

Philbert flexed the whip, taking a practice swipe. It made a satisfying sound as it smacked the ground, ripping up pieces of earth and grass. A gasp went up from the crowd.

Philbert, feeling an extraordinary sense of power surging through him, advanced on Bute. He let fly with the whip speculatively. It cut into the flesh of the nigger's side, leaving a deep incision in his skin. Philbert was amazed. He struck again, and the lash tore a lump of flesh out of Bute's arm.

"I say, what fun!"

The whip sliced into Bute's buttocks. The crowd groaned. Bute twisted in pain, blood trickling down his thigh into the mud.

"That's enough," roared Carlton. "You're just tickling him." He snatched the whip from Philbert's hand. "Caspar, take it!"

Caspar's blows were strong and steady, inspired by his own hatred for what Bute had done. The whip seared down on Bute with a speed which, in seconds, scarred his smooth back so it resembled a bloodied nutmeg grater.

"That's it," called Carlton, who was watching closely. "I don't want him to lose consciousness." He stepped over to Bute's body, tapping the slave on his face with his foot.

"Bute?"

Bute opened his eyes and gazed up in terror.

Carlton kneeled down. "It was rape wasn't it, Bute?"

Bute searched the Bondmaster's face, not understanding.

"It was rape, Bute! You forced Miss Laura to go to the cabin with you!"

A single tear slipped from Bute's scared eyes. It meandered down his cheek, merging with the mud and blood splattered on his face.

Carlton snapped upright. "You see," he glared at the faces watching him. "Where's Constance?" The huge slave shuffled forward from his vantage point by the veranda. He carried a leather sack under his arm.

Carlton nodded.

Constance squatted down beside Bute, studying the nigger professionally. His eyes gleamed. He reached in his bag. The slaves at the railing craned their necks to see what Constance was going to do. Ella watched impassively while Hayes clung to Mingoson in excitement.

The Earl of Philbert was puzzled by the thick iron rod which Constance drew from his sack with a flourish.

Carlton grinned. He pointed at the Earl. Constance held out the rod with pride, offering it to Philbert. The Earl tugged at his mustache nervously.

"Take it!" hissed Carlton. "It's your right."

"What is it?" gulped Philbert, acceping the rod thrust it into his hands. He inspected it with fascination. It had been crudely hammered into the shape of an enormous penis. The end was still warm from the blacksmith's fire.

"There!" Carlton pointed at Bute.

"I don't know what you mean!" Philbert stammered.

"By the devil!" Caspar exploded with fury, ignoring the Bondmaster's glance of surprise. "Laura was to be your bride. You must take your revenge."

Philbert hesitated.

"Dammit, Earl! If you won't take your revenge like a man, then I will!"

Caspar seized the rod from Philbert's trembling hand. He advanced on Bute, gripping the shaft firmly in front of him. Carlton swallowed anxiously as Caspar plunged the rod between Bute's buttocks, splitting him open.

The crowd wailed. Bute's scream was worse than they had ever heard. Children in the nursery began to cry. The naked bucks standing on the veranda clutched themselves in terror.

Caspar stood back, shaking, as Carlton stooped down beside Bute and hissed into his ear.

"See how it feels, nigger! You die in agony just as I and my daughter must live in agony, forever remembering what you did to us."

Carlton spat into Bute's face and stood up and turned away. With his shoulders hunched in sorrow, he walked slowly back to the house, alone.

Chapter 30

Laura scuttled down the trail to Layou. The pale glare of the moon outlined her erratic progress. Harodine, clutching Laura's reticule, scurried after her. They carried no light or protection against the snakes and jumbies which both believed moved in the forest at night. Laura's resoluteness was their only defense.

She had awakened Harodine at midnight. Stealthily they had quit the house without disturbing the Bondmaster dozing on the gallery. Laura was resolved to flee and make her own life. She was no longer going to be subjected to her father's edicts as though she were one of his breeding wenches. She would marry whom she wanted to without being ordered by Carlton.

Laura's outrage was also directed at Caspar. It was intolerable to her that he should have behaved so callously. When he discovered Bute with her, she expected him to be filled with remorse at her plight, consoling her with affectionate tenderness. Instead, he accused her of enjoying the experience! If she did, it was he, Caspar, who had schooled her in such matters.

Laura was determined to prove to Caspar and to her father that she had a will of her own and that she was quite capable of conducting her own *affaires de coeur* without their surveillance.

"I am not sure what I intend to do," Laura had explained to Harodine when they were safely out of the house. "But I shall do something to make them realize I am a woman, not a filly."

Nothing was more inviting to Laura that night than the lanterns of Layou which greeted her as she hastened around the last bend in the trail. Although it was after midnight, the river town resounded with activity, shouts and roars of drunken sailors, shrieks of their women, and the raucous music of concertinas and goatskin drums.

Laura stopped so suddenly that Harodine bumped into her.

"Oh, Miss Laura," wailed Harodine, overawed by the sounds from the townlet. "What are we going to do?"

Before Laura could answer, the jangle of horsemen galloping along the trail caused Laura to pull Harodine close to her. Two horses pounded toward them, the leading rider calling a halt as he observed them cowering in the bushes.

"Whoa!" A man's voice shouted confidently. He reined in his horse, stopping by Laura's side. He peered down at her.

"By Old Horny! What have we here? A white witch by her tail?" The man chuckled at the Negro who accompanied him.

"If I were a witch, you would be a toad!" snapped Laura, annoyed by the man's arrogance. She stepped out of the shadow, beckoning Harodine to follow.

"Ho, ho, *m'selle!* A sprightly night walker indeed. May I ask where you are bound?" The man's tone softened as the moon glow suggested Laura's dainty features.

"You may ask," said Laura firmly. "But I am not obliged to answer!" She considered the man quickly. From his mount and the dress of his Negro, Laura could see the man was no renegade. She, too, softened her attitude.

"We are going to Layou. To visit a sick cousin."

"Walking abroad without escort in these dangerous times?" The man sounded amazed. "It is not far now, by Jove, but I insist on offering you my protection." The man swung out of his saddle, leaving the Negro to grasp the reins.

"There are maroons who would like to ravish a beauty such as yourself, *m'selle*. Who is your cousin who is so sick, pray, that you leave your bed at this hour?"

Laura saw that the man doubted her. "May Gregg," she answered, giving the first name which entered her head.

The man's bluff courtesy vanished instantly. "May Gregg!" he exclaimed. "Why, she was in good enough shape when I left her not an hour ago." He stared at Laura.

"If it's May Gregg's you be bound for, you can not fool me about your errand. She's a sly one, that whore," he mused aloud.

"She never mentioned she had a new girl. Been serving the Bondmaster, have you? It's like May to save you for that Cock of the Niggers."

Laura was appalled by what the man said. She was on the verge of protesting most vociferously when it occurred to her that perhaps it would suit her purpose to permit the man to delude himself.

"Oh, sir!" she pleaded, putting her hand on his arm as she imagined a whore might do. "Do not say a word to May Gregg, please. She does not know I am coming to her. I was at Roxborough, but the Bondmaster treated me so cruelly, I am indeed fleeing from him."

"By Old Horny! What luck! The Bondmaster's strumpet on my arm! That bugger's father stole my inheritance, wench. He made Roxborough from the land he swindled out of my father. It's sweet revenge to have his harlot at my side!"

Laura was intrigued. They reached the houses surrounding the trail and by the light from the lanterns hanging at the open bars she assessed the man's features. He was tolerably good-looking in a rough fashion, with a firm jaw and a leathery complexion.

His brown hair flowed down his head in a mane which he tossed arrogantly when he spoke. He was nearly a foot taller than she and appeared to be bursting with muscles. Watching him made her forget her own nervousness at her flight. She felt she had an ally in this white giant.

"Here's Mary Gregg's house," said the man. "Her mam's casino is over there." He looked down at Laura and rubbed his cheek appreciatively. "What a dainty bird you are, and no mistake. The Bondmaster is sure to be enraged when he finds you have flown from his nest!"

"That's his concern," Laura sniffed. "Thank you for your trouble."

"Trouble be blowed!" The man slapped his thigh. "There's more thank-you to come from your rosebud lips."

The man swooped down and placed his mouth on Laura's so fast she had no time to draw away. Startled, she put up her hands to fend him off, only to remember the role as a fleeing whore. The man's tongue was demanding entry.

"Fie!" she said, pulling her head back. "Do you take me for a common courtesan to be taken on the public highway?"

"Ha! I like your spirit." The man held Laura around her waist. "You," he said, turning to Harodine. "Go about your business. My Negro will take care of you."

"You hear, Harodine," murmured Laura. "Do as the gentleman says." Harodine was watching Laura in panic.

"You are fortunate to have such a stalwart nigger to cover you, wench."

Laura turned away quickly so she did not have to watch the Negro dragging Harodine across the road to the darkness of the beach. Laura abandoned herself to the man whose arm now clasped her firmly around her waist.

The man steered her up the steps to the interior of the house where Mary Gregg and the other casino whores entertained their clients.

"Mary!" roared the man as he stepped into the reception room. "See who I have here!"

Mary looked up from the couch on which she was reclining while a sailor nibbled her toes. She blinked in the dim light of the lantern, recognizing Laura. She cocked her head in inquiry.

"I see who you have, Fletcher. What do you intend to do with her?"

"Do?" Fletcher slapped his thigh. "By Jove, is

there anything else one does to a girl in a whore-house? I want a room, Mary!"

Mary shrugged her shoulders. There was no accounting for what whim Fletcher would get up to next. He had smashed two sailors to a pulp that evening for insulting him. He was one of the casino's best customers. Mary Gregg always gave him what he demanded. If he had persuaded Laura Todd to spend the night with him in her brothel, it was not her concern. He would pay.

"Have my room," she smiled, patting the sailor's head. "Tar here is Spanish and will spend his time groveling in vain at my ankles, trying to raise a rod that's hard. I'll have no need for the bed tonight."

Laura wrinkled her nose at the smell and the filth of the brothel. She held Fletcher's hand tightly. A drunken planter was retching over the landing rail as a whore, her blouse ripped across her breasts, kicked at his ankles causing him to topple in a heap at her feet. The whore cackled.

From the rooms leading off the passageway came grunts and mirthless giggles. The stench of un-washed, sweating bodies wafted over her. Laura closed her eyes. It was settled.

She smiled coquettishly as Fletcher hurried to unfasten his breeches. "We have plenty of time!" Laura crooned, holding out her arm for him to join her as she perched on the edge of Mary Gregg's bed.

"Yes! Yes!" bellowed Fletcher, grasping her. She fell back on the bed as he pawed at her bodice.

She kissed him ardently the way she had learned from Caspar. He wriggled beside her, desire mount-ing him.

"By Jove! You are a busy wench!" he gasped.

"This ain't the time for romance. Open your legs, girl, it's Fletcher you have riding you, not some sissified rawhider."

He took her like a fiend, rolling off abruptly after he had spent himself. Within seconds, he was snoring. Laura frowned at the darkness, listening to the creaks and curses coming from the other rooms. Although she felt so unsatisfied, for all his brutishness, Fletcher had stirred something within Laura. She gazed at him with adoration, stroking his cheek. She snuggled into his arms and fell asleep.

The smell of Fletcher's foul breath woke Laura. She opened her eyes to see him puffing into her face, his own eyes tightly closed. He clambered on top of her.

Daylight was sneaking through the jalousies.

Fletcher drove at Laura, taking her selfishly but, in the laziness of awakening, with a tamed strength which brought her to a new pitch as he strained and bucked within her.

The crash of the door being flung open and the switch of a leather blade slicing into Laura's shoulder suddenly swelled her climax. She stared up in terror. A black hurricane began to tear the bed apart, a whip whistling through the air as Laura shrank back fearfully.

Black hands hauled at Fletcher before he could raise his head to see his assailants. His massive body was flung like a dead rat's into the corner of the boudoir. Shrieks of the occupants of the brothel filled the air, almost drowning the curses of the Negroes spilling into the room.

A whip slashed down, tearing Fletcher's silk shirt to shreds and slicing into the soft flesh of his stomach. He howled with pain, groping for his pistol. Another whip cracked, and the pistol shot out of his grasp. The lash curled around his thigh. He rolled into a ball with his head on his knees, clutching his body to protect himself.

Laura stared at the man flogging Fletcher mercilessly. It was Caspar.

She tried to scream his name, but the huge hands of the dumb Constance seized her. Constance swung her over his shoulder as though she were a sack of flour and barged out of the room. A Negro ran in front of him scything a path with his supplejack through the whores and sailors cowering in the hallway.

Caspar kicked Fletcher heartily in the crotch, splitting the skin. He bolted out of the room, leaving the man writhing and cursing on the floor.

The wagon was already in motion when Caspar hit the street and jumped for the tailboard. Samboth helped Asaph to pull him up while Caliste whipped the horses into a gallop. Ella sat on the floor of the wagon clutching Laura's reluctant head to her bosom, crooning softly. Constance leered, remembering the feel of Laura's thigh against his cheek as he carried her from the brothel.

Fletcher, his face dripping blood from the cuts of Caspar's whip, glared from the window of Mary's boudoir. His threats were lost in the clatter of the wagon and the jubilant shouts of the slaves on board.

"I'll get you, you black bastard," he choked, clutching his bleeding genitals. "You'll swing by your grain for this!"

Chapter 31

ROGER PYE FOLDED HIS ARMS ACROSS HIS CHEST. He leaned back against the trunk of the coconut tree and gazed down at the head of the slave girl at his thighs. The contrast of the wench's black skin as she champed his own white flesh amazed him.. "Do these hottentots really have emotions and brains just like us?" he wondered.

He raised his head to peer through the sugar cane. The ship on which he had arrived an hour before was sweeping out of the river basin, a light wind billowing out its sails. It was a solemn moment for Pye when he realized that his link with the real world was literally drifting away. He glanced down at the wench. She had nearly finished. He bucked away from the tree, his knees weakening, gripping the girl's head as she tried to pull back.

"That's better, gel!" he said as he withdrew, fascinated by the color of his semen smeared across the girl's dark lips. He fastened his trousers, buckled up his belt, and bent down to pick up his hat and his bag.

Fumbling in his pocket, he pulled out a shilling which he tossed to the girl, still drooling on her

334

knees. His tall hat on his head, he stepped jauntily out of the cane field and continued his walk up the hill path to Roxborough Hall.

Roger Pye's arrival at Roxborough had been expected. He had been in correspondence with Carlton concerning the position of a tutor for Hayes. He had seen the advertisement while browsing through *The Roseau Gazette* in the neighboring island of Antigua.

"I am no genius," he readily admitted to Carlton as the two men faced each other across the drawing room floor.

"You might even say I am a young man of fortune, without a fortune, of course. I work well for my pay, though, I can assure you. I can read, write and add, and even subtract. Boys like me, girls adore me, and as a tutor you'll find me admirable."

"Harrumph," grunted Carlton, eyeing the man suspiciously. "You from England, you say. Never been in the West Indies before? Not trying to fool me, are you? You're not a white nigger trying to worm your way into my trust?"

"I say, steady on, Mister Todd." Pye was shocked. "You have my references. My family may not be much, but my aunt does know Lady Mountjoy. You can write to her if you wish."

"I have to be sure about you, boy," Carlton growled.

"I have my daughter here. She is not married, Pye. She is sixteen . . ." His voice trailed off with an unspoken threat. His eyes bored into Pye's.

Pye felt himself blushing at the implication. He blinked, nodding his head rapidly to show he understood.

"Good. You'll keep away from her. You will have plenty to do. My son Hayes is ten. He has been mollycoddled too long and needs an education. He is my heir, Pye."

"I will be delighted to provide that education, sir."

"You don't have much luggage," sniffed Carlton. "No books?"

"Indeed, I don't, sir. I left England in rather a hurry, and I wasn't aware that I was destined to become a tutor."

"We had a doctor here before you who left a set of books. You will have his cabin. The front room is a schoolroom." Carlton leaned forward and lowered his voice. "My daughter won't attend your schoolroom, Pye. She keeps to her boudoir."

In spite of Carlton's warning, the first visitor to Roger Pye's cabin later that afternoon was Laura herself. She swept in without knocking and sidled silently into the bedroom. Pye was combing his dark hair in a mirror propped up on the dressing table. He did not see her as she stood in the doorway studying him.

He was younger than Laura had expected, younger than Fletcher but older than Caspar. He was slim. And attractive.

"Welcome to Roxborough," Laura said sarcastically. "Have you been allocated a bed wench yet?"

Pye jumped with surprise at the sound of her voice. "You frightened me!" he said with a laugh.

"If that's all it takes to frighten you, you're going to have a very nervous time here." Laura sniggered and sat down on the bed.

Pye peered around the partition into the front

336

room. "I say, you don't have a chaperone with you? There's no swarthy Hercules lurking outside to chop off my head if I make you scream?"

The sadness in Laura's eyes vanished for a few seconds. She frowned, intrigued by the young man.

"So you've heard already?"

"The tale of how the Bondmaster's daughter was rescued from a Layou brothel is on every sailor's lips."

"I wasn't rescued!" Laura pounded the bed crossly. "I was captured." She gazed at Pye. "Do you know Fletcher?" she asked hopefully.

"Never set eyes on the bounder. Nor do I want to."

"He seems to have disappeared. I can get no word of him from anyone."

"You hardly think he would come here, do you? Your father would kill him."

Laura sighed again, depression returning to her eyes. Pye felt sorry for her.

"Are you sure there is no hottentot armed to the teeth skulking outside the window?"

Laura shook her head miserably.

"Then let me show you your Fletcher is but one of many men."

Pye fell on the bed beside Laura, seizing her in his arms. He kissed her passionately. Laura gave a token shrug of resistance, then slowly subsided into his arms, returning his kiss.

"You give a girl precious little opportunity to scream for help, Roger Pye, if you plug her lips so energetically with your tongue!" Laura gasped, intrigued by Pye's boldness.

"That's because I'm a coward." He kissed her again. Laura eased herself down onto the bed. Pye broke away from the embrace, cursing himself for having fooled with the slave girl earlier.

"I'm interested in living to a ripe old age, Laura. Perhaps we should meet again at a more auspicious time, not in the middle of the afternoon with the door of the cabin wide open."

Laura laughed, not harshly as before but with a sense of happiness. "I think that I am going to enjoy your sojourn here, Roger Pye. I was frightened about what you would be like. No white men ever come here except the revenue collectors." She pouted.

"It is so lonely with only blacks to gaze at all the time. And Caspar, of course." Laura bit her lip.

Pye raised his eyebrows, wondering what she meant.

Laura rose from the bed suddenly and smoothed down her dress. She swept past Pye and out of the room.

He scampered after her to the door of the cabin. "When will I see you again?"

"At supper, I suppose."

"I mean . . ." Pye winked.

"I know what you mean, Roger Pye." She smiled. "This cabin has memories for me, Pye. I haunt it!" She tripped lightly down the steps from the cabin and hurried across the yard to the house. She felt she was flying.

Ella, spying from the kitchen, observed the spring in Laura's walk. She gloated. "Ah does be happy about dat Mister Pye," she declared to Caspar. "Miss Laura done lose she vexation a'ready."

Caspar scowled. "It makes no difference to me." He shrugged his shoulders. Since they had brought

Laura back from Layou, she had ignored him. Now he would forget her.

Roger Pye was baffled. He had been at Roxborough for a week but had not seen Laura since the afternoon of his arrival. He glowered at Hayes, who was sitting at his desk in the school cabin, trying to pronounce aloud the words from a book. His dark shadow, Mingoson, sat behind Hayes, mouthing the words silently.

Pye corrected Hayes's pronunciation in a perfunctory fashion, gazing out of the window to the balcony outside Laura's room. "Was that a glimpse of her dress swirling along the gallery around the corner of the house?" he daydreamed.

"What happened to your sister, Hayes?" Pye demanded suddenly. "I haven't seen her since my first day here."

Hayes liked Roger Pye. He was funny and did not lose his temper. "That's the way she does be, sah," he replied.

" 'Is', Hayes. 'That's the way she is, sir.' Say 'sir,' not 'sah.' "

"Sir."

"Right, now what do you mean?"

"She does. . . ." Hayes stumbled with his sentence when Pye uttered a groan. "She stays, sir, she stays in her boudoir, sir. Do you like her, *sir?*"

"Very good, Hayes. Yes, of course I like her, don't you? She is beautiful. You can tell her that from me. Maybe it will prise her from her fortress."

"Perhaps I can persuade her to have supper wid us tonight, sir."

"*With* us, not wid. Capital idea. Do you think you can?"

Pye loathed mealtimes at Roxborough. The Bond-master himself, when he condescended to acknowl-edge Pye's presence, seemed capable of talking only about the sex life of his slaves. Hayes had appalling table manners and ate as though he were snuffling at a trough. Slaves hovered nervously at the table, apparently terrified. The whole atmosphere was one of gloom instead of conviviality.

Worse, for Pye, was having to sit with the Bond-master on the gallery after supper and serve as audience for Carlton's rambling discourses on Negro morals. If only Laura would emerge from her boudoir, thought Pye on these occasions, at least there would be the distraction of trying to lay her.

As well as the eccentric behavior of the Bond-master and Laura, Pye had to contend with the slaves. The one called Tita appeared to be spying on him; the overseer, Caspar, treated him with total contempt; and the cook, Ella, was forever offering herb teas. The house slaves moved with respectful silence and gracious smiles, yet Pye could not stifle the impres-sion that they were smiling out of habit rather than true feeling.

To cap it all, the women who interested him were either confined to the paddock or billeted in the village stud farm. Whenever he walked around the plantation in the hope of finding a wench to dally with in the sugar cane, the youth called Sam-both followed him, no doubt to report on his every movement to the overseer. If his life at Rox-borough was to continue in that vein, Pye was quite prepared to forgo the doubtful luxury of his job and seek his fortune elsewhere.

Unknown to Pye, however, other plans were afoot. Pye's casual remark to Hayes about his sister had been speedily relayed to Laura herself. She, in turn, had sought out her father as he dozed in the gallery after dinner that day.

"Daddy," she announced brusquely while Carlton was half asleep, "I want to marry Roger Pye."

"Harrumph!" Carlton roused himself. "Who the devil is he?"

"The new tutor."

"The tutor, egad! Do you think he'd have you?"

"He claims to adore me."

"Hah! I knew the boy was stupid the moment I saw him! I can't say he impresses me very much. What do you want to marry him for?"

"What else can I do?"

"Yes, you are right about that, I'll grant you."

"Will you arrange it for me, please, Daddy? I'm sure you can!" Laura's smile at her father was bereft of warmth. She left him as abruptly as she had come.

"Boy!" bellowed Carlton without rising from his chair. "Boy!" he stamped his foot impatiently on the floorboards of the gallery.

"Massa!" a voice answered from below the house.

"Tell Caspar I want him up here right away."

"Yassa!"

Carlton sank back in the chair to contemplate. Laura's suggestion had merit. Pye was about five years her senior. He appeared to be a genuine Englishman. He could probably be procured to marry Laura quite cheaply.

"That fellow Pye," Carlton addressed Caspar as soon as he appeared on the gallery. "What's he like?"

Caspar sniffed disparagingly. "He is not a gentleman."

"I know that, dammit! What does he do at night? Not rolling around with the bucks, is he? Like that Doctor!"

Caspar shook his head. "He gave Tency a shilling, and Sam says he has been trying to find wenches in the field gangs."

"That's a relief." Carlton shifted in his chair, relaxing a bit.

"Laura has a mind to marry that Pye. Knowing how she is, we must arrange it as quickly as possible. Send a message to Reverend Audain at once. I doubt if I could get any better for her now."

Caspar seemed despondent.

"If this marriage goes through, Caspar, I'll be able to go to Trinidad with a coffle again. I need to sell a score of slaves to recover what I invested in Bute. It was a mistake to slaughter that nigger before he had a fight." Carlton scowled at Caspar, then broke into a grin as a thought occurred to him.

"Do you realize, Caspar, that if we install Pye here, we get an extra white man for nothing! He will be a tutor for Hayes and a husband to keep Laura out of the niggers' breeches. I believe I am growing to like young Mister Pye."

In spite of his remarks, Carlton has his misgivings about Pye. That night, Laura joined them for supper, and Carlton observed that Pye's eyes were focused exclusively on the low-cut bodice of her gown. Pye was intent on passing one dish of vegetables after another across to her, each time inquiring if she wanted more.

"For the devil's sake, boy!" Carlton blurted out when he could stand Pye's ogling no longer. "Laura is perfectly capable of serving herself."

"Yes, Mister Todd," retorted Pye cheerfully, determined not to be intimidated. "But it is my pleasure to serve her myself."

Hayes laughed, picked up a piece of dasheen and hurled it at a slave who was leaving the room. Carlton chose not to notice his son's behavior.

"I see that you like it here with us, Pye," he muttered, attempting to stimulate the conversation.

"Indeed, I do, sir." Pye winked at Laura, ignoring the sauce which Hayes tipped down his sleeve.

"Ever think of settling down in a place like this, Pye? Such a country could offer a lot of opportunities for a young man like you." Carlton picked his teeth with a dirty fingernail, his eyes fixed on Pye.

"Yes, it could." Pye leered at Laura, pushing his plate forward.

"You have finished already, Mister Pye?" Laura sounded concerned. "I hope nothing is wrong?"

"Nothing at all, Miss Laura. I just don't feel like eating very much." He smiled sheepishly. "I say, there's an absolutely cracking moon out tonight. It makes the palm trees and the jungle look jolly romantic. I suppose you wouldn't care for a postprandial stroll, Miss Laura."

"Heavens!" said Laura. "I would hesitate to venture anywhere without my father's permission."

"Granted!" said Carlton quickly.

"Can I go, too?" piped up Hayes. "I'll take Mingoson."

"No, son!" Carlton snorted.

Pye rose from the table and waited for Laura

to do likewise. He took her elbow to escort her through the drawing room and down the front steps. Carlton rubbed his chin thoughtfully.

"What they gon' do, Da'?"

Carlton picked up an orange from the fruit dish and hurled it at Hayes's head. "Go and play with your nigger and stop asking daft questions, boy!"

When they reached the bottom step, Pye pulled Laura into the shadows under the gallery and kissed her. She made no attempt to resist. His hands began to invade her body.

"Roger!" she said, breaking away. "I thought you said a stroll in the moonlight."

"I don't believe we have time for preliminaries."

"Whatever do you mean?"

"I never see you. But now I've got you, I'm not going to let you go."

"I accept."

"What?" Pye paused in his efforts to unfasten Laura's bodice. "What do you accept?" he asked in confusion.

"Your proposition."

"Did I make a proposition?"

"You said that you are not going to let me go."

"Oh, well, yes. Come on, Laura, let's go to my cabin." He released his hands from her body.

"Of course, we can discuss the details there."

"If that's what you want to call it."

Pye snatched up Laura's hand and led her in great haste across the yard. She halted suddenly and gazed up at the sky.

"Come! What's the matter? Your father might send his nigger charlies after us if we don't hurry."

"Do look at the moon, Roger. It really is romantic. See, there is a silver halo around it."

"You'll see it better from my bed. We can open the window and gaze at it above us. Come on!" He pulled her, and she followed him into the cabin.

He wrapped his arms around her and held her tightly, close to his body. "Laura! I love you."

"I don't believe you!"

"I do, I do, I do. Now let's go in the bedroom and lie down and look at the moon."

"No, Roger, I think we'll stay here and talk. Sit there, and I'll sit here at your desk as the tutor." She moved over to his desk and climbed onto the stool.

"What about the moon? Come on, Laura, this isn't the time for playing school. I've been doing that all day with your wretched brother and his nigger. I've wanted you ever since that first time I saw you, Laura. Why are we waiting?"

"There'll be plenty of time for that when we are married."

"Married!" Pye was startled. "Who said anything about marriage?"

"You did! You said you would never let me go."

"That's a figure of speech, Laura." He laughed. "You had me worried."

He grasped her hand. "Come on, Laura, let's go in there. You want me as much as I want you. I've heard about you, Laura."

"I don't think I understand you."

"Come on, Laura, you do not have to pretend you are a virgin with me! We do not have time to waste before your father calls you."

"He hasn't spoken to you?"

"Yes, frequently. About his need for new slave

blood. He suggested I could take my pick of the hottentots in his paddock and breed him a half-white whelp."

"What did you tell him, Roger?"

"I declined. I'm not a slave stud."

He seized her hand and began kissing it rapidly, gnawing his way up her arm to the soft inside of her elbow. He bit her gently. To Laura's consternation, she felt her whole body quivering.

"I'm going, Roger!" She jumped up, pulling her arm away from him. She ran quickly out of the cabin.

"Come back!" He dived out of the door after her. "Laura, I'm sorry. Did I offend you?" He caught her by the arm and tried to kiss her.

"No!" she hissed. "No! Not until we are married."

"Married! What is this, Laura?"

He gazed at her face as a cloud drifted away from the moon. Laura's pale lips fluttered as a firefly with its luminous glow hovered above her blond hair. Holding her slender waist, Pye felt that if he pressed his hands together, he would squeeze the life out of her.

"Married? Laura, you would marry *me*? Really?"

Pye did not know what made him speak like that. He lowered his lips to Laura's, feeling the romance which was stirred in the air by the gentle breeze and the passionate moonlight.

"Yes!" she breathed. "Yes!"

She slipped out of his grasp before his lips brushed hers. She darted across the yard toward the front steps, shouting gleefully.

"Daddy! Daddy! Roger Pye has asked me to marry him!" she cried.

A *crapaud* croaked plaintively in the darkness of the jungle as Roger gazed after her. He cursed the moonlight for making him foolish.

Chapter 32

THE SWIRL OF HORSEMEN GALLOPING UP THE path to the house had Hayes and Mingoson scrambling for the window of the schoolroom. They both ignored Pye's shout to sit down. Pye grabbed Hayes by the seat of the pants and hauled him back into the cabin.

"Who's there, Mingoson?" shouted Hayes, struggling to free himself.

"A stranger! I don't know he at all."

"I don't know *him,*" corrected Pye wearily, loosening his hold on Hayes. The boy wriggled free and dashed out of the cabin.

Pye watched from the door as the two horsemen cantered up to the steps. One slipped out of his saddle quickly and steadied the other horse so that the rider could dismount. He was a portly man dressed soberly in a black coat and a wide-brimmed black hat. He eased himself with great effort out of the saddle and plopped onto the ground, mopping his brow. Hayes watched him in awe.

"Where's your daddy, my young whippersnapper!" panted the man after almost a minute trying to catch his breath.

Carlton, attracted by the noise of the horsemen, leaned over the gallery rail. "Audain!" he exclaimed with pleasure. "Come up, come up!"

"Just getting my wind, Carlton. Hope you've got a good screw awaiting me. Rode down from Colihaut as soon as I got your letter." He spoke in short bursts as he climbed the steps, pausing frequently.

Carlton shook the Reverend Audain's hand warmly and escorted him to the gallery chair. "Boy!" he shouted unnecessarily, for Pip was already crossing the drawing room floor with the decanter and glasses.

"What about your man?" asked Carlton, indicating the other rider, who remained downstairs.

Audain accepted the glass of rum from Pip and drained it in a gulp, belching noisily. "Got a wench you can lend him? Shan't be staying long, you see."

"Of course. Pip, tell Ella to send a filly to meet the Reverend's man in the stable."

"Got your letter, Carlton. Came as quick as I could. In bloom, is she?"

"No idea."

"Heard about Fletcher." Audain poured himself a second rum. "Unfortunate business. That rascal is headed for a bad end." Audain chuckled wheezily, gulping the rum.

"I know his mother. The good lady has packed him off to Antigua, out of the way. After what your niggers did, not even a two-bit whore will look at him. Lashed him from head to toe, I hear!" Audain's bulky frame shook with merriment. "You must be on your guard for Fletcher, Carlton. The rogue has vowed revenge, by all accounts. He is not the man to let any slave shame him."

"Really?" Carlton sounded bored.

"No one says you were wrong, Carlton!" Audain added hastily when he sensed Carlton's displeasure. "Even God himself would agree."

"Pah!" Carlton scoffed. "Laura is very much like her dead mother. She's taken a fancy to another chap now. I want to get her spliced to him before the bugger gives her the slip."

"Splendid idea. Let her start a family. Children keep a lady from straying. Are they ready?"

"Got your books, have you?"

"Never bother with them, Carlton. What service do you want? I can elaborate Mass in French, read the liturgy of the Church of England, spracken the Dutch service, or chant the Methodists'. No extra charge."

The laughter of the two men drowned the sound of Tita hurrying across the creaking floorboards at the other side of the gallery. The news that Laura was to be married stunned her. She bit her lower lip, wondering what to do.

"With Miss Laura married and Hayes and Mingoson growing older," she thought, "what use will Mas Carlton have for me?" She knew Carlton could send her out to live in the slave quarters if he had a mind to do so. Ella would be supreme at Roxborough then. It was important, Tita decided, that the marriage should not take place.

Hoisting up her dress, she trotted quickly down the back steps, aware that Ella's eyes were on her as she hastened to Pye's cabin.

"Mingoson!" she called loudly, to allay Ella's curiosity about the reason for her visit to the cabin.

"My mother is calling me, sir," Mingoson said,

looking up from his book and accentuating every word with care.

"Very good, Mingoson. Yes, I hear her. You may go." Pye sighed. He was not going to get very far with those children this morning.

Tita appeared at the doorway.

"Yes, ma'am?" Mingoson inquired obediently.

"Go to Mas Hayes, boy. Ah think he does need yo'."

Mingoson dashed off quickly, and Tita entered the cabin.

"Massa Pye, sah." Tita gazed at Pye coyly. "Ah does have somethin' to tell yo'."

"I *have* some*thing* to tell *you*, Tita." Pye corrected her automatically.

"What dat, sah?"

"No, I mean that you say 'I have something to tell you.'"

"Yassa?" Tita looked at Pye and waited expectantly.

"What is it?" Pye assumed the expression of disinterest which he used whenever the slaves sought his advice or came to him with some kind of farfetched tale.

"Mah message, sah?" Tita wanted to make sure that she had the buckra's attention.

"Yes."

"Ah hear how yo' does be gon' wed Miss Laura, sah."

"Indeed, Tita?"

"Does yo' know about she, sah? Ah was be she nanny befoh she done go to Trinidad fuh she schooling."

"Go on." Pye sat patiently at the desk, wondering what the old wench was trying to tell him.

351

"Ah does be de one dat suckle she like she mah own whelp, sah. Mah own whelp does be dat boy Samboth by Claudius what does be dead, sah. Mas Carlton don't know dat, sah. Mas Carlton done take me as wet nurse fuh Miss Laura, and ah leave dat boy Samboth in Layou. He don't know ah does be he dam." She paused to see if Pye understood her.

"When Laura's mam met she death, ah does be de one what care fuh Laura like she mah own slave blood, sah!"

"I understand." Pye wished the wench would finish so he could see who was on the balcony.

"She not a virgin, sah!"

"What? I didn't catch that." Pye stifled a yawn.

"Miss Laura, sah. She not virgin!" Tita exulted in the mischief of her revelation. The buckra would not marry Laura now.

"I'm pleased to hear it," said Pye languidly. "Is that all?"

Tita was puzzled. "Yo' understand me, sah?"

When Pye showed no concern, Tita decided to impart the final horror of Laura's shame. "It does be a slave buck what burst she maid, sah!"

Pye grinned. "Really? How quaint that you should know all those details, Tita. I'm really most terribly grateful to you. Look, here's a penny for your trouble."

The marriage of Laura Todd and Roger Pye was performed in the drawing room of Roxborough Hall that afternoon. Carlton, fortified by large measures of rum and the convivial company at dinner of the Reverend Audain, swayed at Laura's side. Laura clasped Pye as though she thought he might attempt

352

to escape. Pye occupied his thoughts with an estimation of the wealth of his father-in-law. Caspar was a reluctant best man, having been declared by Audain to be an honorary free mulatto for the occasion.

The house slaves were allowed to crowd into the drawing room to watch the ceremony. Tita was instructed to keep Hayes and Mingoson quiet. She herself witnessed the proceedings with a malevolent scowl, fearful that this union would somehow lead to a lessening of her influence.

The solemnity with which the ceremony began was shattered by the Reverend Audain himself. As he garbled the words of the service, Audain suddenly spied a vessel tacking in the river basin. He peered again through the open window over the cane fields.

"Good Lord!" he said, interrupting himself. Caspar turned sharply in the direction the vicar was staring. A schooner was sailing into the bay with a demasted barque laden with sugar and rum from Guadeloupe. Audain coughed to cover his lack of concentration, muttered a closing prayer, and declared Roger and Laura man and wife.

"Do forgive me, Carlton." Audain grabbed Carlton's hand and pumped it. "I must hasten down to Layou immediately. It seems that my schooner has been blessed with bounty!"

Audain pushed his way through the slaves and bellowed for his horse. He puffed down the steps with a cheerful wave. "God bless you, children! Send for me again, any time."

"Our vicar is both priest and privateer, it seems!" chuckled Pye, hugging Laura. "Now, Mistress Pye, a kiss for your husband!"

The slaves applauded as Roger embraced Laura.

The sound roused Carlton, who stared bleary-eyed at Pye. He shook his head to recover his wits. "You married her?" he demanded gruffly.

"Yes, sir!" Pye grinned. "We did it with the help of our best man here." He clapped Caspar on his shoulder in a gesture of affection.

Caspar smiled politely and moved away.

"Let me tell you this, boy." Carlton waved his finger drunkenly across his chest. "Now you've got my daughter, get me a grandson out of her!"

"Stop that, Daddy!" Laura stamped her foot. "We're not a pair of your wretched breeding niggers. I suppose you'll tell Roger you'll give him a gold piece if I get a bright-eyed pickaninny, and I'll get a bolt of cloth for a new dress. For God's sake, Daddy, we are a man and a woman, not a couple of rutting slaves."

"Splendid, Laura!" Pye applauded.

Caspar cleared his throat and spat contemptuously on the floor by Pye's boot.

Carlton glanced at his daughter in astonishment, squinting as he focused his eyes on her. "If there is anything which you despise in me, Laura, remember it may manifest itself in you some day. Hah! Look how you've got your mother's worst qualities!" Carlton pushed himself out of his chair and faced Laura.

"Your mother was devoured by Ibos, and so was her nigger stallion. You have got yourself spliced to an itinerant libertine whose only merit seems to be that he has a white skin and blue eyes. Think yourself fortunate, daughter. You could have been skewered alongside your black paramour.

"I ask this knave here to get a grandson out of

you! That's not slave talk, Laura. It's you and Roxborough I'm thinking of."

Laura lay beside Pye, her head resting on his arm as his hand playfully caressed her naked breasts.

He stared up at the ceiling framed by the drapes of the four-poster bed. "Twice before midnight," Pye thought proudly. He would let the woman sleep now before revealing the pleasures of Pye in the early morning.

"I was so scared, Roger," breathed Laura as Pye sank exhausted into sleep. She nibbled his earlobe to wake him.

"Scared," he said drowsily. "Whatever for?"

"For what you'd think of me."

"For goodness sake, haven't I shown you what I think of you? I love you, Laura. Now go to sleep."

"My father thought you would not have me. After the things I have done."

"We all have our secrets, Laura. I knew yours, but no one asked me mine. I'm not such a good catch, Laura."

"Oh, Roger, what do you mean? Don't tell me you are already married!" Laura raised her head to look directly into his eyes.

"No!" Pye smiled. "Not that."

"Oh, Roger, you've made me so happy." She kissed his lips, his chin, then let her mouth explore his chest, her tongue rooting out his nipple under a forest of tawny hair. Her hand gently fondled him back to life.

"I want this to go on forever," she said, her lips creeping lower.

The next day, Carlton patrolled the estate with

355

Caspar. The sugar cane was nearing maturity, and there was work to be done in the mill. New coopers were being trained by the old ones who were no longer able to work. Hogsheads were being assembled under their watchful eyes with materials imported from England. A gang under Asaph were scouring and scrubbing the huge sugar vats.

Carlton made a detailed inspection, approving the preparation for the cane harvest. When he toured the slave quarters, he noticed a new warmth in the greetings from the slaves.

"How d'ye, massa? How de misses?" asked one colt as he bounced jauntily along the trail.

"Fine. Your filly take yet?"

"Jus' now, jus' now. The slave grinned impishly.

"Good," muttered Carlton. "What do you make of that, Caspar? The Negroes seem happy today."

"Laura," Caspar answered laconically.

"Laura? Dammit, what's she got to do with the slaves?"

"Plenty. They are pleased she has found a husband." Caspar patted his horse. "They would be even happier if you had one."

"The devil they would!"

"I mean a wife." Caspar smiled.

"I fail to see how that should be of any interest to the niggers, Caspar."

"Slaves like their owners to be married," Caspar spoke with conviction. "It promotes an additional sense of security. Now the slaves are waiting for Pye to take a bed wench so he will be a real buckra master."

"I don't care a damn what a herd of slaves think, Caspar. What goes on in our family is our business. Perhaps they expect that rascal Pye to become the

Bondmaster!" Carlton slashed angrily at a branch as they rode under a clump of trees.

"Yes, I see why they want him to have a bed wench. They feel that they will have a way to influence him through the slave filly he choses. They are mistaken, Caspar."

Caspar reined in his horse to listen.

"I don't want Pye to have anything to do with the slaves at all, Caspar. That's for you and Ella. He is tutor to Hayes, and that's his status at Roxborough. A scoundrel fresh out from England is not going to disrupt the system I have worked years to achieve. Don't worry, he'll have his hands full with Laura."

Caspar sighed with relief. Now that Pye's role on the plantation had been defined, he was satisfied.

Pye himself had his own ideas. He indulged Laura's whims and fantasies for the first days of their marriage. The effect was dramatic. The whole household had been concerned lest Pye reject Laura as his bride and precipitate another crisis in the domestic routine. When it was apparent from Laura's ecstatic simpers that the marriage had started well, a new cheerfulness descended on the household.

Carlton was astonished to hear the slaves singing in the kitchen, something they had not done for months.

"Marriage agreeing with you as much as it does with Laura?" Carlton asked Pye one evening as they sat on the balcony. "She is putting you through your paces, what?" He guffawed.

"I'm endeavoring to keep Laura happy," replied Pye, helping himself to rum from the decanter presented to them by Pip. Carlton observed that Pye did not offer it to himself first. Pye swung his legs up on the railing as he had seen Carlton do, and sighed arrogantly.

"You have such a large plantation here, Father. A lot of land which you could work. I suppose you have been short of a white man to share the responsibility with you. Well, now I'm here, why don't you let me take on the job?"

"Hum!" Carlton murmured sarcastically. "Mighty good of you to offer. Let me tell you, Pye." He leaned across in his chair and stared into Pye's eyes.

"I hired you as a tutor for my son, Hayes. That's your job, Pye, and nothing else." Carlton tapped him on his arm. "You may have married my daughter, but I'm the Bondmaster to you the same way that I am to everyone else. I am not your father, boy!'

Pye blinked, aware that he had made the wrong approach. "Of course, of course, sir, I understand. As tutor for Hayes, I have a great responsibility, and I will discharge it properly. However, any time you may have need of my assistance, I would like you to know that I am willing."

Pye put down his glass and tried again. "Sir, there is the matter of . . . well, being a worthy husband for your daughter. I feel she deserves a husband less impecunious than my own humble self."

Carlton sat back in his chair and beamed. "Pye, you rogue! I wondered how long it would take you! I admire your tactics. You show me how you have tamed Laura before you ask for the reward!" He chuckled into his rum glass.

"Pye," he continued, smirking to himself, "if my precious daughter wishes her husband to be impecunious, that is her affair. I have given Laura an annuity, Pye, from which she could give you an allowance, if she so wishes."

Carlton reached for the decanter, amused by Pye's crestfallen face. "Now you have married Laura, Roger Pye, you have to please her. She calls the tune!"

Pye's plans were delayed rather than changed. It was no hardship for him to make love to Laura, even though she demanded it so frequently. Pye was willing to tend to her whims with diligence. He knew now that it was through her that the way to her father's wealth lay.

After the first blush of their marriage faded, Laura appreciated the power she held over Pye, thanks to her father's arrangements. She gave Pye money when he asked, because he was giving her what she wanted, too. She was not so stupid as to be unaware that should dissension enter into their marriage, Pye would do what she asked simply for recompense.

To Pye's chagrin, as well as a delay in getting his hands on the Bondmaster's wealth, his own daily routine remained the same in spite of his marriage. Hayes, tailed by Mingoson, attended for his lessons in the school cabin as before. Each day, Samboth sat like a sentinel on the steps outside.

Tired of Samboth's perpetual presence, Pye called him into the cabin one morning. "Every day," he told him, "you sit on the step listening to us, boy. I want to see if you have learned anything."

"No!" Hayes jumped up. "Slaves ain't supposed to be learning!" he spluttered. "If they read and write, they are bound to get too fresh." His sallow complexion reddened with indignation.

Pye rounded on him. "I decide what goes on here, young Hayes, not you! And call me 'Sir' when you address me, if you please."

"You don't have no right to speak to me like that!" Hayes retorted.

"Oh, I don't, eh! We'll see about that." Pye advanced suddenly on Hayes and clipped him around his ear.

Hayes stared at Pye. His body shook, and he burst into tears.

"Bite him, boy, bite him!" he screamed at Mingoson.

Mingoson's cheerful face clouded with consternation. He shifted uncertainly in his seat. "He don't do me nothing!"

Pye held Hayes by his ear, pulling him off the Negro. "Go to your room, boy, until you have learned to behave. I'll speak to your father about this."

Hayes brought up his fist with a crushing blow into Pye's crotch and ran off to the house.

The crisis passed with the start of the cane harvest. Lessons were canceled so that Hayes could accompany Carlton to the mill. It was around this time that Laura began to spend her afternoons with Tita while Pye drank rum by himself in his cabin.

Ella, observing these developments, studied Laura's demeanor with interest. After a few days, she was certain she was right. She let Carlton know her suspicion. Laura was pregnant.

Chapter 33

ROGER PYE STOOD ON THE BALCONY AND watched the schooner far down in the river mouth weigh anchor. He smiled grimly. The Bondmaster was on the vessel with a coffle of slaves he was taking to Trinidad. Pye had heard Carlton and Caspar discussing the arrangements every evening for months. He had bided his time patiently, waiting for the day the Bondmaster would sail and leave him in charge of the plantation. The fact that Carlton said Caspar and Ella were responsible for the slaves and the estate did not intimidate him. At last, with the Bondmaster away, he could live his own life.

"Boy!" He stamped his foot on the balcony floor.

Pip, who was in the kitchen, heard the cry. He glanced at Ella. "He don't take long!" he observed dryly.

"Is true," agreed Ella. "Now we does see Massa Pye trying de Bon'massa boots. He does want rum. Take he de rum wid de pepper in it. See if he can drink dat screw!" She chuckled. "Ah does put soursop leaf in de callaloo to cool he down."

Pye was surprised when Pip brought him the decanter. "You know my wishes good, boy," he told him, pouring a large measure and tipping it down his throat with relish.

"Yassa," said Pip with mock servility.

"Fine. Tell that stable boy to saddle a horse so I can look around this plantation."

"Beg pard'n, sah. Mas Caspar does be down Layou."

"So what? I don't need that halfbreed know-all to escort me, boy."

"Are you going out, darling?" Laura rose from her seat in the drawing room. She stood behind Pye, entwining her arms around his waist. "What about the lessons?"

"No class today!" Pye twisted out of Laura's grasp. "I've been cooped up in this gloomy house for too long. I want to ride and see what we have here."

"I would like to come with you, Roger," Laura said, holding her stomach. "But the baby."

"Yes, I've been thinking about that." Pye leaned backwards against the railing, folding his arms across his chest. He eyed his wife's figure.

"I think I'll move back to the school cabin to sleep until you've had that get."

"Roger!" Laura was shocked. "Why do you want to do that?"

"It will be better for you. I might make too much demand on you."

"That's never too much for me, Roger." She put out her arms to hold him again, leaning forward and kissing the tip of his nose. "Forget that silly idea, Roger."

"Silly idea, is it? What about me? Do you think I want to have a bloated whale in bed beside me every night? It's sickening." He jerked himself away from her grasp. A tear of shock pricked her eyes.

"I'm going out for the day. Tell Ella to send my dinner over to the cabin this afternoon!"

Pye had no idea of what he expected to find when he rode around the plantation. The slaves were working efficiently in the field gangs. The drivers bade him good day respectfully, and the old wenches he met in the path bobbed their heads and smiled a greeting. His irritability vanished before such esteem.

He squared his shoulders with new pride, casting his eyes with pleasure around the plantation. The success of Carlton and Caspar in keeping a neat and profitable estate was everywhere apparent. That he had a share in it by marriage boosted Pye's ego as much as the scrapings and salutations of the slaves.

He reined in his horse by the paddock fence. Children were playing happily in the bright sunshine, romping like monkeys. Wet nurses sat on the veranda with the babes they were suckling cradled in their arms. He took in the whole paddock area, including the near-naked young wenches sitting in the shade of a saman tree. He slid out of the saddle and sauntered into the pen for a closer inspection.

Children capered around his heels laughing, shouting and pulling at his trousers. They were talking in a tongue he could barely understand, although he recognized the word *beké,* white man. The youngsters pushed forward a boy about five years old. Pye halted in astonishment.

Unlike the grinning niggerlings surrounding him, this was a white boy. The child was watching him sullenly.

"What the hell are you doing here?" Pye stooped

down and brought his face level with the boy's eyes. "Who are you?"

"Brett." The boy spoke without a trace of nervousness. "What are you doing here?" His yellow eyes regarded Pye with contempt.

"Why, you're a fresh young whelp!" Pye snapped his horsewhip down on the child's bare bottom. The children jeered and pulled Brett away. Pye pushed them aside and walked to where the girls were sitting under the tree.

"Stand up!" They scrambled to their feet immediately.

Pye pursed his lips. Since the day he had arrived in Antigua and met a free Negro called Prince who told him about plantation life, Pye had wanted to pick out a young black virgin for himself. He scratched his head. There was a score to chose from here.

He cast his eyes around the group, who were regarding him doubtfully. One girl had a complexion the color of cured tobacco. Her lips, in contrast, were a delicate crimson. Her breasts were half-formed, and her thighs looked lusty.

"You!" Pye decided, pointing at her with his whip handle. "Bathe yourself in the river and then go to the school cabin. Wait for me there."

"Yassa." The girl looked up, started to speak, and then hung her head down again.

"What is it, wench?"

"Please, sah, Mas Caspar does say ah does be he wench. He does be coming fuh me when de wench he does have now does be full." The other girls chorused their agreement.

"She does be allocated, sah," protested a big girl with a broad nose. "Ah does be ready to be

364

burst, sah." She held her crotch obscenely while the others shrieked with laughter.

Pye cracked the whip over their heads. "Damn you all for your insolence. I want that wench. You know who I am? I don't take second place to that slave Caspar." He glared at them.

"Get to the river and bathe and then go up to my cabin at once, wench."

Pye completed his ride around the estate and returned to relax in the school cabin. Pip carried over his dinner along with the decanter of rum. Pye was content. While the Bondmaster was away, he was going to have his pick of all the wenches on the estate, beginning that very afternoon.

There was a tap on the cabin door. Pye stretched extravagantly. "Come in," he bellowed, reaching over the side of the bed for the decanter and pouring himself another shot of the rum.

"I'm in the bedroom," he called as he heard the door open and someone enter the cabin. A black hand gripped the side of the partition. Pye sighed with anticipation, ready for the wench.

"What the hell are you doing here!" he shouted when he saw Samboth's head poke around the doorway. "Get out!"

"Ah does have a message fuh yo' from Mas Caspar," said Samboth firmly. "He does say yo' to come see he on de gallery."

"What!" Pye sat up angrily. "That nigger overseer summons me to him! Who does he think he is? You can tell that slave, if he wants to see me he can come here!" Pye snorted. "But I don't want to see him so that's the end of it."

"He does be plenty vex', sah," Samboth commented. "Miss Laura does be wid he, sah."

"That does not concern me. Get out!"

Samboth shrugged his shoulders and backed out of the cabin, slamming the door shut. Pye hastily poured another shot of rum. The interruption irritated him. He resolved to drain his anger on the paddock wench when she came.

He gulped more rum. It was fiery in his throat and spread quickly through his body making his limbs feel weak, dulling his brain. After a while, he spun into a drunken doze. A crash, as the cabin door banged open, roused him. A bundle of clothes flopped onto the bed.

"You can sleep out here as long as you want, Roger Pye," shrieked Laura, standing over him shaking her fist. He groaned.

"I know what your plan is! Because the Bondmaster is away, you want to burst every little black wench that takes your fancy. If that's what's in your mind, then you'll stay out here, Roger Pye, under guard. Caspar and I ain't going to have any nonsense from you!"

Pye peered behind Laura's shoulder. He could see the huge bulk of Caspar blocking the doorway, a stern expression on his face.

"Oh, leave me alone, Laura! Can't you see I'm tired of you. Let me have some peace!"

"Oh, yes, you can have peace, Roger. Don't try to come in my boudoir again, that's all!"

"Woman!" Pye sat up drunkenly. "When you want me, you'll bang down this cabin for me. Have a rum." He picked up the decanter and held it to his lips, before extending it to Laura. She slammed it out of his hand and it shattered on the floor.

Caspar whispered into Laura's ear. She frowned.

"Caspar says you should remember the Bondmaster's right. Daddy is very particular about who takes his virgins."

"Oh, gawd!" said Pye, falling back on the mattress. "Leave me in peace. When I'm drinking my rum, don't speak to me." He covered his eyes with his hand.

"Oh gawd! Oh gawd! Oh gawd!" he uttered until he was certain that both Laura and Caspar had gone out of the cabin. He rolled across the mattress and hung his head over the edge. He vomited.

If Pye had thought his wife would relent and try to persuade him to come back into the house, he had not bargained for Tita. The old nanny was the first to offer comfort to Laura, nodding her head sympathetically as Laura poured out her story to her later that same afternoon.

"I have never seen him like that before," Laura declared. "He was such a beast. He doesn't usually drink so much rum."

"All men does be like dat." Tita sat behind her mistress brushing her hair. "Now yo' does finish crying, ah gon' brush yuh hair like ah done do when yo' was be a chil'.

"Ah must tell yo', Miss Laura, dat dere ain't no good in men at all. Because yo' does be a *beké,* yo' does have to marry wid one, ah know. Tita done see a lot of things, Miss Laura, and ah tell yo' dat bucks are de curse of we fillies, yassa!"

Laura found Tita's brisk stroking of her hair very soothing. She half-listened to Tita's words, but her mind was on Roger sprawled on his cabin bed. Alone. Laura had no doubt that he was alone, because Caspar had posted Samboth and Asaph to guard the cabin.

"You are probably right, Tita," drawled Laura. "But how can a woman do without a man?"

"Dat does be easy, Miss Laura." Tita caressed the back of Laura's neck tenderly.

Laura raised her eyes to the slave and pouted at her in consternation. "Oh, what shall I do? I do so love Roger, Tita. I shall miss him at my side tonight."

"Dat does be small matters, Miss Laura. Tita gon' come keep yo' company tonight in a way dat gon' make yo' never want dat man again."

Laura looked quizzically at Tita.

"If yo' does want me to, ma'am?"

Laura bent her head forward into Tita's soft, caring hands. Gently Tita massaged her ears, cooing words of endearment. Laura, with her eyes closed, tilted her head back and abandoned herself to Tita's caresses.

The old Negress leaned over and brought her lips down onto Laura's half-open mouth.

Pye was not short of rum. He found an unexpected ally in Tita. It was Tita who arranged for Mingoson to carry his meals over for him every day as well as provide him with rum when he needed it.

Pye did not know that Tita did this as a means of keeping Pye from returning to the house and interrupting her own liaison with Laura. Whatever her reasons, Pye did not care. He was convinced his wife would have to send for him in the end. When she did, he would stipulate his own terms.

Pye sat on the step of his cabin, a bottle of rum in his hand, scowling at the sun setting over the village down at the rivermouth. He had lost count of the days he had been in his cabin. Each day he drank the rum brought to him by Mingoson until he passed out in a drunken stupor. This evening, he told himself, it would be different. He was going to have that wench in the paddock even if he had to drag her to his cabin by her bushy hair.

He took a slow deliberate swig from the bottle, placed it on the cabin floor with care, and stood up. He gripped the door jamb to steady himself, then lurched uncertainly down the steps. Samboth, crouching under the house gallery, observed his stumbling progress in the direction of the paddock.

He got up and followed.

Pye reached the gate of the paddock and paused, his head down low. Night was falling quickly, the somber shadows of the trees merging with the dim twilight. A rush of cold air wafted down the valley, sending a chill of foreboding through the paddock.

The children glanced at Pye swaying by the gate. They fell silent. The younger ones ran inside the nursery where the lamps were being lit. The older children huddled closer together under the trees. They waited.

Samboth saw Pye fumbling to open the gate. He ran to call Caspar.

In his befuddled mind Pye knew what he wanted. He wove his way toward the cluster of dark shadows at the far side of the paddock. Although they saw him coming, none of the children got up to run. They sat silently, waiting. He came so close to them they could smell the stench of rum and sweat on his grimy clothes.

"Where is she?" he demanded, putting out his hand to steady himself against the trunk of the tree. He squinted at the black faces watching him. They stared back, eyeing the whip in his hand.

None of them answered. He peered again. The swarm of swarthy faces swam in front of his eyes as the children shifted nervously. He raised his whip and cracked it down in the center of the group. They sprang to life.

"Who dat, massa? Which she yo' does want?"

"You know the one I crave, you cunning nigger brats." Pye spoke with effort. "She's here somewhere."

He dived unsteadily into the middle of the group, grabbing a girl by her arm. He gaped at her, then thrust her aside when he realized she was not the one he sought.

"Come on," he said impatiently, waving the whip. "Where ish she?"

With drunken agility, Pye pounced through the group, holding the first body he encountered. He looked at the girl's face, turned away, and then looked back, peering again at these brown features and bright lips.

"Ah-ha!" he exclaimed triumphantly. "So there you are, my litter nigger wench! Lesh go."

He held the girl by her wrist and dragged her out of the group. The others watched from under lowered eyelashes, each one of them afraid to interfere in case the *beké* picked on them instead.

"I've got you now, my black maiden!" Pye blundered across the paddock jerking the girl along behind him.

He stumbled when a little boy collided with his legs in the near-dark. He flicked at him with his whip to drive him away. To his amazement the boy fastened his hands around his ankle and held on, anchoring his foot to the ground.

"What!" said Pye. "Damn brats all over the

plashe." He lifted his leg to shake off the boy. Seizing her opportunity to escape, the girl pulled her hand out of his grasp. Pye grabbed at the girl to keep her from running. He lost his balance, toppled over the boy, and landed with a thump on the ground.

He struck out angrily at the boy entangled in his legs. The blow caught the boy on his shoulder as he was trying to wriggle away. The boy flopped to the ground, howling with pain.

Pye peered in the gloom at the child who had foiled his plan. He realized it was the white brat he had come across before.

Angrily, Pye drew back his wrist and sliced his whip through the air. It landed with a stinging thwack on the boy's cheek, silencing him.

Pye's brow was heavy with rage. He pulled himself to his feet and stood over the tiny figure. He cracked down the whip in a sizzling blow across the boy's throat. Pye took careful aim and swung his boot into the child's waist. The boy's scream turned to a breathless gasp of terror.

"For gawd's sake, shut up!" shouted Pye, lifting his boot to stamp on the child's head.

Pye felt the swish of air before the thick leather tongue of the bullwhip cut into his cheek, curling around his neck. He tried to hold his balance but the whip pulled him backwards and he crashed down onto the hard mud of the paddock.

Instinct made him roll over quickly as the whip lashed again. He scrambled to his feet and crouched low as he peered into the moonless night in the direction of his attacker. He recognized the hulking shadow which loomed over him.

"Caspar!" he yelled. "How dare you attack a white man! I'll have you hanged for this!"

The whip snaked down and cut across his chest.

"Stop it now, stop it, Caspar. I order you!" Pye panicked. The impact of the whip as it ripped into the side of his head blinded him with agony.

"Caspar, Caspar!" His voice changed to a whine. "Stop it, I beg of you." He curled himself up like a child as Caspar stood over him.

He waited for the next lash. None came. Slowly Pye opened his eyes. He was staring at Caspar's mud-spattered riding boot. He raised his head cautiously, squinting at Caspar's leg.

In his mind he sized up the chances of banging his head into Caspar's crotch and then making a dash for the house. He could get one of the Bondmaster's pistols and finish the nigger off for good. Pye risked a glance upwards so he could judge how to aim the blow. His heart stopped.

Caspar's cutlass was poised above his head.

Pye's shriek of fear was cut off by the swipe of the blade driven into the side of his neck.

Blood spurted out of the wound onto Caspar's trousers. Caspar cursed gently in patois as he chopped the blade down again, severing Pye's head from his body.

He stood over the bloodied corpse and gaped at the faces watching him. Ella cradled Brett in her arms. The child was sobbing silently.

"He'll live," whispered Ella.

Tita clutched Laura who gazed helplessly at her husband's body.

"You killed him!" said Laura without emotion.

Caspar shrugged his shoulders.

"I'll have to hang you."

He stared at her. Suddenly she pounced at him, pounding her fists against his chest.

"You killed him! she shrieked.

Her cry changed to a moan of pain. She gripped her belly and slid slowly down his body and collapsed on the earth at his feet beside Roger.

"De baby!" gasped Tita. "She gon' drop de whelp!"

Chapter 34

Laura's son, Vincent, was born prematurely two days later in the bed Laura had shared for eight months with Roger Pye. Laura's confinement saved Caspar.

For the second time, Caspar had deprived Laura of her man and she had determined to report Caspar to the authorities for slaughtering Pye. But without her father at home, Laura was trapped.

Ella and the slaves combined to prevent her having contact with the outside world. She was forced to depend on Caspar, although loathing had replaced the affection she once felt for him. She blamed Caspar for all her troubles.

Tita, who might have been tempted to act as Laura's messenger, was overjoyed with the baby. She moved into Laura's bedroom, spending every minute with her. The baby slept between them in the big four-poster bed.

It was Tita who helped Laura over the shock of Pye's death. Tita made certain that her presence was essential to Laura and the baby. In the baby's birth and Pye's death, Tita saw security for herself at least until Hayes inherited the mantle of the Bondmaster. Then she could use her influence with Hayes to oust Ella and put her in full control.

Ella nursed the injured Brett. She gave him her bed, sleeping on a mat on the stone floor beside him every night. She gave him bush baths with *shandella* or *gercy toute* leaves in the water; she massaged his body each night with soft candle and burnt rum and nutmeg. Ella smeared unguents, made from obeah recipes passed down to her from her mother, on the child's wounds and bruises. Brett recovered, but he bore a livid weal streaking across his white skin from his ear to his throat. It was to scar him for the rest of his life.

"He does be a' right, *oui?*" announced Ella when Brett walked into the kitchen and stood shyly by the pantry door. It was a few days before Carlton's return.

"Come, boy."

Brett regarded Caspar suspiciously. With a faint smile, he ran instead to Ella, clasping her around her waist. Ella wiped her hands on her apron where she stood at the stove.

"Yo' don't want yuh Da', Brett?" laughed Ella. "Go 'n' show he how yo' does be well, now." Ella pushed the child toward Caspar.

"Come, Brett!" grinned Caspar as the boy frowned. "Surely you are not afraid of your dad?"

"No." Brett brushed at his tousled hair as it strayed across his eyes.

"Son!" said Caspar proudly. "You look like my boy again. Let me tell you, here is your home now. You are going to live here in the house with Miss Ella and Pip to look after you. You ain't going back to the pen with the whelps."

Brett did not speak.

"He has had a big shock," Caspar said, facing Ella.

"He'll take his time to get over it."

"He ain't gon' like no white man after dat!" Ella exclaimed. "De boy gon' distrust every buckra he does see from now. He does be white-skinned like he mam, Caspar, but he does have yuh black heart."

Brett put out his hand to touch Caspar's arm. He stroked it, feeling the soft hair on his father's brown skin. He sucked at his lower lip and raised his head. "Why yo' does have hair on yuh arm, Da'?"

Caspar picked up Brett, raising him above his head with a shout. He danced around the kitchen shaking the boy until he laughed.

"Careful!" scolded Ella. "Yo' don't know if he does be cured yet."

"My boy is cured, not so, Brett?"

"Yes, Da'."

"Yo' know yo' must be de one to tell Mas Carlton dat Pye done die? Before Laura does see she father?"

Ella's words stopped Caspar spinning round the kitchen. He placed Brett on the floor and regarded Ella shrewdly.

"Miss Laura does be a determined wench, and Tita does be in she boudoir wid she all de time," Ella said. "Who does know what dey does be scheming?"

"Don't worry about that, Ella," Caspar bragged, "I know how to handle Mas Carlton better than Laura."

"So yo' does say." Ella chewed thoughtfully on a piece of dry codfish. "Mas Carlton does be vex' when he does discover he have Miss Laura here widout she husband."

Caspar heeded Ella's warning. A few days later, he took Brett with him and went to Layou to meet Carlton. Samboth had brought the news of the Bondmaster's return before breakfast. Laura and Tita were still in the boudoir with the baby, so Caspar would have a chance to present his side of the story before Laura said her piece.

Carlton was alone when the skiff landed him at the jetty. He gripped Caspar's arm affectionately as he clambered ashore. He glared at Brett, who stood on the jetty watching silently.

"What the devil is that whelp doing out of the paddock? What have you been doing with the plantation while I have been in Trinidad, Caspar?"

"I'm pleased to see you back," Caspar said softly. "I've taken Brett out of the pen. There is some bad news."

"What!" Carlton glanced around before venting his anger. The usual idlers were shuffling at the end of the jetty.

"I have your horse here," said Caspar. "Samboth and Asaph will look after your boxes." He pushed the way through the crowd, waiting while Carlton mounted his horse. He jumped on his own and put Brett in front of him.

"Roger Pye is dead," he said quickly. "And Laura has had a son."

"I thought you said bad news. Now what's that boy doing with you?"

"If it were not for Brett here, Roger Pye would have raped the paddock wenches." Caspar explained in detail what had occurred.

"Laura said she will see me hanged," he concluded as they reached the house.

"The devil she will!" Carlton jumped down from his horse and flung the reins to Caliste.

"Pip!" he shouted as he hurried up the steps. "Get the rum out. Where's Hayes?"

Hearing his name called, Hayes ran through the drawing room to greet his father. Mingoson chased after him and hid behind a chair as Carlton cuffed Hayes affectionately.

"How are you, son? No one took a lash at you, I suppose?"

"Mister Pye did, dad, but I made Mingoson take it."

"Oh, he did, did he? Seems like that Pye was a dedicated trouble hound." Carlton snatched the decanter off the tray as Pip sidled up. He splashed rum into his glass, knocking it back quickly.

"Hmm," he commented to Caspar. "That the new screw? Not bad, not bad at all. Now where is Laura?"

He strode across to his daughter's bedroom and kicked open the door. Laura was sitting in the bed, suckling Vincent. Tita hovered over her. "Get out, scalawag!" he shouted at Tita. He hustled her out of the door and shut it, drawing the bolt across.

Without speaking to Laura, he walked around the room closing the shutters. The room was dim, lit only by the shafts of sunlight which seeped through the cracks in the boards.

"Tita is the babe's nanny, daddy. She could stay."

"And I'm the babe's grandfather, Laura. I want to talk to you." He paused, stroking his chin as he studied the child.

378

"Well, there's no doubt about that, Laura. He has the eyes! And my hair. What a bonnie baby!"

Carlton sat down on the bed beside Laura and put his arm around her shoulder. He felt her body go tense.

"Laura, in spite of everything, I am still your father. I am happy. You have born a son." He squeezed her shoulder, but Laura gazed at him with a blank expression.

"You must hang Caspar. He killed Roger. You punished Bute for what he did to me. Now you must punish Caspar, too."

"Oh, yes?" Carlton rose. He strolled over to the armchair and sat down, staring at his daughter. He stroked his chin.

"I follow your logic very clearly, Laura. For a slave to kill a white man, a painful death is the punishment. Yet the law says, Laura, that a slave who protects his master's property will be rewarded.

"Is it not true that Roger Pye was attacking my property at the time?" he asked.

"You won't hang him?" Laura patted the baby on his back. Her voice showed no emotion.

"No, I won't hang him. And I am letting Brett live with us in the house."

"Very well, then."

"I don't like your tone, Laura."

"You are not expected to."

"You have something on your mind, Laura?"

Carlton gazed at the ceiling. He remembered at that moment how thirty years before, he had been a young boy about the same age as Hayes, quartered in that same room without a care in the world. His own father was alive then. The old man was ruthless with slaves.

379

Carlton frowned when it occurred to him that if old Hayes was still the Bondmaster he would have hanged Caspar by his heels, whipped him two hundred times, and left him to bleed to death.

"I shall go to the authorities myself." Laura stood up and placed the child in the center of the bed.

"I don't believe you!"

"Why not? You shall see. I will take Caliste and ride to Layou. If there is no agent there, I will hire a drogher to sail me to Roseau. Roger's death must be avenged."

"Damme, Laura! What's come over you? The fellow was a scoundrel wanted by the authorities in England for embezzlement. He only escaped the gallows himself through fleeing England in the nick of time, according to a letter I've had about him. It's my speculation that Caspar has done you a favor. The rascal would have swindled you and me out of everything we possess."

"He has not done me a favor, Daddy, Caspar has robbed me of a man."

"Hah! A man! You call an embezzler a man? He is better dead, Laura. You will get another man, a real man."

"White or black?"

"A white man, Laura," replied Carlton with a heavy sigh. "Not a Negro animal."

"Those you call animals are the only men here. You cannot deter me, Daddy. A crime has taken place. I must report it and see justice done."

"You would see Caspar hang? You know what Caspar is to this plantation. Hang Caspar and we have no plantation." Carlton fidgeted uneasily in the chair.

"Of course, when he is older, Hayes will take

over. After Hayes, who knows, it could be little Vincent here. I tell you, Laura," he lowered his voice, "if Caspar is hanged, we are as good as finished."

"Oh, I understand you, Daddy." Laura smoothed the baby's hair, a forced smile softening her tense features. "But you don't understand me. Where are the white men here to replace Roger?"

Carlton was perplexed. "There aren't any right now, of course. I'll hire a new tutor for Hayes."

"Am I to go through that again? Can't I choose who I want?"

"Laura! Your husband has not been dead for more than a month, and you are talking about putting another man in your bed before it is cold. If you were in England you would be wearing widow's weeds."

"Well, that's in England, Daddy. I'm a creole wench, you know!" Laura smiled.

"Creole wench! You'll be telling me you want a black lover next."

"A Negro animal, Daddy? What would you say if I did?"

"Say?" Carlton stood up, eyeing his daughter suspiciously. "What does that mean?"

"If I did have a black lover, Daddy, would you skewer him to death like you did Bute?"

"Bute raped you!"

"Oh yes, Daddy, so he did. But if a black buck came to my room at my request, what would you do?"

"You must be mad! The baby, everything that has happened, has been a strain for you. I shall call Ella and ask her to make a herb tea to calm you down. You need rest."

"There's nothing wrong with me, Daddy. I want to get something very clear, that's all. I have no man, Daddy, because of what Caspar did. If I have no man, you cannot believe I will remain at home in seclusion, like a Papist nun. I must either acquaint the authorities with the atrocity against my husband or I will be forced to seek comfort in the arms of others."

Laura pouted. "Those others will be your slaves."

"It's preposterous!" Carlton sank back, staring at his daughter. He shook his head, swallowing hard.

Laura picked up Vincent, who was gurgling happily. "Keep Caspar to run the plantation. I will say nothing. I'll choose my companion to compensate me for my loss. And, Daddy," she added as Carlton's face turned to crimson, "you can have Vincent as your son, your own son."

She thrust the baby at Carlton and unbolted the door, sweeping out into the drawing room.

"Tita, Tita!" she called. "Tell Caliste to saddle a horse. I want to ride!"

Carlton carried the baby to the door. The child was cooing happily, his tiny hands waving at Carlton's face.

"Caspar," Carlton croaked wretchedly, "escort Miss Laura. She is going to select a buck for herself."

Chapter 35

Hayes and Mingoson sauntered across the yard, arms around each other. Hayes was growing. His legs were lanky like his father's, and his thin shoulders were beginning to expand. His hair, which had been long, was shriveling up and becoming wiry, a phenomenon which Tita explained to Ella was caused by the boy playing in the sun without his hat.

He wore a ragged pair of pants, revealing an adolescent body of a pale brown color: color caused, claimed Tita, by constant exposure to the sunlight.

In contrast, Mingoson's complexion was the liver brown of a Negro, his hair a cap of tight black whorls. He had filled out faster than Hayes, and his young body was tough and muscular. He walked with a lithe swagger, carrying his head arrogantly. His features were more European than Negro, the nose slender and the lips thin.

Glimpsing the two boys from the kitchen, Carlton was disgusted by the apparent intimacy between them. "Look at that son of mine, Ella. You'd think he's out strolling with his brother, not his slave."

"He does be raised wid he, dat's why. Tita de

383

one encouraging dat. She ain't got no respect fuh de massa like de slave should, Carlton."

They were alone in the kitchen. A few minutes before, Carlton had ridden in from the provision gardens in the hills. He shrugged his shoulders at Ella's observation and strolled across the kitchen to the water filter.

He raised the lid of the coral stone upper filter and saw that someone had recently filled it with rainwater. This was percolating through into the shallowed and thicker lower filter and into the marble basin below. He picked up the calabash from the ledge and dipped it into the basin. He drank the cool water directly from the calabash.

Studying him carefully, Ella smiled. Carlton surely knew he was drinking from a slave cup, she thought. He transgressed his own rules for segregating slaves and whites more than anyone.

In fact, Carlton had no defined white standards in his home. He ate the same food as the slaves and worked alongside them. Ella knew most creole whites favored imported salt beef over local meat, wanted brandy to drink instead of local rum, and generally furnished their homes as though they had been transplanted by accident from England.

Carlton was different. Although he was white, he lived as naturally in his comforts and tastes as any slave. He lived in the manner to which he had been born. Perhaps, reasoned Ella, this was why the Governor and English officials never came to call. Whites, generally, kept away from Roxborough Hall unless they were slave traders in search of stock.

Carlton set his rules by instinct. A slave could feel his wrath quite unwittingly when Carlton, as though by caprice, decided that some kind of behavior was irregular.

"I don't understand that boy, Ella. You would expect Hayes to use me as an example. I take him around with me when I go on the plantation. He gabbles away with the slaves in patois, like he was one of them, instead of being reserved and aloof." Carlton splashed the cool water on his face.

"I've told him, Ella, that those slaves he laughs and jokes with will be the same slaves who will slit his throat. Then he hugs Mingoson and shakes with laughter at my old-fashioned ways!"

"He does be growing, Carlton. He gon' take time to understand."

"At his age, I was helping my dad to run the plantation. I was lusting for wenches, riding my horse, and beating idle niggers. Of course, Ella, I did not have a nursemaid and a playboy to dote on me all the time!" He wiped his face.

"My father sold Prince—he was my playboy—when I was thirteen. I never did have a nanny."

"De times change, Carlton."

"It was harder then! We had only raw dandas in the fields, and not so many females, either. It was vigilance all the time. You were here, though. You must remember."

"Yas, massa!" Ella rolled her eyes and flashed him a wide grin exposing her white teeth to ridicule his seriousness. "When yo' was be a boy, Carlton, yo' was be mingling wid de slaves like Hayes does be now."

Carlton placed the calabash back on the ledge. "That was for the sake of the plantation, Ella. I was building up stock and learning. That was not friendship. I knew that I was going to be the Bond-master one day." He shook his head wearily.

"There seems to be something wrong with Hayes. He does not have my mettle. He seizes on every chance to enjoy himself with the niggers, never thinking about learning how to carry on the slave-breeding."

Brett ran into the kitchen from the back door. He did not observe Carlton standing in the corner by the water filter.

"Ma!" he cried, grabbing Ella's apron. "Ah done feed de swine wid Dukey this morning an', Ma, dere does be two fillies done drop in de nursery!"

"Is dat so, Brett?" Ella patted his shoulder. "Yo' don't see de Bon'massa does be here?"

"Good morning, sir!" Brett said politely in English, shuffling in awe behind Ella.

"Come here, boy. Let me look at you." Carlton beckoned Brett to the center of the kitchen. "You don't have to be afraid of me, boy."

"No, sir." Brett replied softly.

"He's a gradely lad, Ella. Of course, even though he is white-skinned, I can see he has slave blood in him, Ella. I can always tell."

Ella cocked her head on one side. She was doubt-ful. "Yo' does know every time?"

"Oh, yes, it's easy to spot. Might be the hair, the nose, even the teeth, the way the body is built, or the ears. Brett is light-skinned, but he'll darken up.

"See, his ears are small, that's sign of Negro blood. His hair is long now, but it will get kinky as he gets older. That's what he got from you, Ella. Now, he has my eyes from Caspar. What he got from the whore who is his mother, I don't know."

Brett listened to the Bondmaster without under-

386

standing all the man said. His voice was kind, and Brett liked the way he ran his hand quickly over his body, squeezing his arms and legs.

Carlton spun him around and patted him on his bare backside. "Go, Brett. Go back and help Dukey tend the swine." Carlton sat down on the bench, stroking his cheek.

"How's the other one? Vincent?"

"He does be growing well, *oui*? He in mah cell sleeping. Ah done send de wet nurse back to de paddock. He does have enough age to do without de breast."

"Not much sense in having Tita in the house now," Carlton mused. "You are raising Vincent, and Hayes has no need of her. Mingoson could go into a field gang until he is ready for breeding." He looked at Ella.

"What should I do with Tita?"

"She does be a company fuh Miss Laura," Ella said pointedly.

"Damme! Laura has all the company she wants! Tita could go to the nursery to tend the whelps there. Or I could sell her. She has kept her figure. Maybe she ain't pretty any more, but she could still get a good price as a child-minder."

Carlton rose. "You'll be pleased at that, won't you, Ella? I know you've never liked her." He hugged Ella affectionately.

"Dere be some way she does get on, like she have a secret over we. Since de day she done come from Antigua wid de two whelps and yuh wife. She does have a wickedness in she, Carlton."

Carlton released Ella and strode out of the kitchen at the same moment as Hayes was trying to get Mingoson to run up the steps.

387

"Hayes!" he called. "Hayes!"

The boy halted and glanced in annoyance at Carlton. Mingoson nodded brightly.

"Hayes, you ain't got time for playing any more, son. I'm going to send Mingoson to the small gang so you are not fooling around with him all day. You have to put your mind on the estate now.

"Come here!" He waited for Hayes to descend the step.

Hayes regarded him sulkily from the corner of his eye.

"Listen, son, every day, I want you to ride around the plantation with Caspar. I want you to help him in his work, Hayes. You'll see all the different things you will have to do, from counting the whelps to repairing a cartwheel. I want you to learn from him, Hayes."

"Are you really going to put Mingoson in the field gang?"

"Of course. The buck's fit. Hard work will put some muscle on him. If he were not so dandified in his face, he might be a fighter in a few years. He has the physique for it." Carlton rubbed his hands across Mingoson's chest and down his arms.

"Tita sure gon' be vexed," pouted Hayes.

"What the hell do I care about that?" He released Mingoson.

"Tita says that Mingoson ain't going to work in the fields as long as she's at Roxbruh."

"Is that so, son!" Carlton chuckled, putting his hand into the boy's mop of frizzy hair. "Tita won't be here much longer, anyway! Hey, what happened to your hair? It's looking kind of niggery."

Hayes raised his hand to his head and brushed

388

his hair down. It sprang back up as soon as he removed his hand.

"Tita says it is because I play in the sun without my hat. She says the sun does burn the oil in my skin."

"Tita! What does she know? Whites don't have oil in their skins like blacks. Your hair ain't like mine, that's for certain. Look, son, mine is fair and curly and soft. And the sun is hitting it all the time."

Carlton's brow wrinkled as he mulled over this peculiarity. "You must have your mother's hair, though I don't recall it ever looking niggery like that. I must ask Ella."

"What have you done to Tita, Daddy?"

Carlton set down his rum glass in surprise. Laura stretched across the table for the soup tureen. She ladled the callaloo into her plate as she waited for a reply. Carlton glanced at Hayes for enlightenment, but the boy was soaking chunks of bread in his soup without listening to the conversation.

"I ain't done nothing to Tita."

"That's not what she says." Laura spoke brusquely between mouthfuls of soup. "I've had her crying on my shoulder the whole afternoon. Hayes told her you are going to sell her. Is that true?"

Carlton glowered at Hayes. "Boy, you say that?" He banged his fist down on the tabletop, making the dishes and cutlery jump. Hayes raised his head out of his soup plate.

"You tell that slave Tita what I said this morning?"

"I done tell you she would be vexed!" Hayes shrugged his shoulders.

"Hayes!" Carlton smacked the boy across his face, sending him tumbling out of his seat. Hayes jumped up quickly, tears in his eyes.

"Boy! You should know that a white man and a slave don't have no business to converse! How can you go and tell a slave something I told you?"

Carlton leveled his finger at Hayes's face. "Now get this in your head, Hayes Todd. You're the son of the Bondmaster, and it's about time you behaved like it.

"You ain't a nigger, and you've got no truck with niggers except to tell them what to do and to whip them when they don't do it."

Hayes stared at Carlton, his face pale with anger.

"Now get out of here and go to your room. I'll come and see you later."

Laura continued to sip at her soup. "It's true, then?" she said when Hayes had slunk out.

"Why that damn boy had to tell her, I don't know. It's not good for a slave to know in advance what's going to happen. They are so damn contrary."

"I don't think you should sell Tita." Laura laid her spoon on the table.

"Why not?"

"How can you ask? She's part of the family."

"I know she gets your slave lovers for you!"

"Daddy, don't be coarse. You've never seen one of them in the house, have you? It makes no difference to you at all."

"When I think of what my daughter is doing!" Carlton thumped the table.

"You've done things, too, we all know that. I don't interfere with you, and we have our agreement, remember? I know you'll sell Tita if you want to; she is your property, after all. I don't think it would be very wise. She knows a lot, you see."

Laura's last sentence hung in midair.

Pip silently removed the dishes. A crash as Carlton pushed back his chair and it toppled to the floor shattered the uneasy silence. He stomped onto the back gallery. He stared down from the railing edge at the dogs sniffing in the pool of light outside the kitchen door. He could hear the gay chatter and grunts of the slaves eating their own supper below.

Carlton raised his head to peer at the dark sky. Stars were blinking in the clear night over the wall of hills surrounding Roxborough. He glanced at the sea at the mouth of the valley and at the townlet where lanterns marked the casinos and bars. Lights bobbed on the masts of vessels anchored in the river.

Carlton paced the gallery floor to the corner of the house and sniffed. He remembered how his father had claimed that he could always tell when a nigger was moving at night by the scent of the wind.

He strode down the gallery, past the room occupied by Hayes and Mingoson, pausing at the opposite corner, outside Laura's room. If he wished, he could walk along the front gallery and down the other side of the house: it was the extent of his world. All around the house, as far as the eye could see in daylight, was the Roxborough plantation.

"Dammit!" Carlton muttered into the night. "This is mine. Why the devil can't I do what I want?"

A shape moving up the front steps was outlined

in the dark by the lantern swinging at the corner of the gallery. Carlton remained motionless. The figure wore a long dress which flopped over the steps and scraped along the floorboards of the balcony. Carlton put out his hand in the dark.

"Oh!' squealed Tita. "Yo' done scare me. sah!"

"I should have scared you years ago. Tita Why were you coming up the front steps? Slaves are supposed to use the back steps, as you well know, Tita! Perhaps you don't think yourself a slave?" He squeezed her wrist.

"Ah does be yuhs, Mas Carlton." Her eyes were wide as they stared at him. "Yo' gon' sell Tita, sah?"

Carlton wondered if there was a threat in the way she spoke.

"Why shouldn't I sell you, Tita?" His voice throbbed with anger.

Tita's tongue strayed across her lips sweeping slowly from side to side. In the dim light from the corner lantern. her face was softened. Unwittingly, Carlton recalled the night many years ago when Tita had come to his bed while his wife, Sybil, lay waiting for him in the next-door room.

"Yo' does recall how Miss Sybil done go to Antigua to have she child Mas Carlton," whispered Tita as though following his thoughts.

"Sybil?" Any mention of his dead wife put him on the defensive.

"Yo' does rem'ber ah done be pregnant, too, an' ah done go wid Miss Sybil as she companion?"

"Yes," Carlton answered suspiciously. "What about it?"

"Yo' does recollec' when we done return Miss Sybil done say Hayes be she child and Mingoson does be mine?" Tita's face was frozen in a smile of mockery as Carlton stared at her.

"That's right," he said, repelled by the doubts which Tita planted in his mind. "You were pregnant by that buck Mingo. I put you to breed with him. Mingo was the sire of your child!"

"Oh, yas, Mas Carlton. Mingo does be de sire of Mingoson, yo' can see dat." Tita grinned. "Mingoson does have white blood in he as well. Not me does be he dam, Mas Carlton. Mingoson does be de whelp of dat Mingo and yuh wife."

Carlton gripped the balcony rail, blood draining from his face. "Go on!" he whispered. "Who is Hayes?"

"Hayes does be yuh son by me, Mas Carlton, not by yuh wife."

"Your son? You changed the babies?" Carlton gripped Tita by her shoulders. "Why?"

"So yo' don't know Miss Sybil done have a slave's whelp, Mas Carlton."

"Is it true?" Carlton's eyes pleaded with Tita. "Hayes is not full white? He has your nigger blood in him?"

"Yas, Mas Carlton."

Carlton gazed out to sea, speechless.

"If yo' does keep me here at Roxbruh, Mas Carlton, yuh secret does be safe wid me. Yo' can have Hayes as yuh heir an' only me does know de truth dat de son of de Bon'massa does be a nigger."

Chapter 36

LAURA GALLOPED DOWN THE PATH. THE MOON was high, shining with a pallor that illuminated her long black dress. Her blond tresses flowed behind her in the wind, while the moonglow accentuated the ivory hardness of her expression.

Her whip cracked in the cacophony of the night. The horse responded by plunging off the track into the undergrowth. Gigantic ferns brushed her face, and creepers caught at her hair. Laura crouched with her head close to the horse's neck as the beast thundered relentlessly through the bush.

Hob heard the crashing of the horse. He cowered beneath the saman tree and clutched the obeah amulet he wore on a leather thong around his neck. His heart was thumping. He trembled as the waffling noise drew nearer and the plantain trees at the edge of the clearing burst apart. He raised his eyes.

In the vague light which streaked into the glade, he glimpsed the savage face of his mistress. He rose slowly to his feet.

"Hob?"

"Ah does be here, Miss Laura."

"Tie the horse!" Laura jumped down. "You really

are a stupid nigger, Hob, cowering under the tree like a softhead. Did you think I was the devil going to canter off to Hades with you?"

"De noise, ma'am," stuttered the youth.

"You knew I was coming, otherwise you would not be here, would you, Hob?"

"No, ma'am. Oh no."

Laura stretched her legs while Hob walked the horse to the edge of the clearing and tied the reins to a calabash tree.

"I really cannot understand Negroes," she said, half to herself. "You have strong bodies and big muscles, yet your minds are weak like children's. You believe every shadow and coincidence is the work of obeah.

"Your *soucoyants* don't scare me, Hob. See, I ride through the night in the full moon, and *loogarous* run before me. Is it because I'm a *soucouyant* myself, Hob?"

The slave, who was walking back toward her, halted in fear.

"Is so dey does say in de quarters, *oui!*"

"Let them speak, Hob. Come, boy, why do you stand so far from me?"

"Yas, ma'am."

Laura stamped the ground with her foot, trampling down the grass at the base of the saman tree. She eased herself down with her back resting against the trunk. She beckoned Hob closer to her. She fumbled with the ribbon securing his pants.

"Hob, I find you are one of my favorites," she said, pulling the pants free. "There's no nonsense about you at all." The pants dropped to the slave's feet.

"Ah, there's my black benefactor. See," she said, grasping him, "see, how hearty he is."

Laura rubbed her face against him. She nudged her nose and lips along his firmness, gasping, as she always did, at his monstrous size. "Hob!" she sighed, "you are never to be sold, you hear? I want you, always, always, always."

He shifted his feet. "Yo' does be tickling me, ma'am."

"Indeed?" She looked up. "Come Hob, sit down. Lie down here, rest your head against the trunk of the tree." She adjusted Hob to her satisfaction so he was lying on his back on the grass, with the tree serving as a pillow for his head.

Laura stood up and regarded him thoughtfully. The moonlight played on his nakedness, the triangle of tight hair glistening where it spread down from his navel. Laura hitched up her dress and clenched it to her side with her elbows. She placed her feet astride Hob, one leg on either side of his waist. She crouched down over him.

Gently, she eased him into her. She had the whip in her hand and, steadying herself with her knees pressed close to his body, reached back to flick his thighs. She moved herself up and down as though riding a horse, jabbing her spurs into his outstretched legs.

"Be here tomorrow night," she said, standing up suddenly and letting her dress fall back into place over her riding boots. "Don't be late!"

Hob, his eyes glazed, remained prostrate while he listened to the sound of the horse plunging out of the glade back to the trail. He clenched his amulet tightly in his fist.

Caspar, who had been standing unseen on the

other side of the saman tree, snaked away into the forest.

"There's four of them that I know of," Caspar reported to Carlton. "Some nights she sees one, some nights she sees two. She never stays with them very long. They seem terrified of her. They think she's a witch."

"Dammit! They know she's my daughter!"

Carlton and Caspar were walking together across the yard from the stables. "That's probably why they're scared, anyway," Carlton added with an ironic chuckle. "They know what happened to Bute."

"None of them are like Bute, Mas Carlton." Caspar tried to explain. "I mean they don't look interested, if you see what I mean. They just do it because she threatens to have them punished if they don't."

"I know, I know. Animals, every one of them," Carlton muttered. "She'll drain them! Spoil my stock! Caspar," he implored. "Something has to be done.

"We have damn good quality slaves being produced here now. I can sell every whelp in the paddock and every buck and filly on the plantation. People want the Roxborough breed.

"If Laura is picking out all my good colts for herself—dammit!—I won't get any new whelps from them at all. All their sap will be dry."

Caspar stepped aside for Carlton to climb the steps in front of him. "Ella believes that when Laura's pregnant again she will change her ways," he said.

"What!" Carlton gazed back at Caspar in alarm. "Pregnant for whom? A slave?"

He shuddered as he pondered the situation. "Those four bucks she has now. I'll make a quick trip to Trinidad to sell them. I hate to lose such ripe stock, but it will restrain her." He shrugged his shoulders with resignation.

"Come here, Hayes!" Carlton called as Hayes strolled idly across the gallery.

Carlton placed his hand under Hayes's chin and tilted up his face toward him. He found himself staring into eyes the color of his own at that age. Carlton sighed. But for his hair and his bronzed complexion, the boy could be his son, not a half-breed slave whelp.

"Boy, how would you like to go to a school in Trinidad?"

"Trinidad? Yes, Da'." Hayes jumped up and down with excitement. "Can Mingoson come, too?"

"I suppose so." Carlton's voice was flat. "Where's Tita?"

"Ah does be here, Mas Carlton." Tita glided around the corner where she had been listening to the conversation.

"Nanny Tita! Mah da' done say he gon' take me and Mingoson to Trinidad fuh school!" Hayes ran to Tita and clasped her hand.

Tita carefully scrutinized Carlton's face, suspecting treachery.

Carlton beamed at her, putting his arm on hers with apparent satisfaction. "You know, Tita, the boy does not get much chance being cooped up here all day. My son deserves a good education. He is bright enough for it. Mingoson should benefit, too, don't you think?"

"I'll tell you what," he added, as though just thinking of an idea. "Why don't you come, too? Not to stay, I mean. Just to see the two boys settled in. You have been like a mother to both of them. They'll miss you."

Caspar frowned with astonishment as he listened to Carlton's proposal.

"Oh, yes, Da'. Please come, Nanny Tita! Mingoson!" Hayes shouted as he galloped down the steps in search of his playboy. "We goin' to Trinidad wid Nanny!"

Tita shrugged her shoulders, her eyes deep with meaning. "Ah ain't have no say, Mas Carlton, sah. Is yo'."

Caspar passed quietly around the balcony and went down the back steps to the kitchen. He banged open the door and threw himself on the bench. Pip and Ella regarded him cautiously. He sucked in air noisily to show his annoyance.

"Pip!" he demanded. "Take a decanter of rum up to Mas Carlton at once." He rubbed his nose while Pip took down his tray from the nail on the wall, placed the decanter on it and rushed up the stairs.

"What the devil do you make of that, Ella!" Caspar exclaimed as soon as Pip had left the kitchen. "I just heard with my own ears the Bondmaster himself ask Tita if she wants to go to Trinidad with him. The man must be sick in his head."

"Oh mah gawd!" Ella sat down. "Is true?"

"Yes. He says he is going to take Hayes and Mingoson to school and Tita can go, too, and come back with him."

Ella shook her head slowly, wiping her hands on her apron. "Ah don't know what does be becoming of mah massa," she wailed. "Tita does be using he, *oui?*"

Ella's worry increased daily. Carlton seemed to be going out of his way to pander to Tita. He ordered dresses in the latest style to be made up for her and sent for shoes for her from Roseau. Tita passed her time bragging about the trip to all the other slaves. She was even encouraged by Carlton.

It was a relief to the household when the schooner that was to take them to Trinidad arrived in the basin. Chests were loaded onto the wagon. Hayes and Mingoson, dressed like young gentlemen, scrambled up on the cart while Tita settled in the front with all the airs of an English lady. The four bucks who were to be sold were rounded up, chained together, and tied to the back of the wagon.

Ella watched with disbelief as the wagon disappeared down the trail to Layou. Her pleasure at Tita's absence, even if only for a few weeks, was marred by her jealousy. Neither Ella nor Caspar could understand the change in Carlton. Why had he taken Tita with him? Why not Ella?

The departure of the Bondmaster from Layou attracted the attention of other observers.

From the door of the rum shop where he was swigging sangaree, Dyce Dobbs watched Carlton and his entourage being transported across the river to the schooner anchored in the mouth.

He cursed quietly to himself. That a man should be blessed with so much wealth caused Dyce considerable discomfort. The sight of Carlton with two superb youths and a richly dressed wench, to say

400

nothing of the four shackled slaves who accompanied him, profoundly disturbed Dyce. He gulped down his sangaree and turned back into the shadows of the rum shop.

"Whose schooner is that?" he demanded of the old man who tended the bar.

The man's wizened face creased into more furrows as he squinted out of the window. He dithered. "I does not know fuh sure, sah. Is de Bondmaster of Roxbruh dat does have de charter, *oui?*"

Dyce slapped down some bits on the counter with impatience. "John-James!" he snapped. "You are a worthless Negro."

"Yas, sah. An', Dyce Dobbs, yo' does be a white lummox!"

Dyce did not hear. He dived out of the rum shop and mingled with the Negroes and seamen strolling through the townlet. He wormed his way through the crowd at the jetty, clutching his purse carefully lest he become a target for pickpockets. He glanced at the people around him. Most were wharf rats jostling to see what pickings could be made from passengers arriving and departing. The mob was thickest around a tall, elegantly dressed mulatto. Dyce edged closer.

This fancy buck, Dyce guessed, was Caspar. He sidled up to him, straining his ears to see what he could overhear above the chatter of the Negroes.

"Come, Sam!" Caspar placed his hand on the youth with him. "Let's return to Roxborough."

"Ah does wish Mas Carlton done take me wid he, sah."

"For what, Sam? You are not content here?"

"Ah does want to see Trinidad, sah. Ah hear so much of dat place a'ready from de nigger-stealers."

401

Dyce smirked to himself; he had heard enough. Clasping his coat around him to ward off the niggers, he sauntered back into the town.

If the Bondmaster was sailing for Trinidad, Dyce reasoned to himself, he would be away from Roxborough for at least a week. There was time for Dyce to complete his business in Layou and then sail down the coast to Roseau to alert his crony, Fletcher.

Fletcher had recently returned to Roseau from Antigua. He would certainly reward him lavishly for the information that the Bondmaster was away from his plantation. Dyce chuckled, an evil glint in his eyes.

A certain mulatto *macquereau* was about to get his comeuppance.

Chapter 37

IN HER EXCITEMENT AT THE VOYAGE, TITA HAD deluded herself into thinking she was being taken to Trinidad as a bed wench for Carlton. She saw it as her reward for keeping secret the true parentage of Hayes and Mingoson. She was astonished, therefore, when Carlton retired to his cabin as soon as he boarded the vessel. During the voyage, he neither spoke nor sent for her. The only time she saw him was a day before their arrival when he was engaged in deep conversation with the captain at the wheel.

Tita forgot her puzzlement about Carlton's behavior when the ship dropped anchor off the coast of Trinidad. She was thrilled. From a sailor, she learned the ship would be going into Port of Spain after the four slaves had been off-loaded at the bay where they were anchored.

Carlton had strolled on deck when the anchor was rolled out. He stood at the rail, staring at a longboat heading for the schooner from the shore.

A white man was sitting in it. Carlton waved to him.

Tita sauntered over to attract his attention. "Morning, Mas Carlton! How d'yo' be? How de day?" She hailed him gaily, strutting along the deck and twirling her parasol.

Carlton glared at her. "Where are the boys?"

"Dey does be in de front of de ship, massa, watching de shore."

"Helloo, Carlton Todd! What a pleasure to see you again!" The white man clambered on deck from the longboat and embraced Carlton.

"James Macreary! You look more prosperous every day!" Carlton shook the man's hand warmly, tugging at his coat with the other. "That's a fine suit. All white. Is that the fashion now?"

"Ho, Carlton! The blacker your business, the whiter your troggery. You have something special for me?"

Carlton held the man's elbow and led him away. Tita scowled after them, wondering why she had been ignored. She observed Carlton whispering something in the man's ear. The man turned, scrutinized her briefly, and then put his arm around Carlton's shoulder as they went below.

"Macreary," began Carlton as soon as they were ensconced in the privacy of his tiny cabin. "I have four prime bucks for you, first-class breeders. They are all capable of breeding *Roxborough quality* stock. It hurts me to sell them."

"Why sell them, dear fellow? Not to please me, I'll be bound."

Carlton shook his head. "I have some problems at home, Macreary. Nothing to do with the stock. Rum?" He poured a large measure into a glass

404

and passed it across to Macreary, serving himself at the same time.

They raised their glasses.

"To niggers!" said Macreary. "May they continue to make us rich."

"To *Roxborough* niggers!" corrected Carlton, with a chuckle.

"Carlton, I'm delighted to get your stock. The market is clamoring. Who will worry if your bucks will breed or not? They have the Bondmaster's brand, so they will sell at a premium."

"That's your side of the business, Macreary. I could not run the risk of selling in Trinidad without you. As your plantation is on the coast, I can deliver the slaves before the revenue men sniff an extra nigger being landed.

"This time, Macreary, we are returning to Dominica this very afternoon. I do not want to be absent from Roxborough a day longer than is necessary." Carlton downed his rum.

"You want to surprise them, eh?" The factor slapped his thigh. "By the by, Carlton, George Tyndall sends you his regards."

"What the devil! The doctor? I once had hopes for that English blunderhead. What's he up to?"

"He is damn popular here, Carlton. Got a thriving practice. Do you know, that is a strange thing! One of those slaves I sold for you years ago is his assistant. The doctor bought the nigger from his first owner here and manumitted him. The boy's being trained to be a doctor himself now."

"I remember the buck." Carlton nodded. "It proves that Roxborough slaves are the best. But freeing slaves is dangerous; gives them fresh ideas. Damme, Macreary, a nigger sawbones! What next?"

Carlton poured himself another shot of rum and handed the bottle across to the factor.

"There's a lot of talk these days about emancipation, Carlton. Are you not worried by it?"

"It won't happen, Macreary. You know that." Carlton sipped his rum. "A Negro is a strong animal. He is built like an ox. He'll only work if he's whipped. Otherwise he'll squat on the ground and scratch his balls."

"The abolitionists say if the nigger is paid he will work."

"Abolitionists!" Carlton spat out of the porthole. "They live in a free society of white gentlemen and artisans, Macreary. They forget that the Negro is not white like them.

"A nigger does not think like you and me. He has no motivation to work. Money means nothing to him. Why, a few years ago, the Negroes were wild savages in the jungles of Africa. They could pull fruit from trees or set a trap for a wild boar for meat. Their life is not so much different in the Caribbees.

"You've seen how free Negroes pass their time aimlessly. They can fish, some have their gardens in the heights, and they need no clothes. They have no instinct for improvement. Why do they need money? Why should they work?"

Carlton drained his glass and smacked his lips to finish the conversation. "Now, Macreary. To business. There is that wench in the fancy clothes you saw on deck. She's a nanny. First-rate, but spoiled. She's pure Fulani, which accounts for her Mediterranean complexion and straight hair. She's been at Roxborough for twenty years." Carlton sighed as a sudden sadness gripped him.

"She doesn't know she is to be sold. I have arranged with the captain for his men to shackle her while we are talking. She is a witch, Macreary. She'll give you the Roxborough history if she thinks it will free her." He placed his hand on the factor's arm.

"Take no notice of her blabberings, I beg of you. I know you're a hard man and a true friend. Whatever she tells you, you can be assured that she is nothing more to me than a worthless nigger."

Macreary guffawed. "I have the place for her, Carlton. Do not worry. There is a sailor's brothel in Port of Spain where she'll be chained like a dog. The men like it that way."

"There are two boys also. Sell the black one. He is fully house-trained. He'll make a fine steward if he gets a good master.

"There's a special favor I ask of you." Carlton lowered his voice.

"Ask what you want. I am indebted to you, Carlton."

"The other boy appears to be white at first sight. The wench is his mother, and I'm his father. His name is Hayes. Do not sell him. Arrange for him to be apprenticed to a trade for seven years. Look upon him as a free mulatto, but not as my son."

A scream shattered the silence. It was accompanied by the gruff oaths of the seamen who were shackling Tita.

Carlton also identified the shocked cries of Mingoson and Hayes. He shrugged his shoulders mournfully, handing over a sheaf of documents to Macreary. "I nearly forgot. Here are the bills of sale."

"Are you coming on deck?" The factor rose to go.

Carlton shook his head. "No. It's your cargo now. I have company here. He held up the rum bottle, trying to close his ears to the screams.

Caspar loped easily along the trail to his cabin. There was no moon, but he knew the path so well that he did not bother to carry a lantern. His day, like the others since the Bondmaster had left for Trinidad. had been uneventful.

Even Laura was subdued. With her favorite bucks removed for sale and with Tita absent she spent her time in her boudoir or lounging on the balcony. She eyed Caspar but did not call him. For his part, he ignored her.

Ella had closed up the house for the night. Caspar glanced back. There was a weak glow of light from Laura's chamber. Caspar imagined that Laura must be sitting on the balcony outside her room, staring defiantly into the night. He hoped she would not choose that evening to stir onto the plantation. He was weary; he wanted to sleep.

However, if Laura did ride out, he would have to follow her in case she was attacked. Caspar's lips twitched. "Who would attack her?" he thought. "The slaves are too docile and believe she's a witch, and the maroons have scattered." He grunted.

There was no welcoming light in his cabin. He was not surprised. That afternoon he had despatched Samboth to Layou to look out for Carlton's return, and probably the boy had stayed there. "It would have been bright to have sent for a wench from the paddock," he thought "instead of spending the night alone." He grunted again, then stopped abruptly.

Caspar's nostrils tightened. He sniffed suspiciously. There was an odd odor in the air. He cocked his head to one side, his eyes narrowed. He stood motionless, peering through the darkness to the shadow of his cabin. He was about ten paces from it. He was puzzled. He sniffed again. There was a smell he just could not identify.

He was careless. He decided to wait until he had lit the lantern in his cabin before looking for the source of the unusual aroma.

He bounded anxiously across the clearing, leaped onto the veranda of the cabin, and pushed open the door. If he sensed danger then, his reflexes were too slow for him to do anything about it.

A blow from a pistol butt cracked him squarely across his head; it felled him instantly. As he fell, he tried to pitch his body away from his attacker. But there was more than one of them. Someone landed with a thump on his back. Another held down his legs. He was pinioned to the floor.

"By Old Horny! Keep down your voices!"

Caspar lashed out desperately. He twisted, he bucked, he cursed. But he could not dislodge the two men on top of him.

There was a flicker of light. The glow of his own lantern spread around the room. Before he could raise his head to see his attackers, Caspar was astonished to feel the cut of an iron bracelet clapped around his ankle. He was being shackled.

"What the devil!" He twisted his head in anger. His eyes saw first the highly polished brown riding boots of the man straddling his shoulders. He glanced upwards.

409

"You're a lively nigger, my beauty!" The white man chuckled evilly as he glared down at him.

Caspar frowned.

The man sitting on his legs clamped on an iron fetter to secure his other ankle.

Was he being captured? Even as the thought flashed through Caspar's mind, he knew it was ridiculous. No nigger-stealers would dare to raid Roxborough.

Drawing on the strength which his panic gave him, Caspar heaved himself off the floor. He dislodged the man sitting on his shoulders and seized the leg of the man who was towering over him. He snatched at the man's foot, toppling him backwards.

Caspar dragged himself across the floor and fell on top of the man. Raising his shackled legs, he pounded his knees into the man's crotch as his fingers flew for the man's throat.

The first blow on his head from behind did not dislodge Caspar. Instead, he clung to the man's neck, summoning the strength to squeeze the life out of him.

"Get the bugger off!" the man squealed.

Another blow on his head made Caspar wince. A third blow drained the force from his fingers. He slumped forward and rolled onto the floor.

"Don't beat him unconscious!"

"Did he hurt you, Fletcher?"

Fletcher! Caspar's mind shrank with fear. Now he could understand.

He opened his eyes slowly. There were three of them. Fletcher was standing above him, dusting dirt off his elegant clothes. The other two men were sitting on him again.

Fletcher sneered.

"Secure him, Dyce."

Caspar's arms were wrenched backwards, almost out of their sockets. His wrists were forced together behind his back and iron manacles snapped around them.

To Caspar's surprise, he felt his chest being lifted off the floor as they pulled his shoulders backwards. His ankles were raised, hoisting his thighs off the floor too. A shackle clinched into place, fastening his wrists behind his back to his ankles. Only Caspar's stomach supported him on the floor.

Fletcher tipped him over with his foot. He was like a pig awaiting slaughter.

"What a troublesome nigger!" Fletcher growled. Dyce and the other man stood back. "I'll wager he'll give us no more trouble!"

"He damn near kicked my balls out!" Dyce rubbed his crotch.

"Small matter." Fletcher leered. "Jepson, take a look outside. See if this beauty's scuffling disturbed the house."

It occurred to Caspar that he could cry out for help. But if he did, who could come to his rescue? The only man in the house was Pip. Asaph and the drivers were in the quarters. There were bucks in the barracoon but they were all locked in with their guard.

Caspar swallowed. He resolved not to give Fletcher the satisfaction of hearing him bleat for help.

"Everything is quiet, Fletcher." Jepson closed the door of the cabin and stood by Dyce. "What do we do now?"

"A taste of the nigger's own medicine, I think." Fletcher cracked his whip above Caspar's head.

"Stand back, Dyce, or you'll taste it, too." The lash snapped out, slicing across Caspar's extended arms. He winced. The lash fell again, cutting his wrists.

"No, that's no damn good," cried Fletcher. "Roll him over the other way."

Dyce and Jepson forced Caspar to roll over so he lay on his side facing Fletcher. His stomach and thighs were the target with his hands and legs grappled behind him.

Fletcher drooled. "Now, my arrogant beauty, let's see how you enjoy this."

The whip cut across Caspar's soft underbelly, ripping open his trousers. The lash fell again, slicing into his thighs. Caspar pitched forward to protect himself. Dyce and Jepson rolled him back and held him in position.

Fletcher studied Caspar's torso, placing his strokes so that the lash gradually tore away his clothes. Caspar's exposed body seemed to enrage Fletcher. He flayed him in a frenzy of hatred. Caspar's once gleaming skin oozed blood as torn flesh shredded onto the floor.

"Cry, you bugger!" roared Fletcher raising his hand to strike again. "Weep, damn you, weep!"

The pain of each slice merged into one blissful agony. Caspar teetered on the brink of oblivion. His teeth bit into his tongue as he tried to keep himself from begging for mercy.

Laura listened to the commotion from outside Caspar's cabin. She was angry. Her horse snorted as she held its reins tightly. Laura had no plan for that night. She just wanted to ride. But she found the sound of activity from Caspar's cabin intolerable.

It was obvious from the noise that someone was being whipped.

Laura assumed that Caspar and his cronies from the slave quarters were indulging in some form of sport. If he could have his, why could she not have hers?

She urged her horse into the clearing, leaping off and striding on to the veranda. She flung open the door crossly.

"Fletcher!"

Laura was taken aback by the sight of the man she had given up hopes of ever seeing again.

Fletcher paused, the whip raised above his head. Dyce and Jepson stood up quickly. They drew their pistols, letting Caspar topple over with a squelch into the pool of blood and flesh on the floor.

"Fletcher!" Laura's cry of pleasure turned to one of terror. "Where's Caspar?"

Fletcher smirked. "There!" he panted, pointing at the floor. "No nigger can do to you and me what he did and get away with it, Laura."

There was a hush.

"Is he dead?"

"No," Fletcher sneered. "Niggers don't die that easy."

He stepped over Caspar's bleeding body and took Laura's arm. "You are even prettier than I remember you, Laura. I thought of you all the time when I was in Antigua. I've come for you, Laura. Mary Gregg told me who you are."

"She did?" Laura turned her eyes coolly to Fletcher.

"I love you, Laura!"

Laura watched him silently. Dyce and Jepson replaced their pistols in their belts. Caspar twitched.

"What will you do with him?" she asked, linking her arm under Fletcher's and leading him out of the cabin onto the veranda.

Fletcher glanced back into the cabin, nodding at Dyce. "Nothing, Laura," he lied.

"Take me away with you, Fletcher! Now!"

"Now?"

"Yes, Fletcher! Let us go!"

Fletcher grinned foolishly to himself in the darkness. He guided Laura past the sugar canes scraping in the night breeze to the coppice where his horse was hidden.

Brett, crouching in the cane, listened to the sound of Laura and the man riding off into the night.

Brett waited. He had come to the cabin to warn Caspar that Laura had ridden off from the house. He rose from his hiding place and moved toward the cabin. Someone was coming out with a lantern. Brett dived back into the shelter of the cane. He peered out nervously.

The man who was holding the lantern had a rope in his hand. He placed the lantern on the ground and slung the rope over the branch of the huge flamboyant tree which spread over the cabin. He tested the rope, fashioning a noose at one end of it. He fastened the other end to the veranda railing.

Brett watched as another man emerged from the cabin dragging something behind him. The two men crouched down and hooked the noose to their burden. Brett heard them laugh as they pushed the shape off the veranda and it spun into the arc of light from the lantern, twisting by its neck above the ground.

The men ran off into the bush.

Brett bolted from his hiding place and dashed

into the cabin. He seized Caspar's cutlass from where it lay on the floor in a pool of blood. He ran out.

Standing on the tips of his toes on the deck of the veranda, he leaned out to reach the rope. Desperately, he hacked at it with the cutlass.

The rope parted, and Caspar's trussed-up body dropped with a thump to the ground.

EPILOGUE

The Troubled Years

1821-1824

Chapter 38

The pile of ledgers on the bureau bored Carlton. He closed the book he was writing in with annoyance and banged down his fist. "Why in hell's name a herd of niggers should involve me in so much writing. I do not know!"

Ella bustled into the drawing room with a pitcher of sangaree.

"Why don't you hire a bookkeeper, Carlton?" she nagged. "If you don't want an overseer to replace Caspar, at least a bookkeeper would help you. You would have more time to supervise the breeding."

"I have all the time I need, dammit, Ella!" He kicked back his chair and stood up. "But why are there so many cussed books for a bunch of slaves, ch? That's what frustrates me." He stalked over to the dresser and filled his tankard with the sangaree.

"The ledgers on the slaves' lineage are interesting. It is the others, Ella." Crossly, he waved his hand at the bureau. "There are books here on stores, accounts, food, medicines, and orders, to say nothing of all the ledgers on rum and sugar."

Ella righted his chair where it had fallen. "If you do not bother with your books, what happens then?"

"What happens?" Carlton strolled the length of the drawing room. Outside, the sun was boring down on the plantation. From the cane fields came the low drone of slaves singing rhythmically as they moved across a field, weeding in the ratoons. Occasionally, there was a louder shout from a driver followed by the crunch of a whip and a slave's yelp of pain.

Birds twitted at each other in the trees around the house. The laughter of Caspar's boy, Brett, as he played with Laura's child, Vincent, drifted up to the gallery from the yard below. Carlton smiled at the irony of Ella's question.

"What happens? Why, nothing!" Sighing, he walked back to face Ella. "Come, sit down with me."

"But ah have de dinner to prepare, Carlton."

"That can wait. Here." He pulled Ella down onto the couch beside him and put his arm around her shoulder. He drew her close.

"Slaves are expensive to rear, Ella. It's a good practice to study the books to gauge my profit. When Caspar was alive, I needed the ledgers to check what was going on." He nudged Ella's neck gently with his nose, cuddling her for comfort.

"Although it is nigh on two years since Caspar was killed, Ella, I still miss him."

"Will dey ever catch dat Fletcher?"

"No!" Carlton was scornful. "Why should those lawmakers in Roseau concern themselves about apprehending a white *gentleman* who slaughters a slave! They could only make him pay Caspar's auction value as compensation.

"Who knows where he is now, Ella? Captain Loring said he took Fletcher and Laura to Antigua. They could be in Jamaica now, or England. Laura

420

is probably whore to his pimp. Serves her right!" He nestled his head on Ella's shoulder.

"Brett says he can still remember the faces of the other two."

"Aye. Wish I knew their names. I cannot take young Brett to every casino in the country to search for them!"

"He swears he will chop them to death if he sets eyes on them when he is older."

"Brett!" Carlton smiled wearily. "He has Caspar's spirit. He and Vincent make a good pair. Vincent will be the Bondmaster one day. When I have given up, Ella. He will do well with Brett by his side."

"Give up!" Ella drew herself away. "What do you mean?"

"Don't be so surprised, Ella. Do you think I want to raise niggers for the rest of my days? No! I want to sit on the gallery with my rum in my hand and a young wench in my bed and let Vincent take care of the plantation. I want to do that before I am too old to enjoy it!"

Ella pouted. "A young wench in yuh bed, *oui*? What about Ella?"

"You? If you were not black and a slave, you would be my wife, Ella. You know that. Are you going to be vexed every time some chit gives relief to the old Bondmaster!"

"Carlton?" Ella was thoughtful.

"Yes?"

"Since yo' came home from England, yo' have sold hundreds of slaves, an' those yo' still own would fetch a fortune. Why don't yo' stop de breeding an' sell dem, too? Think what a life yo' could have."

Carlton pulled Ella close to him. "Ella, you don't

421

understand, do you?" he smiled with affection. "Slaves are a booming business. What inheritance would there be for Vincent if I stop now?"

He stretched out on the couch and laid his head on Ella's lap. She caressed his thinning hair, smiling down as she would to a child.

"Yas, massa!" she said in patois. "Yas, sah!"

Carlton's thoughts drifted. After the bitterness at Caspar's murder and Laura's departure had been blunted by time, it was the loneliness which assailed Carlton most of all. The evenings were the depressing times at Roxborough. Of course, he could pick any wench on the plantation to pleasure him, but frequently he slept alone, or summoned Ella.

The thrill of mastery no longer impressed him, especially when a wench lay limply on his mattress with her legs up while he strained to work himself off. Carlton yearned now for the company of people with whom he could talk in the evenings. Without Caspar, he had only the fireflies darting in the darkness for companionship.

He blinked open his eyes and sat up, swinging around to face Ella on the couch. "I've just remembered!" he exclaimed. "There is to be an auction in Colihaut next week. Beautour is selling his plantation. I will go and see what prices his stock fetches. Maybe I will find some cheap whelps."

Ella regarded him sadly as he stood up and paced the floor. She understood his great need. She sighed, knowing that she would not be the one who would fulfill it and bring peace to the Bondmaster.

Carlton journeyed up the west coast of the island to Colihaut by horse. It was a day's ride along a trail which followed the lowlands of the coast. He was accompanied by Asaph, one of the drivers, and by Vulcan, the newest kitchen boy. They arrived in Colihaut at nightfall the day before the auction.

Colihaut was a lively township with its taverns and billiard rooms and a mixed white and colored population of English and French descent. Since the days of the Caribs, Colihaut had attracted missionaries and other white men, the first settlers having arrived a hundred years before.

Beautour the elder was one of the earliest planters to establish himself. His property had been handed down in a direct line through his sons and grandsons. Two of the Beautour sons had been involved in the French uprising thirty years previously. They were banished from Dominica in consequence. Now another link with that French past was to be severed with the sale of the Beautour property.

Carlton was well-known in Colihaut and it did not take him very long to secure lodgings at a house that overlooked the square and belonged to a creole widow.

Asaph and Vulcan were directed to sleep with the horses in the stable. Carlton declined the widow's suggestion that he should chain them. He explained to Widow Foy that his slaves had ample chance to run at Roxborough and Roxborough slaves did not run.

"The Bondmaster's branded R for Roxborough on their shoulders, Mistress Foy, always brings them back to me." Carlton indicated the letter which had been scorched into Vulcan's shoulder when he was a child. "That's the sign of quality!"

"You'll not find anything of that standard at the Beautour plantation," commented Widow Foy with a sniff.

"They say the French are better for their slaves than the English, but not that Beautour grandson! He was loath even to feed them, but on Sundays he forced them to attend church. They have religion, Carlton, but not an ounce of flesh!"

Widow Foy was in her fifties, a large, garrulous woman in voluminous skirts and a pristine bonnet. She showed Carlton his room. It was simply furnished with a large bed, a dresser on which stood the water jug and basin, and a rocking chair. A flight of stairs led from the gallery outside the chamber down into the square below.

"This was Mister Foy's room," sniffed the widow with disgust. "It was the goings on he had in here that killed him." Carlton followed her eyes to look across the square to the taverns on the opposite side.

"He used to roll home at all times with a whore on either side of him. He died with his nose under a strumpet's skirt!" She spat piously into the gutter below the house. "You can do what you like here, Carlton. I'm beyond shocking."

That night Carlton toured the taverns and the billiard rooms. He was greeted by several planters whom he knew and, as befitted his status bought rounds of wine and rum for them all. He ignored the blandishments of the harlots who hung around him like flies around an Ibo's eyes.

He was enjoying the company of men with similar problems and interests to his own so much that he could not bother with a Colihaut tart. He drank heartily, finally passing out and having to be carried back to his lodgings by the faithful Asaph and Vulcan.

When he viewed the Beautour stock the next

morning, Carlton was appalled. One glance at the creatures in the stockade convinced him that there was nothing of value. Every slave exhibited welts and scars from lashings and injuries Each had the beaten look of perpetual hunger in his lifeless eyes.

Carlton upbraided Jonas Henderson, the auctioneer. "How can a man expect to get work out of a beast without muscle and fat? You'll be fortunate to find buyers for this lot, Henderson. I wouldn't soil my hands fingering them!"

"Slaves are scarce, Carlton," Henderson whined. "People will bid high, you'll see. A few days grazing and they will be fit for years in the cane fields."

"That's your view, Henderson," Carlton replied scornfully. "Beautour is a Papist. Religion does not make good slaves."

Henderson took Carlton by his elbow to steer him out of earshot of the other planters. "There is one slave you may be interested in, Carlton I've penned her separately, she is rather special." He leaned toward Carlton's ear.

"She is a mulatto, raised as maid to the old Madame Beautour who died recently. She is about thirteen years of age and," Henderson gripped Carlton's elbow tightly. "she is a virgin!"

"Bah! I don't believe it. Not in a French household."

"It is true, Carlton. Madame Beautour would not let the girl sleep anywhere but with her Kept her with her all the time, she did, until the minute she died. She has been with the priest ever since."

"You sure the priest has not blessed her?"

Henderson ignored Carlton's remark and escorted him to a room adjoining the kitchen. A girl was squatting on the floor with her head bowed. Carlton stared at her long black hair and yellow skin, a delightful combination.

"Stand up, wench!" said the auctioneer. The girl rose obediently. She had well-formed, slender limbs. She stood meekly with her hands clasped in front of the dirty linen shift she was wearing.

"Come, wench, let's see your face!" ordered Carlton, placing his fingers under the girl's chin and raising her head. Her dark eyes flickered sadly.

Her face intrigued Carlton. Her complexion showed the taint of her Negro background, while her delicate features were from her white ancestry. Carlton found her enchanting.

"Lift your shift, wench."

She looked at him perplexed. He repeated the command in French, and still the girl gawked at him.

"She has a very shy nature, Carlton. The old *madame*, you see, protected her from the realities."

"Oh, yes? She will soon discover them, won't she?" Carlton smirked, lifting the front of the girl's dress and kneeling on his haunches to peer at her. He placed his fingers between her legs.

"She is a fine specimen, is she not, Carlton? Those thighs, that bottom, those breasts so perfectly formed!"

"Henderson, you are slobbering so much you should buy the wench yourself." Carlton stood up, letting the girl's dress fall.

The brightness of her complexion had drained away. The girl swayed toward Carlton. He caught her and held her in his arms.

"I'll take her, Henderson. How much?"

426

"She is supposed to go into the auction."

"You said that you saved her for me, Henderson. Now you have changed your mind because I approve and you want me to give cachet to this vendue of carrion." Carlton snorted.

"I'll give you a hundred currency. You will never get so much from this crowd of paupers here. I don't want that lecherous clan of libertines fingering this wench all day!"

Henderson raised his eyebrows, backing out of the room and leaving Carlton with his purchase.

Uncertain what to do with the prize and doubtful if he could entrust the wench to Asaph and Vulcan, Carlton left the vendue and escorted the girl back to his lodgings himself. He locked her in his room and stepped across the square to the nearest tavern for a shot of rum.

It was late afternoon when Carlton stumbled up the stairs onto Widow Foy's gallery. He carried a flagon of rum in one hand and a roasted chicken in the other.

The wench scrambled to her feet in terror when he barged into the room.

"No, no!" muttered Carlton effusively. "Quite all right. Sit down, sit down! Don't worry about a silly ol' bugger like me!"

He placed the chicken and the flagon very carefully on the dresser. He gave the wench a little wave as though trying to cheer her up, then closed and locked the door from the inside.

"What a day! What a day!" Carlton was almost singing. He glanced at the wench. She was regarding him more confidently now.

He removed his long coat and threw it on the

bed, standing before her in his shirt and trousers. With effort, he rolled up his sleeves.

"See these arms, wench? See how they be brown from the years I've worked close to the soil. When I clench my fist like so, see the muscles move? I'm a working planter, wench, not a sissified Frenchie like those Beautours who raised you."

"Madame Beautour was very good to me, sah!"

"Hah! Hah! The wench speaks. And such pretty English!" Carlton bowed his head mockingly before her. "Have you more words to say, wench?"

The girl bit her lip.

"Don't be frightened, wench. I'm jus' a silly ol' bugger!"

Carlton stumbled as he moved to the dresser. He reached for the flagon of rum, found a glass by the basin, and poured himself a large measure which he downed immediately. It seemed to fortify him. He tore off a leg from the chicken and carried it toward the girl.

"You see the Bondmaster thinks of you, wench. Eat!" He thrust the leg at her. "Go on, take it." He was relieved when she accepted the leg and began to gnaw at it ravenously.

He nodded his head, trying to focus his bleary eyes on the image of the honey-limbed fledgling crouched on the rocking chair. His breathing was heavy. The outline of the girl's naked body under her mousseline shift disturbed him.

He advanced toward her, taking the chicken bone from her hand and throwing it on the floor. He took her arms in his hands and pulled her to her feet.

She gaped at him in alarm.

"All right, wench, all right!" he belched, letting

the girl slip from his grasp. She fell back into the rocking chair, bouncing backwards and forwards.

Carlton got down on his knees slowly and steadied the chair. He placed his hands on the girl's ankles and clamped her feet firmly to the floor.

"Wench!" He stared into her eyes. "You are the Bondmaster's now. You are mine!"

Forcing her legs apart with his body, Carlton brushed the girl's shift up to her waist. He eased himself closer to her. He was on his knees, his eyes level with hers as she sat on the chair. He untied the flap of his trousers and rose from his kneeling position.

He pulled the girl to the edge of the cedarwood chair so that she was poised in line with him. He grimaced triumphantly as he put pressure on the arms of the rocking chair and the girl rocked down onto him. He pressed the back of the chair; the girl rocked backwards and he rose up with her.

The wench's shriek when the chair rocked down again gave way to a whimper of confusion. She raised her legs, locking them behind Carlton's waist as the chair rocked faster up and down.

Ella was puzzled when she saw the filly Carlton had bought. While she was arranging a pallet on the floor for the wench to sleep in Carlton's dressing room, she questioned her. The answers the young wench gave confirmed Ella's doubts. She left the girl in Carlton's chamber and sought him out on the gallery.

"De wench," she queried. "What yo' does know about she?"

"Ella, don't start on me! I still feel the same way

429

about you!" There was a note of exasperation in Carlton's voice.

"Look, Ella. I've bought her and she is to be my bed wench for a time. That's all there is to it!"

"Oh, Carlton, ah does not be worried about me," Ella said, smiling. She sat down in the chair beside Carlton to emphasize her almost equal status.

"Ah does be pleased yo' does have a new wench. Yo' done be so grumpy lately, a new wench may make yo' a sweeter master!"

"Don't be so foolish, Ella!"

"It may be yo' who does be foolish, Carlton." Ella spoke slowly. "Yo' does remember when yo' done go away to England wid Caspar, ah done tell yo' ah does be full fuh yo'?"

"That's a damn long time to speak about. I don't recall that at all." Carlton scowled.

"Maybe yo' don't but ah done birth a whelp, a sweet little picaninny de color of sunshine. Ol' Massa Hayes done sell she because he done say we do have too many whelps."

"He never told me." Carlton yawned.

"He done say he gon' tell yo' when yo' come back, but he done die." Ella paused. "He done sell de whelp to Madame Beautour."

Carlton's yawning stopped abruptly. He turned to face Ella. "What was the whelp's name?"

"Miranda."

"What's the name of that wench I bought?"

"Miranda."

"Dammit!" swore Carlton. "That means I paid a hundred pounds for my own daughter!"

"What yo' gon' do, Carlton?"

430

"Do? I'll mount the wench every night until I get a whelp out of her. I've got to make back the money I paid for her!"

Chapter 39

"SEE, MIRANDA! SEE HOW HE IS GROWING!"

Carlton smiled proudly and lifted Vincent off the ground. He held him above his head.

"You're getting heavy, boy," he laughed, placing the child on the flagstones at the foot of the front steps.

Vincent raised his head to gaze up at Carlton. "Gran'pa! Will you take me riding with you today?"

"The boy's as keen as the pox, Miranda! Ella has raised Brett the same way. That's Bondmaster blood!" He ruffled the boy's hair.

"Vincent, you must be five now, eh, boy? I was like you at that age." Carlton crouched down to bring his eyes level with Vincent.

"No, Vincent, I cannot ride today. I have to do battle with the ledgers. Have you had your breakfast?"

"Yes, Gran'pa."

"Find Brett, boy. You can play with him while I work at my books."

"Gran'pa?" Vincent hung his head awaiting Carlton's reply.

"Yes, boy, what is it?"

"Can I go to the river?"

"Sure, son. But only if Brett is with you. Find him first."

"Yes, Gran'pa!" Vincent scuttled around the side of the house shouting for Brett.

"You see, Miranda," said Carlton, rising and helping his wench up the front steps, "what a fine heir I have in Vincent."

"What about my whelp, Mas Carlton?" Miranda patted her swollen belly. "It does be coming at the turn of de moon. Dat does be what Ella does say."

Carlton paused when he reached the top of the steps. He beamed at Miranda. Her childish ways and tender features had matured in the two years since he had brought her to Roxborough. In place of her youth, Miranda's face was radiant with approaching motherhood. Her eyes flickered under his scrutiny.

"Your child will be free, Miranda. I promise you."

She touched him on the arm, returning his smile. Miranda adored Carlton. She knew that she was completely his. He was her father, and he would be the father of her child. The thought of what might happen to her if ever he spurned her was the only hazard to her happiness.

She tended for Carlton with complete devotion. At Ella's behest, she had dedicated herself to Carlton, knowing that any cause she gave him for exasperation could bring calamity for her and the slaves.

"I'll be so pleased when I've had yuh child, Mas Carlton. I does be wanting yo', plenty."

"Ella was the same," chuckled Carlton. "Insatiable."

"Is that pretty?"

He slapped her bottom tenderly. "Go, Miranda. Tell that mother of yours to send up the sangaree. Let me work on those cussed ledgers this morning."

It was eleven years since Carlton had returned to the plantation. The ledgers piled up on the bureau in front of him chronicled every event during that period. He turned to them with a heavy heart. It was a fact that his slave breeding had kept him going when coffee and sugar prices were falling, causing the ruination of other plantations. But Carlton had paid a high price. Without Ella and Miranda to sustain him, and Vincent to give him hope for the future. he would be alone in a world which he himself had created.

Carlton sighed and pulled the stock books toward him. There were three more births to record. It was his custom to name the whelps himself. He dredged his mind. Every name had to be different to avoid confusion.

He checked the dam's name. It was Liza, so the new female would be Lizette. The two males? Carlton had Arrowsmith's atlas on his bookshelf. He opened it at random for inspiration. The page showed Africa. His eye searched a line from Saldanha Bay to the Grain Coast. He would call the new Negroes Benin and Biafra, he decided. He inked the names carefully in the stock book and then turned to the stores ledger to prepare an order for his agent in Bristol.

While Carlton worked, Vincent toddled across the yard, holding Brett's hand. The movement caught Carlton's eye. He smiled with pleasure. Brett was talking solicitously to Vincent, obviously explaining something about the estate.

"They are good whelps," Carlton acknowledged to himself. "They complete my contentment." Or did they? Carlton was forty-four; he had wealth, an heir, everything he could wish for, yet he was acutely aware that his life was empty.

He gazed after Brett and Vincent until they disappeared down the path to the river. The morning was already heavy with the heat of the sun. Down in the valley the sea appeared motionless, a sheen of dark blue rising to the lighter blue of the cloudless sky. There was no breeze. The leaves of the trees hung limply in the air. Even the birds were silent. Carlton stroked his jaw and pondered.

Vincent was prattling to Brett as they walked. Brett answered the boy's questions with a seriousness which belied his ten years. Brett carried a spear which he made for himself out of a wooden shaft and an iron rod Constance had forged for him.

"Yo' gon' fishing, Brett?" Vincent demanded.

"Yes. De Wagenies done show me where dey does have crayfish, long like yuh arm," Brett measured from his hand to his elbow to show Vincent what he meant.

"What de Wagenies, Brett?"

"De Wagenies does be de river slaves, Vincent. Dey does be de niggers what does catch fish for de *cou,* an' row de hogsheads to Layou."

Vincent considered this. "What about yo', Brett? Is yo' a river slave or a land slave?"

"I ain't a slave!"

"But yo' does sleep in de slave quarters under de house, Brett. Not in a chamber like me an' mah gran'pa."

"Dat does be becuz I does be staying wid Ella an' she does be mah mama, Vincent. Ella does

435

say de day does be coming when dere ain't slaves no more!" he confided.

"Brett!" Vincent tugged at the boy's arm to make sure he got an answer. "Yo' afraid of mah gran'pa?"

With his free hand, Brett fingered the weal cutting across his neck. "I does respect yuh grand'pa, Vincent. He is mah Bon'massa. But he does be mah gran'pa, too. I ain't afraid he. Yo' does see dis?" He indicated the scar.

"Mah da', Caspar, he done kill de buckra what cut me dere. He was not afraid of any buckra. One day, I gon' chop de men dat kill he. I ain't afraid of dem!"

Vincent regarded Brett with awe. He liked the way the boy's bright eyes seemed to notice everything. He liked his strong sun-blackened arms; he liked his musty smell. "I'm gon' help yo', Brett," he pledged.

The river gurgled through the channel of trees down to Layou. It was cooler in the shade, and Vincent walked carefully behind Brett as they trod the path along the riverbank. They came to a clearing where Brett announced he would look for crayfish. He cautioned Vincent to wait for him by the water's edge, slipped out of his pants, and ran naked into the river. He carried his spear proudly.

Vincent sat down on a boulder and gazed at Brett as he floated with his head down, peering into the water. The sun filtering through the bamboo leaves on the opposite bank dappled his body with shadows.

Vincent glanced at the bank: someone was staring at him through the bamboo pales. Although he could not see the person properly, Vincent felt frightened. He called for Brett to come back, but the boy had his head under the water and could not hear him.

He wondered if he should run back to the house or wade into the river and get Brett.

The bush was thick around the clearing and the river at his feet was flowing fast. Vincent bit his thumb. The river was too deep for him. He yelled at Brett as the boy floated out of sight around a bend.

Vincent plucked up his courage to glance at the bamboo cluster again. He saw no one this time, which made him more scared as he realized he was completely alone. Perhaps it had not been a real person at all, but a *soucouyant*. He shuddered as a cloud blotted out the sun. He plunged into the bush, fighting his way along the narrow trail winding through the tall, dark trees.

"Where you going so fast, little one?"

A woman blocked his path. She caught him by his shoulder as he ran blindly into her. A cloak with a hood covered her hair and most of her face. She gripped him fiercely, kneeling down to face him.

Vincent trembled. This was the face he had seen staring at him through the bamboo.

"There ain't no need to be frightened, boy. A big boy like you!" The woman's voice grated hard on his ears. It was not kind and happy like the voices of Ella and Miranda. The strange woman spoke in English, not in the familiar creole patois of the plantation. Her fingers dug into his flesh.

"Yo' does be hurting me!"

"Oh dear, am I really? What's your name, little boy?"

"What for!" Vincent could feel the tears pricking his eyes.

"Because I may be your mother."

"Yo' ain't mah mam!" Vincent was puzzled. "She does be gone a long time."

"Aha!" the woman exclaimed. "So you *are* Vincent!" Her eyes gleamed with evil below her hood.

The glint made Vincent cower. "Please let me go," he begged.

"Oh, yes!" The woman stood up and transferred her grip from Vincent's shoulder to his hand. "You shall go, Vincent," she murmured.

"I have been longing to see you. You won't remember me, Vincent, because I went away when you were still a baby. For a long time I have been dreaming that one day I would return and we would meet like this." The woman snickered.

"Does Gran'pa know yo' does be here?" Vincent demanded.

The woman was leading him along the path. "Where we going?" He struggled when the woman suddenly tried to drag him off the path into a thicket.

"Come, Vincent," the woman croaked. "Don't be scared of me. We are going where we shall be private and you can talk to me. I do not want anybody to see us together.

"Mas Carlton is an evil man, Vincent. He would not be pleased if he saw us together. Come, Vincent, I have something for you." She tugged at his arm again.

Vincent's curiosity got the better of him. "What do you have for me?" he asked, allowing himself to be pulled into the trees.

"Come, you shall see!" The woman guided him through the foliage to a small clearing which she seemed to recognize. She smiled at Vincent.

"Yes, let us sit here, shall we?" She eased herself down against the trunk of a saman tree, maintaining her hold on Vincent's wrist. She pulled him closer. "Sit, boy. I am your mother. Why are you so scared?"

"I ain't afraid of no one!" cried Vincent defiantly, remembering what Brett had said. He wished Brett would come and see this lady. He would know if she was his mother or a forest witch.

"Oh, you are a brave boy!" The woman snorted. "That's the Bondmaster's arrogance for you. How is the celebrated Bondmaster of Roxborough, Vincent? Is he in good health?"

"He does be fine, thank you." Vincent was thoughtful. "If yo' does be mah mam like yo' does say, come to de *cou* wid me. Mah gran'pa is partial to me, an' he gon' be so pleased to see yo' wid me."

Vincent's skin tingled as the woman sniggered. He tried to jerk his hand free of her spancel-like grip.

"Loose me!" he sniveled, frightened now. "Yo' does be hurting me!"

"Hush, brat!" The woman lifted her head and listened. Under the shadow of her hood, her eyes darted around the glade.

"I have no time to lose," she muttered. "Here, boy, I have these marbles for you."

Out of the voluminous folds of her cloak, she produced a collection of small glass beads, each one exquisitely colored. She rolled them from her hand onto the ground, where they nestled in the grass.

Vincent's eyes lit up with delight. The woman released his hand and he fell on the beads, scooping them up with a shriek of joy.

He looked up to thank the woman, but his shout of pleasure died on his lips. The woman was standing above him brandishing a whip and a cutlass.

439

When Brett returned to the glade by the river where he had left Vincent playing, he was unconcerned that the boy was no longer there. He picked up his pants and carried them in his hand together with his spear and the crayfish he had caught. He assumed that Vincent had started back along the path to the *cou* by himself.

Brett stepped out swiftly to catch up with Vincent. After a few yards, he was surprised to see, ahead of him, a woman in a cloak standing in the shade of a tree beside the trail. She appeared to be a stranger.

"Good day, ma'am," he called politely.

The woman's cloak was fastened tightly around her; she was clutching the hood across her face like a leper. Brett could only see her eyes. In her hand she carried a package of plantain leaves bound with vine. She beckoned to Brett.

Brett advanced cautiously. He was aware of her eyes lingering on him, making him conscious of his nakedness.

"Yo' does be a fine buck!" the woman croaked, nodding her head. "Here! Take dis message to de Bon'massa " She thrust the package at him. "Run, boy!" The woman cackled behind her hood.

"Yes, ma'am." Brett needed no bidding to run away from the woman as fast as he could.

He dropped his spear, the crayfish, and his pants, feeling the woman's gaze on him until he was out of sight of the tree where she lurked. He shuddered, clutching the package close to his body as he ran.

"Mas Carlton! Mas Carlton!" Brett panted as he crossed the cobbled courtyard in front of the house.

"What is it, boy?" Carlton drawled wearily from his chair on the gallery.

440

"A strange woman in a cloak done give me a message fuh yo', sah!"

"In a cloak, on a day like this?" Carlton snorted with disbelief, looking up at the blazing sun. "You must be dreaming, boy." He glanced over the balcony rail as Brett raced up to the front steps. "Oh, very well. Come up, boy!"

Ella, who had heard the commotion, bustled up the back stairs to see what it was all about.

"Maybe she was a *soucouyant,* Mas Carlton. All I could see were her eyes. They were black, like midnight!"

"Indeed?" Carlton feigned interest. He squinted at the plantain leaf package which the boy clutched to his chest. "I suppose you have brought me some obeah jujube." He held out his hand for the package.

"No!" shrieked Ella. "Don't touch dat!"

Carlton looked up sharply. "Why ever not, Ella?"

"Carlton, dere does be blood! See, Brett has blood on he chest where he done hold the package."

"What the devil is in it? Has a slave sent me a cock's head?" Carlton did not know whether to be angry or laugh.

"Put it on the floor, Brett," Ella commanded. She slipped to her knees and crouched over the package. She began to mutter a soft incantation.

"That's enough of that nonsense, Ella!" Carlton snapped. "Open the damned thing!"

Cautiously, Ella picked at the vine which tied the package. With mounting horror, she unfolded the large green plantain leaf to reveal a mess of blood inside.

"What the hell is that?" Carlton felt a chill of fear. "Take that obeah paraphernalia off the gallery!"

441

He squinted at the bits of bloody flesh in the package.

Ella screamed.

She lunged at Brett and hugged him close to her in fright. "Quick, boy," she pleaded. "What de woman look like?"

"Like a witch, mam. I could see she eyes."

"She white or she black?"

"I don't rightly know. Her complexion was be fair like mine. But she hands was be dark and bony. She done look like I see she befuh, Ella."

Brett frowned. He recognized the pieces of flesh smeared onto the plantain leaf laid out on the gallery deck.

"Mas Carlton!" he gasped. "Dat does be Vincent!"

"What, boy!" Carlton's heart leaped.

"Yes." He bent down and scooped up the flesh, shaking off the blood. "See, it does be a prick an' a grain." There was a hush.

"Mas Carlton, the witch done cut Vincent."

"Tita!" exclaimed Ella, understanding who the mysterious woman was. "Tita done take she revenge."

Carlton clutched his chest, gasping for breath. He twisted. Blood drained from his face as his legs folded under him and he collapsed on the floor of the gallery. His half-open lips turned blue and he gurgled incoherently. He lapsed into silence, his tongue protruding obscenely from his mouth.

Carlton alternated between unconsciousness and delirium. Vincent's mutilated body was buried by Ella and Brett in a hole next to Old Massa Hayes and Caspar.

Ella tended Carlton, working every kind of remedy she knew in an effort to revive him. Soil from old

Hayes's grave was spread at the four corners of Carlton's bed. Ground parrots' beaks and eggshells were placed in the dirt, while Ella spent hours at Carlton's bedside keening obeah spells in the hope of speeding his recovery. With Brett's help, she forced Carlton to swallow broth made with herbs gathered in the moonlight and laced with blood from the liver of a freshly slaughtered manicoo.

Carlton lay in his bed, sometimes with his eyes open without speaking, and sometimes in a deep, troubled sleep.

Ella also cared for Miranda, who was struggling in childbirth. The midwives from the paddock came over to help. Meanwhile, the field slaves drifted to their tasks each day and the drivers' whips rose and fell.

Brett roamed the plantation every morning, imagining what he would do if he was the Bondmaster. In the afternoons, he sat on a chair in Carlton's chamber, keeping watch.

Carlton's cheeks had shrunk, revealing the fine bone structure under his skin. His once gold hair had turned to silver; his eyelids were red and tightly closed.

One afternoon, as Brett stared at Carlton, the stillness of the house erupted with a hubbub of confused voices. Wenches were chattering loudly amongst themselves. Brett rose from his chair to bawl at them to keep quiet.

"Miranda done drop a *beké* whelp, *oui*!" a wench called to him when he opened the door.

Ella swept across the floor into Carlton's room, pushing past Brett and the other slaves. She held the pink baby in her arms. She smiled reassuringly at Brett and walked over to Carlton's bedside.

"Carlton!" she called. "Carlton, you have a new heir. Miranda done birth a male whelp for yo'!"

Carlton's chest heaved. He opened his lips as though to speak at last. Ella dangled the baby in front of his eyes, bending her head forward to catch his words. There was no sound.

Through his half-opened eyes, Carlton could see her tired old black head hanging over him. It reminded him of the vultures hovering over the slave dump in Trinidad. He sighed.

The sigh was long, draining all the breath from his body. He squeezed his eyes shut, to close out that black visage which seemed to be harrying him to his grave.

Carlton Todd was not going to die! He was the Bondmaster, the Bondmaster of Roxborough!

"Get out!" He sat bolt upright, his voice bellowing from the depths of his being. He lashed out at Ella's prying face and cuffed her with his clenched fist.

"Get out!" He shouted at the black faces filling the room. "Get out!"

He coughed, dragging the phlegm up into his mouth. He glared at the bright pink monstrosity clutched in Ella's black fingers. He drew back his head and spat into the baby's face.

"Ain't no whelp with slave blood going to be my heir!" he shouted, throwing off the covers. He swung his legs over the edge of the bed as the slaves crowding the room scrambled to get out through the door.

Brett stepped over quickly to steady Carlton!

"Boy, get my boots."

"Where yo' does be going, Carlton?"

"I does be *Master* Carlton to you, Ella!" he

snapped. "Where I choose to go is of no concern of yours!"

Ella regarded him sulkily and backed out of the room with the baby.

Brett placed his boots at his feet and knelt down to help Carlton put them on.

"We are going riding, Brett, you and I. To Roseau. I am weary of the company of slaves. It is time for me to take a white wife and produce a real heir to the Bondmaster."

"Yes, Mas Carlton, sir!" Brett answered happily, stepping back as Carlton jumped to his feet.

"I'm coming!"

THE BEST OF THE BESTSELLERS
FROM WARNER BOOKS!

THE BEST OF THE BESTSELLERS
FROM WARNER BOOKS!

FIRE AND ICE by Andrew Tobias   **(82-409, $2.25)**
The bestselling **Fire And Ice** is a fascinating inside view of Charles Revson, the cosmetics magnate who built the Revlon empire. "The perfect book; a book about a first-class s.o.b. . . . Full of facts and gossip . . . absorbing."—Wall Street Journal. 32 pages of photographs

MY HEART BELONGS by Mary Martin   **(89-355, $1.95)**
"An effervescent story about a little lady who believes in the magic of make-believe and maintains a childlike enthusiasm, a sparkling joy for life she can barely contain."—St. Louis Globe. Almost 100 photos from Mary Martin's private scrapbook.

THE CAMERONS by Robert Crichton   **(82-497, $2.25)**
The Camerons is the story of the indomitable Maggie Drum, who washes the grime of coal-mining Pitmungo town from her beautiful face and sets out to find a man worthy of fathering her family. It is the story of the big, poor-but-proud Highlander who marries her, gives her seven children, and challenges her with an unyielding spirit of his own.

THE HAMLET WARNING by Leonard Sanders   **(89-370, $1.95)**
An international terrorist group has built an atom bomb and is using it to blackmail the United States. "A doomsday thriller." —The New York Times

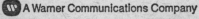 A Warner Communications Company

Please send me the books I have checked.

Enclose check or money order only, no cash please. Plus 35¢ per copy to cover postage and handling. N.Y. State residents add applicable sales tax.

Please allow 2 weeks for delivery.

WARNER BOOKS
P.O. Box 690
New York, N.Y. 10019

Name ....

Address ....

City .... State .... Zip ....

_____ Please send me your free mail order catalog

THE BEST OF THE BESTSELLERS
FROM WARNER BOOKS!